MARK TWAIN

ADVENTURES OF HUCKLEBERRY FINN

THE MARK TWAIN LIBRARY

The Library offers for the first time popular editions of Mark Twain's best works just as he wanted them to be read. These moderately priced volumes, faithfully reproduced from the California scholarly editions and printed on acid-free paper, are sparingly annotated and include all the original illustrations that Mark Twain commissioned and enjoyed.

"Huck waited for no particulars. He sprang away
and sped down the hill as fast as his
legs could carry him."

—THE ADVENTURES OF TOM SAWYER

FROM THE BUST BY KARL GERHARDT.

HUCKLEBERRY FINN.

MARK TWAIN

ADVENTURES
OF
HUCKLEBERRY
FINN

TOM SAWYER'S COMRADE

Scene: The Mississippi Valley
Time: Forty to Fifty Years Ago

Edited by
Walter Blair and Victor Fischer

A publication of the
Mark Twain Project of The Bancroft Library

Published in cooperation with the
University of Iowa

University of California Press

Berkeley   Los Angeles   London

The text of this Mark Twain Library edition of *Adventures of Huckleberry Finn* is identical with the text of the scholarly edition of *Adventures of Huckleberry Finn*, edited by Walter Blair and Victor Fischer (University of California Press, 1985, forthcoming). It is based on the author's manuscript in the Buffalo and Erie County Public Library, and was established in accord with the standards of the Center for Scholarly Editions (CSE). Editorial work was supported by generous grants from the Hedco Foundation and the Program for Editions of the National Endowment for the Humanities.

Library of Congress Cataloging-in-Publication Data

Twain, Mark, 1835–1910.
    Adventures of Huckleberry Finn.
    (The Mark Twain Library)
    Bibliography: p.
    I. Blair, Walter, 1900–   . II. Fischer, Victor, 1942–   . III. Bancroft Library. IV. Title.
PS1305.A2B53   1986   813'.4   84–40713
ISBN 0–520–05337–0 (alk. paper)
ISBN 0–520–05520–9 (pbk. : alk. paper)

University of California Press
Berkeley and Los Angeles
University of California Press, Ltd.
London

Manufactured in the United States of America.

1 2 3 4 5 6 7 8 9 0

The Mark Twain Library is designed by Steve Renick.

The text of this Mark Twain Library edition of
Adventures of Huckleberry Finn
is drawn from the Mark Twain Project's complete edition of
The Works and Papers of Mark Twain.
Editorial work for this volume has been supported by a grant to
The Friends of The Bancroft Library from the

HEDCO FOUNDATION

and by matching funds from the
PROGRAM FOR EDITIONS,
NATIONAL ENDOWMENT FOR THE HUMANITIES,
an independent federal agency.

Without such generous support, these editions could
not have been produced.

The members of the Mark Twain Project
affectionately dedicate this
volume to

JAMES D. HART

in appreciation and celebration
of his distinguished scholarship, his unswerving
loyalty, and his surpassing enterprise as
Director and Friend
of The Bancroft Library
1985

CONTENTS

ILLUSTRATIONS

FOREWORD

Mark Twain began *Adventures of Huckleberry Finn* in July 1876. He wrote about a fourth of it that summer, shelved the manuscript for three years or so, and thereafter worked at it "by fits and starts" until late summer 1883, when he wrote to his publisher: "I've just finished writing a book; & modesty compels me to say it's a rattling good one, too." The product of this seven-year process, most scholars and critics agree, is his best book and one of America's four or five greatest novels.

The author, at the summit of his powers, made use of a lesson he had learned: that for him, intermittent composition was best—that when a book gets "tired, . . . when the tank runs dry you've only to leave it alone and it will fill up again, in time, while you are asleep—also while you are at work at other things, and are quite unaware that this unconscious and profitable cerebration is going on." He found a particularly useful stock of materials in vivid memories of his boyhood in Hannibal, Missouri, and of his years as a Mississippi River pilot. So in a narrative that begins in St. Petersburg, a fictional version of Hannibal, and moves down the river deep into the South, Mark Twain recreated a wide range of scenes, people, and events, movingly evoking for readers a bygone time, place, and way of life.

He had learned, however, to shape his recollections so as to enhance his story, and he had discovered how important it was for him to choose the right fictional point of view. He decided that he wanted a boy to tell this story in the first person—"not Tom Sawyer," because "he would not be a good character for it," but the less conventional social outcast Huckleberry Finn. Huck's prototype was a poor white Hannibal contemporary, Tom Blankenship, about whom the author said: "He was ignorant, unwashed, insufficiently fed; but he had as good a heart as ever any boy had." Huck's way of talking was a backwoods style that had already been adapted by narrators, including Mark Twain, to the telling of short stories, sketches, and tales. But for a longer work Huck had to be given keen perceptive powers, great sensitivity, and a mastery of words and rhythms. Here, in a fairly typical passage, the youth of "thirteen or fourteen or along there" tells us how it feels to be lost in his canoe in a river fog:

I kept quiet, with my ears cocked, about fifteen minutes, I reckon. I was floating along, of course, four or five mile an hour; but you don't ever think of that. No, you *feel* like you are laying dead still on the water; and if a little glimpse of a snag slips by, you don't think to yourself how fast *you're* going, but you catch your breath and think, my! how that snag's tearing along. If you think it ain't dismal and lonesome out in a fog that way, by yourself, in the night, you try it once—you'll see.

Here, as in even more idiosyncratic passages, the homely vocabulary, the faulty grammar, the details, and the talk-like rhythms of a unique and vivid personality all help the reader, directly addressed, share the character's experiences, sensations, and responses. And the innovative decision to use Huck's style throughout a whole novel has been hailed by critics, among them T. S. Eliot, who wrote that in *Huckleberry Finn*, Mark Twain "reveals himself to be one of those writers . . . who have discovered a new way of writing, valid not only for themselves but for others. I should place him, . . . with Dryden and Swift, as one of those rare writers who have brought their language up to date, and in so doing, 'purified the dialect of the tribe.' "

Huck takes off from the St. Petersburg of the 1840s to escape from "a persecuting good widow" and her stern sister, who want to make "a nice, truth-telling, respectable boy of him," and from a brutal father who literally threatens to kill him. He is accompanied by Jim, a slave running away to avoid being sold down the river. In their flight downstream, they encounter folk of many sorts—poor whites, enslaved blacks, confidence men, workmen, middle-class men and women, the "quality"—the world, as Mark Twain saw it, in miniature.

Mark Twain's panoramic narrative shows that his varied experiences, wide reading, and tireless thinking made of him, untrained though he was, a philosopher who ponders such ancient problems as these: What are the wellsprings of human action? How does man decide what is virtuous? And how should he decide? Although Huck rarely speaks directly for Mark Twain, the boy's depictions of riverside dwellers, his reporting of their remarks, and his own interior debates imply what the author's answers would be. Colonel Sherburn, in his speech in chapter 22, for instance, condemns, as Mark Twain would, "the average all around." And the most famous passage in the novel, Huck's account in chapter 31 of his struggle to decide whether he will report Jim's whereabouts, memorably contrasts the attitudes of "authorities" concerning right and wrong. Mark Twain characterized Huck's quandary in a notebook entry: "In a crucial moral emergency . . . a sound heart & a deformed conscience come into collision & conscience suffers defeat":

In those old slave-holding days the whole community was agreed as to one thing—the awful sacredness of slave property. To help steal a horse or a cow was a low crime, but to help a hunted slave, or feed him or shelter him, or hide him, or comfort him, in his troubles, his terrors, his despair, or hesitate to promptly betray him to the slave-catcher when opportunity offered was a much baser crime, & carried with it a stain, a moral smirch which nothing could wipe away. . . . It shows that that strange thing, the conscience—that unerring monitor—can be trained to approve any wild thing you *want* it to approve if you begin its education early & stick to it.

Nevertheless, although Huck follows the promptings of his "sound heart" and does what is right, he believes that he sins and must suffer horrible punishment: "All right, then," he says, "I'll *go* to hell."

Neither the book's concern with such philosophical problems nor its epic sweep prevents it from being a humorous classic. Huck is an Americanized version of a timeless comic character—the sometimes silly but frequently wise uneducated rustic. This sober recorder of hilarious events is ideal for unfolding a deadpan narrative—always an American specialty. The raftsmen in the passage that this edition restores to chapter 16, with their extravagant boasts and avoidance of a showdown, are naturalized representatives of another stereotype as old as comedy—the cowardly braggart. Still another traditional comic figure—the fancy-talking confidence man—is represented by the king and the duke. And Huck's vernacular, brilliantly adapted by a master funmaker, makes the most of these and other laugh-provoking characters.

Adventures of Huckleberry Finn was first published in England and Canada on 10 December 1884, and in the United States on 18 February 1885, with illustrations by Edward Windsor Kemble, a young cartoonist whose work had so delighted Mark Twain that he had insisted to his publisher, "*That* is the man I want to try." The appeal of high, medium, and low humor of the novel has helped keep it in print for one hundred years and make it a best seller. In English and in translation into more than fifty languages, it has sold an estimated twenty million copies.

Throughout its history, nevertheless, it has been America's most controversial classic. Well into the twentieth century, zealous protectors of juvenile virtue fought to keep it out of children's hands for fear they might follow Huck's example and use faulty grammar, play hookey, steal, lie, and run away. In time, this fear subsided, only to be replaced by another: school boards, teachers, librarians, and public officials decided that the book fostered racism, and removed it from library shelves and curricula. They were answered by defenders of the book, who claim that far from encouraging racial prejudice, it fiercely advocates (as its author did), complete and unstinting tolerance and civil rights.

Another long-lasting quarrel was about the novel's literary merit. Even before the first editions appeared, excerpts were described as "pitched in but one key, and that is the key of a vulgar and abhorrent life," as well as "a transcript from nature" that "will not easily be surpassed" and "the best book ever written." Early reviewers called it "grotesque," "a pitiable exhibition of irreverence and vulgarity," and reported that "a search expedition for humorous qualities" yielded nothing but blood-curdling and unfunny episodes. Others, though, called it the crowning achievement of "a literary artist of a very high order," a "tour de force," a "minute and faithful picture," and hailed its evocation of the "lawless, mysterious, wonderful Mississippi" and of the "startlingly real" riverside people who "do not have the air of being invented, but of being found." As the years passed, attacks on the book's artistry came to be fewer and fewer, and scores of thoughtful analyses of its form and structure revealed newly perceived riches. At *Huckleberry Finn*'s hundredth birthday, most critics and scholars unite in praising it as a landmark in American literature and a great world masterpiece. It is also the most popular and best-loved among a small group of American novels considered by general agreement the country's finest.

Walter Blair
Victor Fischer

MARK TWAIN

ADVENTURES
OF
HUCKLEBERRY
FINN

NOTICE

PERSONS attempting to find a motive in this narrative will be prosecuted; persons attempting to find a moral in it will be banished; persons attempting to find a plot in it will be shot.

BY ORDER OF THE AUTHOR
PER G. G., CHIEF OF ORDNANCE.

EXPLANATORY

In this book a number of dialects are used, to wit: the Missouri negro dialect; the extremest form of the backwoods South-Western dialect; the ordinary "Pike-County" dialect; and four modified varieties of this last. The shadings have not been done in a haphazard fashion, or by guess-work; but pains-takingly, and with the trustworthy guidance and support of personal familiarity with these several forms of speech.

I make this explanation for the reason that without it many readers would suppose that all these characters were trying to talk alike and not succeeding.

THE AUTHOR.

The Adventures of Huckleberry Finn.
Chapter I.

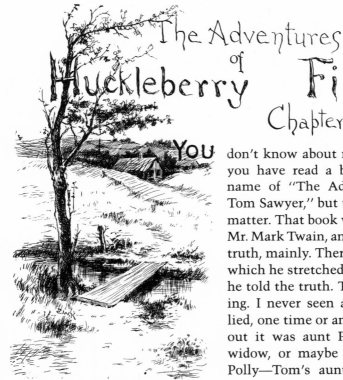

THE WIDOW'S.

YOU don't know about me, without you have read a book by the name of "The Adventures of Tom Sawyer," but that ain't no matter. That book was made by Mr. Mark Twain, and he told the truth, mainly. There was things which he stretched, but mainly he told the truth. That is nothing. I never seen anybody but lied, one time or another, without it was aunt Polly, or the widow, or maybe Mary. Aunt Polly—Tom's aunt Polly, she is—and Mary, and the widow Douglas, is all told about in that book—which is mostly a true book; with some stretchers, as I said before.

Now the way that the book winds up, is this: Tom and me found the money that the robbers hid in the cave, and it made us rich. We got six thousand dollars apiece—all gold. It was an awful sight of money when it was piled up. Well, Judge Thatcher, he took it and put it out at interest, and it fetched us a dollar a day apiece, all the year round—more than a body could tell what to do with. The widow Douglas, she took me for her son, and allowed she would sivilize me; but it was rough living in the house all the time, considering how dismal regular and decent the widow was in all her ways; and so when I couldn't stand it no longer, I lit out. I got into my old rags, and my sugar-hogshead again, and was free and satisfied. But Tom Sawyer, he hunted me up and said he was going to

start a band of robbers, and I might join if I would go back to the
widow and be respectable. So I went back.

The widow she cried over me, and called me a poor lost lamb, and
she called me a lot of other names, too, but she never meant no harm
by it. She put me in them new clothes again, and I couldn't do
nothing but sweat and sweat, and feel all cramped up. Well, then,
the old thing commenced again. The widow rung a bell for supper,
and you had to come to time. When you got to the table you couldn't
go right to eating, but you had to wait for the widow to tuck down

LEARNING ABOUT MOSES AND THE "BULRUSHERS."

her head and grumble a little over the victuals, though there warn't
really anything the matter with them. That is, nothing only everything was cooked by itself. In a barrel of odds and ends it is different;
things get mixed up, and the juice kind of swaps around, and the
things go better.

After supper she got out her book and learned me about Moses
and the Bulrushers; and I was in a sweat to find out all about him;
but by and by she let it out that Moses had been dead a considerable
long time; so then I didn't care no more about him; because I don't
take no stock in dead people.

Pretty soon I wanted to smoke, and asked the widow to let me. But she wouldn't. She said it was a mean practice and wasn't clean, and I must try to not do it any more. That is just the way with some people. They get down on a thing when they don't know nothing about it. Here she was a bothering about Moses, which was no kin to her, and no use to anybody, being gone, you see, yet finding a power of fault with me for doing a thing that had some good in it. And she took snuff too; of course that was all right, because she done it herself.

Her sister, Miss Watson, a tolerable slim old maid, with goggles

Miss Watson

on, had just come to live with her, and took a set at me now, with a spelling-book. She worked me middling hard for about an hour, and then the widow made her ease up. I couldn't stood it much longer. Then for an hour it was deadly dull, and I was fidgety. Miss Watson would say, "Don't put your feet up there, Huckleberry;" and "don't scrunch up like that, Huckleberry—set up straight;" and pretty soon she would say, "Don't gap and stretch like that, Huckleberry— why don't you try to behave?" Then she told me all about the bad place, and I said I wished I was there. She got mad, then, but I didn't mean no harm. All I wanted was to go somewheres; all I wanted was a change, I warn't particular. She said it was wicked to say what I said; said she wouldn't say it for the whole world; *she* was going to live so as to go to the good place. Well, I couldn't see no advantage in going where she was going, so I made up my mind I wouldn't try for it. But I never said so, because it would only make trouble, and wouldn't do no good.

Now she had got a start, and she went on and told me all about the good place. She said all a body would have to do there was to go around all day long with a harp and sing, forever and ever. So I didn't think much of it. But I never said so. I asked her if she reckoned Tom Sawyer would go there, and she said, not by a considerable sight. I was glad about that, because I wanted him and me to be together.

Miss Watson she kept pecking at me, and it got tiresome and lonesome. By and by they fetched the niggers in and had prayers, and then everybody was off to bed. I went up to my room with a piece of candle and put it on the table. Then I set down in a chair by the window and tried to think of something cheerful, but it warn't no use. I felt so lonesome I most wished I was dead. The stars was shining, and the leaves rustled in the woods ever so mournful; and I heard an owl, away off, who-whooing about somebody that was dead, and a whippowill and a dog crying about somebody that was going to die; and the wind was trying to whisper something to me and I couldn't make out what it was, and so it made the cold shivers run over me. Then away out in the woods I heard that kind of a sound that a ghost makes when it wants to tell about something that's on its mind and can't make itself understood, and so can't rest easy in its grave and has to go about that way every night grieving. I got so down-hearted and scared, I did wish I had some company. Pretty soon a spider went crawling up my shoulder, and I flipped it off and it lit in the candle; and before I could budge it was all shriveled up. I didn't need anybody to tell me that that was an awful bad sign and would fetch me some bad luck, so I was scared and most shook the clothes off of me. I got up and turned around in my tracks three times and crossed my breast every time; and then I tied up a little lock of my hair with a thread to keep witches away. But I hadn't no confidence. You do that when you've lost a horse-shoe that you've found, instead of nailing it up over the door, but I hadn't ever heard anybody say it was any way to keep off bad luck when you'd killed a spider.

I set down again, a shaking all over, and got out my pipe for a smoke; for the house was all as still as death, now, and so the widow wouldn't know. Well, after a long time I heard the clock away off in the town go boom—boom—boom—twelve licks—and all still again—stiller than ever. Pretty soon I heard a twig snap, down in the dark amongst the trees—something was a stirring. I set still and listened. Directly I could just barely hear a *"me-yow! me-yow!"* down there. That was good! Says I, *"me-yow! me-yow!"* as soft as I could, and then I put out the light and scrambled out of the window onto the shed. Then I slipped down to the ground and crawled in amongst the trees, and sure enough there was Tom Sawyer waiting for me.

HUCK STEALING AWAY.

Chapter II.

We went tip-toeing along a path amongst the trees back towards the end of the widow's garden, stooping down so as the branches wouldn't scrape our heads. When we was passing by the kitchen I fell over a root and made a noise. We scrouched down and laid still. Miss Watson's big nigger, named Jim, was setting in the kitchen door; we could see him pretty clear, because there was a light behind him. He got up and stretched his neck out about a minute, listening. Then he says,

"Who dah?"

He listened some more; then he come tip-toeing down and stood right between us; we could a touched him, nearly.

THEY TIP-TOED ALONG.

Well, likely it was minutes and minutes that there warn't a sound, and we all there so close together. There was a place on my ankle that got to itching; but I dasn't scratch it; and then my ear begun to itch; and next my back, right between my shoulders. Seemed like I'd die if I couldn't scratch. Well, I've noticed that thing plenty of times since. If you are with the quality, or at a funeral, or trying to go to sleep when you ain't sleepy—if you are anywheres where it won't do for you to scratch, why you will itch all over in upwards of a thousand places. Pretty soon Jim says:

"Say—who is you? Whar is you? Dog my cats ef I didn' hear sumf'n. Well, I knows what I's gwyne to do. I's gwyne to set down here and listen tell I hears it agin."

So he set down on the ground betwixt me and Tom. He leaned his back up against a tree, and stretched his legs out till one of them most touched one of mine. My nose begun to itch. It itched till the tears come into my eyes. But I dasn't scratch. Then it begun to itch on the inside. Next I got to itching underneath. I didn't know how I was going to set still. This miserableness went on as much as six or seven minutes; but it seemed a sight longer than that. I was itching in eleven different places now. I reckoned I couldn't stand it more'n a minute longer, but I set my teeth hard and got ready to try. Just then Jim begun to breathe heavy; next he begun to snore—and then I was pretty soon comfortable again.

Tom he made a sign to me—kind of a little noise with his mouth—and we went creeping away on our hands and knees. When we was ten foot off, Tom whispered to me and wanted to tie Jim to the tree for fun; but I said no; he might wake and make a disturbance, and then they'd find out I warn't in. Then Tom said he hadn't got candles enough, and he would slip in the kitchen and get some more. I didn't want him to try. I said Jim might wake up and come. But Tom wanted to resk it; so we slid in there and got three candles, and Tom laid five cents on the table for pay. Then we got out, and I was in a sweat to get away; but nothing would do Tom but he must crawl to where Jim was, on his hands and knees, and play something on him. I waited, and it seemed a good while, everything was so still and lonesome.

As soon as Tom was back, we cut along the path, around the garden fence, and by and by fetched up on the steep top of the hill the other side of the house. Tom said he slipped Jim's hat off of his head and hung it on a limb right over him, and Jim stirred a little, but he didn't wake. Afterwards Jim said the witches bewitched him and put him in a trance, and rode him all over the State, and then set him under the trees again and hung his hat on a limb to show who done it. And next time Jim told it he said they rode him down to New Orleans; and after that, every time he told it he spread it more and more, till by and by he said they rode him all over the world, and tired him most to death, and his back was all over saddle-boils. Jim was monstrous proud about it, and he got so he wouldn't hardly notice the other niggers. Niggers would come miles to hear Jim tell about it, and he was more looked up to than any nigger in that country. Strange niggers would stand with their mouths open and look him all over, same as if he was a wonder. Niggers is always talking about witches in the dark by the kitchen fire; but whenever one was talking and letting on to know all about such things, Jim would happen in and say, "Hm! What you know 'bout witches?" and that nigger was corked up and had to take a back seat. Jim always kept that five-center piece around his neck with a string and said it

JIM.

was a charm the devil give to him with his own hands and told him he could cure anybody with it and fetch witches whenever he wanted to, just by saying something to it; but he never told what it was he said to it. Niggers would come from all around there and give Jim any-thing they had, just for a sight of that five-center piece; but they wouldn't touch it, because the devil had had his hands on it. Jim was most ruined, for a servant, because he got so stuck up on account of having seen the devil and been rode by witches.

Well, when Tom and me got to the edge of the hill-top, we looked away down into the vil-lage and could see three or four lights twinkling, where there was sick folks, may be; and the stars over us was sparkling ever so fine; and down by the village was the river, a whole mile broad, and awful still and grand. We went down the hill and found Jo Harper, and Ben Rogers, and two or three more of the boys, hid in the old tanyard. So we unhitched a skiff and pulled down the river two mile and a half, to the big scar on the hillside, and went ashore.

We went to a clump of bushes, and Tom made everybody swear to keep the secret, and then showed them a hole in the hill, right in the thickest part of the bushes. Then we lit the candles and crawled in on our hands and knees. We went about two hundred yards, and then the cave opened up. Tom poked about amongst the passages and pretty soon ducked under a wall where you wouldn't a noticed that there was a hole. We went along a narrow place and got into a kind of room, all damp and sweaty and cold, and there we stopped. Tom says:

"Now we'll start this band of robbers and call it Tom Sawyer's Gang. Everybody that wants to join has got to take an oath, and write his name in blood."

Everybody was willing. So Tom got out a sheet of paper that he had wrote the oath on, and read it. It swore every boy to stick to the band, and never tell any of the secrets; and if anybody done anything to any boy in the band, whichever boy was ordered to kill that person and his family must do it, and he mustn't eat and he mustn't sleep till he had killed them and hacked a cross in their breasts, which was the sign of the band. And nobody that didn't belong to the band could use that mark, and if he did he must be sued; and if he done it again he must be killed. And if anybody that belonged to the band told the secrets, he must have his throat cut, and then have his carcass burnt up and the ashes scattered all around, and his name blotted off of the list with blood and never mentioned again by the gang, but have a curse put on it and be forgot, forever.

TOM SAWYER'S BAND OF ROBBERS.

Everybody said it was a real beautiful oath, and asked Tom if he got it out of his own head. He said, some of it, but the rest was out of pirate books, and robber books, and every gang that was high-toned had it.

Some thought it would be good to kill the *families* of boys that told the secrets. Tom said it was a good idea, so he took a pencil and wrote it in. Then Ben Rogers says:

"Here's Huck Finn, he hain't got no family—what you going to do 'bout him?"

"Well, hain't he got a father?" says Tom Sawyer.

"Yes, he's got a father, but you can't never find him, these days. He used to lay drunk with the hogs in the tanyard, but he hain't been seen in these parts for a year or more."

They talked it over, and they was going to rule me out, because they said every boy must have a family or somebody to kill, or else it wouldn't be fair and square for the others. Well, nobody could think of anything to do—everybody was stumped, and set still. I was most ready to cry; but all at once I thought of a way, and so I offered them Miss Watson—they could kill her. Everybody said:

"Oh, she'll do, she'll do. That's all right. Huck can come in."

Then they all stuck a pin in their fingers to get blood to sign with, and I made my mark on the paper.

"Now," says Ben Rogers, "what's the line of business of this Gang?"

"Nothing only robbery and murder," Tom said.

"But who are we going to rob? houses—or cattle—or—"

"Stuff! stealing cattle and such things ain't robbery, it's burglary," says Tom Sawyer. "We ain't burglars. That ain't no sort of style. We are highwaymen. We stop stages and carriages on the road, with masks on, and kill the people and take their watches and money."

"Must we always kill the people?"

"Oh, certainly. It's best. Some authorities think different, but mostly it's considered best to kill them. Except some that you bring to the cave here and keep them till they're ransomed."

"Ransomed? What's that?"

"I don't know. But that's what they do. I've seen it in books; and so of course that's what we've got to do."

"But how can we do it if we don't know what it is?"

"Why blame it all, we've *got* to do it. Don't I tell you it's in the books? Do you want to go to doing different from what's in the books, and get things all muddled up?"

"Oh, that's all very fine to *say*, Tom Sawyer, but how in the nation are these fellows going to be ransomed if we don't know how to do it to them? that's the thing *I* want to get at. Now what do you *reckon* it is?"

"Well I don't know. But per'aps if we keep them till they're ransomed, it means that we keep them till they're dead."

"Now, that's something *like*. That'll answer. Why couldn't you said that before? We'll keep them till they're ransomed to death— and a bothersome lot they'll be, too, eating up everything and always trying to get loose."

"How you talk, Ben Rogers. How can they get loose when there's a guard over them, ready to shoot them down if they move a peg?"

"A guard. Well, that *is* good. So somebody's got to set up all night and never get any sleep, just so as to watch them. I think that's foolishness. Why can't a body take a club and ransom them as soon as they get here?"

"Because it ain't in the books so—that's why. Now Ben Rogers, do you want to do things regular, or don't you?—that's the idea. Don't you reckon that the people that made the books knows what's the correct thing to do? Do you reckon *you* can learn 'em anything? Not by a good deal. No, sir, we'll just go on and ransom them in the regular way."

"All right. I don't mind; but I say it's a fool way, anyhow. Say—do we kill the women, too?"

"Well, Ben Rogers, if I was as ignorant as you I wouldn't let on. Kill the women? No—nobody ever saw anything in the books like that. You fetch them to the cave, and you're always as polite as pie to them; and by and by they fall in love with you and never want to go home any more."

"Well, if that's the way, I'm agreed, but I don't take no stock in it. Mighty soon we'll have the cave so cluttered up with women, and fellows waiting to be ransomed, that there won't be no place for the robbers. But go ahead, I ain't got nothing to say."

Little Tommy Barnes was asleep, now, and when they waked him

up he was scared, and cried, and said he wanted to go home to his
ma, and didn't want to be a robber any more.

So they all made fun of him, and called him cry-baby, and that
made him mad, and he said he would go straight and tell all the
secrets. But Tom give him five cents to keep quiet, and said we
would all go home and meet next week and rob somebody and kill
some people.

Ben Rogers said he couldn't get out much, only Sundays, and so
he wanted to begin next Sunday; but all the boys said it would be
wicked to do it on Sunday, and that settled the thing. They agreed
to get together and fix a day as soon as they could, and then we
elected Tom Sawyer first captain and Jo Harper second captain of
the Gang, and so started home.

I clumb up the shed and crept into my window just before day
was breaking. My new clothes was all greased up and clayey, and I
was dog-tired.

HUCK CREEPS INTO HIS WINDOW.

Chapter III.

MISS WATSON'S LECTURE.

WELL, I got a good going-over in the morning, from old Miss Watson, on account of my clothes; but the widow she didn't scold, but only cleaned off the grease and clay and looked so sorry that I thought I would behave a while if I could. Then Miss Watson she took me in the closet and prayed, but nothing come of it. She told me to pray every day, and whatever I asked for I would get it. But it warn't so. I tried it. Once I got a fish-line, but no hooks. It warn't any good to me without hooks. I tried for the hooks three or four times, but somehow I couldn't make it work. By and by, one day, I asked Miss Watson to try for me, but she said I was a fool. She never told me why, and I couldn't make it out no way.

I set down, one time, back in the woods, and had a long think about it. I says to myself, if a body can get anything they pray for, why don't Deacon Winn get back the money he lost on pork? Why can't the widow get back her silver snuff-box that was stole? Why can't Miss Watson fat up? No, says I to myself, there ain't nothing in it. I went and told the widow about it, and she said the thing a body could get by praying for it was "spiritual gifts." This was too many for me, but she told me what she meant—I must help other people, and do everything I could for other people, and look out for them all the time, and never think about myself. This was including Miss Watson, as I took it. I went out in the woods and turned it over in my mind a long time, but I couldn't see no advantage about it— except for the other people—so at last I reckoned I wouldn't worry about it any more, but just let it go. Sometimes the widow would take me one side and talk about Providence in a way to make a body's mouth water; but maybe next day Miss Watson would take hold and knock it all down again. I judged I could see that there was two Providences, and a poor chap would stand considerable show with the widow's Providence, but if Miss Watson's got him there warn't no help for him any more. I thought it all out, and reckoned I would belong to the widow's, if he wanted me, though I couldn't make out how he was agoing to be any better off then than what he was before, seeing I was so ignorant and so kind of low-down and ornery.

Pap he hadn't been seen for more than a year, and that was comfortable for me; I didn't want to see him no more. He used to always whale me when he was sober and could get his hands on me; though I used to take to the woods most of the time when he was around. Well, about this time he was found in the river drowned, about twelve mile above town, so people said. They judged it was him, anyway; said this drowned man was just his size, and was ragged, and had uncommon long hair—which was all like pap—but they couldn't make nothing out of the face, because it had been in the water so long it warn't much like a face at all. They said he was floating on his back in the water. They took him and buried him on the bank. But I warn't comfortable long, because I happened to think of something. I knowed mighty well that a drownded man don't float on his back, but on his face. So I knowed, then, that this warn't pap, but a woman dressed up in a man's clothes. So I was uncomfortable again. I judged the old man would turn up again by and by, though I wished he wouldn't.

We played robber now and then about a month, and then I re-signed. All the boys did. We hadn't robbed nobody, we hadn't killed any people, but only just pretended. We used to hop out of the woods and go charging down on hog-drovers and women in carts taking garden stuff to market, but we never hived any of them. Tom Sawyer called the hogs "ingots," and he called the turnips and stuff "julery" and we would go to the cave and pow-wow over what we had done and how many people we had killed and marked. But I couldn't see no profit in it. One time Tom sent a boy to run about town with a blazing stick, which he called a slogan (which was the sign for the

Gang to get together), and then he said he had got secret news by his spies that next day a whole parcel of Spanish merchants and rich A-rabs was going to camp in Cave Hollow with two hundred elephants, and six hundred camels, and over a thousand "sumter" mules, all loaded down with di'monds, and they didn't have only a guard of four hundred soldiers, and so we would lay in ambuscade, as he called it, and kill the lot and scoop the things. He said we must slick up our swords and guns, and get ready. He never could go after even a turnip-cart but he must have the swords and guns all scoured up for it; though they was only lath and broom-sticks, and you might scour at them till you rotted and then they warn't worth a mouthful of ashes more than what they was before. I didn't believe we could lick such a crowd of Spaniards and A-rabs, but I wanted to see the camels and elephants, so I was on hand next day, Saturday, in the ambuscade; and when we got the word, we rushed out of the woods and down the hill. But there warn't no Spaniards and A-rabs, and there warn't no camels nor no elephants. It warn't anything but a Sunday-school picnic, and only a primer-class at that. We busted it up, and chased the children up the hollow; but we never got anything but some doughnuts and jam, though Ben Rogers got a rag doll, and Jo Harper got a hymn-book and a tract; and then the teacher charged in and made us drop everything and cut. I didn't see no di'monds, and I told Tom Sawyer so. He said there was loads of them there, anyway; and he said there was A-rabs there, too, and elephants and things. I said, why couldn't we see them, then? He said if I warn't so ignorant, but had read a book called "Don Quixote," I would know without asking. He said it was all done by enchantment. He said there was hun-

THE ROBBERS DISPERSED.

dreds of soldiers there, and elephants and treasure, and so on, but we had enemies which he called magicians, and they had turned the whole thing into an infant Sunday school, just out of spite. I said, all right, then the thing for us to do was to go for the magicians. Tom Sawyer said I was a numskull.

"Why," says he, "a magician could call up a lot of genies, and they would hash you up like nothing before you could say Jack Robinson. They are as tall as a tree and as big around as a church."

"Well," I says, "s'pose we got some genies to help *us*—can't we lick the other crowd then?"

"How you going to get them?"

"I don't know. How do *they* get them?"

"Why they rub an old tin lamp or an iron ring, and then the genies come tearing in, with the thunder and lightning a-ripping around and the smoke a-rolling, and everything they're told to do they up and do it. They don't think nothing of pulling a shot tower up by the roots, and belting a Sunday-school superintendent over the head with it—or any other man."

"Who makes them tear around so?"

"Why, whoever rubs the lamp or the ring. They belong to whoever rubs the lamp or the ring, and they've got to do whatever he says. If he tells them to build a palace forty miles long, out of di'monds, and fill it full of chewing gum, or whatever you want, and fetch an emperor's daughter from China for you to marry, they've got to do it—and they've got to do it before sun-up next morning, too. And more—they've got to waltz that palace around over the country wherever you want it, you understand."

"Well," says I, "I think they are a pack of flatheads for not keeping the palace themselves 'stead of fooling them away like that. And what's more—if I was one of them I would see a man in Jericho before I would drop my business and come to him for the rubbing of an old tin lamp."

"How you talk, Huck Finn. Why, you'd *have* to come when he rubbed it, whether you wanted to or not."

"What, and I as high as a tree and as big as a church? All right, then; I *would* come; but I lay I'd make that man climb the highest tree there was in the country."

"Shucks, it ain't no use to talk to you, Huck Finn. You don't seem to know anything, somehow—perfect sap-head."

I thought all this over for two or three days, and then I reckoned I would see if there was anything in it. I got an old tin lamp and an iron ring and went out in the woods and rubbed and rubbed till I sweat like an Injun, calculating to build a palace and sell it; but it warn't no use, none of the genies come. So then I judged that all that stuff was only just one of Tom Sawyer's lies. I reckoned he believed in the A-rabs and the elephants, but as for me I think different. It had all the marks of a Sunday school.

RUBBING THE LAMP.

Chapter IV.

!!!!!

WELL, three or four months run along, and it was well into the winter, now. I had been to school most all the time, and could spell, and read, and write just a little, and could say the multiplication table up to six times seven is thirty-five, and I don't reckon I could ever get any further than that if I was to live forever. I don't take no stock in mathematics, anyway.

At first I hated the school, but by and by I got so I could stand it. Whenever I got uncommon tired I played hookey, and the hiding I got next day done me good and cheered me up. So the longer I went to school the easier it got to be. I was getting sort of used to the widow's ways, too, and they warn't so raspy on me. Living in a house, and sleeping in a bed, pulled on me pretty tight, mostly, but before the cold weather I used to slide out and sleep in the woods, sometimes, and so that was a rest to me. I liked the old ways best, but I was getting so I liked the new ones, too, a little bit. The widow said I was coming along slow but sure, and doing very satisfactory. She said she warn't ashamed of me.

One morning I happened to turn over the salt-cellar at breakfast. I reached for some of it as quick as I could, to throw over my left shoulder and keep off the bad luck, but Miss Watson was in ahead of me, and crossed me off. She says, "Take your hands away, Huckleberry—what a mess you are always making." The widow put in a good word for me, but that warn't going to keep off the bad luck, I knowed that well enough. I started out, after breakfast, feeling worried and shaky, and wondering where it was going to fall on me, and what it was going to be. There is ways to keep off some kinds of bad luck, but this wasn't one of them kind; so I never tried to do anything, but just poked along low-spirited and on the watch-out.

I went down the front garden and clumb over the stile, where you go through the high board fence. There was an inch of new snow on the ground, and I seen somebody's tracks. They had come up from the quarry and stood around the stile a while, and then went on around the garden fence. It was funny they hadn't come in, after standing around so. I couldn't make it out. It was very curious, somehow. I was going to follow around, but I stooped down to look at the tracks first. I didn't notice anything at first, but next I did. There was a cross in the left boot-heel made with big nails, to keep off the devil.

I was up in a second and shinning down the hill. I looked over my shoulder every now and then, but I didn't see nobody. I was at Judge Thatcher's as quick as I could get there. He said:

"Why, my boy, you are all out of breath. Did you come for your interest?"

"No sir," I says; "is there some for me?"

"Oh, yes, a half-yearly is in, last night. Over a hundred and fifty dollars. Quite a fortune for you. You better let me invest it along with your six thousand, because if you take it you'll spend it."

"No sir," I says, "I don't want to spend it. I don't want it at all—nor the six thousand, nuther. I want you to take it; I want to give it to you—the six thousand and all."

He looked surprised. He couldn't seem to make it out. He says:

"Why, what can you mean, my boy?"

I says, "Don't you ask me no questions about it, please. You'll take it—won't you?"

He says:

"Well I'm puzzled. Is something the matter?"

"Please take it," says I, "and don't ask me nothing—then I won't have to tell no lies."

He studied a while, and then he says:

"Oho-o. I think I see. You want to *sell* all your property to me—not give it. That's the correct idea."

JUDGE THATCHER SURPRISED.

Then he wrote something on a paper and read it over, and says:

"There—you see it says 'for a consideration.' That means I have bought it of you and paid you for it. Here's a dollar for you. Now, you sign it."

So I signed it, and left.

Miss Watson's nigger, Jim, had a hair-ball as big as your fist, which had been took out of the fourth stomach of an ox, and he used to do magic with it. He said there was a spirit inside of it, and it knowed everything. So I went to him that night and told him pap was here again, for I found his tracks in the snow. What I wanted to know, was, what he was going to do, and was he going to stay? Jim got out his hair-ball, and said something over it, and then he held it up and dropped it on the floor. It fell pretty solid, and only rolled about an inch. Jim tried it again, and then another time, and it acted just the same. Jim got down on his knees and put his ear against it and listened. But it warn't no use; he said it wouldn't talk. He said sometimes it wouldn't talk without money. I told him I had an old slick counterfeit quarter that warn't no good because the brass showed through the silver a little, and it wouldn't pass nohow, even if the brass didn't show, because it was so slick it felt greasy, and so that would tell on it every time. (I reckoned I wouldn't say nothing about the dollar I got from the judge.) I said it was pretty bad money, but maybe the hair-ball would take it, because maybe it wouldn't know the difference. Jim smelt it, and bit it, and rubbed it, and said he would manage so the hair-ball would think it was good. He said he would split open a raw Irish potato and stick the quarter in between and keep it there all night, and next morning you couldn't see no brass, and it wouldn't feel greasy no more, and so anybody in town would take it in a minute, let alone a hair-ball. Well, I knowed a potato would do that, before, but I had forgot it.

Jim put the quarter under the hair-ball and got down and listened again. This time he said the hair-ball was all right. He said it would tell my whole fortune if I wanted it to. I says, go on. So the hair-ball talked to Jim, and Jim told it to me. He says:

"Yo' ole father doan' know, yit, what he's a-gwyne to do. Sometimes he spec he'll go 'way, en den agin he spec he'll stay. De bes'

JIM LISTENING.

way is to res' easy en let de ole man take his own way. Dey's two angels hoverin' roun' 'bout him. One uv 'em is white en shiny, en t'other one is black. De white one gits him to go right, a little while, den de black one sail in en bust it all up. A body can't tell, yit, which one gwyne to fetch him at de las'. But you is all right. You gwyne to have considable trouble in yo' life, en considable joy. Sometimes you gwyne to git hurt, en sometimes you gwyne to git sick; but every time you's gwyne to git well agin. Dey's two gals flyin' 'bout you in yo' life. One uv 'em's light en t'other one is dark. One is rich en t'other is po'. You's gwyne to marry de po' one fust en de rich one by en by. You wants to keep 'way fum de water as much as you kin, en don't run no resk, 'kase it's down in de bills dat you's gwyne to git hung."

When I lit my candle and went up to my room that night, there set pap, his own self!

Chapter V.

I HAD SHUT the door to. Then I turned around, and there he was. I used to be scared of him all the time, he tanned me so much. I reckoned I was scared now, too; but in a minute I see I was mistaken. That is, after the first jolt, as you may say, when my breath sort of hitched—he being so unexpected; but right away after, I see I warn't scared of him worth bothering about.

He was most fifty, and he looked it. His hair was long and tangled and greasy, and hung down, and you could see his eyes shining through like he was behind vines. It was all black, no

"PAP."

gray; so was his long, mixed-up whiskers. There warn't no color in his face, where his face showed; it was white; not like another man's white, but a white to make a body sick, a white to make a body's flesh crawl—a tree-toad white, a fish-belly white. As for his clothes—just rags, that was all. He had one ankle resting on t'other knee; the boot on that foot was busted, and two of his toes stuck through, and he worked them now and then. His hat was laying on the floor; an old black slouch with the top caved in, like a lid.

I stood a-looking at him; he set there a-looking at me, with his chair tilted back a little. I set the candle down. I noticed the window was up; so he had clumb in by the shed. He kept a-looking me all over. By and by he says:

"Starchy clothes—very. You think you're a good deal of a big-bug, *don't* you?"

"Maybe I am, maybe I ain't," I says.

"Don't you give me none o' your lip," says he. "You've put on considerble many frills since I been away. I'll take you down a peg before I get done with you. You're educated, too, they say; can read and write. You think you're better'n your father, now, don't you, because he can't? *I'll* take it out of you. Who told you you might meddle with such hifalut'n foolishness, hey?—who told you you could?"

"The widow. She told me."

"The widow, hey?—and who told the widow she could put in her shovel about a thing that ain't none of her business?"

"Nobody never told her."

"Well, I'll learn her how to meddle. And looky here—you drop that school, you hear? I'll learn people to bring up a boy to put on airs over his own father and let on to be better'n what *he* is. You lemme catch you fooling around that school again, you hear? Your mother couldn't read, and she couldn't write, nuther, before she died. None of the family couldn't, before *they* died. *I* can't; and here you're a-swelling yourself up like this. I ain't the man to stand it—you hear? Say—lemme hear you read."

I took up a book and begun something about General Washington and the wars. When I'd read about a half a minute, he fetched the book a whack with his hand and knocked it across the house. He says:

"It's so. You can do it. I had my doubts when you told me. Now looky here; you stop that putting on frills. I won't have it. I'll lay for you, my smarty; and if I catch you about that school I'll tan you good. First you know you'll get religion, too. I never see such a son."

He took up a little blue and yaller picture of some cows and a boy, and says:

"What's this?"

"It's something they give me for learning my lessons good."

He tore it up, and says—

"I'll give you something better—I'll give you a cowhide."

He set there a-mumbling and a-growling a minute, and then he says—

"*Ain't* you a sweet-scented dandy, though? A bed; and bed-clothes; and a look'n-glass; and a piece of carpet on the floor—and your own father got to sleep with the hogs in the tanyard. I never see such a son. I bet I'll take some o' these frills out o' you before I'm done with you. Why there ain't no end to your airs—they say you're rich. Hey?—how's that?"

"They lie—that's how."

"Looky here—mind how you talk to me; I'm a-standing about all I can stand, now—so don't gimme no sass. I've been in town two

HUCK AND HIS FATHER.

days, and I hain't heard nothing but about you bein' rich. I heard about it away down the river, too. That's why I come. You git me that money to-morrow—I want it."

"I hain't got no money."

"It's a lie. Judge Thatcher's got it. You git it. I want it."

"I hain't got no money, I tell you. You ask Judge Thatcher; he'll tell you the same."

"All right. I'll ask him; and I'll make him pungle, too, or I'll know the reason why. Say—how much you got in your pocket? I want it."

"I hain't got only a dollar, and I want that to—"

"It don't make no difference what you want it for—you just shell it out."

He took it and bit it to see if it was good, and then he said he was going down town to get some whisky; said he hadn't had a drink all day. When he had got out on the shed, he put his head in again, and cussed me for putting on frills and trying to be better than him; and when I reckoned he was gone, he come back and put his head in again, and told me to mind about that school, because he was going to lay for me and lick me if I didn't drop that.

Next day he was drunk, and he went to Judge Thatcher's and bullyragged him and tried to make him give up the money, but he couldn't, and then he swore he'd make the law force him.

The judge and the widow went to law to get the court to take me away from him and let one of them be my guardian; but it was a new judge that had just come, and he didn't know the old man; so he said courts mustn't interfere and separate families if they could help it; said he'd druther not take a child away from its father. So Judge Thatcher and the widow had to quit on the business.

That pleased the old man till he couldn't rest. He said he'd cowhide me till I was black and blue if I didn't raise some money for him. I borrowed three dollars from Judge Thatcher, and pap took it and got drunk and went a-blowing around and cussing and whooping and carrying on; and he kept it up all over town, with a tin pan, till most midnight; then they jailed him, and next day they had him before court, and jailed him again for a week. But he said *he* was satisfied; said he was boss of his son, and he'd make it warm for *him*.

When he got out the new judge said he was agoing to make a man of him. So he took him to his own house, and dressed him up clean and nice, and had him to breakfast and dinner and supper with the family, and was just old pie to him, so to speak. And after supper he talked to him about temperance and such things till the old man cried, and said he'd been a fool, and fooled away his life; but now he was agoing to turn over a new leaf and be a man nobody wouldn't be ashamed of, and he hoped the judge would help him and not look down on him. The judge said he could hug him for them words; so *he* cried, and his wife she cried again; pap said he'd been a man that had always been misunderstood before, and the judge said he believed it. The old man said that what a man wanted that was down, was sympathy; and the judge said it was so; so they cried again. And when it was bedtime, the old man rose up and held out his hand, and says:

"Look at it gentlemen, and ladies all; take ahold of it; shake it. There's a hand that was the hand of a hog; but it ain't so no more; it's the hand of a man that's started in on a new life, and 'll die before he'll go back. You mark them words—don't forget I said them. It's a clean hand now; shake it—don't be afeard."

So they shook it, one after the other, all around, and cried. The judge's wife she kissed it. Then the old man he signed a pledge—

REFORMING THE DRUNKARD.

made his mark. The judge said it was the holiest time on record, or something like that. Then they tucked the old man into a beautiful room, which was the spare room, and in the night sometime he got powerful thirsty and clumb out onto the porch-roof and slid down a stanchion and traded his new coat for a jug of forty-rod, and clumb back again and had a good old time; and towards daylight he crawled out again, drunk as a fiddler, and rolled off the porch and broke his left arm in two places and was most froze to death when somebody found him after sun-up. And when they come to look at that spare room, they had to take soundings before they could navigate it.

The judge he felt kind of sore. He said he reckoned a body could reform the ole man with a shot-gun, maybe, but he didn't know no other way.

FALLING FROM GRACE.

Chapter VI

GETTING OUT OF THE WAY.

WELL, pretty soon the old man was up and around again, and then he went for Judge Thatcher in the courts to make him give up that money, and he went for me, too, for not stopping school. He catched me a couple of times and thrashed me, but I went to school just the same, and dodged him or out-run him most of the time. I didn't want to go to school much, before, but I reckoned I'd go now to spite pap. That law trial was a slow business; appeared like they warn't ever going to get started on it; so every now and then I'd borrow two or three dollars off of the judge for him, to keep from getting a cowhiding. Every time he got money he got drunk; and every time he got drunk he raised Cain around town; and every time he raised Cain he got jailed. He was just suited—this kind of thing was right in his line.

He got to hanging around the widow's too much, and so she told him at last, that if he didn't quit using around there she would make trouble for him. Well, *wasn't* he mad? He said he would show who was Huck Finn's boss. So he watched out for me one day in the spring, and catched me, and took me up the river about three mile, in a skiff, and crossed over to the Illinois shore where it was woody and there warn't no houses but an old log hut in a place where the timber was so thick you couldn't find it if you didn't know where it was.

He kept me with him all the time, and I never got a chance to run off. We lived in that old cabin, and he always locked the door and put the key under his head, nights. He had a gun which he had stole, I reckon, and we fished and hunted, and that was what we lived on. Every little while he locked me in and went down to the store, three miles, to the ferry, and traded fish and game for whisky and fetched it home and got drunk and had a good time, and licked me. The widow she found out where I was, by and by, and she sent a man over to try to get hold of me, but pap drove him off with the gun, and

SOLID COMFORT.

it warn't long after that till I was used to being where I was, and liked it, all but the cowhide part.

It was kind of lazy and jolly, laying off comfortable all day, smoking and fishing, and no books nor study. Two months or more run along, and my clothes got to be all rags and dirt, and I didn't see how I'd ever got to like it so well at the widow's, where you had to wash, and eat on a plate, and comb up, and go to bed and get up regular, and be forever bothering over a book and have old Miss Watson pecking at you all the time. I didn't want to go back no more. I had stopped cussing, because the widow didn't like it; but now I took to it again because pap hadn't no objections. It was pretty good times up in the woods there, take it all around.

But by and by pap got too handy with his hick'ry, and I couldn't stand it. I was all over welts. He got to going away so much, too, and locking me in. Once he locked me in and was gone three days. It was dreadful lonesome. I judged he had got drowned and I wasn't ever going to get out any more. I was scared. I made up my mind I would fix up some way to leave there. I had tried to get out of that cabin many a time, but I couldn't find no way. There warn't a window to it big enought for a dog to get through. I couldn't get up the chimbly, it was too narrow. The door was thick solid oak slabs. Pap was pretty careful not to leave a knife or anything in the cabin when he was away; I reckon I had hunted the place over as much as a hundred times; well, I was 'most all the time at it, because it was about the only way to put in the time. But this time I found something at last; I found an old rusty wood-saw without any handle; it was laid in between a rafter and the clapboards of the roof. I greased it up and went to work. There was an old horse-blanket nailed against the logs at the far end of the cabin behind the table, to keep the wind from blowing through the chinks and putting the candle out. I got under the table and raised the blanket and went to work to saw a section of the big bottom log out, big enough to let me through. Well, it was a good long job, but I was getting towards the end of it when I heard pap's gun in the woods. I got rid of the signs of my work, and dropped the blanket and hid my saw, and pretty soon pap come in.

Pap warn't in a good humor—so he was his natural self. He said he was down to town, and everything was going wrong. His lawyer said he reckoned he would win his lawsuit and get the money, if they ever got started on the trial; but then there was ways to put it off a long time, and Judge Thatcher knowed how to do it. And he said people allowed there'd be another trial to get me away from him and give me to the widow for my guardian, and they guessed it would win, this time. This shook me up considerable, because I didn't want to go back to the widow's any more and be so cramped up and sivilized, as they called it. Then the old man got to cussing, and cussed everything and everybody he could think of, and then cussed them all over again to make sure he hadn't skipped any, and after that he polished off with a kind of a general cuss all round, including a considerable parcel of people which he didn't know the names of, and so called them what's-his-name, when he got to them, and went right along with his cussing.

He said he would like to see the widow get me. He said he would watch out, and if they tried to come any such game on him he knowed of a place six or seven mile off, to stow me in, where they might hunt till they dropped and they couldn't find me. That made me pretty uneasy again, but only for a minute; I reckoned I wouldn't stay on hand till he got that chance.

The old man made me go to the skiff and fetch the things he had got. There was a fifty-pound sack of corn meal, and a side of bacon, ammunition, and a four-gallon jug of whisky, and an old book and two newspapers for wadding, besides some tow. I toted up a load, and went back and set down on the bow of the skiff to rest. I thought it all over, and I reckoned I would walk off with the gun and some lines, and take to the woods when I run away. I guessed I wouldn't stay in one place, but just tramp right across the country, mostly

THINKING IT OVER.

night times, and hunt and fish to keep alive, and so get so far away that the old man nor the widow couldn't ever find me any more. I judged I would saw out and leave that night if pap got drunk enough, and I reckoned he would. I got so full of it I didn't notice how long I was staying, till the old man hollered and asked me whether I was asleep or drownded.

I got the things all up to the cabin, and then it was about dark. While I was cooking supper the old man took a swig or two and got sort of warmed up, and went to ripping again. He had been drunk over in town, and laid in the gutter all night, and he was a sight to look at. A body would a thought he was Adam, he was just all mud. Whenever his liquor begun to work, he most always went for the govment. This time he says:

"Call this a govment! why, just look at it and see what it's like. Here's the law a-standing ready to take a man's son away from him—a man's own son, which he has had all the trouble and all the anxiety and all the expense of raising. Yes, just as that man has got that son raised at last, and ready to go to work and begin to do suthin' for *him* and give him a rest, the law up and goes for him. And they call *that* govment! That ain't all, nuther. The law backs that old Judge Thatcher up and helps him to keep me out o' my property. Here's what the law does. The law takes a man worth six thousand dollars and upards, and jams him into an old trap of a cabin like this, and lets him go round in clothes that ain't fitten for a hog. They call that govment! A man can't get his rights in a govment like this. Sometimes I've a mighty notion to just leave the country for good and all. Yes, and I *told* 'em so; I told old Thatcher so to his face. Lots of 'em heard me, and can tell what I said. Says I, for two cents I'd leave the blamed country and never come anear it agin. Them's the very words. I says, look at my hat—if you call it a hat—but the lid raises up and the rest of it goes down till it's below my chin, and then it ain't rightly a hat at all, but more like my head was shoved up through a jint o' stove-pipe. Look at it, says I—such a hat for me to wear—one of the wealthiest men in this town, if I could git my rights.

"Oh, yes, this is a wonderful govment, wonderful. Why, looky here. There was a free nigger there, from Ohio; a mulatter, most as white as a white man. He had the whitest shirt on you ever see, too, and the shiniest hat; and there ain't a man in that town that's got as fine clothes as what he had; and he had a gold watch and chain, and a silver-headed cane—the awfulest old gray-headed nabob in the State. And what do you think? they said he was a p'fessor in a

college, and could talk all kinds of languages, and knowed everything. And that ain't the wust. They said he could *vote*, when he
was at home. Well, that let me out. Thinks I, what is the country a-
coming to? It was 'lection day, and I was just about to go and vote,
myself, if I warn't too drunk to get there; but when they told me
there was a State in this country where they'd let that nigger vote, I
drawed out. I says I'll never vote agin. Them's the very words I said;
they all heard me; and the country may rot for all me—I'll never
vote agin as long as I live. And to see the cool way of that nigger—
why, he wouldn't a give me the road if I hadn't shoved him out o'
the way. I says to the people, why ain't this nigger put up at auction
and sold?—that's what I want to know. And what do you reckon
they said? Why, they said he couldn't be sold till he'd been in the
State six months, and he hadn't been there that long yet. There,
now—that's a specimen. They call that a govment that can't sell a
free nigger till he's been in the State six months. Here's a govment
that calls itself a govment, and lets on to be a govment, and thinks
it is a govment, and yet's got to set stock-still for six whole months
before it can take ahold of a prowling, thieving, infernal, white-
shirted free nigger, and—"

Pap was agoing on so, he never noticed where his old limber legs
was taking him to, so he went head over heels over the tub of salt
pork, and barked both shins, and the rest of his speech was all the
hottest kind of language—mostly hove at the nigger and the govment, though he give the tub some, too, all along, here and there.
He hopped around the cabin considerable, first on one leg and then
on the other, holding first one shin and then the other one, and at
last he let out with his left foot all of a sudden and fetched the tub a
rattling kick. But it warn't good judgment, because that was the
boot that had a couple of his toes leaking out of the front end of it;
so now he raised a howl that fairly made a body's hair raise, and
down he went in the dirt, and rolled there, and held his toes; and the
cussing he done then laid over anything he had ever done previous.
He said so his own self, afterwards. He had heard old Sowberry
Hagan in his best days, and he said it laid over him, too; but I reckon
that was sort of piling it on, maybe.

After supper pap took the jug, and said he had enough whisky
there for two drunks and one delirium tremens. That was always

his word. I judged he would be blind drunk in about an hour, and
then I would steal the key, or saw myself out, one or t'other. He
drank, and drank, and tumbled down on his blankets, by and by; but

RAISING A HOWL.

luck didn't run my way. He didn't go sound asleep, but was uneasy.
He groaned, and moaned, and thrashed around this way and that,
for a long time. At last I got so sleepy I couldn't keep my eyes open,
all I could do, and so before I knowed what I was about I was sound
asleep, and the candle burning.

I don't know how long I was asleep, but all of a sudden there was
an awful scream and I was up. There was pap, looking wild and
skipping around every which way and yelling about snakes. He said
they was crawling up his legs; and then he would give a jump and
scream, and say one had bit him on the cheek—but I couldn't see
no snakes. He started and run round and round the cabin, hollering
"take him off! take him off! he's biting me on the neck!" I never see
a man look so wild in the eyes. Pretty soon he was all fagged out,
and fell down panting; then he rolled over and over, wonderful fast,

kicking things every which way, and striking and grabbing at the air with his hands, and screaming, and saying there was devils ahold of him. He wore out, by and by, and laid still a while, moaning. Then he laid stiller, and didn't make a sound. I could hear the owls and the wolves, away off in the woods, and it seemed terrible still. He was laying over by the corner. By and by he raised up, part way, and listened, with his head to one side. He says very low:

"Tramp—tramp—tramp; that's the dead; tramp—tramp—tramp; they're coming after me; but I won't go— Oh, they're here! don't touch me—don't! hands off—they're cold; let go— Oh, let a poor devil alone!"

Then he went down on all fours and crawled off begging them to let him alone, and he rolled himself up in his blanket and wallowed in under the old pine table, still a-begging; and then he went to crying. I could hear him through the blanket.

By and by he rolled out and jumped up on his feet looking wild, and he see me and went for me. He chased me round and round the place, with a clasp-knife, calling me the Angel of Death and saying he would kill me and then I couldn't come for him no more. I begged, and told him I was only Huck, but he laughed such a screechy laugh, and roared and cussed, and kept on chasing me up. Once when I turned short and dodged under his arm he made a grab and got me by the jacket between my shoulders, and I thought I was gone; but I slid out of the jacket quick as lightning, and saved myself. Pretty soon he was all tired out, and dropped down with his back against the door, and said he would rest a minute and then kill me. He put his knife under him, and said he would sleep and get strong, and then he would see who was who.

So he dozed off, pretty soon. By and by I got the old split-bottom chair and clumb up, as easy as I could, not to make any noise, and got down the gun. I slipped the ramrod down it to make sure it was loaded, and then I laid it across the turnip barrel, pointing towards pap, and set down behind it to wait for him to stir. And how slow and still the time did drag along.

CHAPTER VII.

"GIT UP!"

"Git up! what you 'bout!"

I opened my eyes and looked around, trying to make out where I was. It was after sun-up, and I had been sound asleep. Pap was standing over me, looking sour—and sick, too. He says—

"What you doin' with this gun?"

I judged he didn't know nothing about what he had been doing, so I says:

"Somebody tried to get in, so I was laying for him."

"Why didn't you roust me out?"

"Well I tried to, but I couldn't; I couldn't budge you."

"Well, all right. Don't stand there palavering all day, but out with you and see if there's a fish on the lines for breakfast. I'll be along in a minute."

He unlocked the door and I cleared out, up the river bank. I noticed some pieces of limbs and such things floating down, and a sprinkling of bark; so I knowed the river had begun to rise. I reckoned I would have great times, now, if I was over at the town. The June rise used to be always luck for me; because as soon as that rise begins, here comes cord-wood floating down, and pieces of log rafts—sometimes a dozen logs together; so all you have to do is to catch them and sell them to the wood yards and the sawmill.

I went along up the bank with one eye out for pap and t'other one out for what the rise might fetch along. Well, all at once, here comes a canoe; just a beauty, too, about thirteen or fourteen foot long, riding high like a duck. I shot head first off of the bank, like a frog, clothes and all on, and struck out for the canoe. I just expected

there'd be somebody laying down in it, because people often done
that to fool folks, and when a chap had pulled a skiff out most to it
they'd raise up and laugh at him. But it warn't so this time. It was a
drift-canoe, sure enough, and I clumb in and paddled her ashore.
Thinks I, the old man will be glad when he sees this—she's worth
ten dollars. But when I got to shore pap wasn't in sight yet, and as I
was running her into a little creek like a gully, all hung over with
vines and willows, I struck another idea; I judged I'd hide her good,
and then, stead of taking to the woods when I run off, I'd go down
the river about fifty mile and camp in one place for good, and not
have such a rough time tramping on foot.

It was pretty close to the shanty, and I thought I heard the old
man coming, all the time; but I got her hid; and then I out and looked
around a bunch of willows, and there was the old man down the
path apiece just drawing a bead on a bird with his gun. So he hadn't
seen anything.

When he got along, I was hard at it taking up a "trot" line. He
abused me a little for being so slow, but I told him I fell in the river
and that was what made me so long. I knowed he would see I was
wet, and then he would be asking questions. We got five cat-fish off
of the lines and went home.

THE SHANTY.

While we laid off, after breakfast, to sleep up, both of us being about wore out, I got to thinking that if I could fix up some way to keep pap and the widow from trying to follow me, it would be a certainer thing than trusting to luck to get far enough off before they missed me; you see, all kinds of things might happen. Well, I didn't see no way for a while, but by and by pap raised up a minute, to drink another barrel of water, and he says:

"Another time a man comes a-prowling round here, you roust me out, you hear? That man warn't here for no good. I'd a shot him. Next time, you roust me out, you hear?"

Then he dropped down and went to sleep again—but what he had been saying give me the very idea I wanted. I says to myself, I can fix it now so nobody won't think of following me.

About twelve o'clock we turned out and went along up the bank. The river was coming up pretty fast, and lots of drift-wood going by on the rise. By and by, along comes part of a log raft—nine logs fast together. We went out with the skiff and towed it ashore. Then we had dinner. Anybody but pap would a waited and seen the day through, so as to catch more stuff; but that warn't pap's style. Nine logs was enough for one time; he must shove right over to town and sell. So he locked me in and took the skiff and started off towing the raft about half-past three. I judged he wouldn't come back that night. I waited till I reckoned he had got a good start, then I out with my saw and went to work on that log again. Before he was t'other side of the river I was out of the hole; him and his raft was just a speck on the water away off yonder.

I took the sack of corn meal and took it to where the canoe was hid, and shoved the vines and branches apart and put it in; then I done the same with the side of bacon; then the whisky jug; I took all the coffee and sugar there was, and all the ammunition; I took the wadding; I took the bucket and gourd, I took a dipper and a tin cup, and my old saw and two blankets, and the skillet and the coffee-pot. I took fish-lines and matches and other things—everything that was worth a cent. I cleaned out the place. I wanted an axe, but there wasn't any, only the one out at the wood pile, and I knowed why I was going to leave that. I fetched out the gun, and now I was done.

I had wore the ground a good deal, crawling out of the hole and dragging out so many things. So I fixed that as good as I could from the outside by scattering dust on the place, which covered up the smoothness and the sawdust. Then I fixed the piece of log back into its place, and put two rocks under it and one against it to hold it there,—for it was bent up at that place, and didn't quite touch ground. If you stood four or five foot away and didn't know it was sawed, you wouldn't ever notice it; and besides, this was the back of the cabin and it warn't likely anybody would go fooling around there.

It was all grass clear to the canoe; so I hadn't left a track. I followed around to see. I stood on the bank and looked out over the river. All safe. So I took the gun and went up a piece into the woods and was hunting around for some birds, when I see a wild pig; hogs soon went wild in them bottoms after they had got away from the prairie farms. I shot this fellow and took him into camp.

I took the axe and smashed in the door—I beat it and hacked it considerable, a-doing it. I fetched the pig in and took him back nearly to the table and hacked into his throat with the axe, and laid him down on the ground to bleed—I say ground, because it *was* ground—hard packed, and no boards. Well, next I took an old sack and put a lot of big rocks in it,—all I could drag—and I started it from the pig and dragged it to the door and through the woods down

SHOOTING THE PIG.

to the river and dumped it in, and down it sunk, out of sight. You could easy see that something had been dragged over the ground. I did wish Tom Sawyer was there, I knowed he would take an interest in this kind of business, and throw in the fancy touches. Nobody could spread himself like Tom Sawyer in such a thing as that.

Well, last I pulled out some of my hair, and bloodied the axe good, and stuck it on the back side, and slung the axe in the corner. Then I took up the pig and held him to my breast with my jacket (so he couldn't drip) till I got a good piece below the house and then dumped him into the river. Now I thought of something else. So I went and got the bag of meal and my old saw out of the canoe and fetched them to the house. I took the bag to where it used to stand, and ripped a hole in the bottom of it with the saw, for there warn't no knives and forks on the place—pap done everything with his clasp-knife, about the cooking. Then I carried the sack about a hundred yards across the grass and through the willows east of the house, to a shallow lake that was five mile wide and full of rushes—and ducks too, you might say, in the season. There was a slough or a creek leading out of it on the other side, that went miles away, I don't know where, but it didn't go to the river. The meal sifted out and made a little track all the way to the lake. I dropped pap's whetstone there too, so as to look like it had been done by accident. Then I tied up the rip in the meal sack with a string, so it wouldn't leak no more, and took it and my saw to the canoe again.

It was about dark, now; so I dropped the canoe down the river under some willows that hung over the bank, and waited for the moon to rise. I made fast to a willow; then I took a bite to eat, and by and by laid down in the canoe to smoke a pipe and lay out a plan. I says to myself, they'll follow the track of that sackful of rocks to the shore and then drag the river for me. And they'll follow that meal track to the lake and go browsing down the creek that leads out of it to find the robbers that killed me and took the things. They won't ever hunt the river for anything but my dead carcass. They'll soon get tired of that, and won't bother no more about me. All right; I can stop anywhere I want to. Jackson's Island is good enough for me; I know that island pretty well, and nobody ever comes there. And then I can paddle over to town, nights, and slink around and pick up things I want. Jackson's Island's the place.

I was pretty tired, and the first thing I knowed, I was asleep. When I woke up I didn't know where I was, for a minute. I set up and looked around, a little scared. Then I remembered. The river looked miles and miles across. The moon was so bright I could a counted the drift logs that went a slipping along, black and still, hundreds of yards out from shore. Everything was dead quiet, and it looked late, and *smelt* late. You know what I mean—I don't know the words to put it in.

I took a good gap and a stretch, and was just going to unhitch and start, when I heard a sound away over the water. I listened. Pretty soon I made it out. It was that dull kind of a regular sound that comes from oars working in rowlocks when it's a still night. I peeped out through the willow branches, and there it was—a skiff, away across the water. I couldn't tell how many was in it. It kept a-coming, and when it was abreast of me I see there warn't but one man in it. Thinks I, maybe it's pap, though I warn't expecting him. He dropped below me, with the current, and by and by he come a-swinging up shore in the easy water, and he went by so close I could a reached out the gun and touched him. Well, it *was* pap, sure enough—and sober, too, by the way he laid to his oars.

I didn't lose no time. The next minute I was a-spinning down stream soft but quick in the shade of the bank. I made two mile and a half, and then struck out a quarter of a mile or more towards the middle of the river, because pretty soon I would be passing the ferry landing and people might see me and hail me. I got out amongst the drift-wood and then laid down in the bottom of the canoe and let her float. I laid there and had a good rest and a smoke out of my pipe, looking away into the sky, not a cloud in it. The sky looks ever so deep when you lay down on your back in the moonshine; I never knowed it before. And how far a body can hear on the water such nights! I heard people talking at the ferry landing. I heard what they said, too, every word of it. One man said it was getting towards the long days and the short nights, now. T'other one said *this* warn't one of the short ones, he reckoned—and then they laughed, and he said it over again and they laughed again; then they waked up another fellow and told him, and laughed, but he didn't laugh; he ripped out something brisk and said let him alone. The first fellow said he 'lowed to tell it to his old woman—she would think it was pretty good; but he said that warn't nothing to some things he had said in his time. I heard one man say it was nearly three o'clock, and he hoped daylight wouldn't wait more than about a week longer. After that, the talk got further and further away, and I couldn't make out the words any more, but I could hear the mumble; and now and then a laugh, too, but it seemed a long ways off.

I was away below the ferry now. I rose up and there was Jackson's Island, about two mile and a half down stream, heavy-timbered and

TAKING A REST.

standing up out of the middle of the river, big and dark and solid, like a steamboat without any lights. There warn't any signs of the bar at the head—it was all under water, now.

It didn't take me long to get there. I shot past the head at a ripping rate, the current was so swift, and then I got into the dead water and landed on the side towards the Illinois shore. I run the canoe into a deep dent in the bank that I knowed about; I had to part the willow branches to get in; and when I made fast nobody could a seen the canoe from the outside.

I went up and set down on a log at the head of the island and looked out on the big river and the black driftwood, and away over to the town, three mile away, where there was three or four lights twinkling. A monstrous big lumber raft was about a mile up stream, coming along down, with a lantern in the middle of it. I watched it come creeping down, and when it was most abreast of where I stood I heard a man say, "Stern oars, there! heave her head to stabboard!" I heard that just as plain as if the man was by my side.

There was a little gray in the sky, now; so I stepped into the woods and laid down for a nap before breakfast.

Chapter VIII.

IN THE WOODS.

The sun was up so high when I waked, that I judged it was after eight o'clock. I laid there in the grass and the cool shade, thinking about things and feeling rested and ruther comfortable and satisfied. I could see the sun out at one or two holes, but mostly it was big trees all about, and gloomy in there amongst them. There was freckled places on the ground where the light sifted down through the leaves, and the freckled places swapped about a little, showing there was a little breeze up there. A couple of squirrels set on a limb and jabbered at me very friendly.

I was powerful lazy and comfortable—didn't want to get up and cook breakfast. Well, I was dozing off again, when I thinks I hears a deep sound of "boom!" away up the river. I rouses up and rests on my elbow and listens; pretty soon I hears it again. I hopped up and went and looked out at a hole in the leaves, and I see a bunch of smoke laying on the water a long ways up—about abreast the ferry. And there was the ferry-boat full of people, floating along down. I knowed what was the matter, now. "Boom!" I see the white smoke squirt out of the ferry-boat's side. You see, they was firing cannon over the water, trying to make my carcass come to the top.

I was pretty hungry, but it warn't going to do for me to start a fire, because they might see the smoke. So I set there and watched the cannon-smoke and listened to the boom. The river was a mile wide, there, and it always looks pretty on a summer morning—so I was

having a good enough time seeing them hunt for my remainders, if
I only had a bite to eat. Well, then I happened to think how they
always put quicksilver in loaves of bread and float them off because
they always go right to the drownded carcass and stop there. So says
I, I'll keep a lookout, and if any of them's floating around after me,
I'll give them a show. I changed to the Illinois edge of the island to
see what luck I could have, and I warn't disappointed. A big double

WATCHING THE BOAT.

loaf come along, and I most got it, with a long stick, but my foot
slipped and she floated out further. Of course I was where the current set in the closest to the shore—I knowed enough for that. But
by and by along comes another one, and this time I won. I took out
the plug and shook out the little dab of quicksilver, and set my teeth
in. It was "baker's bread"—what the quality eat—none of your low-
down corn-pone.

I got a good place amongst the leaves, and set there on a log, munching the bread and watching the ferry-boat, and very well satisfied. And then something struck me. I says, now I reckon the widow or the parson or somebody prayed that this bread would find me, and here it has gone and done it. So there ain't no doubt but there is something in that thing. That is, there's something in it when a body like the widow or the parson prays, but it don't work for me, and I reckon it don't work for only just the right kind.

I lit a pipe and had a good long smoke and went on watching. The ferry-boat was floating with the current, and I allowed I'd have a chance to see who was aboard when she come along, because she would come in close, where the bread did. When she'd got pretty well along down towards me, I put out my pipe and went to where I fished out the bread, and laid down behind a log on the bank in a little open place. Where the log forked I could peep through.

By and by she come along, and she drifted in so close that they could a run out a plank and walked ashore. Most everybody was on the boat. Pap, and Judge Thatcher, and Becky Thatcher, and Jo Harper, and Tom Sawyer, and his old aunt Polly, and Sid and Mary, and plenty more. Everybody was talking about the murder, but the captain broke in and says:

"Look sharp, now; the current sets in the closest here, and maybe he's washed ashore and got tangled amongst the brush at the water's edge. I hope so, anyway."

I didn't hope so. They all crowded up and leaned over the rails, nearly in my face, and kept still, watching with all their might. I could see them first-rate, but they couldn't see me. Then the captain sung out:

"Stand away!" and the cannon let off such a blast right before me that it made me deef with the noise and pretty near blind with the smoke, and I judged I was gone. If they'd a had some bullets in, I reckon they'd a got the corpse they was after. Well, I see I warn't hurt, thanks to goodness. The boat floated on and went out of sight around the shoulder of the island. I could hear the booming, now and then, further and further off, and by and by after an hour, I didn't hear it no more. The island was three mile long. I judged they had got to the foot, and was giving it up. But they didn't yet a while. They turned around the foot of the island and started up the channel on the Missouri side, under steam, and booming once in a while as they went. I crossed over to that side and watched them. When they got abreast the head of the island they quit shooting and dropped over to the Missouri shore and went home to the town.

I knowed I was all right now. Nobody else would come a-hunting after me. I got my traps out of the canoe and made me a nice camp in the thick woods. I made a kind of a tent out of my blankets to put my things under so the rain couldn't get at them. I catched a cat-fish and haggled him open with my saw, and towards sundown I started my camp fire and had supper. Then I set out a line to catch some fish for breakfast.

When it was dark I set by my camp fire smoking, and feeling pretty satisfied; but by and by it got sort of lonesome, and so I went and set on the bank and listened to the currents washing along, and counted the stars and drift-logs and rafts that come down, and then went to bed; there ain't no better way to put in time when you are lonesome; you can't stay so, you soon get over it.

And so for three days and nights. No difference—just the same thing. But the next day I went exploring around down through the island. I was boss of it; it all belonged to me, so to say, and I wanted to know all about it; but mainly I wanted to put in the time. I found plenty strawberries, ripe and prime; and green summer-grapes, and green razberries; and the green blackberries was just beginning to show. They would all come handy by and by, I judged.

Well, I went fooling along in the deep woods till I judged I warn't far from the foot of the island. I had my gun along, but I hadn't shot nothing; it was for protection; thought I would kill some game nigh home. About this time I mighty near stepped on a good sized snake, and it went sliding off through the grass and flowers, and I after it, trying to get a shot at it. I clipped along, and all of a sudden I bounded right on to the ashes of a camp fire that was still smoking.

My heart jumped up amongst my lungs. I never waited for to look further, but uncocked my gun and went sneaking back on my tip-toes as fast as ever I could. Every now and then I stopped a second, amongst the thick leaves, and listened; but my breath come so hard I couldn't hear nothing else. I slunk along another piece further, then listened again; and so on, and so on; if I see a stump, I took it for a man; if I trod on a stick and broke it, it made me feel like a person had cut one of my breaths in two and I only got half, and the short half, too.

When I got to camp I warn't feeling very brash, there warn't much sand in my craw; but I says, this ain't no time to be fooling around. So I got all my traps into my canoe again so as to have them out of sight, and I put out the fire and scattered the ashes around to look like an old last year's camp, and then clumb a tree.

I reckon I was up in the tree two hours; but I didn't see nothing, I didn't hear nothing—I only *thought* I heard and seen as much as a

DISCOVERING THE CAMP FIRE.

thousand things. Well, I couldn't stay up there forever; so at last I got down, but I kept in the thick woods and on the lookout all the time. All I could get to eat was berries and what was left over from breakfast.

By the time it was night I was pretty hungry. So when it was good and dark, I slid out from shore before moonrise and paddled over to the Illinois bank—about a quarter of a mile. I went out in the woods and cooked a supper, and I had about made up my mind I would stay there all night, when I hear a *plunkety-plunk*, *plunkety-plunk*, and says to myself, horses coming; and next I hear people's voices. I got everything into the canoe as quick as I could, and then went creeping through the woods to see what I could find out. I hadn't got far when I hear a man say:

"We better camp here, if we can find a good place; the horses is about beat out. Let's look around."

I didn't wait, but shoved out and paddled away easy. I tied up in the old place, and reckoned I would sleep in the canoe.

I didn't sleep much. I couldn't, somehow, for thinking. And every time I waked up I thought somebody had me by the neck. So the sleep didn't do me no good. By and by I says to myself, I can't live this way; I'm agoing to find out who it is that's here on the island with me; I'll find it out or bust. Well, I felt better, right off.

So I took my paddle and slid out from shore just a step or two, and then let the canoe drop along down amongst the shadows. The moon was shining, and outside of the shadows it made it most as light as day. I poked along well onto an hour, everything still as rocks and sound asleep. Well by this time I was most down to the foot of the island. A little ripply, cool breeze begun to blow, and that was as good as saying the night was about done. I give her a turn with the paddle and brung her nose to shore; then I got my gun and slipped out and into the edge of the woods. I set down there on a log and looked out through the leaves. I see the moon go off watch and the darkness begin to blanket the river. But in a little while I see a pale streak over the tree-tops, and knowed the day was coming. So I took my gun and slipped off towards where I had run across that camp fire, stopping every minute or two to listen. But I hadn't no luck, somehow; I couldn't seem to find the place. But by and by, sure enough, I catched a glimpse of fire, away through the trees. I went for it, cautious and slow. By and by I was close enough to have a look, and there laid a man on the ground. It most give me the fan-tods. He had a blanket around his head, and his head was nearly in the fire. I set there behind a clump of bushes, in about six foot of him, and kept my eyes on him steady. It was getting gray daylight, now. Pretty soon he gapped, and stretched himself, and hove off the blanket, and it was Miss Watson's Jim! I bet I was glad to see him. I says:

"Hello, Jim!" and skipped out.

He bounced up and stared at me wild. Then he drops down on his knees, and puts his hands together and says:

"Doan' hurt me—don't! I hain't ever done no harm to a ghos'. I awluz liked dead people, en done all I could for 'em. You go en git in

JIM AND THE GHOST.

de river agin, whah you b'longs, en doan' do nuffn to Ole Jim, 'at 'uz awluz yo' fren'."

Well, I warn't long making him understand I warn't dead. I was ever so glad to see Jim. I warn't lonesome, now. I told him I warn't afraid of *him* telling the people where I was. I talked along, but he only set there and looked at me; never said nothing. Then I says:

"It's good daylight. Le's get breakfast. Make up your camp fire good."

"What's de use er makin' up de camp fire to cook strawbries en sich truck? But you got a gun, hain't you? Den we kin git sumfn better den strawbries."

"Strawberries and such truck," I says. "Is that what you live on?"

"I couldn' git nuffn else," he says.

"Why, how long you been on the island, Jim?"

"I come heah de night arter you's killed."

"What, all that time?"

"Yes-indeedy."

"And ain't you had nothing but that kind of rubbage to eat?"

"No, sah—nuffn else."

"Well, you must be most starved, ain't you?"

"I reck'n I could eat a hoss. I think I could. How long you ben on de islan'?"

"Since the night I got killed."

"No! W'y, what has you lived on? But you got a gun. Oh, yes, you got a gun. Dat's good. Now you kill sumfn en I'll make up de fire."

So we went over to where the canoe was, and while he built a fire in a grassy open place amongst the trees, I fetched meal and bacon and coffee, and coffee-pot and frying-pan, and sugar and tin cups, and the nigger was set back considerable, because he reckoned it was all done with witchcraft. I catched a good big cat-fish, too, and Jim cleaned him with his knife, and fried him.

When breakfast was ready, we lolled on the grass and eat it smoking hot. Jim laid it in with all his might, for he was most about starved. Then when we had got pretty well stuffed, we laid off and lazied.

By and by Jim says:

"But looky here, Huck, who wuz it dat 'uz killed in dat shanty, ef it warn't you?"

Then I told him the whole thing, and he said it was smart. He said Tom Sawyer couldn't get up no better plan than what I had. Then I says:

"How do you come to be here, Jim, and how'd you get here?"

He looked pretty uneasy, and didn't say nothing for a minute. Then he says:

"Maybe I better not tell."

"Why, Jim?"

"Well, dey's reasons. But you wouldn' tell on me ef I 'uz to tell you, would you, Huck?"

"Blamed if I would, Jim."

"Well, I b'lieve you, Huck. I—I run off."

"Jim!"

"But mind, you said you wouldn't tell—you know you said you wouldn't tell, Huck."

"Well, I did. I said I wouldn't, and I'll stick to it. Honest injun I will. People would call me a low down Ablitionist and despise me for keeping mum—but that don't make no difference. I ain't agoing to tell, and I ain't agoing back there anyways. So now, le's know all about it."

"Well, you see, it 'uz dis way. Ole Missus—dat's Miss Watson—she pecks on me all de time, en treats me pooty rough, but she awluz said she wouldn' sell me down to Orleans. But I noticed dey wuz a nigger trader roun' de place considable, lately, en I begin to git oneasy. Well, one night I creeps to de do', pooty late, en de do' warn't quite shet, en I hear ole missus tell de widder she gwyne to sell me down to Orleans, but she didn' want to, but she could git eight hund'd dollars for me, en it 'uz sich a big stack o' money she couldn' resis'. De widder she try to git her to say she wouldn' do it, but I never waited to hear de res'. I lit out mighty quick, I tell you.

"I tuck out en shin down de hill en 'spec to steal a skift 'long de sho' som'ers 'bove de town, but dey wuz people a-stirrin' yit, so I hid in de ole tumble-down cooper shop on de bank to wait for everybody to go 'way. Well, I wuz dah all night. Dey wuz somebody roun' all de time. 'Long 'bout six in de mawnin', skifts begin to go by, en 'bout eight er nine every skift dat went 'long wuz talkin' 'bout how yo' pap come over to de town en say you's killed. Dese las' skifts wuz full o' ladies en genlmen agoin' over for to see de place. Sometimes dey'd pull up at de sho' en take a res' b'fo' dey started acrost, so by de talk I got to know all 'bout de killin'. I 'uz powerful sorry you's killed, Huck, but I ain't no mo', now.

"I laid dah under de shavins all day. I 'uz hungry, but I warn't afeared; bekase I knowed ole missus en de widder wuz goin' to start to de camp-meetn' right arter breakfas' en be gone all day, en dey knows I goes off wid de cattle 'bout daylight, so dey wouldn' 'spec to see me roun' de place, en so dey wouldn' miss me tell arter dark in de evenin'. De yuther servants wouldn' miss me, kase dey'd shin out en take holiday, soon as de ole folks 'uz out'n de way.

"Well, when it come dark I tuck out up de river road, en went 'bout two mile er more to whah dey warn't no houses. I'd made up my mine 'bout what I's agwyne to do. You see ef I kep' on tryin' to git away afoot, de dogs 'ud track me; ef I stole a skift to cross over, dey'd miss dat skift, you see, en dey'd know 'bout whah I'd lan' on de yuther side en whah to pick up my track. So I says, a raff is what I's arter; it doan' *make* no track.

"I see a light a-comin' roun' de p'int, bymeby, so I wade' in en shove' a log ahead o' me, en swum more'n half-way acrost de river, en got in 'mongst de drift-wood, en kep' my head down low, en kinder swum agin de current tell de raff come along. Den I swum to de stern uv it, en tuck aholt. It clouded up en 'uz pooty dark for a little while. So I clumb up en laid down on de planks. De men 'uz all 'way yonder in de middle, whah de lantern wuz. De river wuz arisin' en dey wuz a good current; so I reck'n'd 'at by fo' in de mawnin' I'd be twenty-five mile down de river, en den I'd slip in, jis' b'fo' daylight, en swim asho' en take to de woods on de Illinoi side.

"But I didn' have no luck. When we 'uz mos' down to de head er de islan', a man begin to come aft wid de lantern. I see it warn't no use fer to wait, so I slid overboad, en struck out fer de islan'. Well, I had a notion I could lan' mos' anywhers, but I couldn't—bank too bluff. I 'uz mos' to de foot er de islan' b'fo' I foun' a good place. I went into de woods en jedged I wouldn' fool wid raffs no mo', long as dey move de lantern roun' so. I had my pipe en a plug er dog-leg, en some matches in my cap, en dey warn't wet, so I 'uz all right."

"And so you ain't had no meat nor bread to eat all this time? Why didn't you get mud-turkles?"

"How you gwyne to git'm? You can't slip up on um en grab um; en how's a body gwyne to hit um wid a rock? How could a body do it in de night? en I warn't gwyne to show mysef on de bank in de daytime."

"Well, that's so. You've had to keep in the woods all the time, of course. Did you hear 'em shooting the cannon?"

"Oh, yes. I knowed dey was arter you. I see um go by heah; watched um thoo de bushes."

Some young birds come along, flying a yard or two at a time and lighting. Jim said it was a sign it was going to rain. He said it was a sign when young chickens flew that way, and so he reckoned it was the same way when young birds done it. I was going to catch some of them, but Jim wouldn't let me. He said it was death. He said his father laid mighty sick once, and some of them catched a bird, and his old granny said his father would die, and he did.

And Jim said you mustn't count the things you are going to cook for dinner, because that would bring bad luck. The same if you shook the table-cloth after sundown. And he said if a man owned a bee-hive, and that man died, the bees must be told about it before sun-up next morning, or else the bees would all weaken down and quit work and die. Jim said bees wouldn't sting idiots; but I didn't believe that, because I had tried them lots of times myself, and they wouldn't sting me.

I had heard about some of these things before, but not all of them. Jim knowed all kinds of signs. He said he knowed most everything. I said it looked to me like all the signs was about bad luck, and so I asked him if there warn't any good-luck signs. He says:

"Mighty few—an' *dey* ain' no use to a body. What you want to know when good luck's a-comin' for? want to keep it off?" And he said: "Ef you's got hairy arms en a hairy breas', it's a sign dat you's agwyne to be rich. Well, dey's some use in a sign like dat, 'kase it's so fur ahead. You see, maybe you's got to be po' a long time fust, en so you might git discourage' en kill yo'sef 'f you didn' know by de sign dat you gwyne to be rich bymeby."

"Have you got hairy arms and a hairy breast, Jim?"

"What's de use to ax dat question? don' you see I has?"

"Well, are you rich?"

"No, but I ben rich wunst, and gwyne to be rich agin. Wunst I had foteen dollars, but I tuck to specalat'n', en got busted out."

"What did you speculate in, Jim?"

"Well, fust I tackled stock."

"What kind of stock?"

"Why, live stock. Cattle, you know. I put ten dollars in a cow. But I ain' gwyne to resk no mo' money in stock. De cow up 'n' died on my han's."

"So you lost the ten dollars."

"No, I didn' lose it all. I on'y los' 'bout nine of it. I sole de hide en taller for a dollar en ten cents."

"You had five dollars and ten cents left. Did you speculate any more?"

"Yes. You know dat one-laigged nigger dat b'longs to ole Misto Bradish? well, he sot up a bank, en say anybody dat put in a dollar would git fo' dollars mo' at de en' er de year. Well, all de niggers went in, but dey didn' have much. I wuz de on'y one dat had much. So I stuck out for mo' dan fo' dollars, en I said 'f I didn' git it I'd start a bank mysef. Well o' course dat nigger want' to keep me out er de business, bekase he say dey warn't business 'nough for two banks, so he say I could put in my five dollars en he pay me thirty-five at de en' er de year.

"So I done it. Den I reck'n'd I'd inves' de thirty-five dollars right off en keep things a-movin'. Dey wuz a nigger name' Bob, dat had ketched a wood-flat, en his marster didn' know it; en I bought it off'n him en told him to take de thirty-five dollars when de en' er de

MISTO BRADISH'S NIGGER.

year come; but somebody stole de wood-flat dat night, en nex' day de one-laigged nigger say de bank 's busted. So dey didn' none uv us git no money."

"What did you do with the ten cents, Jim?"

"Well, I 'uz gwyne to spen' it, but I had a dream, en de dream tole me to give it to a nigger name' Balum—Balum's Ass dey call him for short, he's one er dem chuckle-heads, you know. But he's lucky, dey say, en I see I warn't lucky. De dream say let Balum inves' de ten cents en he'd make a raise for me. Well, Balum he tuck de money, en when he wuz in church he hear de preacher say dat whoever give to de po' len' to de Lord, en boun' to git his money back a hund'd times. So Balum he tuck en give de ten cents to de po', en laid low to see what wuz gwyne to come of it.''

"Well, what did come of it, Jim?''

"Nuffn' never come of it. I couldn' manage to k'leck dat money no way; en Balum he couldn'. I ain' gwyne to len' no mo' money 'dout I see de security. Boun' to git yo' money back a hund'd times, de preacher says! Ef I could git de ten *cents* back, I'd call it squah, en be glad er de chanst.''

"Well, it's all right, anyway, Jim, long as you're going to be rich again some time or other.''

"Yes—en I's rich now, come to look at it. I owns mysef, en I's wuth eight hund'd dollars. I wisht I had de money, I wouldn' want no mo'.''

Chapter IX.

I wanted to go and look at a place right about the middle of the island, that I'd found when I was exploring; so we started, and soon got to it, because the island was only three miles long and a quarter of a mile wide.

This place was a tolerable long steep hill or ridge, about forty foot high. We had a rough time getting to the top, the sides was so steep and the bushes so thick. We tramped and clumb around all over it, and by and by found a good big cavern in the rock, most up to the top on the side towards Illinois. The cavern was as big as two or three rooms

EXPLORING THE CAVE.

bunched together, and Jim could stand up straight in it. It was cool in there. Jim was for putting our traps in there, right away, but I said we didn't want to be climbing up and down there all the time.

Jim said if we had the canoe hid in a good place, and had all the traps in the cavern, we could rush there if anybody was to come to the island, and they would never find us without dogs. And besides, he said them little birds had said it was going to rain, and did I want the things to get wet?

So we went back and got the canoe and paddled up abreast the cavern, and lugged all the traps up there. Then we hunted up a place close by to hide the canoe in, amongst the thick willows. We took some fish off of the lines and set them again, and begun to get ready for dinner.

The door of the cavern was big enough to roll a hogshead in, and on one side of the door the floor stuck out a little bit and was flat and a good place to build a fire on. So we built it there and cooked dinner.

We spread the blankets inside for a carpet, and eat our dinner in there. We put all the other things handy at the back of the cavern. Pretty soon it darkened up and begun to thunder and lighten; so the birds was right about it. Directly it begun to rain, and it rained like all fury, too, and I never see the wind blow so. It was one of these regular summer storms. It would get so dark that it looked all blue-black outside, and lovely; and the rain would thrash along by so thick that the trees off a little ways looked dim and spider-webby; and here would come a blast of wind that would bend the trees down and turn up the pale underside of the leaves; and then a perfect ripper of a gust would follow along and set the branches to tossing their arms as if they was just wild; and next, when it was just about the bluest and blackest—*fst!* it was as bright as glory and you'd have a little glimpse of tree-tops a-plunging about, away off yonder in the storm, hundreds of yards further than you could see before; dark as sin again in a second, and now you'd hear the thunder let go with an awful crash and then go rumbling, grumbling, tumbling down the sky towards the under side of the world, like rolling empty barrels

IN THE CAVE.

down stairs, where it's long stairs and they bounce a good deal, you know.

"Jim, this is nice," I says. "I wouldn't want to be nowhere else but here. Pass me along another hunk of fish and some hot corn-bread."

"Well, you wouldn't a ben here, 'f it hadn't a ben for Jim. You'd a ben down dah in de woods widout any dinner, en gittn' mos' drownded, too, dat you would, honey. Chickens knows when it's gwyne to rain, en so do de birds, chile."

The river went on raising and raising for ten or twelve days, till at last it was over the banks. The water was three or four foot deep on the island in the low places and on the Illinois bottom. On that side it was a good many miles wide; but on the Missouri side it was the same old distance across—a half a mile—because the Missouri shore was just a wall of high bluffs.

Daytimes we paddled all over the island in the canoe. It was mighty cool and shady in the deep woods even if the sun was blazing outside. We went winding in and out amongst the trees; and sometimes the vines hung so thick we had to back away and go some other way. Well, on every old broken-down tree, you could see rabbits, and snakes, and such things; and when the island had been overflowed a day or two, they got so tame, on account of being hungry, that you could paddle right up and put your hand on them if you wanted to; but not the snakes and turtles—they would slide off in the water. The ridge our cavern was in, was full of them. We could a had pets enough if we'd wanted them.

One night we catched a little section of a lumber raft—nice pine planks. It was twelve foot wide and about fifteen or sixteen foot long, and the top stood above water six or seven inches, a solid level floor. We could see saw-logs go by in the daylight, sometimes, but we let them go; we didn't show ourselves in daylight.

Another night, when we was up at the head of the island, just before daylight, here comes a frame house down, on the west side. She was a two-story, and tilted over, considerable. We paddled out and got aboard—clumb in at an up-stairs window. But it was too dark to see yet, so we made the canoe fast and set in her to wait for daylight.

The light begun to come before we got to the foot of the island.

Then we looked in at the window. We could make out a bed, and a table, and two old chairs, and lots of things around about on the floor; and there was clothes hanging against the wall. There was something laying on the floor in the far corner that looked like a man. So Jim says:

"Hello, you!"

But it didn't budge. So I hollered again, and then Jim says:

"De man ain't asleep—he's dead. You hold still—I'll go en see."

He went and bent down and looked, and says:

"It's a dead man. Yes, indeedy; naked, too. He's ben shot in de

JIM SEES A DEAD MAN.

back. I reck'n he's ben dead two er three days. Come in, Huck, but doan' look at his face—it's too gashly."

I didn't look at him at all. Jim throwed some old rags over him, but he needn't done it; I didn't want to see him. There was heaps of old greasy cards scattered around over the floor, and old whisky bottles, and a couple of masks made out of black cloth; and all over the walls was the ignorantest kind of words and pictures, made with charcoal. There was two old dirty calico dresses, and a sun-bonnet, and some women's under-clothes, hanging against the wall, and some men's clothing, too. We put the lot into the canoe; it might come good. There was a boy's old speckled straw hat on the floor; I took that too. And there was a bottle that had had milk in it; and it had a rag stopper for a baby to suck. We would a took the bottle, but it was broke. There was a seedy old chest, and an old hair trunk with the hinges broke. They stood open, but there warn't nothing left in them that was any account. The way things was scattered about, we reckoned the people left in a hurry and warn't fixed so as to carry off most of their stuff.

We got an old tin lantern, and a butcher knife without any handle, and a bran-new Barlow knife worth two bits in any store, and a lot of tallow candles, and a tin candlestick, and a gourd, and a tin cup, and a ratty old bed-quilt off the bed, and a reticule with needles and pins and beeswax and buttons and thread and all such truck in it, and a hatchet and some nails, and a fish-line as thick as my little finger, with some monstrous hooks on it, and a roll of buckskin, and a leather dog-collar, and a horse-shoe, and some vials of medicine that didn't have no label on them; and just as we was leaving I found a tolerable good curry-comb, and Jim he found a ratty old fiddle-bow, and a wooden leg. The straps was broke off of it, but barring that, it was a good enough leg, though it was too long for me and not long enough for Jim, and we couldn't find the other one, though we hunted all around.

And so, take it all around, we made a good haul. When we was ready to shove off, we was a quarter of a mile below the island, and it was pretty broad day; so I made Jim lay down in the canoe and cover up with the quilt, because if he set up, people could tell he was a nigger a good ways off. I paddled over to the Illinois shore, and drifted down most a half a mile doing it. I crept up the dead water under the bank, and hadn't no accidents and didn't see nobody. We got home all safe.

Chapter X.

THEY FOUND EIGHT DOLLARS.

AFTER breakfast I wanted to talk about the dead man and guess out how he come to be killed, but Jim didn't want to. He said it would fetch bad luck; and besides, he said, he might come and ha'nt us; he said a man that warn't buried was more likely to go a-ha'nting around than one that was planted and comfortable. That sounded pretty reasonable, so I didn't say no more; but I couldn't keep from studying over it and wishing I knowed who shot the man, and what they done it for.

We rummaged the clothes we'd got, and found eight dollars in silver sewed up in the lining of an old blanket overcoat. Jim said he reckoned the people in that house stole the coat, because if they'd a knowed the money was there they wouldn't a left it. I said I reckoned they killed him, too; but Jim didn't want to talk about that. I says:

"Now you think it's bad luck; but what did you say when I fetched in the snake-skin that I found on the top of the ridge day before yesterday? You said it was the worst bad luck in the world to touch a snake-skin with my hands. Well, here's your bad luck! We've raked in all this truck and eight dollars besides. I wish we could have some bad luck like this every day, Jim."

"Never you mind, honey, never you mind. Don't you git too peart. It's a-comin'. Mind I tell you, it's a-comin'."

It did come, too. It was a Tuesday that we had that talk. Well, after dinner Friday, we was laying around in the grass at the upper end of the ridge, and got out of tobacco. I went to the cavern to get some, and found a rattlesnake in there. I killed him, and curled him up on the foot of Jim's blanket, ever so natural, thinking there'd be some fun when Jim found him there. Well, by night I forgot all about the snake, and when Jim flung himself down on the blanket while I struck a light, the snake's mate was there, and bit him.

He jumped up yelling, and the first thing the light showed was the varmint curled up and ready for another spring. I laid him out in

JIM AND THE SNAKE.

a second with a stick, and Jim grabbed pap's whisky jug and begun to pour it down.

He was barefooted, and the snake bit him right on the heel. That all comes of my being such a fool as to not remember that wherever you leave a dead snake its mate always comes there and curls around it. Jim told me to chop off the snake's head and throw it away, and then skin the body and roast a piece of it. I done it, and he eat it and said it would help cure him. He made me take off the rattles and tie them around his wrist, too. He said that that would help. Then I slid out quiet and throwed the snakes clear away amongst the bushes; for I warn't going to let Jim find out it was all my fault, not if I could help it.

Jim sucked and sucked at the jug, and now and then he got out of his head and pitched around and yelled; but every time he come to himself he went to sucking at the jug again. His foot swelled up pretty big, and so did his leg; but by and by the drunk begun to come, and so I judged he was all right; but I'd druther been bit with a snake than pap's whisky.

Jim was laid up for four days and nights. Then the swelling was all gone and he was around again. I made up my mind I wouldn't ever take aholt of a snake-skin again with my hands, now that I see what had come of it. Jim said he reckoned I would believe him next time. And he said that handling a snake-skin was such awful bad luck that maybe we hadn't got to the end of it yet. He said he druther see the new moon over his left shoulder as much as a thousand times than take up a snake-skin in his hand. Well, I was getting to feel that way myself, though I've always reckoned that looking at the new moon over your left shoulder is one of the carelessest and foolishest things a body can do. Old Hank Bunker done it once, and bragged about it; and in less than two years he got drunk and fell off of the shot tower and spread himself out so that he was just a kind of a layer, as you may say; and they slid him edgeways between two barn doors for a coffin, and buried him so, so they say, but I didn't see it. Pap told me. But anyway, it all come of looking at the moon that way, like a fool.

Well, the days went along, and the river went down between its banks again; and about the first thing we done was to bait one of the big hooks with a skinned rabbit and set it and catch a cat-fish that was as big as a man, being six foot two inches long, and weighed over two hundred pounds. We couldn't handle him, of course; he would a flung us into Illinois. We just set there and watched him rip and tear around till he drownded. We found a brass button in his stomach, and a round ball, and lots of rubbage. We split the ball open

with the hatchet, and there was a spool in it. Jim said he'd had it
there a long time, to coat it over so and make a ball of it. It was as
big a fish as was ever catched in the Mississippi, I reckon. Jim said
he hadn't ever seen a bigger one. He would a been worth a good deal
over at the village. They peddle out such a fish as that by the pound
in the market house there; everybody buys some of him; his meat's
as white as snow and makes a good fry.

Next morning I said it was getting slow and dull, and I wanted to

OLD HANK BUNKER.

get a stirring up, some way. I said I reckoned I would slip over the
river and find out what was going on. Jim liked that notion; but he
said I must go in the dark and look sharp. Then he studied it over
and said, couldn't I put on some of them old things and dress up like
a girl? That was a good notion, too. So we shortened up one of the
calico gowns and I turned up my trowser-legs to my knees and got
into it. Jim hitched it behind with the hooks, and it was a fair fit. I
put on the sun-bonnet and tied it under my chin, and then for a body

to look in and see my face was like looking down a joint of stove-
pipe. Jim said nobody would know me, even in the daytime, hardly.
I practiced around all day to get the hang of the things, and by and
by I could do pretty well in them, only Jim said I didn't walk like a
girl; and he said I must quit pulling up my gown to get at my britches
pocket. I took notice, and done better.

I started up the Illinois shore in the canoe just after dark.

I started across to the town from a little below the ferry landing,
and the drift of the current fetched me in at the bottom of the town.
I tied up and started along the bank. There was a light burning in a
little shanty that hadn't been lived in for a long time, and I wondered
who had took up quarters there. I slipped up and peeped in at the

"A FAIR FIT."

window. There was a woman about forty year old in there, knitting
by a candle that was on a pine table. I didn't know her face; she was
a stranger, for you couldn't start a face in that town that I didn't
know. Now this was lucky, because I was weakening; I was getting
afraid I had come; people might know my voice and find me out.
But if this woman had been in such a little town two days she could
tell me all I wanted to know; so I knocked at the door, and made up
my mind I wouldn't forget I was a girl.

Chapter XI.

"COME IN."

Come in," says the woman, and I did. She says:

"Take a cheer."

I done it. She looked me all over with her little shiny eyes, and says:

"What might your name be?"

"Sarah Williams."

"Where 'bouts do you live? In this neighborhood?"

"No'm. In Hookerville, seven mile below. I've walked all the way and I'm all tired out."

"Hungry, too, I reckon. I'll find you something."

"No'm, I ain't hungry. I was so hungry I had to stop two mile below here at a farm; so I ain't hungry no more. It's what makes me so late. My mother's down sick, and out of money and everything, and I come to tell my uncle Abner Moore. He lives at the upper end of the town, she says. I hain't ever been here before. Do you know him?"

"No; but I don't know everybody yet. I haven't lived here quite two weeks. It's a considerable ways to the upper end of the town. You better stay here all night. Take off your bonnet."

"No," I says, "I'll rest a while, I reckon, and go on. I ain't afeard of the dark."

She said she wouldn't let me go by myself, but her husband would be in by and by, maybe in a hour and a half, and she'd send him along with me. Then she got to talking about her husband, and about her relations up the river, and her relations down the river, and about how much better off they used to was, and how they didn't know but they'd made a mistake coming to our town, instead of letting well alone—and so on and so on, till I was afeard *I* had made a mistake coming to her to find out what was going on in the town; but by and by she dropped onto pap and the murder, and then I was pretty willing to let her clatter right along. She told about me and Tom Sawyer finding the six thousand dollars (only she got it ten) and all about pap and what a hard lot he was, and what a hard lot I was, and at last she got down to where I was murdered. I says:

"Who done it? We've heard considerable about these goings on, down in Hookerville, but we don't know who 'twas that killed Huck Finn."

"Well, I reckon there's a right smart chance of people *here* that 'd like to know who killed him. Some thinks old Finn done it himself."

"No—is that so?"

"Most everybody thought it at first. He'll never know how nigh he come to getting lynched. But before night they changed around and judged it was done by a runaway nigger named Jim."

"Why *he*—"

I stopped. I reckoned I better keep still. She run on, and never noticed I had put in at all.

"The nigger run off the very night Huck Finn was killed. So there's a reward out for him—three hundred dollars. And there's a reward out for old Finn too—two hundred dollars. You see, he come to town the morning after the murder, and told about it, and was out with 'em on the ferry-boat hunt, and right away after he up and left. Before night they wanted to lynch him, but he was gone, you see. Well, next day they found out the nigger was gone; they found out he hadn't ben seen sence ten o'clock the night the murder was done. So then they put it on him, you see, and while they was full of it, next day back comes old Finn and went boo-hooing to Judge Thatcher to get money to hunt for the nigger all over Illinois with. The judge give him some, and that evening he got drunk and was around till after midnight with a couple of mighty hard looking strangers, and then went off with them. Well, he hain't come back sence, and they ain't looking for him back till this thing blows over a little, for people thinks now that he killed his boy and fixed things so folks would think robbers done it, and then he'd get Huck's money without having to bother a long time with a lawsuit. People do say he warn't any too good to do it. Oh, he's sly, I reckon. If he don't come back for a year, he'll be all right. You can't prove anything on him, you know; everything will be quieted down then, and he'll walk into Huck's money as easy as nothing."

"Yes, I reckon so, 'm. I don't see nothing in the way of it. Has everybody quit thinking the nigger done it?"

"Oh, no, not everybody. A good many thinks he done it. But they'll get the nigger pretty soon, now, and maybe they can scare it out of him."

"Why, are they after him yet?"

"Well, you're innocent, ain't you! Does three hundred dollars lay round every day for people to pick up? Some folks thinks the nigger ain't far from here. I'm one of them—but I hain't talked it around. A few days ago I was talking with an old couple that lives next door in the log shanty, and they happened to say hardly anybody ever goes to that island over yonder that they call Jackson's Island. Don't anybody live there? says I. No, nobody, says they. I didn't say any more, but I done some thinking. I was pretty near certain I'd seen smoke over there, about the head of the island, a day or two before that, so I says to myself, like as not that nigger's hiding over there; anyway, says I, it's worth the trouble to give the place a hunt. I hain't seen any smoke sence, so I reckon maybe he's gone, if it was him; but husband's going over to see—him and another man. He was gone up the river; but he got back to-day and I told him as soon as he got here two hours ago."

I had got so uneasy I couldn't set still. I had to do something with my hands; so I took up a needle off of the table and went to threading it. My hands shook, and I was making a bad job of it. When the woman stopped talking, I looked up, and she was looking at me pretty curious, and smiling a little. I put down the needle and thread and let on to be interested—and I was, too—and says:

"Three hundred dollars is a power of money. I wish my mother could get it. Is your husband going over there to-night?"

"Oh, yes. He went up town with the man I was telling you of, to get a boat and see if they could borrow another gun. They'll go over after midnight."

"Couldn't they see better if they was to wait till daytime?"

"Yes. And couldn't the nigger see better, too? After midnight he'll likely be asleep, and they can slip around through the woods and hunt up his camp fire all the better for the dark, if he's got one."

"I didn't think of that."

"HIM AND ANOTHER MAN."

The woman kept looking at me pretty curious, and I didn't feel a bit comfortable. Pretty soon she says:

"What did you say your name was, honey?"

"M—Mary Williams."

Somehow it didn't seem to me that I said it was Mary before, so I didn't look up; seemed to me I said it was Sarah; so I felt sort of cornered, and was afeared maybe I was looking it, too. I wished the woman would say something more; the longer she set still, the uneasier I was. But now she says:

"Honey, I thought you said it was Sarah when you first come in?"

"Oh, yes'm, I did. Sarah Mary Williams. Sarah's my first name. Some calls me Sarah, some calls me Mary."

"Oh, that's the way of it?"

"Yes'm."

I was feeling better, then, but I wished I was out of there, anyway. I couldn't look up yet.

Well, the woman fell to talking about how hard times was, and how poor they had to live, and how the rats was as free as if they owned the place, and so forth, and so on, and then I got easy again. She was right about the rats. You'd see one stick his nose out of a hole in the corner every little while. She said she had to have things handy to throw at them when she was alone, or they wouldn't give her no peace. She showed me a bar of lead, twisted up into a knot, and said she was a good shot with it generly, but she'd wrenched her arm a day or two ago, and didn't know whether she could throw true, now. But she watched for a chance, and directly she banged away at a rat, but she missed him wide, and said "Ouch!" it hurt her arm so. Then she told me to try for the next one. I wanted to be getting away before the old man got back, but of course I didn't let on. I got the thing, and the first rat that showed his nose I let drive, and if he'd a stayed where he was he'd a been a tolerable sick rat. She said that that was first-rate, and she reckoned I would hive the next one. She went and got the lump of lead and fetched it back and brought along a hank of yarn, which she wanted me to help her with. I held up my two hands and she put the hank over them and went on talking about her and her husband's matters. But she broke off to say:

"Keep your eye on the rats. You better have the lead in your lap, handy."

So she dropped the lump into my lap, just at that moment, and I clapped my legs together on it and she went on talking. But only about a minute. Then she took off the hank and looked me straight in the face, but very pleasant, and says:

"Come, now—what's your real name?"

"Wh-what, mum?"

"What's your real name? Is it Bill, or Tom, or Bob?—or what is it?"

I reckon I shook like a leaf, and I didn't know hardly what to do. But I says:

"Please to don't poke fun at a poor girl like me, mum. If I'm in the way, here, I'll—"

"No, you won't. Set down and stay where you are. I ain't going to hurt you, and I ain't going to tell on you, nuther. You just tell me your secret, and trust me. I'll keep it; and what's more, I'll help you. So'll my old man, if you want him to. You see, you're a runaway 'prentice—that's all. It ain't anything. There ain't any harm in it. You've been treated bad, and you made up your mind to cut. Bless you, child, I wouldn't tell on you. Tell me all about it, now—that's a good boy."

So I said it wouldn't be no use to try to play it any longer, and I would just make a clean breast and tell her everything, but she mustn't go back on her promise. Then I told her my father and mother was dead, and the law had bound me out to a mean old farmer in the country thirty mile back from the river, and he treated me so bad I couldn't stand it no longer; he went away to be gone a couple of days, and so I took my chance and stole some of his daughter's old clothes, and cleared out, and I had been three nights coming the thirty miles; I traveled nights, and hid day-times and slept, and the bag of bread and meat I carried from home lasted me all the way and I had a plenty. I said I believed my uncle Abner Moore would take care of me, and so that was why I struck out for this town of Goshen.

"Goshen, child? This ain't Goshen. This is St. Petersburg. Goshen's ten mile further up the river. Who told you this was Goshen?"

"Why, a man I met at day-break this morning, just as I was going to turn into the woods for my regular sleep. He told me when the roads forked I must take the right hand, and five mile would fetch me to Goshen."

"He was drunk I reckon. He told you just exactly wrong."

"Well, he did act like he was drunk, but it ain't no matter now. I got to be moving along. I'll fetch Goshen before day-light."

"Hold on a minute. I'll put you up a snack to eat. You might want it."

So she put me up a snack, and says:

"Say—when a cow's laying down, which end of her gets up first? Answer up prompt, now—don't stop to study over it. Which end gets up first?"

"The hind end, mum."

"Well, then, a horse?"

"The for'rard end, mum."

"Which side of a tree does the most moss grow on?"

"North side."

"If fifteen cows is browsing on a hillside, how many of them eats with their heads pointed the same direction?"

"The whole fifteen, mum."

SHE PUTS UP A SNACK.

"Well, I reckon you *have* lived in the country. I thought maybe you was trying to hocus me again. What's your real name, now?"

"George Peters, mum."

"Well, try to remember it, George. Don't forget and tell me it's Elexander before you go, and then get out by saying it's George-Elexander when I catch you. And don't go about women in that old calico. You do a girl tolerable poor, but you might fool men, maybe. Bless you, child, when you set out to thread a needle, don't hold the thread still and fetch the needle up to it; hold the needle still and poke the thread at it—that's the way a woman most always does;

but a man always does t'other way. And when you throw at a rat or anything, hitch yourself up a tip-toe, and fetch your hand up over your head as awkard as you can, and miss your rat about six or seven foot. Throw stiff-armed from the shoulder, like there was a pivot there for it to turn on—like a girl; not from the wrist and elbow, with your arm out to one side, like a boy. And mind you, when a girl tries to catch anything in her lap, she throws her knees apart; she don't clap them together, the way you did when you catched the lump of lead. Why, I spotted you for a boy when you was threading the needle; and I contrived the other things just to make certain. Now trot along to your uncle, Sarah Mary Williams George Elexander Peters, and if you get into trouble you send word to Mrs. Judith Loftus, which is me, and I'll do what I can to get you out of it. Keep the river road, all the way, and next time you tramp, take shoes and socks with you. The river road's a rocky one, and your feet 'll be in a condition when you get to Goshen, I reckon."

I went up the bank about fifty yards, and then I doubled on my tracks and slipped back to where my canoe was, a good piece below the house. I jumped in and was off in a hurry. I went up stream far enough to make the head of the island, and then started across. I took off the sun-bonnet, for I didn't want no blinders on, then. When I was about the middle, I hear the clock begin to strike; so I stops and listens; the sound come faint over the water, but clear—eleven. When I struck the head of the island I never waited to blow, though I was most winded, but I shoved right into the timber where my old camp used to be, and started a good fire there on a high-and-dry spot.

Then I jumped in the canoe and dug out for our place a mile and a half below, as hard as I could go. I landed, and slopped through the timber and up the ridge and into the cavern. There Jim laid, sound asleep on the ground. I roused him out and says:

"Git up and hump yourself, Jim! There ain't a minute to lose. They're after us!"

Jim never asked no questions, he never said a word; but the way he worked for the next half an hour showed about how he was scared. By that time everything we had in the world was on our raft and she was ready to be shoved out from the willow cove where she was hid. We put out the camp fire at the cavern the first thing, and didn't show a candle outside after that.

I took the canoe out from shore a little piece and took a look, but
if there was a boat around I couldn't see it, for stars and shadows
ain't good to see by. Then we got out the raft and slipped along down
in the shade, past the foot of the island dead still, never saying a
word.

"HUMP YOURSELF!"

Chapter XII

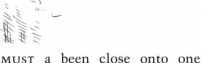

ON THE RAFT.

MUST a been close onto one o'clock when we got below the island at last, and the raft did seem to go mighty slow. If a boat was to come along, we was going to take to the canoe and break for the Illinois shore; and it was well a boat didn't come, for we hadn't ever thought to put the gun into the canoe, or a fishing-line or anything to eat. We was in ruther too much of a sweat to think of so many things. It warn't good judgment to put *everything* on the raft.

If the men went to the island, I just expect they found the camp fire I built, and watched it all night for Jim to come. Anyways, they stayed away from us, and if my building the fire never fooled them it warn't no fault of mine. I played it as low-down on them as I could.

When the first streak of day begun to show, we tied up to a tow-head in a big bend on the Illinois side, and hacked off cotton-wood branches with the hatchet and covered up the raft with them so she looked like there had been a cave-in in the bank there. A tow-head is a sand-bar that has cotton-woods on it as thick as harrow-teeth.

We had mountains on the Missouri shore and heavy timber on the Illinois side, and the channel was down the Missouri shore at that place, so we warn't afraid of anybody running across us. We laid there all day and watched the rafts and steamboats spin down the Missouri shore, and up-bound steamboats fight the big river in the middle. I told Jim all about the time I had jabbering with that woman; and Jim said she was a smart one, and if she was to start after us herself *she* wouldn't set down and watch a camp fire—no, sir, she'd fetch a dog. Well, then, I said, why couldn't she tell her husband to fetch a dog? Jim said he bet she did think of it by the time the men was ready to start, and he believed they must a gone up town to get a dog and so they lost all that time, or else we wouldn't be here on a tow-head sixteen or seventeen mile below the village— no, indeedy, we would be in that same old town again. So I said I didn't care what was the reason they didn't get us, as long as they didn't.

When it was beginning to come on dark, we poked our heads out of the cottonwood thicket and looked up, and down, and across; nothing in sight; so Jim took up some of the top planks of the raft and built a snug wigwam to get under in blazing weather and rainy, and to keep the things dry. Jim made a floor for the wigwam, and raised it a foot or more above the level of the raft, so now the blankets and all the traps was out of the reach of steamboat waves. Right in the middle of the wigwam we made a layer of dirt about five or six inches deep with a frame around it for to hold it to its place; this was to build a fire on in sloppy weather or chilly; the wigwam would keep it from being seen. We made an extra steering oar, too, because one of the others might get broke, on a snag or something. We fixed up a short forked stick to hang the old lantern on; because we must always light the lantern whenever we see a steamboat coming down stream, to keep from getting run over; but we wouldn't have to light it for up-stream boats unless we see we was in what they call a "crossing;" for the river was pretty high yet, very low banks being still a little under water; so up-bound boats didn't always run the channel, but hunted easy water.

This second night we run between seven and eight hours, with a current that was making over four mile an hour. We catched fish, and talked, and we took a swim now and then to keep off sleepiness. It was kind of solemn, drifting down the big still river, laying on our backs looking up at the stars, and we didn't ever feel like talking loud, and it warn't often that we laughed, only a little kind of a low chuckle. We had mighty good weather, as a general thing, and nothing ever happened to us at all, that night, nor the next, nor the next.

Every night we passed towns, some of them away up on black hillsides, nothing but just a shiny bed of lights, not a house could you see. The fifth night we passed St. Louis, and it was like the whole world lit up. In St. Petersburg they used to say there was twenty or thirty thousand people in St. Louis, but I never believed it till I see that wonderful spread of lights at two o'clock that still night. There warn't a sound there; everybody was asleep.

HE SOMETIMES LIFTED A CHICKEN.

Every night, now, I used to slip ashore, towards ten o'clock, at some little village, and buy ten or fifteen cents' worth of meal or bacon or other stuff to eat; and sometimes I lifted a chicken that warn't roosting comfortable, and took him along. Pap always said, take a chicken when you get a chance, because if you don't want him yourself you can easy find somebody that does, and a good deed ain't ever forgot. I never see pap when he didn't want the chicken himself, but that is what he used to say, anyway.

Mornings, before daylight, I slipped into corn fields and borrowed a watermelon, or a mushmelon, or a punkin, or some new corn, or things of that kind. Pap always said it warn't no harm to borrow things, if you was meaning to pay them back, sometime; but the widow said it warn't anything but a soft name for stealing, and no decent body would do it. Jim said he reckoned the widow was partly right and pap was partly right; so the best way would be for us to pick out two or three things from the list and say we wouldn't borrow them any more—then he reckoned it wouldn't be no harm to borrow the others. So we talked it over all one night, drifting along down the river, trying to make up our minds whether to drop the watermelons, or the cantelopes, or the mushmelons, or what. But towards daylight we got it all settled satisfactory, and concluded to drop crabapples and p'simmons. We warn't feeling just right, before that, but it was all comfortable now. I was glad the way it come out, too, because crabapples ain't ever good, and the p'simmons wouldn't be ripe for two or three months yet.

We shot a water-fowl, now and then, that got up too early in the morning or didn't go to bed early enough in the evening. Take it all around, we lived pretty high.

The fifth night below St. Louis we had a big storm after midnight, with a power of thunder and lightning, and the rain poured down in a solid sheet. We stayed in the wigwam and let the raft take care of itself. When the lightning glared out we could see a big straight river ahead, and high rocky bluffs on both sides. By and by says I, "Hel-lo, Jim, looky yonder!" It was a steamboat that had killed herself on a rock. We was drifting straight down for her. The lightning showed her very distinct. She was leaning over, with part of her upper deck above water, and you could see every little chimbly-guy clean and clear, and a chair by the big bell, with an old slouch hat hanging on the back of it when the flashes come.

Well, it being away in the night, and stormy, and all so mysterious-like, I felt just the way any other boy would a felt, when I see that wreck laying there so mournful and lonesome in the middle of the river: I wanted to get aboard of her and slink around a little, and see what there was there. So I says:

"Le's land on her, Jim."

But Jim was dead against it, at first. He says:

"I doan want to go fool'n 'long er no wrack. We's doin' blame' well, en we better let blame' well alone, as de good book says. Like as not dey's a watchman on dat wrack."

"Watchman your grandmother," I says; "there ain't nothing to watch but the texas and the pilot house; and do you reckon anybody's going to resk his life for a texas and a pilot house such a night as this, when it's likely to break up and wash off down the river any minute?" Jim couldn't say nothing to that, so he didn't try. "And besides," I says, "we might borrow something worth having, out of the captain's stateroom. Seegars, *I* bet you—and cost five cents apiece, solid cash. Steamboat captains is always rich, and get sixty dollars a month, and *they* don't care a cent what a thing costs, you know, long as they want it. Stick a candle in your pocket; I can't rest, Jim, till we give her a rummaging. Do you reckon Tom Sawyer would ever go by this thing? Not for pie, he wouldn't. He'd call it an adventure—that's what he'd call it; and he'd land on that wreck if it was his last act. And wouldn't he throw style into it?— wouldn't he spread himself, nor nothing? Why, you'd think it was Christopher C'lumbus discovering Kingdom-Come. I wish Tom Sawyer *was* here."

Jim he grumbled a little, but give in. He said we mustn't talk any more than we could help, and then talk mighty low. The lightning showed us the wreck again, just in time, and we fetched the starboard derrick, and made fast there.

The deck was high out, here. We went sneaking down the slope of it to labboard, in the dark, towards the texas, feeling our way slow with our feet, and spreading our hands out to fend off the guys, for it was so dark we couldn't see no sign of them. Pretty soon we struck the forward end of the skylight, and clumb onto it; and the next step fetched us in front of the captain's door, which was open; and by jimminy, away down through the texas hall we see a light! and all in the same second we seem to hear low voices in yonder!

Jim whispered and said he was feeling powerful sick; and told me to come along. I says, all right; and was going to start for the raft; but just then I heard a voice wail out and say:

"O, please don't, boys; I swear I won't ever tell!"

Another voice said, pretty loud:

"It's a lie, Jim Turner. You've acted this way before. You always want more'n your share of the truck, and you've always got it, too, because you've swore 't if you didn't you'd tell. But this time you've said it jist one time too many. You're the meanest, treacherousest hound in this country."

By this time Jim was gone for the raft. I was just a-biling with curiosity; and I says to myself, Tom Sawyer wouldn't back out now, and so I won't either; I'm agoing to see what's going on here. So I dropped on my hands and knees, in the little passage, and crept aft in the dark, till there warn't but about one stateroom betwixt me and the cross-hall of the texas. Then, in there I see a man stretched on the floor and tied hand and foot, and two men standing over him, and one of them had a dim lantern in his hand, and the other one had a pistol. This one kept pointing the pistol at the man's head on the floor and saying,—

"I'd *like* to! And I orter, too, a mean skunk!"

The man on the floor would shrivel up and say, "O, please don't, Bill—I hain't ever goin' to tell."

And every time he said that, the man with the lantern would laugh, and say:

" 'Deed you *ain't!* You never said no truer thing 'n that, you bet you." And once he said: "Hear him beg! and yit if we hadn't got the best of him and tied him, he'd a killed us both. And what *for?* Jist for noth'n'. Jist because we stood on our *rights*—that's what for. But I lay you ain't agoin' to threaten nobody any more, Jim Turner. Put *up* that pistol, Bill."

"PLEASE DON'T, BILL."

Bill says:

"I don't want to, Jake Packard. I'm for killin' him—and didn't he kill old Hatfield jist the same way—and don't he deserve it?"

"But I don't *want* him killed, and I've got my reasons for it."

"Bless yo' heart for them words, Jake Packard!—I'll never forgit you, long's I live!" says the man on the floor, sort of blubbering.

Packard didn't take no notice of that, but hung up his lantern on a nail, and started towards where I was, there in the dark, and motioned Bill to come. I crawfished as fast as I could, about two yards, but the boat slanted so that I couldn't make very good time; so, to keep from getting run over and catched, I crawled into a stateroom on the upper side. The men come a-pawing along in the dark, and when Packard got to my stateroom, he says:

"Here—come in here."

And in he come, and Bill after him. But before they got in, I was up in the upper berth, cornered, and sorry I come. Then they stood there, with their hands on the ledge of the berth, and talked. I couldn't see them, but I could tell where they was, and how close they was, by the whisky they'd been having. I was glad I didn't drink whisky; but it wouldn't made much difference, anyway, because most of the time they couldn't a treed me, because I didn't breathe. I was too scared. And besides, a body *couldn't* breathe, and hear such talk. They talked low and earnest. Bill wanted to kill Turner. He says:

"He's said he'll tell, and he will. If we was to give both our shares to him, *now*, it wouldn't make no difference, after the row, and the way we've served him. Shore's you're born, he'll turn State's evidence, now you hear *me*. I'm for putting him out of his troubles."

"So'm I," says Packard, very quiet.

"Blame it, I'd sorter begun to think you wasn't. Well, then, that's all right. Le's go and do it."

"Hold on, a minute; I hain't had my say, yit. You listen to me. Shooting's good, but there's quieter ways, if the thing's *got* to be done. But what *I* say, is this: it ain't good sense to go court'n around after a halter, if you can git at what you're up to in some way that's jist as good and at the same time don't bring you into no resks. Ain't that so?"

"You bet it is. But how you goin' to manage it this time?"

"Well, my idea is this: we'll rustle around and gether up whatever pickins we've overlooked in the staterooms, and shove for shore and hide the truck. Then we'll wait. Now I say it ain't agoin' to be more'n two hours befo' this wrack breaks up and washes off down the river. See? He'll be drownded, and won't have nobody to blame for it but his own self. I reckon that's a considerble sight better'n killin' of him. I'm unfavorable to killin' a man as long as you can git around it; it ain't good sense, it ain't good morals. Ain't I right?"

"IT AIN'T GOOD MORALS."

"Yes—I reck'n you are. But s'pose she *don't* break up and wash off?"

"Well, we can wait the two hours, anyway, and see, can't we?"

"All right, then; come along."

So they started, and I lit out, all in a cold sweat, and scrambled forward. It was dark as pitch there; but I said, in a kind of a coarse whisper, "Jim!" and he answered up, right at my elbow, with a sort of a moan, and I says:

"Quick, Jim, it ain't no time for fooling around and moaning; there's a gang of murderers in yonder, and if we don't hunt up their boat and set her drifting down the river so these fellows can't get away from the wreck, there's one of 'em going to be in a bad fix. But if we find their boat we can put *all* of 'em in a bad fix—for the Sheriff 'll get 'em. Quick—hurry! I'll hunt the labboard side, you hunt the stabboard. You start at the raft, and—"

"O my lordy, lordy! *Raf'*? Dey ain' no raf' no mo', she done broke loose en gone!—en here we is!"

"O MY LORDY, LORDY!"

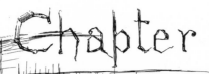

IN A FIX.

WELL, I catched my breath, and most fainted. Shut up on a wreck with such a gang as that! But it warn't no time to be sentimentering. We'd *got* to find that boat, now—had to have it for ourselves. So we went a-quaking and shaking down the stabboard side, and slow work it was, too—seemed a week before we got to the stern. No sign of a boat. Jim said he didn't believe he could go any further—so scared he hadn't hardly any strength left, he said. But I said come on, if we get left on this wreck, we are in a fix, sure. So on we prowled, again. We struck for the stern of the texas, and found it, and then scrabbled along forwards on the skylight, hanging on from shutter to shutter, for the edge of the skylight was in the water. When we got pretty close to the cross-hall door, there was the skiff, sure enough!—I could just barely see her. I felt ever so thankful. In another second I would a been aboard of her; but just then the door opened. One of the men stuck his head out, only about a couple of foot from me, and I thought I was gone; but he jerked it in again, and says:

"Heave that blame lantern out o' sight, Bill!"

He flung a bag of something into the boat, and then got in, himself, and set down. It was Packard. Then Bill *he* come out and got in. Packard says, in a low voice:

"All ready—shove off!"

I couldn't hardly hang on to the shutters, I was so weak. But Bill says:

"Hold on—'d you go through him?"

"No. Didn't you?"

"No. So he's got his share o' the cash, yet."

"Well, then, come along—no use to take truck and leave money."

"Say—won't he suspicion what we're up to?"

"Maybe he won't. But we got to have it anyway. Come along."

So they got out and went in.

The door slammed to, because it was on the careened side; and in a half second I was in the boat, and Jim come a-tumbling after me. I out with my knife and cut the rope, and away we went!

We didn't touch an oar, and we didn't speak nor whisper, nor hardly even breathe. We went gliding swift along, dead silent, past the tip of the paddle-box, and past the stern; then in a second or two more we was a hundred yards below the wreck, and the darkness soaked her up, every last sign of her, and we was safe, and knowed it.

When we was three or four hundred yards down stream, we see the lantern show like a little spark at the texas door, for a second, and we knowed by that that the rascals had missed their boat, and was beginning to understand that they was in just as much trouble, now, as Jim Turner was.

Then Jim manned the oars, and we took out after our raft. Now was the first time that I begun to worry about the men—I reckon I hadn't had time to, before. I begun to think how dreadful it was, even for murderers, to be in such a fix. I says to myself, there ain't no telling but I might come to be a murderer myself, yet, and then how would _I_ like it? So says I to Jim:

"The first light we see, we'll land a hundred yards below it or above it, in a place where it's a good hiding place for you and the skiff, and then I'll go and fix up some kind of a yarn, and get somebody to go for that gang and get them out of their scrape, so they can be hung when their time comes."

But that idea was a failure; for pretty soon it begun to storm again, and this time worse than ever. The rain poured down, and never a light showed; everybody in bed, I reckon. We boomed along down

the river, watching for lights and watching for our raft. After a long
time the rain let up, but the clouds staid, and the lightning kept
whimpering, and by and by a flash showed us a black thing ahead,
floating, and we made for it.

It was the raft, and mighty glad was we to get aboard of it again.
We seen a light, now, away down to the right, on shore. So I said I
would go for it. The skiff was half full of plunder which that gang
had stole, there on the wreck. We hustled it onto the raft in a pile,
and I told Jim to float along down, and show a light when he judged
he had gone about two mile, and keep it burning till I come; then I
manned my oars and shoved for the light. As I got down towards it,
three or four more showed—up on a hillside. It was a village. I closed
in above the shore-light, and laid on my oars and floated. As I went
by, I see it was a lantern hanging on the jackstaff of a double-hull
ferry boat. Everything was dead still, nobody stirring. I floated in
under the stern, made fast, and clumb aboard. I skimmed around
for the watchman, a-wondering whereabouts he slept; and by and
by I found him roosting on the bitts, forward, with his head down
between his knees. I give his shoulder two or three little shoves,
and begun to cry.

He stirred up, in a kind of a startlish way; but when he see it was
only me, he took a good gap and stretch, and then he says:

"Hello, what's up? Don't cry, bub. What's the trouble?"

I says:

"Pap, and mam, and sis, and—"

Then I broke down. He says:

"O, dang it, now, *don't* take on so, we all has to have our troubles,
and this'n 'll come out all right. What's the matter with 'em?"

"They're—they're—are you the watchman of the boat?"

"Yes," he says, kind of pretty-well-satisfied like, "I'm the captain, and the owner, and the mate, and the pilot, and watchman,
and head deck-hand; and sometimes I'm the freight and passengers.
I ain't as rich as old Jim Hornback, and I can't be so blame' generous
and good to Tom, Dick and Harry as what he is, and slam around
money the way he does, but I've told him a many a time 't I wouldn't
trade places with him; for, says I, a sailor's life's the life for me, and
I'm derned if *I*'d live two mile out o' town, where there ain't nothing

ever goin' on, not for all his spondulicks and as much more on top of it. Says I—"

I broke in and says:

"They're in an awful peck of trouble, and—"

"*Who* is?"

"Why, pap, and mam, and sis, and Miss Hooker; and if you'd take your ferry boat and go up there—"

"Up where? Where are they?"

"On the wreck."

"HELLO, WHAT'S UP?"

"What wreck?"

"Why, there ain't but one."

"What, you don't mean the *Walter Scott?*"

"Yes."

"Good land! what are they doin' *there*, for gracious sakes?"

"Well, they didn't go there a-purpose."

"I bet they didn't! Why, great goodness, there ain't no chance for 'em if they don't git off mighty quick! Why, how in the nation did they ever git into such a scrape?"

"Easy enough. Miss Hooker was a-visiting, up there to the town—"

"Yes, Booth's Landing—go on."

"She was a visiting, there at Booth's Landing, and just in the edge of the evening she started over with her nigger woman in the horse-ferry, to stay all night at her friend's house, Miss What-you-may-call-her, I disremember her name, and they lost their steering-oar, and swung around and went a-floating down, stern-first, about two mile, and saddle-baggsed on the wreck, and the ferry man and the nigger woman and the horses was all lost, but Miss Hooker she made a grab and got aboard the wreck. Well, about an hour after dark, we come along down in our trading-scow, and it was so dark we didn't notice the wreck till we was right on it; and so *we* saddle-baggsed; but all of us was saved but Bill Whipple—and oh, he *was* the best cretur!—I most wish't it had been me, I do."

"My George! it's the beatenest thing I ever struck. And *then* what did you all do?"

"Well, we hollered and took on, but it's so wide, there, we couldn't make nobody hear. So pap said somebody got to get ashore and get help, somehow. I was the only one that could swim; so I made a dash for it, and Miss Hooker she said if I didn't strike help sooner, come here and hunt up her uncle, and he'd fix the thing. I made the land about a mile below, and been fooling along ever since, trying to get people to do something, but they said, 'What, in such a night and such a current? there ain't no sense in it; go for the steam-ferry.' Now if you'll go, and—"

"By Jackson, I'd *like* to, and blame it I don't know but I will; but who in the dingnation's agoin' to *pay* for it? Do you reckon your pap—"

"Why *that's* all right. Miss Hooker she told me, *particular*, that her uncle Hornback—"

"Great guns! is *he* her uncle? Looky here, you break for that light over yonder-way, and turn out west when you git there, and about a quarter of a mile out you'll come to the tavern; tell 'em to dart you out to Jim Hornback's, and he'll foot the bill. And don't you fool around any, because he'll want to know the news. Tell him I'll have his niece all safe before he can get to town. Hump yourself, now; I'm agoing up around the corner, here, to roust out my engineer."

I struck for the light, but as soon as he turned the corner I went back and got into my skiff and bailed her out and then pulled up shore in the easy water about six hundred yards, and tucked myself in among some woodboats; for I couldn't rest easy till I could see the ferryboat start. But take it all around, I was feeling ruther comfortable, on accounts of taking all this trouble for that gang, for not many would a done it. I wished the widow knowed about it. I judged she would be proud of me for helping these rapscallions, because rapscallions and dead beats is the kind the widow and good people takes the most interest in.

Well, before long, here comes the wreck, dim and dusky, sliding

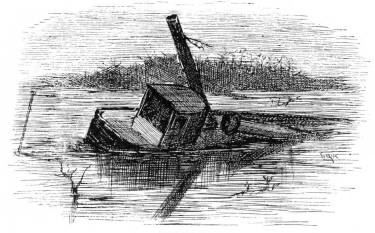

THE WRECK.

along down! A kind of cold shiver went through me, and then I struck out for her. She was very deep, and I see in a minute there warn't much chance for anybody being alive in her. I pulled all around her, and hollered a little, but there wasn't any answer; all dead still. I felt a little bit heavy-hearted about the gang, but not much, for I reckoned if they could stand it, I could.

Then here comes the ferryboat; so I shoved for the middle of the river on a long down-stream slant; and when I judged I was out of eye-reach, I laid on my oars, and looked back and see her go and smell around the wreck for Miss Hooker's remainders, because the captain would know her uncle Hornback would want them; and

then pretty soon the ferryboat give it up and went for shore, and I
laid into my work and went a-booming down the river.

It did seem a powerful long time before Jim's light showed up;
and when it did show, it looked like it was a thousand mile off. By
the time I got there the sky was beginning to get a little gray in the
east; so we struck for an island, and hid the raft, and sunk the skiff,
and turned in and slept like dead people.

WE TURNED IN AND SLEPT.

Chapter XIV.

TURNING OVER THE TRUCK.

B Y AND BY, when we got up, we turned over the truck the gang had stole off of the wreck, and found boots, and blankets, and clothes, and all sorts of other things, and a lot of books, and a spyglass and three boxes of seegars. We hadn't ever been this rich before, in neither of our lives. The seegars was prime. We laid off all the afternoon in the woods, talking, and me reading the books, and having a general good time. I told Jim all about what happened inside the wreck, and at the ferryboat; and I said these kinds of things was adventures; but he said he didn't want no more adventures. He said that when I went in the texas and he crawled back to get on the raft and found her gone, he nearly died; because he judged it was all up with *him*, anyway it could be fixed; for if he didn't get saved he would get drownded; and if he did get saved, whoever saved him would send him back home so as to get the reward, and then Miss Watson would sell him south, sure. Well, he was right; he was most always right; he had an uncommon level head, for a nigger.

I read considerable to Jim about kings, and dukes, and earls and such, and how gaudy they dressed and how much style they put on, and called each other your majesty, and your grace, and your lordship, and so on, 'stead of mister; and Jim's eyes bugged out, and he was interested. He says:

"I didn' know dey was so many un um. I hain't hearn 'bout none un um, skasely, but ole king Sollermun, onless you counts dem kings dat's in a pack er k'yards. How much do a king git?"

"Get?" I says; "why, they get a thousand dollars a month if they want it; they can have just as much as they want; everything belongs to them."

"*Ain'* dat gay? En what dey got to do, Huck?"

"*They* don't do nothing! Why, how you talk. They just set around."

"No—is dat so?"

"Of course it is. They just set around. Except maybe when there's a war; then they go to the war. But other times they just lazy around; or go hawking—just hawking and sp— Sh!—d' you hear a noise?"

We skipped out and looked; but it warn't nothing but the flutter of a steamboat's wheel away down coming around the point; so we come back.

"Yes," says I, "and other times, when things is dull, they fuss with the parlyment; and if everybody don't go just so, he whacks their heads off. But mostly they hang round the harem."

"Roun' de which?"

"Harem."

"What's de harem?"

"The place where he keeps his wives. Don't you know about the harem? Solomon had one; he had about a million wives."

"Why, yes, dat's so; I—I'd done forgot it. A harem's a bo'd'n house, I reck'n. Mos' likely dey has rackety times in de nussery. En I reck'n de wives quarrels considable; en dat 'crease de racket. Yit dey say Sollermun de wises' man dat ever live'. I doan' take no stock in dat. Bekase why: would a wise man want to live in de mids' er sich a blimblammin' all de time? No—'deed he wouldn't. A wise man 'ud take en buil' a biler-factry; en den he could shet *down* de biler-factry when he want to res'."

"Well, but he *was* the wisest man, anyway; because the widow she told me so, her own self."

"I doan k'yer what de widder say, he *warn't* no wise man, nuther. He had some er de dad-fetchedes' ways I ever see. Does you know 'bout dat chile dat he 'uz gwyne to chop in two?"

"Yes; the widow told me all about it."

"*Well*, den! Warn' dat de beatenes' notion in de worl'? You jis'

take en look at it a minute. Dah's de stump, dah—dat's one er de
women; heah's you—dat's de yuther one; I's Sollermun; en dish-
yer dollar bill's de chile. Bofe un you claims it. What does I do? Does
I shin aroun' mongs' de neighbors en fine out which un you de bill
do b'long to, en han' it over to de right one, all safe en soun', de way

SOLOMON AND HIS MILLION WIVES.

dat anybody dat had any gumption would? No—I take en whack de
bill in *two*, en give half un it to you, en de yuther half to de yuther
woman. Dat's de way Sollermun was gwyne to do wid de chile. Now
I want to ast you: what's de use er dat half a bill?—can't buy noth'n
wid it. En what use is a half a chile? I would'n give a dern for a
million un um."

"But hang it, Jim, you've clean missed the point—blame it,
you've missed it a thousand mile."

"Who? Me? Go 'long. Doan talk to *me* 'bout yo' pints. I reck'n I
knows sense when I sees it; en dey ain' no sense in sich doin's as
dat. De 'spute warn't 'bout a half a chile, de 'spute was 'bout a whole
chile; en de man dat think he kin settle a 'spute 'bout a whole chile
wid a half a chile, doan know enough to come in out'n de rain. Doan
talk to me 'bout Sollermun, Huck, I knows him by de back."

"But I tell you you don't get the point."

"Blame de pint! I reck'n I knows what I knows. En mine you, de *real* pint is down furder—it's down deeper. It lays in de way Sollermun was raised. You take a man dat's got on'y one er two chillen: is dat man gwyne to be waseful o' chillen? No, he ain't; he can't 'ford it. *He* know how to value 'em. But you take a man dat's got 'bout

THE STORY OF "SOLLERMUN."

five million chillen runnin' roun' de house, en it's diffunt. *He* as soon chop a chile in two as a cat. Dey's plenty mo'. A chile er two, mo' er less, warn't no consekens to Sollermun, dad fetch him!"

I never see such a nigger. If he got a notion in his head once, there warn't no getting it out again. He was the most down on Solomon of any nigger I ever see. So I went to talking about other kings, and let Solomon slide. I told about Louis Sixteenth that got his head cut off in France long time ago; and about his little boy the dolphin, that would a been a king, but they took and shut him up in jail, and some say he died there.

"Po' little chap."

"But some says he got out and got away, and come to America."

"Dat's good! But he'll be pooty lonesome—dey ain' no kings here, is dey, Huck?"

"No."

"Den he cain't git no situation. What he gwyne to do?"

"Well, I don't know. Some of them gets on the police, and some of them learns people how to talk French."

"Why, Huck, doan de French people talk de same way we does?"

"*No*, Jim; you couldn't understand a word they said—not a single word."

"Well, now, I be ding-busted! How do dat come?"

"*I* don't know; but it's so. I got some of their jabber out of a book. Spose a man was to come to you and say *Polly-voo-franzy*—what would you think?"

"I wouldn' think nuff'n; I'd take en bust him over de head. Dat is, ef he warn't white. I wouldn't 'low no nigger to call me dat."

"Shucks, it ain't calling you anything. It's only saying, do you know how to talk French."

"Well, den, why couldn't he *say* it?"

"Why, he *is* a-saying it. That's a Frenchman's *way* of saying it."

"Well, it's a blame' ridicklous way, en I doan want to hear no mo' 'bout it. Dey ain' no sense in it."

"Looky here, Jim, does a cat talk like we do?"

"No, a cat don't."

"Well, does a cow?"

"No, a cow don't, nuther."

"Does a cat talk like a cow, or a cow talk like a cat?"

"No, dey don't."

"It's natural and right for 'em to talk different from each other, ain't it?"

"'Course."

"And ain't it natural and right for a cat and a cow to talk different from *us?*"

"Why, mos' sholy it is."

"Well, then, why ain't it natural and right for a *Frenchman* to talk different from us?—you answer me that."

"Is a cat a man, Huck?"

"No."

"Well, den, dey ain't no sense in a cat talkin' like a man. Is a cow a man? —er is a cow a cat?"

"No, she ain't either of them."

"Well, den, she ain' got no business to talk like either one er the yuther of 'em. Is a Frenchman a man?"

"Yes."

"*Well*, den! Dad blame it, why doan he *talk* like a man?—you answer me *dat!*"

I see it warn't no use wasting words—you can't learn a nigger to argue. So I quit.

Chapter XV.

"WE WOULD SELL THE RAFT."

WE JUDGED that three nights more would fetch us to Cairo, at the bottom of Illinois, where the Ohio River comes in, and that was what we was after. We would sell the raft and get on a steamboat and go way up the Ohio amongst the free States, and then be out of trouble.

Well, the second night a fog begun to come on, and we made for a tow-head to tie to, for it wouldn't do to try to run in fog; but when I paddled ahead in the canoe, with the line, to make fast, there warn't anything but little saplings to tie to. I passed the line around one of them right on the edge of the cut bank, but there was a stiff current, and the raft come booming down so lively she tore it out by the roots and away she went. I see the fog closing down, and it made me so sick and scared I couldn't budge for most a half a minute it seemed to me—and then there warn't no raft in sight; you couldn't see twenty yards. I jumped into the canoe and run back to the stern and grabbed the paddle and set her back a stroke. But she didn't come. I was in such a hurry I hadn't untied her. I got up and tried to untie her, but I was so excited my hands shook so I couldn't hardly do anything with them.

As soon as I got started I took out after the raft, hot and heavy, right down the tow-head. That was all right as far as it went, but the tow-head warn't sixty yards long, and the minute I flew by the foot of it I shot out into the solid white fog, and hadn't no more idea which way I was going than a dead man.

Thinks I, it won't do to paddle; first I know I'll run into the bank or a tow-head or something; I got to set still and float, and yet it's mighty fidgety business to have to hold your hands still at such a time. I whooped and listened. Away down there, somewheres, I hears a small whoop, and up comes my spirits. I went tearing after it, listening sharp to hear it again. The next time it come, I see I warn't heading for it but heading away to the right of it. And the next time, I was heading away to the left of it—and not gaining on it much, either, for I was flying around, this way and that and t'other, but it was going straight ahead all the time.

I did wish the fool would think to beat a tin pan, and beat it all the time, but he never did, and it was the still places between the whoops that was making the trouble for me. Well, I fought along, and directly I hears the whoop *behind* me. I was tangled good, now. That was somebody else's whoop, or else I was turned around.

I throwed the paddle down. I heard the whoop again; it was behind me yet, but in a different place; it kept coming, and kept changing its place, and I kept answering, till by and by it was in front of me again and I knowed the current had swung the canoe's head down stream and I was all right, if that was Jim and not some other raftsman hollering. I couldn't tell nothing about voices in a fog, for nothing don't look natural nor sound natural in a fog.

The whooping went on, and in about a minute I come a booming down on a cut bank with smoky ghosts of big trees on it, and the current threw me off to the left and shot by, amongst a lot of snags that fairly roared, the current was tearing by them so swift.

In another second or two it was solid white and still again. I set perfectly still, then, listening to my heart thump, and I reckon I didn't draw a breath while it thumped a hundred.

I just give up, then. I knowed what the matter was. That cut bank was an island, and Jim had gone down t'other side of it. It warn't no tow-head, that you could float by in ten minutes. It had the big timber of a regular island; it might be five or six mile long and more than a half a mile wide.

I kept quiet, with my ears cocked, about fifteen minutes, I reckon. I was floating along, of course, four or five mile an hour; but you don't ever think of that. No, you *feel* like you are laying dead still on the water; and if a little glimpse of a snag slips by, you don't think to yourself how fast *you're* going, but you catch your breath and

AMONG THE SNAGS.

think, my! how that snag's tearing along. If you think it ain't dismal and lonesome out in a fog that way, by yourself, in the night, you try it once—you'll see.

Next, for about a half an hour, I whoops now and then; at last I hears the answer a long ways off, and tries to follow it, but I couldn't do it, and directly I judged I'd got into a nest of tow-heads, for I had little dim glimpses of them on both sides of me, sometimes just a narrow channel between; and some that I couldn't see, I knowed was there, because I'd hear the wash of the current against the old dead brush and trash that hung over the banks. Well, I warn't long losing the whoops, down amongst the tow-heads; and I only tried to chase them a little while, anyway, because it was worse than chasing a Jack-o-lantern. You never knowed a sound dodge around so, and swap places so quick and so much.

I had to claw away from the bank pretty lively, four or five times, to keep from knocking the islands out of the river; and so I judged the raft must be butting into the bank every now and then, or else it would get further ahead and clear out of hearing—it was floating a little faster than what I was.

Well, I seemed to be in the open river again, by and by, but I couldn't hear no sign of a whoop nowheres. I reckoned Jim had fetched up on a snag, maybe, and it was all up with him. I was good and tired, so I laid down in the canoe and said I wouldn't bother no more. I didn't want to go to sleep, of course; but I was so sleepy I couldn't help it; so I thought I would take just one little cat-nap.

But I reckon it was more than a cat-nap, for when I waked up the stars was shining bright, the fog was all gone, and I was spinning down a big bend stern first. First I didn't know where I was; I thought I was dreaming; and when things begun to come back to me, they seemed to come up dim out of last week.

It was a monstrous big river here, with the tallest and the thickest kind of timber on both banks; just a solid wall, as well as I could see, by the stars. I looked away down stream, and seen a black speck on the water. I took out after it; but when I got to it it warn't nothing but a couple of saw-logs made fast together. Then I see another speck, and chased that; then another, and this time I was right. It was the raft.

ASLEEP ON THE RAFT.

When I got to it Jim was setting there with his head down between his knees, asleep, with his right arm hanging over the steering oar. The other oar was smashed off, and the raft was littered up with leaves and branches and dirt. So she'd had a rough time.

I made fast and laid down under Jim's nose on the raft, and begun to gap, and stretch my fists out against Jim, and says:

"Hello, Jim, have I been asleep? Why didn't you stir me up?"

"Goodness gracious, is dat you, Huck? En you ain' dead—you ain' drownded—you's back agin? It's too good for true, honey, it's too good for true. Lemme look at you, chile, lemme feel o' you. No, you ain' dead! you's back agin, live en soun', jis de same ole Huck—de same ole Huck, thanks to goodness!"

"What's the matter with you, Jim? You been a drinking?"

"Drinkin'? Has I ben a drinkin'? Has I had a chance to be a drinkin'?"

"Well, then, what makes you talk so wild?"

"How does I talk wild?"

"*How?* why, hain't you been talking about my coming back, and all that stuff, as if I'd been gone away?"

"Huck—Huck Finn, you look me in de eye; look me in de eye. *Hain't* you ben gone away?"

"Gone away? Why, what in the nation do you mean? *I* hain't been gone anywheres. Where would I go to?"

"Well, looky here, boss, dey's sumf'n wrong, dey is. Is I *me*, or who *is* I? Is I heah, or whah *is* I? Now dat's what I wants to know."

"Well, I think you're here, plain enough, but I think you're a tangle-headed old fool, Jim."

"I is, is I? Well you answer me dis. Didn't you tote out de line in de canoe, fer to make fas' to de tow-head?"

"No, I didn't. What tow-head? I hain't seen no tow-head."

"You hain't seen no tow-head? Looky here—didn't de line pull loose en de raf' go a hummin' down de river, en leave you en de canoe behine in de fog?"

"What fog?"

"Why *de* fog. De fog dat's ben aroun' all night. En didn't you whoop, en didn't I whoop, tell we got mix' up in de islands en one un us got los' en t'other one was jis' as good as los', 'kase he didn' know whah he wuz? En didn't I bust up agin a lot er dem islands en have a turrible time en mos' git drownded? Now ain' dat so, boss—ain't it so? You answer me dat."

"Well, this is too many for me, Jim. I hain't seen no fog, nor no islands, nor no troubles, nor nothing. I been setting here talking with you all night till you went to sleep about ten minutes ago, and I reckon I done the same. You couldn't a got drunk in that time, so of course you've been dreaming."

"Dad fetch it, how is I gwyne to dream all dat in ten minutes?"

"Well, hang it all, you did dream it, because there didn't any of it happen."

"But Huck, it's all jis' as plain to me as—"

"It don't make no difference how plain it is, there ain't nothing in it. I know, because I've been here all the time."

Jim didn't say nothing for about five minutes, but set there studying over it. Then he says:

"Well, den, I reck'n I did dream it, Huck; but dog my cats ef it ain't de powerfullest dream I ever see. En I hain't ever had no dream b'fo' dat's tired me like dis one."

"Oh, well, that's all right, because a dream does tire a body like everything, sometimes. But this one was a staving dream—tell me all about it, Jim."

So Jim went to work and told me the whole thing right through, just as it happened, only he painted it up considerable. Then he said he must start in and " 'terpret" it, because it was sent for a warning. He said the first tow-head stood for a man that would try to do us some good, but the current was another man that would get us away from him. The whoops was warnings that would come to us every now and then, and if we didn't try hard to make out to understand them they'd just take us into bad luck, 'stead of keeping us out of it. The lot of tow-heads was troubles we was going to get into with quarrelsome people and all kinds of mean folks, but if we minded our business and didn't talk back and aggravate them, we would pull through and get out of the fog and into the big clear river, which was the free States, and wouldn't have no more trouble.

It had clouded up pretty dark just after I got onto the raft, but it was clearing up again, now.

"Oh, well, that's all interpreted well enough, as far as it goes, Jim," I says; "but what does *these* things stand for?"

It was the leaves and rubbish on the raft, and the smashed oar. You could see them first rate, now.

Jim looked at the trash, and then looked at me, and back at the trash again. He had got the dream fixed so strong in his head that he couldn't seem to shake it loose and get the facts back into its place again, right away. But when he did get the thing straightened around, he looked at me steady, without ever smiling, and says:

"What do dey stan' for? I's gwyne to tell you. When I got all wore out wid work, en wid de callin' for you, en went to sleep, my heart wuz mos' broke bekase you wuz los', en I didn' k'yer no mo' what become er me en de raf'. En when I wake up en fine you back agin, all safe en soun', de tears come en I could a got down on my knees en kiss' yo' foot I's so thankful. En all you wuz thinkin 'bout wuz how you could make a fool uv ole Jim wid a lie. Dat truck dah is *trash;* en trash is what people is dat puts dirt on de head er dey fren's en makes 'em ashamed."

Then he got up slow, and walked to the wigwam, and went in there, without saying anything but that. But that was enough. It made me feel so mean I could almost kissed *his* foot to get him to take it back.

It was fifteen minutes before I could work myself up to go and humble myself to a nigger—but I done it, and I warn't ever sorry for it afterwards, neither. I didn't do him no more mean tricks, and I wouldn't done that one if I'd a knowed it would make him feel that way.

Chapter XVI

"IT *AMOUNTED* TO SOMETHING BEING A RAFTSMAN."

W E SLEPT most all day, and started out at night, a little ways behind a monstrous long raft that was as long going by as a procession. She had four long sweeps at each end, so we judged she carried as many as thirty men, likely. She had five big wigwams aboard, wide apart, and an open camp fire in the middle, and a tall flagpole at each end. There was a power of style about her. It *amounted* to something being a raftsman on such a craft as that.

We went drifting down into a big bend, and the night clouded up and got hot. The river was very wide, and was walled with solid timber on both sides; you couldn't see a break in it hardly ever, or a light. We talked about Cairo, and wondered whether we would know it when we got to it. I said likely we wouldn't, because I had heard say there warn't but about a dozen houses there, and if they didn't happen to have them lit up, how was we going to know we was passing a town? Jim said if the two big rivers joined together there, that would show. But I said maybe we might think we was passing the foot of an island and coming into the same old river again. That disturbed Jim—and me too. So the question was, what to do? I said, paddle ashore the first time a light showed, and tell them pap was behind, coming along with a trading-scow, and was a green hand at the business, and wanted to know how far it was to Cairo. Jim thought it was a good idea, so we took a smoke on it and waited.

But you know a young person can't wait very well when he is impatient to find a thing out. We talked it over, and by and by Jim said it was such a black night, now, that it wouldn't be no risk to swim down to the big raft and crawl aboard and listen,—they would talk about Cairo, because they would be calculating to go ashore there for a spree, maybe, or anyway they would send boats ashore to buy whisky or fresh meat or something. Jim had a wonderful level head, for a nigger: he could most always start a good plan when you wanted one.

I stood up and shook my rags off and jumped into the river, and struck out for the raft's light. By and by, when I got down nearly to

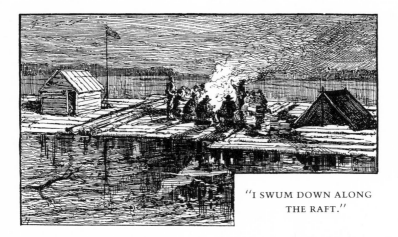

"I SWUM DOWN ALONG
THE RAFT."

her, I eased up and went slow and cautious. But everything was all right—nobody at the sweeps. So I swum down along the raft till I was most abreast the camp fire in the middle, then I crawled aboard and inched along and got in amongst some bundles of shingles on the weather side of the fire. There was thirteen men there—they was the watch on deck of course. And a mighty rough-looking lot, too. They had a jug, and tin cups, and they kept the jug moving. One man was singing—roaring, you may say; and it wasn't a nice song— for a parlor anyway. He roared through his nose, and strung out the last word of every line very long. When he was done they all fetched a kind of Injun war-whoop, and then another was sung. It begun:

"There was a woman in our towdn,
   In our towdn did dwed'l,
She loved her husband dear-i-lee,
   But another man twyste as wed'l.

Singing too, riloo, riloo, riloo,
   Ri-too, riloo, rilay - - - e,
She loved her husband dear-i-lee,
   But another man twyste as wed'l."

And so on—fourteen verses. It was kind of poor, and when he was
going to start on the next verse one of them said it was the tune the
old cow died on; and another one said, "Oh, give us a rest." And
another one told him to take a walk. They made fun of him till he
got mad and jumped up and begun to cuss the crowd, and said he
could lam any thief in the lot.

They was all about to make a break for him, but the biggest man
there jumped up and says:

"Set whar you are, gentlemen. Leave him to me; he's my meat."

Then he jumped up in the air three times and cracked his heels

"HE JUMPED UP IN THE AIR."

together every time. He flung off a buckskin coat that was all hung with fringes, and says, "You lay thar tell the chawin-up's done;" and flung his hat down, which was all over ribbons, and says, "You lay thar tell his sufferins is over."

Then he jumped up in the air and cracked his heels together again and shouted out:

"Whoo-oop! I'm the old original iron-jawed, brass-mounted, copper-bellied corpse-maker from the wilds of Arkansaw!—Look at me! I'm the man they call Sudden Death and General Desolation! Sired by a hurricane, dam'd by an earthquake, half-brother to the cholera, nearly related to the small-pox on the mother's side! Look at me! I take nineteen alligators and a bar'l of whisky for breakfast when I'm in robust health, and a bushel of rattlesnakes and a dead body when I'm ailing! I split the everlasting rocks with my glance, and I squench the thunder when I speak! Whoo-oop! Stand back and give me room according to my strength! Blood's my natural drink, and the wails of the dying is music to my ear! Cast your eye on me, gentlemen!—and lay low and hold your breath, for I'm 'bout to turn myself loose!"

All the time he was getting this off, he was shaking his head and looking fierce, and kind of swelling around in a little circle, tucking up his wrist-bands, and now and then straightening up and beating his breast with his fist, saying, "Look at me, gentlemen!" When he got through, he jumped up and cracked his heels together three times, and let off a roaring "whoo-oop! I'm the bloodiest son of a wildcat that lives!"

Then the man that had started the row tilted his old slouch hat down over his right eye; then he bent

"WENT AROUND IN A LITTLE CIRCLE."

stooping forward, with his back sagged and his south end sticking out far, and his fists a-shoving out and drawing in in front of him, and so went around in a little circle about three times, swelling himself up and breathing hard. Then he straightened, and jumped up and cracked his heels together three times before he lit again (that made them cheer), and he begun to shout like this:

"Whoo-oop! bow your neck and spread, for the kingdom of sorrow's a-coming! Hold me down to the earth, for I feel my powers a-working! whoo-oop! I'm a child of sin, *don't* let me get a start! Smoked glass, here, for all! Don't attempt to look at me with the naked eye, gentlemen! When I'm playful I use the meridians of longitude and parallels of latitude for a seine, and drag the Atlantic Ocean for whales! I scratch my head with the lightning and purr myself to sleep with the thunder! When I'm cold, I bile the Gulf of Mexico and bathe in it; when I'm hot I fan myself with an equinoctial storm; when I'm thirsty I reach up and suck a cloud dry like a sponge; when I range the earth hungry, famine follows in my tracks! Whoo-oop! Bow your neck and spread! I put my hand on the sun's face and make it night in the earth; I bite a piece out of the moon and hurry the seasons; I shake myself and crumble the mountains! Contemplate me through leather—*don't* use the naked eye! I'm the man with a petrified heart and biler-iron bowels! The massacre of isolated communities is the pastime of my idle moments, the destruction of nationalities the serious business of my life! The boundless vastness of the great American desert is my enclosed property, and I bury my dead on my own premises!" He jumped up and cracked his heels together three times before he lit (they cheered him again), and as he come down he shouted out: "Whoo-oop! bow your neck and spread, for the pet child of calamity's a-coming!"

Then the other one went to swelling around and blowing again—the first one—the one they called Bob; next, the Child of Calamity chipped in again, bigger than ever; then they both got at it at the same time, swelling round and round each other and punching their fists most into each other's faces, and whooping and jawing like Injuns; then Bob called the Child names, and the Child called him names back again: next, Bob called him a heap rougher names and the Child come back at him with the very worst kind of language; next, Bob knocked the Child's hat off, and the Child picked it up and kicked Bob's ribbony hat about six foot; Bob went and got it and said never mind, this warn't going to be the last of this thing, because he was a man that never forgot and never forgive, and so the Child better look out, for there was a time a-coming, just as sure as he was a living man, that he would have to answer to him with the best blood in his body. The Child said no man was willinger than he was for that time to come, and he would give Bob fair warning, *now*, never to cross his path again, for he could never rest till he had waded in his blood, for such was his nature, though he was sparing him now on account of his family, if he had one.

Both of them was edging away in different directions, growling and shaking their heads and going on about what they was going to do; but a little black-whiskered chap skipped up and says:

"Come back here, you couple of chicken-livered cowards, and I'll thrash the two of ye!"

And he done it, too. He snatched them, he jerked them this way and that, he booted them around, he knocked them sprawling faster

"HE KNOCKED THEM SPRAWLING."

than they could get up. Why, it warn't two minutes till they begged like dogs—and how the other lot did yell and laugh and clap their hands all the way through, and shout "Sail in, Corpse-Maker!" "Hi! at him again, Child of Calamity!" "Bully for you, little Davy!" Well, it was a perfect pow-wow for a while. Bob and the Child had red noses and black eyes when they got through. Little Davy made them own up that they was sneaks and cowards and not fit to eat with a dog or drink with a nigger; then Bob and the Child shook hands with each other, very solemn, and said they had always respected each other and was willing to let bygones be bygones. So then they washed their faces in the river; and just then there was a loud order to stand by for a crossing, and some of them went forward to man the sweeps there, and the rest went aft to handle the after-sweeps.

I laid still and waited for fifteen minutes, and had a smoke out of a pipe that one of them left in reach; then the crossing was finished, and they stumped back and had a drink around and went to talking and singing again. Next they got out an old fiddle, and one played, and another patted juba, and the rest turned themselves loose on a regular old-fashioned keel-boat break-down. They couldn't keep that up very long without getting winded, so by and by they settled around the jug again.

They sung "jolly, jolly raftsman's the life for me," with a rousing chorus, and then they got to talking about differences betwixt hogs, and their different kind of habits; and next about women and their different ways; and next about the best ways to put out houses that was afire; and next about what ought to be done with the Injuns; and next about what a king had to do, and how much he got; and next about how to make cats fight; and next about what to do when a man has fits; and next about differences betwixt clear-water rivers and muddy-water ones. The man they called Ed said the muddy Mississippi water was wholesomer to drink than the clear water of the Ohio; he said if you let a pint of this yaller Mississippi water settle, you would have about a half to three quarters of an inch of mud in the bottom, according to the stage of the river, and then it warn't no better than Ohio water—what you wanted to do was to keep it stirred up—and when the river was low, keep mud on hand to put in and thicken the water up the way it ought to be.

The Child of Calamity said that was so; he said there was nutritiousness in the mud, and a man that drunk Mississippi water could grow corn in his stomach if he wanted to. He says:

"You look at the graveyards; that tells the tale. Trees won't grow worth shucks in a Cincinnati graveyard, but in a Sent Louis graveyard they grow upwards of eight hundred foot high. It's all on

AN OLD-FASHIONED BREAK-DOWN.

account of the water the people drunk before they laid up. A Cincinnati corpse don't richen a soil any."

And they talked about how Ohio water didn't like to mix with Mississippi water. Ed said if you take the Mississippi on a rise when the Ohio is low, you'll find a wide band of clear water all the way down the east side of the Mississippi for a hundred mile or more, and the minute you get out a quarter of a mile from shore and pass the line, it is all thick and yaller the rest of the way across. Then they talked about how to keep tobacco from getting mouldy, and from that they went into ghosts and told about a lot that other folks had seen; but Ed says:

"Why don't you tell something that you've seen yourselves? Now let me have a say. Five years ago I was on a raft as big as this, and right along here it was a bright moonshiny night, and I was on watch and boss of the stabboard oar forrard, and one of my pards was a man named Dick Allbright, and he come along to where I was sitting, forrard—gaping and stretching, he was—and stooped down on the edge of the raft and washed his face in the river, and come and set down by me and got out his pipe, and had just got it filled, when he looks up and says,—

" 'Why looky-here,' he says, 'ain't that Buck Miller's place, over yander in the bend?'

" 'Yes,' says I, 'it is—why?' He laid his pipe down and leant his head on his hand, and says,—

" 'I thought we'd be furder down.' I says,—

" 'I thought it too, when I went off watch'—we was standing six hours on and six off—'but the boys told me,' I says, 'that the raft didn't seem to hardly move, for the last hour,'—says I, 'though she's a slipping along all right, now,' says I. He give a kind of a groan, and says,—

" 'I've seed a raft act so before, along here,' he says, ' 'pears to me the current has most quit above the head of this bend durin' the last two years,' he says.

"Well, he raised up two or three times, and looked away off and around on the water. That started me at it, too. A body is always doing what he sees somebody else doing, though there mayn't be no sense in it. Pretty soon I see a black something floating on the water away off to stabboard and quartering behind us. I see he was looking at it, too. I says,—

" 'What's that?' He says, sort of pettish,—

" 'Tain't nothing but an old empty bar'l.'

" 'An empty bar'l!' says I, 'why,' says I, 'a spy-glass is a fool to *your* eyes. How can you tell it's an empty bar'l?' He says,—

" 'I don't know; I reckon it ain't a bar'l, but I thought it might be,' says he.

" 'Yes,' I says, 'so it might be, and it might be anything else, too; a body can't tell nothing about it, such a distance as that,' I says.

"We hadn't nothing else to do, so we kept on watching it. By and by I says,—

" 'Why looky-here, Dick Allbright, that thing's a-gaining on us, I believe.'

"He never said nothing. The thing gained and gained, and I judged

it must be a dog that was about tired out. Well, we swung down into
the crossing, and the thing floated across the bright streak of the
moonshine, and, by George, it *was* a bar'l. Says I,—

" 'Dick Allbright, what made you think that thing was a bar'l,
when it was a half a mile off,'
says I. Says he,—

" 'I don't know.' Says I,—

" 'You tell me, Dick All-
bright.' He says,—

" 'Well, I knowed it was a
bar'l; I've seen it before; lots
has seen it; they says it's a
ha'nted bar'l.'

"I called the rest of the
watch, and they come and
stood there, and I told them
what Dick said. It floated
right along abreast, now, and
didn't gain any more. It was
about twenty foot off. Some
was for having it aboard, but
the rest didn't want to. Dick

THE MYSTERIOUS BARREL.

Allbright said rafts that had fooled with it had got bad luck by it.
The captain of the watch said he didn't believe in it. He said he
reckoned the bar'l gained on us because it was in a little better
current than what we was. He said it would leave by and by.

"So then we went to talking about other things, and we had a
song, and then a breakdown; and after that the captain of the watch
called for another song; but it was clouding up, now, and the bar'l
stuck right thar in the same place, and the song didn't seem to have
much warm-up to it, somehow, and so they didn't finish it, and
there warn't any cheers, but it sort of dropped flat, and nobody said
anything for a minute. Then everybody tried to talk at once, and
one chap got off a joke, but it warn't no use, they didn't laugh, and
even the chap that made the joke didn't laugh at it, which ain't
usual. We all just settled down glum, and watched the bar'l, and was
oneasy and oncomfortable. Well, sir, it shut down black and still,
and then the wind begin to moan around, and next the lightning

begin to play and the thunder to grumble. And pretty soon there was a regular storm, and in the middle of it a man that was running aft stumbled and fell and sprained his ankle so that he had to lay up. This made the boys shake their heads. And every time the lightning come, there was that bar'l with the blue lights winking around it.

"SOON THERE WAS A REGULAR STORM."

We was always on the look-out for it. But by and by, towards dawn, she was gone. When the day come we couldn't see her anywhere, and we warn't sorry, neither.

"But next night about half-past nine, when there was songs and high jinks going on, here she comes again, and took her old roost on the stabboard side. There warn't no more high jinks. Everybody got solemn; nobody talked; you couldn't get anybody to do anything but set around moody and look at the bar'l. It begun to cloud up again. When the watch changed, the off watch stayed up, 'stead of turning in. The storm ripped and roared around all night, and in the middle of it another man tripped and sprained his ankle, and had to knock off. The bar'l left towards day, and nobody see it go.

"Everybody was sober and down in the mouth all day. I don't mean the kind of sober that comes of leaving liquor alone,—not that. They was quiet, but they all drunk more than usual,—not together,—but each man sidled off and took it private, by himself.

"After dark the off watch didn't turn in; nobody sung, nobody talked; the boys didn't scatter around, neither; they sort of huddled together, forrard; and for two hours they set there, perfectly still, looking steady in the one direction, and heaving a sigh once in a while. And then, here comes the bar'l again. She took up her old place. She staid there all night; nobody turned in. The storm come on again, after midnight. It got awful dark; the rain poured down; hail, too; the thunder boomed and roared and bellowed; the wind blowed a hurricane; and the lightning spread over everything in big sheets of glare, and showed the whole raft as plain as day; and the river lashed up white as milk as far as you could see for miles, and there was that bar'l jiggering along, same as ever. The captain ordered the watch to man the after sweeps for a crossing, and nobody would go,—no more sprained ankles for them, they said. They wouldn't even *walk* aft. Well then, just then the sky split wide open, with a crash, and the lightning killed two men of the after watch, and crippled two more. Crippled them how, says you? Why, *sprained their ankles!*

"The bar'l left in the dark betwixt lightnings, towards dawn. Well, not a body eat a bite at breakfast that morning. After that the men loafed around, in twos and threes, and talked low together. But none of them herded with Dick Allbright. They all give him the cold shake. If he come around

"THE LIGHTNING
KILLED TWO MEN."

where any of the men was, they split up and sidled away. They wouldn't man the sweeps with him. The captain had all the skiffs hauled up on the raft, alongside of his wigwam, and wouldn't let the dead men be took ashore to be planted; he didn't believe a man that got ashore would come back; and he was right.

"After night come, you could see pretty plain that there was going to be trouble if that bar'l come again; there was such a muttering going on. A good many wanted to kill Dick Allbright, because he'd seen the bar'l on other trips, and that had an ugly look. Some wanted to put him ashore. Some said, let's all go ashore in a pile, if the bar'l comes again.

"This kind of whispers was still going on, the men being bunched together forrard watching for the bar'l, when, lo and behold you, here she comes again. Down she comes, slow and steady, and settles into her old tracks. You could a heard a pin drop. Then up comes the captain, and says:

" 'Boys, don't be a pack of children and fools; I don't want this bar'l to be dogging us all the way to Orleans, and *you* don't; well, then, how's the best way to stop it? Burn it up,—that's the way. I'm going to fetch it aboard,' he says. And before anybody could say a word, in he went.

"He swum to it, and as he come pushing it to the raft, the men spread to one side. But the old man got it aboard and busted in the head, and there was a baby in it! Yes sir, a stark naked baby. It was Dick Allbright's baby; he owned up and said so.

" 'Yes,' he says, a-leaning over it, 'yes, it is my own lamented darling, my poor lost Charles William Allbright deceased,' says he,—for he could curl his tongue around the bulliest words in the language when he was a mind to, and lay them before you without a jint started, anywheres. Yes, he said he used to live up at the head of this bend, and one night he choked his child, which was crying, not intending to kill it,—which was prob'ly a lie,—and then he was scared, and buried it in a bar'l, before his wife got home, and off he went, and struck the northern trail and went to rafting; and this was the third year that the bar'l had chased him. He said the bad luck always begun light, and lasted till four men was killed, and then the bar'l didn't come any more after that. He said if the men would stand it one more night,—and was agoing on like that,—but the men had got enough. They started to get out a boat to take him ashore and lynch him, but he grabbed the little child all of a sudden and jumped overboard with it hugged up to his breast and shedding tears, and we never see him again in this life, poor old suffering soul, nor Charles William neither."

"*Who* was shedding tears?" says Bob; "was it Allbright or the baby?"

"Why, Allbright, of course; didn't I tell you the baby was dead? Been dead three years—how could it cry?"

"Well, never mind how it could cry—how could it *keep* all that time?" says Davy. "You answer me that."

"I don't know how it done it," says Ed. "It done it though—that's all I know about it."

"Say—what did they do with the bar'l?" says the Child of Calamity.

"Why, they hove it overboard, and it sunk like a chunk of lead."

"Edward, did the child look like it was choked?" says one.

"GRABBED THE LITTLE CHILD."

"Did it have its hair parted?" says another.

"What was the brand on that bar'l, Eddy?" says a fellow they called Bill.

"Have you got the papers for them statistics, Edmund?" says Jimmy.

"Say, Edwin, was you one of the men that was killed by the lightning?" says Davy.

"Him? O, no, he was both of 'em," says Bob. Then they all haw-hawed.

"Say, Edward, don't you reckon you'd better take a pill? You look bad—don't you feel pale?" says the Child of Calamity.

"O, come, now, Eddy," says Jimmy, "show up; you must a kept

part of that bar'l to prove the thing by. Show us the bunghole—*do*—
and we'll all believe you."

"Say, boys," says Bill, "less divide it up. Thar's thirteen of us. I
can swaller a thirteenth of the yarn, if you can worry down the rest."

Ed got up mad and said they could all go to some place which he
ripped out pretty savage, and then walked off aft cussing to himself,
and they yelling and jeering at him, and roaring and laughing so you
could hear them a mile.

"ED GOT UP MAD."

"Boys, we'll split a watermelon
on that," says the Child of Calamity; and he come rummaging
around in the dark amongst the
shingle bundles where I was, and
put his hand on me. I was warm and
soft and naked; so he says "Ouch!" and jumped back.

"Fetch a lantern or a chunk of fire here, boys—there's a snake
here as big as a cow!"

So they run there with a lantern and crowded up and looked in
on me.

"Come out of that, you beggar!" says one.

"Who are you?" says another.

"What are you after here? Speak up prompt, or overboard you
go."

"Snake him out, boys. Snatch him out by the heels."

I began to beg, and crept out amongst them trembling. They looked me over, wondering, and the Child of Calamity says:

"A cussed thief! Lend a hand and less heave him overboard!"

"No," says Big Bob, "less get out the paint-pot and paint him a sky blue all over from head to heel, and *then* heave him over!"

"Good! that's it. Go for the paint, Jimmy."

When the paint come, and Bob took the brush and was just going to begin, the others laughing and rubbing their hands, I begun to cry,

"WHO ARE YOU?"

and that sort of worked on Davy, and he says:

" 'Vast there! He's nothing but a cub. I'll paint the man that tetches him!"

So I looked around on them, and some of them grumbled and growled, and Bob put down the paint, and the others didn't take it up.

"Come here to the fire, and less see what you're up to here," says Davy. "Now set down there and give an account of yourself. How long have you been aboard here?"

"Not over a quarter of a minute, sir," says I.

"How did you get dry so quick?"

"I don't know, sir. I'm always that way, mostly."

"Oh, you are, are you? What's your name?"

I warn't going to tell my name. I didn't know what to say, so I just says:

"Charles William Allbright, sir."

Then they roared—the whole crowd; and I was mighty glad I said that, because maybe laughing would get them in a better humor.

When they got done laughing, Davy says:

"CHARLES WILLIAM ALLBRIGHT, SIR."

"It won't hardly do, Charles William. You couldn't have growed this much in five year, and you was a baby when you come out of the bar'l, you know, and dead at that. Come, now, tell a straight story, and nobody'll hurt you, if you ain't up to anything wrong. What *is* your name?"

"Aleck Hopkins, sir. Aleck James Hopkins."

"Well, Aleck, where did you come from, here?"

"From a trading scow. She lays up the bend yonder. I was born on her. Pap has traded up and down here all his life; and he told me to swim off here, because when you went by he said he would like to get some of you to speak to a Mr. Jonas Turner, in Cairo, and tell him—"

"Oh, come!"

"Yes, sir, it's as true as the world; Pap he says—"

"Oh, your grandmother!"

They all laughed, and I tried again to talk, but they broke in on me and stopped me.

"Now, looky-here," says Davy; "you're scared, and so you talk wild. Honest, now, do you live in a scow, or is it a lie?"

"Yes, sir, in a trading scow. She lays up at the head of the bend. But I warn't born in her. It's our first trip."

"Now you're talking! What did you come aboard here, for? To steal?"

"No, sir, I didn't. It was only to get a ride on the raft. All boys does that."

"Well, I know that. But what did you hide for?"

"Sometimes they drive the boys off."

"So they do. They might steal. Looky-here; if we let you off this time, will you keep out of these kind of scrapes hereafter?"

" 'Deed I will, boss. You try me."

"All right, then. You ain't but little ways from shore. Overboard with you, and don't you make a fool of yourself another time this way. Blast it, boy, some raftsmen would rawhide you till you were black and blue!"

I didn't wait to kiss good-bye, but went overboard and broke for shore. When Jim come along by and by, the  big raft was away out of sight around the point. I swum out and got aboard, and was mighty glad to see home again.

There warn't nothing to do, now, but to look out sharp for the town, and not pass it without seeing it. He said he'd be mighty sure to see it, because he'd be a free man the minute he seen it, but if he missed it he'd be in the slave country again and no more show for freedom. Every little while he jumps up and says:

"Dah she is!"

But it warn't. It was Jack-o-lanterns, or lightning-bugs; so he set down again, and went to watching, same as before. Jim said it made him all over trembly and feverish to be so close to freedom. Well, I can tell you it made me all over trembly and feverish, too, to hear him, because I begun to get it through my head that he *was* most free—and who was to blame for it? Why, *me*. I couldn't get that out of my conscience, no how nor no way. It got to troubling me so I couldn't rest; I couldn't stay still in one place. It hadn't ever come home to me before, what this thing was that I was doing. But now it did; and it staid with me, and scorched me more and more. I tried to make out to myself that *I* warn't to blame, because *I* didn't run Jim off from his rightful owner; but it warn't no use, conscience up and says, every time, "But you knowed he was running for his freedom, and you could a paddled ashore and told somebody." That was so— I couldn't get around that, noway. That was where it pinched. Conscience says to me, "What had poor Miss Watson done to you, that you could see her nigger go off right under your eyes and never say one single word? What did that poor old woman do to you, that you could treat her so mean? Why, she tried to learn you your book, she tried to learn you your manners, she tried to be good to you every way she knowed how. *That's* what she done."

I got to feeling so mean and so miserable I most wished I was dead. I fidgeted up and down the raft, abusing myself to myself, and Jim was fidgeting up and down past me. We neither of us could keep still. Every time he danced around and says, "Dah's Cairo!" it went through me like a shot, and I thought if it *was* Cairo I reckoned I would die of miserableness.

Jim talked out loud all the time while I was talking to myself. He was saying how the first thing he would do when he got to a free State he would go to saving up money and never spend a single cent, and when he got enough he would buy his wife, which was owned on a farm close to where Miss Watson lived; and then they would both work to buy the two children, and if their master wouldn't sell them, they'd get an Ab'litionist to go and steal them.

It most froze me to hear such talk. He wouldn't ever dared to talk such talk in his life before. Just see what a difference it made in him the minute he judged he was about free. It was according to the old saying, "give a nigger an inch and he'll take an ell." Thinks I, this is what comes of my not thinking. Here was this nigger which I had as good as helped to run away, coming right out flat-footed and saying he would steal his children—children that belonged to a man I didn't even know; a man that hadn't ever done me no harm.

I was sorry to hear Jim say that, it was such a lowering of him. My conscience got to stirring me up hotter than ever, until at last I says to it, "Let up on me—it ain't too late, yet—I'll paddle ashore at the first light, and tell." I felt easy, and happy, and light as a feather, right off. All my troubles was gone. I went to looking out sharp for a light, and sort of singing to myself. By and by one showed. Jim sings out:

"We's safe, Huck, we's safe! Jump up and crack yo' heels, dat's de good ole Cairo at las', I jis knows it!"

I says:

"I'll take the canoe and go see, Jim. It mightn't be, you know."

He jumped and got the canoe ready, and put his old coat in the bottom for me to set on, and give me the paddle; and as I shoved off, he says:

"Pooty soon I'll be a-shout'n for joy, en I'll say, it's all on accounts o' Huck; I's a free man, en I couldn't ever ben free ef it hadn' ben for Huck; Huck done it. Jim won't ever forgit you, Huck; you's de bes' fren' Jim's ever had; en you's de *only* fren' ole Jim's got now."

I was paddling off, all in a sweat to tell on him; but when he says this, it seemed to kind of take the tuck all out of me. I went along slow then, and I warn't right down certain whether I was glad I started or whether I warn't. When I was fifty yards off, Jim says:

"Dah you goes, de ole true Huck; de on'y white genlman dat ever kep' his promise to ole Jim."

Well, I just felt sick. But I says, I *got* to do it—I can't get *out* of it. Right then, along comes a skiff with two men in it, with guns, and they stopped and I stopped. One of them says:

"What's that, yonder?"

"A piece of a raft," I says.

"Do you belong on it?"

"Yes, sir."

"Any men on it?"

"Only one, sir."

"Well, there's five niggers run off to-night, up yonder above the head of the bend. Is your man white or black?"

I didn't answer up prompt. I tried to, but the words wouldn't come. I tried, for a second or two, to brace up and out with it, but I warn't man enough—hadn't the spunk of a rabbit. I see I was weakening; so I just give up trying, and up and says—

"He's white."

"I reckon we'll go and see for ourselves."

"I wish you would," says I, "because it's pap that's there, and maybe you'd help me tow the raft ashore where the light is. He's sick—and so is mam and Mary Ann."

"Oh, the devil! we're in a hurry, boy. But I s'pose we've got to. Come—buckle to your paddle, and let's get along."

I buckled to my paddle and they laid to their oars. When we had made a stroke or two, I says:

"Pap'll be mighty much obleeged to you, I can tell you. Everybody goes away when I want them to help me tow the raft ashore, and I can't do it by myself."

"Well, that's infernal mean. Odd, too. Say, boy, what's the matter with your father?"

"It's the—a—the—well, it ain't anything, much."

They stopped pulling. It warn't but a mighty little ways to the raft, now. One says:

"Boy, that's a lie. What *is* the matter with your pap? Answer up square, now, and it'll be the better for you."

"I will, sir, I will, honest—but don't leave us, please. It's the—the—gentlemen, if you'll only pull ahead, and let me heave you the head-line, you won't have to come a-near the raft—please do."

"BOY, THAT'S A LIE."

"Set her back, John, set her back!" says one. They backed water. "Keep away, boy—keep to looard. Confound it, I just expect the wind has blowed it to us. Your pap's got the small-pox, and you know it precious well. Why didn't you come out and say so? Do you want to spread it all over?"

"Well," says I, a-blubbering, "I've told everybody before, and then they just went away and left us."

"Poor devil, there's something in that. We are right down sorry for you, but we—well, hang it, we don't want the small-pox, you see. Look here, I'll tell you what to do. Don't you try to land by yourself, or you'll smash everything to pieces. You float along down about twenty miles and you'll come to a town on the left-hand side of the river. It will be long after sun-up, then, and when you ask for help, you tell them your folks are all down with chills and fever. Don't be a fool again, and let people guess what is the matter. Now we're trying to do you a kindness; so you just put twenty miles between us, that's a good boy. It wouldn't do any good to land yonder where the light is—it's only a wood-yard. Say—I reckon your father's poor, and I'm bound to say he's in pretty hard luck. Here—I'll put a twenty dollar gold piece on this board, and you get it when it floats by. I feel mighty mean to leave you, but my kingdom! it won't do to fool with small-pox, don't you see?"

"Hold on, Parker," says the other man, "here's a twenty to put on the board for me. Good-bye, boy, you do as Mr. Parker told you, and you'll be all right."

"That's so, my boy—good-bye, good-bye. If you see any runaway niggers, you get help and nab them, and you can make some money by it."

"Good-bye, sir," says I, "I won't let no runaway niggers get by me if I can help it."

They went off, and I got aboard the raft, feeling bad and low, because I knowed very well I had done wrong, and I see it warn't no use for me to try to learn to do right; a body that don't get *started* right when he's little, ain't got no show—when the pinch comes there ain't nothing to back him up and keep him to his work, and so he gets beat. Then I thought a minute, and says to myself, hold on,— s'pose you'd a done right and give Jim up; would you felt better than what you do now? No, says I, I'd feel bad—I'd feel just the same way

I do now. Well, then, says I, what's the use you learning to do right, when it's troublesome to do right and ain't no trouble to do wrong, and the wages is just the same? I was stuck. I couldn't answer that. So I reckoned I wouldn't bother no more about it, but after this always do whichever come handiest at the time.

I went into the wigwam; Jim warn't there. I looked all around; he warn't anywhere. I says:

"Jim!"

"Here I is, Huck. Is dey out o' sight yit? Don't talk loud."

"HERE I IS, HUCK."

He was in the river, under the stern oar, with just his nose out. I told him they was out of sight, so he come aboard. He says:

"I was a-listenin' to all de talk, en I slips into de river en was gwyne to shove for sho' if dey come aboard. Den I was gwyne to swim to de raf' agin when dey was gone. But lawsy, how you did fool 'em, Huck! Dat *wuz* de smartes' dodge! I tell you, chile, I 'speck it save' ole Jim—ole Jim ain't gwyne to forgit you for dat, honey."

Then we talked about the money. It was a pretty good raise, twenty dollars apiece. Jim said we could take deck passage on a steamboat now, and the money would last us as far as we wanted to go in the free States. He said twenty mile more warn't far for the raft to go, but he wished we was already there.

Towards daybreak we tied up, and Jim was mighty particular about hiding the raft good. Then he worked all day fixing things in bundles, and getting all ready to quit rafting.

That night about ten we hove in sight of the lights of a town away down in a left-hand bend.

I went off in the canoe, to ask about it. Pretty soon I found a man out in the river with a skiff, setting a trot-line. I ranged up and says:

"Mister, is that town Cairo?"

"Cairo? no. You must be a blame' fool."

"What town is it, mister?"

"If you want to know, go and find out. If you stay here botherin' around me for about a half a minute longer, you'll get something you won't want."

I paddled to the raft. Jim was awful disappointed, but I said never mind, Cairo would be the next place, I reckoned.

We passed another town before daylight, and I was going out again; but it was high ground, so I didn't go. No high ground about Cairo, Jim said. I had forgot it. We laid up for the day, on a tow-head tolerable close to the left-hand bank. I begun to suspicion something. So did Jim. I says:

"Maybe we went by Cairo in the fog that night."

He says:

"Doan' less talk about it, Huck. Po' niggers can't have no luck. I awluz 'spected dat rattle-snake skin warn't done wid its work."

"I wish I'd never seen that snake-skin, Jim—I do wish I'd never laid eyes on it."

"It ain't yo' fault, Huck; you didn' know. Don't you blame yo'self 'bout it."

When it was daylight, here was the clear Ohio water in shore, sure enough, and outside was the old regular Muddy! So it was all up with Cairo.

We talked it all over. It wouldn't do to take to the shore; we couldn't take the raft up the stream, of course. There warn't no way but to wait for dark, and start back in the canoe and take the chances. So we slept all day amongst the cotton-wood thicket, so as to be fresh for the work, and when we went back to the raft about dark the canoe was gone!

We didn't say a word for a good while. There warn't anything to say. We both knowed well enough it was some more work of the rattle-snake skin; so what was the use to talk about it? It would only look like we was finding fault, and that would be bound to fetch more bad luck—and keep on fetching it, too, till we knowed enough to keep still.

By and by we talked about what we better do, and found there warn't no way but just to go along down with the raft till we got a chance to buy a canoe to go back in. We warn't going to borrow it when there warn't anybody around, the way pap would do, for that might set people after us.

So we shoved out, after dark, on the raft.

Anybody that don't believe yet, that it's foolishness to handle a snake-skin, after all that that snake-skin done for us, will believe it now, if they read on and see what more it done for us.

The place to buy canoes is off of rafts laying up at shore. But we didn't see no rafts laying up; so we went along during three hours and more. Well, the night got gray, and ruther thick, which is the next meanest thing to fog. You can't tell the shape of the river, and you can't see no distance. It got to be very late and still, and then along comes a steamboat up the river. We lit the lantern, and judged she would see it. Up-stream boats didn't generly come close to us; they go out and follow the bars and hunt for easy water under the reefs; but nights like this they bull right up the channel against the whole river.

We could hear her pounding along, but we didn't see her good till she was close. She aimed right for us. Often they do that and try to see how close they can come without touching; sometimes the wheel bites off a sweep, and then the pilot sticks his head out and laughs, and thinks he's mighty smart. Well, here she comes, and we said she was going to try to shave us; but she didn't seem to be sheering off a bit. She was a big one, and she was coming in a hurry, too, looking like a black cloud with rows of glow-worms around it; but all of a sudden she bulged out, big and scary, with a long row of wide-open furnace doors shining like red-hot teeth, and her monstrous bows and guards hanging right over us. There was a yell at us, and a jingling of bells to stop the engines, a pow-wow of cussing, and whistling of steam—and as Jim went overboard on one side and I on the other, she come smashing straight through the raft.

I dived—and I aimed to find the bottom, too, for a thirty-foot wheel had got to go over me, and I wanted it to have plenty of room. I could always stay under water a minute; this time I reckon I staid under water a minute and a half. Then I bounced for the top in a hurry, for I was nearly busting. I popped out to my arm-pits and blowed the water out of my nose, and puffed a bit. Of course there was a booming current; and of course that boat started her engines again ten seconds after she stopped them, for they never cared much for raftsmen; so now she was churning along up the river, out of sight in the thick weather, though I could hear her.

I sung out for Jim about a dozen times, but I didn't get any answer; so I grabbed a plank that touched me while I was "treading water," and struck out for shore, shoving it ahead of me. But I made out to see that the drift of the current was towards the left-hand shore, which meant that I was in a crossing; so I changed off and went that way.

It was one of these long, slanting, two-mile crossings; so I was a good long time in getting over. I made a safe landing, and clum up the bank. I couldn't see but a little ways, but I went poking along over rough ground for a quarter of a mile or more, and then I run across a big old-fashioned double log house before I noticed it. I was going to rush by and get away, but a lot of dogs jumped out and went to howling and barking at me, and I knowed better than to move another peg.

CLIMBING UP THE BANK.

Chapter XVII.

"WHO'S THERE?"

IN ABOUT half a minute somebody spoke out of a window, without putting his head out, and says:

"Be done, boys! Who's there?"

I says:

"It's me."

"Who's me?"

"George Jackson, sir."

"What do you want?"

"I don't want nothing, sir. I only want to go along by, but the dogs won't let me."

"What are you prowling around here this time of night, for—hey?"

"I warn't prowling around, sir; I fell overboard off of the steamboat."

"Oh, you did, did you? Strike a light there, somebody. What did you say your name was?"

"George Jackson, sir. I'm only a boy."

"Look here; if you're telling the truth, you needn't be afraid—nobody 'll hurt you. But don't try to budge; stand right where you are. Rouse out Bob and Tom, some of you, and fetch the guns. George Jackson, is there anybody with you?"

"No, sir, nobody."

I heard the people stirring around in the house, now, and see a light. The man sung out:

"Snatch that light away, Betsy, you old fool—ain't you got any sense? Put it on the floor behind the front door. Bob, if you and Tom are ready, take your places."

"All ready."

"Now, George Jackson, do you know the Shepherdsons?"

"No, sir—I never heard of them."

"Well, that may be so, and it mayn't. Now, all ready. Step forward, George Jackson. And mind, don't you hurry—come mighty slow. If there's anybody with you, let him keep back—if he shows himself he'll be shot. Come along, now. Come slow; push the door open, yourself—just enough to squeeze in, d' you hear?"

I didn't hurry, I couldn't if I'd a wanted to. I took one slow step at a time, and there warn't a sound, only I thought I could hear my heart. The dogs were as still as the humans, but they followed a little behind me. When I got to the three log door-steps, I heard them unlocking and unbarring and unbolting. I put my hand on the door and pushed it a little and a little more, till somebody said, "There, that's enough—put your head in." I done it, but I judged they would take it off.

The candle was on the floor, and there they all was, looking at me, and me at them, for about a quarter of a minute. Three big men with guns pointed at me, which made me wince, I tell you; the oldest, gray and about sixty, the other two thirty or more—all of them fine and handsome—and the sweetest old gray-headed lady, and back of her two young women which I couldn't see right well. The old gentleman says:

"There—I reckon it's all right. Come in."

As soon as I was in, the old gentleman he locked the door and barred it and bolted it, and told the young men to come in with their guns, and they all went in a big parlor that had a new rag carpet on the floor, and got together in a corner that was out of range of the front windows—there warn't none on the side. They held the candle, and took a good look at me, and all said, "Why _he_ ain't a Shepherdson—no, there ain't any Shepherdson about him." Then the old man said he hoped I wouldn't mind being searched for arms, because he didn't mean no harm by it—it was only to make sure. So he didn't pry into my pockets, but only felt outside with his hands, and said it was all right. He told me to make myself easy and at home, and tell all about myself; but the old lady says:

"Why bless you, Saul, the poor thing's as wet as he can be; and don't you reckon it may be he's hungry?"

"True for you, Rachel—I forgot."

So the old lady says:

"Betsy" (this was a nigger woman), "you fly around and get him something to eat, as quick as you can, poor thing; and one of you girls go and wake up Buck and tell him— Oh, here he is himself.

"BUCK."

Buck, take this little stranger and get the wet clothes off from him and dress him up in some of yours that's dry."

Buck looked about as old as me—thirteen or fourteen or along there, though he was a little bigger than me. He hadn't on anything but a shirt, and he was very frowsy-headed. He come in gaping and digging one fist into his eyes, and he was dragging a gun along with the other one. He says:

"Ain't they no Shepherdsons around?"

They said, no, 'twas a false alarm.

"Well," he says, "if they'd a ben some, I reckon I'd a got one."

They all laughed, and Bob says:

"Why, Buck, they might have scalped us all, you've been so slow in coming."

"Well, nobody come after me, and it ain't right. I'm always kep' down; I don't get no show."

"Never mind, Buck, my boy," says the old man, "you'll have show enough, all in good time, don't you fret about that. Go 'long with you now, and do as your mother told you."

When we got up stairs to his room, he got me a coarse shirt and a roundabout and pants of his, and I put them on. While I was at it he asked me what my name was, but before I could tell him, he started to telling me about a blue jay and a young rabbit he had catched in the woods day before yesterday, and he asked me where Moses was when the candle went out. I said I didn't know; I hadn't heard about it before, no way.

"Well, guess," he says.

"How'm I going to guess," says I, "when I never heard tell about it before?"

"But you can guess, can't you? It's just as easy."

"*Which* candle?" I says.

"Why, any candle," he says.

"I don't know where he was," says I; "where was he?"

"Why he was in the *dark!* That's where he was!"

"Well, if you knowed where he was, what did you ask me for?"

"Why, blame it, it's a riddle, don't you see? Say, how long are you going to stay here? You got to stay always. We can just have booming times—they don't have no school now. Do you own a dog? I've got a dog—and he'll go in the river and bring out chips that you throw in. Do you like to comb up, Sundays, and all that kind of foolishness? You bet I don't, but ma she makes me. Confound these ole britches, I reckon I'd better put 'em on, but I'd ruther not, it's so warm. Are you all ready? All right—come along, old hoss."

Cold corn-pone, cold corn-beef, butter and butter-milk—that is what they had for me down there, and there ain't nothing better that ever I've come across yet. Buck and his ma and all of them smoked cob pipes, except the nigger woman, which was gone, and the two young women. They all smoked and talked, and I eat and talked. The young women had quilts around them, and their hair down their backs. They all asked me questions, and I told them how pap and me and all the family was living on a little farm down at the bottom of Arkansaw, and my sister Mary Ann run off and got married and never was heard of no more, and Bill went to hunt them and he warn't heard of no more, and Tom and Mort died, and then there warn't nobody but just me and pap left, and he was just trimmed down to nothing, on account of his troubles; so when he died I took what there was left, because the farm didn't belong to us, and started up the river, deck passage, and fell overboard; and that was how I come to be here. So they said I could have a home there as long as I wanted it. Then it was most daylight, and everybody went to bed, and I went to bed with Buck, and when I waked up in the morning, drat it all, I had forgot what my name was. So I laid there about an hour trying to think, and when Buck waked up, I says:

"Can you spell, Buck?"

"Yes," he says.

"I bet you can't spell my name," says I.

"I bet you what you dare I can," says he.

"All right," says I, "go ahead."

"G-o-r-g-e J-a-x-o-n—there now," he says.

"Well," says I, "you done it, but I didn't think you could. It ain't no slouch of a name to spell—right off without studying."

I set it down, private, because somebody might want *me* to spell it, next, and so I wanted to be handy with it and rattle it off like I was used to it.

It was a mighty nice family, and a mighty nice house, too. I hadn't seen no house out in the country before that was so nice and had so much style. It didn't have an iron latch on the front door, nor a wooden one with a buckskin string, but a brass knob to turn, the same as houses in a town. There warn't no bed in the parlor, not a sign of a bed; but heaps of parlors in towns has beds in them. There was a big fireplace that was bricked on the bottom, and the bricks was kept clean and red by pouring water on them and scrubbing them with another brick; sometimes they washed them over with red water-paint that they call Spanish-brown, same as they do in town. They had big brass dog-irons that could hold up a saw-log. There was a clock on the middle of the mantel-piece, with a picture of a town painted on the bottom half of the glass front, and a round place in the middle of it for the sun, and you could see the pendulum swing behind it. It was beautiful to hear that clock tick; and sometimes when one of these peddlers had been along and scoured her up and got her in good shape, she would start in and strike a hundred and fifty before she got tuckered out. They wouldn't took any money for her.

Well, there was a big outlandish parrot on each side of the clock, made out of something like chalk, and painted up gaudy. By one of the parrots was a cat made of crockery, and a crockery dog by the other; and when you pressed down on them they squeaked, but didn't open their mouths nor look different nor interested. They squeaked through underneath. There was a couple of big wild-turkey-wing fans spread out behind those things. On a table in the middle of the room was a kind of a lovely crockery basket that had apples and oranges and peaches and grapes piled up in it which was much redder and yellower and prettier than real ones is, but they warn't real because you could see where pieces had got chipped off and showed the white chalk or whatever it was, underneath.

This table had a cover made out of beautiful oil-cloth, with a red and blue spread-eagle painted on it, and a painted border all around. It come all the way from Philadelphia, they said. There was some books too, piled up perfectly exact, on each corner of the table. One was a big family Bible, full of pictures. One was "Pilgrim's Progress," about a man that left his family it didn't say why. I read considerable in it now and then. The statements was interesting, but tough. Another was "Friendship's Offering," full of beautiful stuff and poetry; but I didn't read the poetry. Another was Henry Clay's Speeches, and another was Dr. Gunn's Family Medicine, which told you all about what to do if a body was sick or dead. There was a Hymn Book, and a lot of other books. And there was nice split-bottom chairs, and perfectly sound, too—not bagged down in the middle and busted, like an old basket.

They had pictures hung on the walls—mainly Washingtons and Lafayettes, and battles, and Highland Marys, and one called "Signing the Declaration." There was some that they called crayons, which one of the daughters which was dead made her own self when she was only fifteen years old. They was different from any pictures I ever see before; blacker, mostly, than is common. One was a woman in a slim black dress, belted small under the arm-pits, with bulges like a cabbage in the middle of the sleeves, and a large black scoop-shovel bonnet with a black veil, and white slim ankles crossed about with black tape, and very wee black slippers, like a chisel, and she was leaning pensive on a tombstone on her right elbow, under a weeping willow, and her other hand hanging down her side holding a white handkerchief and a reticule, and underneath the picture it said "Shall I Never See Thee More Alas." Another one was a young lady with her hair all combed up straight to the top of her head, and knotted there in front of a comb like a chair-back, and she was crying into a handkerchief and had a dead bird laying on its back in her other hand with its heels up, and underneath the picture it said "I Shall Never Hear Thy Sweet Chirrup More Alas." There was one where a young lady was at a window looking up at the moon, and tears running down her cheeks; and she had an open letter in one hand with black sealing-wax showing on one edge of it, and she was mashing a locket with a chain to it against her mouth, and underneath the picture it said "And Art Thou Gone Yes Thou Art Gone Alas." These was all nice pictures, I reckon, but I didn't somehow seem to take to them, because if ever I was down a little, they always give me the fan-tods. Everybody was sorry she died, because she had laid out a lot more of these pictures to do, and a body could see by what she had done what they had lost. But I reckoned, that with her disposition, she was having a better time in the graveyard. She was at work on what they said was her greatest picture when she took sick, and every day and every night it was her prayer to be allowed to live till she got it done, but she

never got the chance. It was a picture of a young woman in a long white gown, standing on the rail of a bridge all ready to jump off, with her hair all down her back, and looking up to the moon, with the tears running down her face, and she had two arms folded across her breast, and two arms stretched out in front, and two more reaching up towards the moon—and the idea was, to see which pair would look best and then scratch out all the other arms; but, as I was saying, she died before she got her mind made

"IT MADE HER LOOK TOO SPIDERY."

up, and now they kept this picture over the head of the bed in her room, and every time her birthday come they hung flowers on it. Other times it was hid with a little curtain. The young woman in the picture had a kind of a nice sweet face, but there was so many arms it made her look too spidery, seemed to me.

This young girl kept a scrap-book when she was alive, and used to paste obituaries and accidents and cases of patient suffering in it out of the *Presbyterian Observer*, and write poetry after them out of her own head. It was very good poetry. This is what she wrote about a boy by the name of Stephen Dowling Bots that fell down a well and was drownded:

ODE TO STEPHEN DOWLING BOTS, DEC'D.

> And did young Stephen sicken,
>   And did young Stephen die?
> And did the sad hearts thicken,
>   And did the mourners cry?
>
> No; such was not the fate of
>   Young Stephen Dowling Bots;
> Though sad hearts round him thickened,
>   'Twas not from sickness' shots.
>
> No whooping-cough did rack his frame,
>   Nor measles drear, with spots;
> Not these impaired the sacred name
>   Of Stephen Dowling Bots.
>
> Despised love struck not with woe
>   That head of curly knots,
> Nor stomach troubles laid him low,
>   Young Stephen Dowling Bots.
>
> O no. Then list with tearful eye,
>   Whilst I his fate do tell.
> His soul did from this cold world fly,
>   By falling down a well.
>
> They got him out and emptied him;
>   Alas it was too late;
> His spirit was gone for to sport aloft
>   In the realms of the good and great.

"THEY GOT HIM OUT AND EMPTIED HIM."

If Emmeline Grangerford could make poetry like that before she was fourteen, there ain't no telling what she could a done by and by. Buck said she could rattle off poetry like nothing. She didn't ever have to stop to think. He said she would slap down a line, and if she couldn't find anything to rhyme with it she would just scratch it out and slap down another one, and go ahead. She warn't particular, she could write about anything you choose to give her to write about, just so it was sadful. Every time a man died, or a woman died, or a child died, she would be on hand with her "tribute" before he was cold. She called them tributes. The neighbors said it was the doctor first, then Emmeline, then the undertaker—the undertaker never got in ahead of Emmeline but once, and then she hung fire on a rhyme for the dead person's name, which was Whistler. She warn't ever the same, after that; she never complained, but she kind of pined away and did not live long. Poor thing, many's the time I made myself go up to the little room that used to be hers and get out her poor old scrap-book and read in it when her pictures had been aggravating me and I had soured on her a little. I liked all that family, dead ones and all, and warn't going to let anything come between us. Poor Emmeline made poetry about all the dead people when she was alive, and it didn't seem right that there warn't nobody to make some about her, now she was gone; so I tried to sweat out a verse or two myself, but I couldn't seem to make it go, somehow. They kept Emmeline's room trim and nice and all the things fixed in it just the way she liked to have them when she was alive, and nobody ever slept there. The old lady took care of the room herself, though there was plenty of niggers, and she sewed there a good deal and read her Bible there, mostly.

Well, as I was saying about the parlor, there was beautiful curtains on the windows: white, with pictures painted on them, of castles with vines all down the walls, and cattle coming down to drink. There was a little old piano, too, that had tin pans in it, I reckon, and nothing was ever so lovely as to hear the young ladies sing, "The Last Link is Broken" and play "The Battle of Prague" on it. The walls of all the rooms was plastered, and most had carpets on the floors, and the whole house was whitewashed on the outside.

It was a double house, and the big open place betwixt them was roofed and floored, and sometimes the table was set there in the middle of the day, and it was a cool, comfortable place. Nothing couldn't be better. And warn't the cooking good, and just bushels of it too!

THE HOUSE.

Chapter XVIII.

COL. GRANGERFORD.

Col. Grangerford was a gentleman, you see. He was a gentleman all over; and so was his family. He was well born, as the saying is, and that's worth as much in a man as it is in a horse, so the widow Douglas said, and nobody ever denied that she was of the first aristocracy in our town; and pap he always said it, too, though he warn't no more quality than a mud-cat, himself. Col. Grangerford was very tall and very slim, and had a darkish-paly complexion, not a sign of red in it anywheres; he was clean-shaved every morning, all over his thin face, and he had the thinnest kind of lips, and the thinnest kind of nostrils, and a high nose, and heavy eyebrows, and the blackest kind of eyes, sunk so deep back that they seemed like they was looking out of caverns at you, as you may say. His forehead was high, and his hair was black and straight, and hung to his shoulders. His hands was long and thin, and every day of his life he put on a clean shirt and a full suit from head to foot made out of linen so white it hurt your eyes to look at it; and on Sundays he wore a blue tail-coat with brass buttons on it. He carried a mahogany cane with a silver head to it. There warn't no frivolishness about him, not a bit, and he warn't ever loud. He was as kind as he could be—you could feel that, you know, and so you had confidence. Sometimes he smiled, and it was good to see; but when he straightened himself up like a liberty-pole, and the lightning begun to flicker out from under his eyebrows you wanted to climb a tree first, and find out what the matter was afterwards. He didn't ever have to tell anybody to mind their manners—everybody was always good mannered where he was. Everybody loved to have him around, too; he was sunshine most always—I mean he made it seem like good weather. When he turned into a cloud-bank it was awful dark for a half a minute and that was enough; there wouldn't nothing go wrong again for a week.

When him and the old lady come down in the morning, all the family got up out of their chairs and give them good-day, and didn't set down again till they had set down. Then Tom and Bob went to the sideboard where the decanters was, and mixed a glass of bitters and handed it to him, and he held it in his hand and waited till Tom's and Bob's was mixed, and then they bowed and said "Our duty to you, sir, and madam;" and *they* bowed the least bit in the world and said thank you, and so they drank, all three, and Bob and Tom poured a spoonful of water on the sugar and the mite of whisky or apple brandy in the bottom of their tumblers, and give it to me and Buck, and we drank to the old people too.

Bob was the oldest, and Tom next. Tall, beautiful men with very broad shoulders and brown faces, and long black hair and black eyes. They dressed in white linen from head to foot, like the old gentleman, and wore broad Panama hats.

Then there was Miss Charlotte, she was twenty-five, and tall and proud and grand, but as good as she could be, when she warn't stirred up; but when she was, she had a look that would make you wilt in your tracks, like her father. She was beautiful.

So was her sister, Miss Sophia, but it was a different kind. She was gentle and sweet, like a dove, and she was only twenty.

Each person had their own nigger to wait on them—Buck, too. My nigger had a monstrous easy time, because I warn't used to having anybody do anything for me, but Buck's was on the jump most of the time.

This was all there was of the family, now; but there used to be more—three sons; they got killed; and Emmeline that died.

The old gentleman owned a lot of farms, and over a hundred niggers. Sometimes a stack of people would come there, horseback, from ten or fifteen mile around, and stay five or six days, and have such junketings round about and on the river, and dances and picnics in the woods, day-times, and balls at the house, nights. These people was mostly kin-folks of the family. The men brought their guns with them. It was a handsome lot of quality, I tell you.

There was another clan of aristocracy around there—five or six families—mostly of the name of Shepherdson. They was as high-toned, and well born, and rich and grand, as the tribe of Granger-fords. The Shepherdsons and the Grangerfords used the same

YOUNG HARNEY SHEPHERDSON.

steamboat landing, which was about two mile above our house; so sometimes when I went up there with a lot of our folks I used to see a lot of the Shepherdsons there, on their fine horses.

One day Buck and me was away out in the woods, hunting, and heard a horse coming. We was crossing the road. Buck says:

"Quick! Jump for the woods!"

We done it, and then peeped down the woods through the leaves. Pretty soon a splendid young man come galloping down the road, setting his horse easy and looking like a soldier. He had his gun across his pommel. I had seen him before. It was young Harney

Shepherdson. I heard Buck's gun go off at my ear, and Harney's hat tumbled off from his head. He grabbed his gun and rode straight to the place where we was hid. But we didn't wait. We started through the woods on a run. The woods warn't thick, so I looked over my shoulder, to dodge the bullet, and twice I seen Harney cover Buck with his gun; and then he rode away the way he come—to get his hat, I reckon, but I couldn't see. We never stopped running till we got home. The old gentleman's eyes blazed a minute—'twas pleasure, mainly, I judged—then his face sort of smoothed down, and he says, kind of gentle:

"I don't like that shooting from behind a bush. Why didn't you step into the road, my boy?"

"The Shepherdsons don't, father. They always take advantage."

Miss Charlotte she held her head up like a queen while Buck was telling his tale, and her nostrils spread and her eyes snapped. The two young men looked dark, but never said nothing. Miss Sophia she turned pale, but the color come back when she found the man warn't hurt.

MISS CHARLOTTE.

Soon as I could get Buck down by the corn-cribs under the trees by ourselves, I says:

"Did you want to kill him, Buck?"

"Well, I bet I did."

"What did he do to you?"

"Him? He never done nothing to me."

"Well, then, what did you want to kill him for?"

"Why nothing—only it's on account of the feud."

"What's a feud?"

"Why, where was you raised? Don't you know what a feud is?"

"Never heard of it before—tell me about it."

"Well," says Buck, "a feud is this way. A man has a quarrel with another man, and kills him; then that other man's brother kills *him*; then the other brothers, on both sides, goes for one another; then the *cousins* chip in—and by and by everybody's killed off, and there ain't no more feud. But it's kind of slow, and takes a long time."

"Has this one been going on long, Buck?"

"Well I should *reckon!* it started thirty year ago, or som'ers along there. There was trouble 'bout something and then a lawsuit to settle it; and the suit went agin one of the men, and so he up and shot the man that won the suit—which he would naturally do, of course. Anybody would."

"What was the trouble about, Buck?—land?"

"I reckon maybe—I don't know."

"Well, who done the shooting?—was it a Grangerford or a Shepherdson?"

"Laws, how do *I* know? it was so long ago."

"Don't anybody know?"

"Oh, yes, pa knows, I reckon, and some of the other old folks; but they don't know, now, what the row was about in the first place."

"Has there been many killed, Buck?"

"Yes—right smart chance of funerals. But they don't always kill. Pa's got a few buck-shot in him; but he don't mind it 'cuz he don't weigh much anyway. Bob's been carved up some with a bowie, and Tom's been hurt once or twice."

"Has anybody been killed this year, Buck?"

"Yes, we got one and they got one. 'Bout three months ago, my cousin Bud, fourteen year old, was riding through the woods, on t'other side of the river, and didn't have no weapon with him, which was blame' foolishness, and in a lonesome place he hears a horse a-coming behind him, and sees old Baldy Shepherdson a-linkin' after him with his gun in his hand and his white hair a-flying in the wind; and 'stead of jumping off and taking to the brush, Bud 'lowed he could outrun him; so they had it, nip and tuck, for five mile or more, the old man a-gaining all the time; so at last Bud seen it warn't any use, so he stopped and faced around so as to have the bullet holes in front, you know, and the old man he rode up and shot him down. But he didn't git much chance to enjoy his luck, for inside of a week our folks laid *him* out."

"I reckon that old man was a coward, Buck."

"I reckon he *warn't* a coward. Not by a blame' sight. There ain't a coward amongst them Shepherdsons—not a one. And there ain't no cowards amongst the Grangerfords, either. Why, that old man kep' up his end in a fight one day, for a half an hour, against three Grangerfords, and come out winner. They was all a-horseback; he lit off of his horse and got behind a little wood-pile, and kep' his horse before him to stop the bullets; but the Grangerfords staid on their horses and capered around the old man, and peppered away at him, and he peppered away at them. Him and his horse both went home pretty leaky and crippled, but the Grangerfords had to be *fetched* home—and one of 'em was dead, and another died the next day. No, sir, if a body's out hunting for cowards, he don't want to fool away any time amongst them Shepherdsons, becuz they don't breed any of that *kind*."

Next Sunday we all went to church, about three mile, everybody a-horseback. The men took their guns along, so did Buck, and kept them between their knees or stood them handy against the wall. The Shepherdsons done the same. It was pretty ornery preaching— all about brotherly love, and such-like tiresomeness; but everybody said it was a good sermon, and they all talked it over going home, and had such a powerful lot to say about faith, and good works, and free grace, and preforeordestination, and I don't know what all, that it did seem to me to be one of the roughest Sundays I had run across yet.

About an hour after dinner everybody was dozing around, some in their chairs and some in their rooms, and it got to be pretty dull. Buck and a dog was stretched out on the grass in the sun, sound asleep. I went up to our room, and judged I would take a nap myself. I found that sweet Miss Sophia standing in her door, which was next to ours, and she took me in her room and shut the door very soft, and asked me if I liked her, and I said I did; and she asked me if I

"AND ASKED ME IF I LIKED HER."

would do something for her and not tell anybody, and I said I would. Then she said she'd forgot her Testament, and left it in the seat at church, between two other books and would I slip out quiet and go there and fetch it to her, and not say nothing to nobody. I said I would. So I slid out and slipped off up the road, and there warn't anybody at the church, except maybe a hog or two, for there warn't any lock on the door, and hogs likes a puncheon floor in summer-time because it's cool. If you notice, most folks don't go to church only when they've got to; but a hog is different.

Says I to myself something's up—it ain't natural for a girl to be in such a sweat about a Testament; so I give it a shake, and out drops a little piece of paper with *"Half-past two"* wrote on it with a pencil. I ransacked it, but couldn't find anything else. I couldn't make anything out of that, so I put the paper in the book again, and when I got home and up stairs, there was Miss Sophia in her door waiting for me. She pulled me in and shut the door; then she looked in the Testament till she found the paper, and as soon as she read it she looked glad; and before a body could think, she grabbed me and give me a squeeze, and said I was the best boy in the world, and not to tell anybody. She was mighty red in the face, for a minute, and her eyes lighted up and it made her powerful pretty. I was a good deal astonished, but when I got my breath I asked her what the paper was about, and she asked me if I had read it, and I said no, and she asked me if I could read writing, and I told her "no, only coarse-hand," and then she said the paper warn't anything but a book-mark to keep her place, and I might go and play now.

I went off down to the river, studying over this thing, and pretty soon I noticed that my nigger was following along behind. When we was out of sight of the house, he looked back and around a second, and then comes a-running, and says:

"Mars Jawge, if you'll come down into de swamp, I'll show you a whole stack o' water-moccasins."

Thinks I, that's mighty curious; he said that yesterday. He ought-er know a body don't love water-moccasins enough to go around hunting for them. What is he up to anyway? So I says—

"All right, trot ahead."

I followed a half a mile, then he struck out over the swamp and waded ankle deep as much as another half mile. We come to a little flat piece of land which was dry and very thick with trees and bushes and vines, and he says—

"You shove right in dah, jist a few steps, mars Jawge, dah's whah dey is. I's seed 'm befo', I don't k'yer to see 'em no mo'."

Then he slopped right along and went away, and pretty soon the trees hid him. I poked into the place a-ways, and come to a little open patch as big as a bedroom, all hung around with vines, and found a man laying there asleep—and by jings it was my old Jim!

I waked him up, and I reckoned it was going to be a grand surprise to him to see me again, but it warn't. He nearly cried, he was so glad, but he warn't surprised. Said he swum along behind me, that night, and heard me yell every time, but dasn't answer, because he didn't want nobody to pick *him* up, and take him into slavery again. Says he—

"I got hurt a little, en couldn't swim fas', so I wuz a considable ways behine you, towards de las'; when you landed I reck'ned I could ketch up wid you on de lan' 'dout havin' to shout at you, but when I see dat house I begin to go slow. I 'uz off too fur to hear what dey say to you—I wuz 'fraid o' de dogs—but when it 'uz all quiet agin, I knowed you's in de house, so I struck out for de woods to wait for day. Early in de mawnin' some er de niggers come along, gwyne to de fields, en dey tuck me en showed me dis place, whah de dogs can't track me on accounts o' de water, en dey brings me truck to eat every night, en tells me how you's a gitt'n along."

"Why didn't you tell my Jack to fetch me here sooner, Jim?"

"Well, 'twarn't no use to 'sturb you, Huck, tell we could do sumfn—but we's all right, now. I ben a-buyin' pots en pans en vittles, as I got a chanst, en a patchin' up de raf', nights, when—"

"*What* raft, Jim?"

"Our ole raf'."

"You mean to say our old raft warn't smashed all to flinders?"

"No, she warn't. She was tore up a good deal—one en' of her was—but dey warn't no great harm done, on'y our traps was mos' all los'. Ef we hadn' dive' so deep en swum so fur under water, en de night hadn' ben so dark, en we warn't so sk'yerd, en ben sich punkin-heads, as de sayin' is, we'd a seed de raf'. But it's jis' as well we didn't, 'kase now she's all fixed up agin mos' as good as new, en we's got a new lot o' stuff, too, in de place o' what 'uz los'."

"Why, how did you get hold of the raft again, Jim—did you catch her?"

"How I gwyne to ketch her, en I out in de woods? No, some er de niggers foun' her ketched on a snag, along heah in de ben', en dey hid her in a crick, 'mongst de willows, en dey wuz so much jawin' 'bout which un 'um she b'long to de mos', dat I come to heah 'bout it pooty soon, so I ups en settles de trouble by tellin' 'um she don't b'long to none uv um, but to you en me; en I ast 'm if dey gwyne to grab a young white genlman's propaty, en git a hid'n for it? Den I gin 'm ten cents apiece, en dey 'uz mighty well satisfied, en wisht some mo' raf's 'ud come along en make 'm rich agin. Dey's mighty good to me, dese niggers is, en whatever I wants 'm to do fur me, I doan' have to ast 'm twice, honey. Dat Jack's a good nigger, en pooty smart."

"Yes, he is. He ain't ever told me you was here; told me to come, and he'd show me a lot of water-moccasins. If anything happens, *he* ain't mixed up in it. He can say he never seen us together, and it'll be the truth."

I don't want to talk much about the next day. I reckon I'll cut it pretty short. I waked up about dawn, and was agoing to turn over and go to sleep again, when I noticed how still it was—didn't seem to be anybody stirring. That warn't usual. Next I noticed that Buck was up and gone. Well, I gets up, a-wondering, and goes down stairs—nobody around; everything as still as a mouse. Just the same outside; thinks I, what does it mean? Down by the wood-pile I comes across my Jack, and says:

"What's it all about?"

Says he:

"Don't you know, mars Jawge?"

"No," says I, "I don't."

"Well, den, Miss Sophia's run off! 'deed she has. She run off in de night, sometime—nobody don't know jis' when—run off to git married to dat young Harney Shepherdson, you know—leastways, so dey 'spec. De fambly foun' it out, 'bout half an hour ago—maybe a little mo'—en I *tell* you dey warn't no time los'. Sich another hurryin' up guns en hosses *you* never see! De women folks has gone for to stir up de relations, en ole mars Saul en de boys tuck dey guns en rode up de river road for to try to ketch dat young man en kill him 'fo' he kin git acrost de river wid Miss Sophia. I reck'n dey's gwyne to be mighty rough times."

"Buck went off 'thout waking me up."

"Well I reck'n he *did!* Dey warn't gwyne to mix you up in it. Mars Buck he loaded up his gun en 'lowed he's gwyne to fetch home a Shepherdson or bust. Well, dey'll be plenty un 'm dah, I reck'n, en you bet you he'll fetch one ef he gits a chanst."

I took up the river road as hard as I could put. By and by I begin to hear guns a good ways off. When I come in sight of the log store and the wood-pile where the steamboats lands, I worked along under the trees and brush till I got to a good place, and then I clumb up into the forks of a cotton-wood that was out of reach, and watched. There was a wood-rank four foot high, a little ways in front of the tree, and first I was going to hide behind that; but maybe it was luckier I didn't.

There was four or five men cavorting around on their horses in the open place before the log store, cussing and yelling, and trying to get at a couple of young chaps that was behind the wood-rank alongside of the steamboat landing—but they couldn't come it.

"BEHIND THE WOOD-RANK."

Every time one of them showed himself on the river side of the wood-pile he got shot at. The two boys was squatting back to back behind the pile, so they could watch both ways.

By and by the men stopped cavorting around and yelling. They started riding towards the store; then up gets one of the boys, draws a steady bead over the wood-rank, and drops one of them out of his saddle. All the men jumped off of their horses and grabbed the hurt one and started to carry him to the store; and that minute the two boys started on the run. They got half-way to the tree I was in before the men noticed. Then the men see them, and jumped on their horses and took out after them. They gained on the boys, but it didn't do no good, the boys had too good a start; they got to the wood-pile that was in front of my tree, and slipped in behind it, and so they had the bulge on the men again. One of the boys was Buck, and the other was a slim young chap about nineteen years old.

The men ripped around awhile, and then rode away. As soon as they was out of sight, I sung out to Buck and told him. He didn't know what to make of my voice coming out of the tree, at first. He was awful surprised. He told me to watch out sharp and let him know when the men come in sight again; said they was up to some devilment or other—wouldn't be gone long. I wished I was out of that tree, but I dasn't come down. Buck begun to cry and rip, and 'lowed that him and his cousin Joe (that was the other young chap) would make up for this day, yet. He said his father and his two brothers was killed, and two or three of the enemy. Said the Shepherdsons laid for them, in ambush. Buck said his father and brothers ought to waited for their relations—the Shepherdsons was too strong for them. I asked him what was become of young Harney and Miss Sophia. He said they'd got across the river and was safe. I was glad of that; but the way Buck did take on because he didn't manage to kill Harney that day he shot at him—I hain't ever heard anything like it.

All of a sudden, bang! bang! bang! goes three or four guns—the men had slipped around through the woods and come in from behind without their horses! The boys jumped for the river—both of them hurt—and as they swum down the current the men run along the bank shooting at them and singing out, "Kill them, kill them!" It made me so sick I most fell out of the tree. I ain't agoing to tell *all* that happened—it would make me sick again if I was to do that. I wished I hadn't ever come ashore that night, to see such things. I ain't ever going to get shut of them—lots of times I dream about them.

I staid in the tree till it begun to get dark, afraid to come down. Sometimes I heard guns away off in the woods; and twice I seen little gangs of men gallop past the log store with guns; so I reckoned the trouble was still agoing on. I was mighty down-hearted; so I made up my mind I wouldn't ever go anear that house again, because I reckoned I was to blame, somehow. I judged that that piece of paper meant that Miss Sophia was to meet Harney somewheres at half-past two and run off; and I judged I ought to told her father about that paper and the curious way she acted, and then maybe he would a locked her up and this awful mess wouldn't ever happened.

When I got down out of the tree, I crept along down the river bank a piece, and found the two bodies laying in the edge of the water, and tugged at them till I got them ashore; then I covered up their faces, and got away as quick as I could. I cried a little when I was covering up Buck's face, for he was mighty good to me.

It was just dark, now. I never went near the house, but struck through the woods and made for the swamp. Jim warn't on his island, so I tramped off in a hurry for the crick, and crowded through the willows, red-hot to jump aboard and get out of that awful country—the raft was gone! My souls, but I was scared! I couldn't get my breath for most a minute. Then I raised a yell. A voice not twenty-five foot from me, says—

"Good lan'! is dat you, honey? Doan' make no noise."

It was Jim's voice—nothing ever sounded so good before. I run along the bank a piece and got aboard, and Jim he grabbed me and hugged me, he was so glad to see me. He says—

"Laws bless you, chile, I 'uz right down sho' you's dead agin. Jack's been heah, he say he reck'n you's ben shot, kase you didn' come home no mo'; so I's jes' dis minute a startin' de raf' down towards de mouf er de crick, so's to be all ready for to shove out en leave soon as Jack comes agin en tells me for certain you *is* dead. Lawsy, I's mighty glad to git you back agin, honey."

I says—

"All right—that's mighty good; they won't find me, and they'll think I've been killed, and floated down the river—there's something up there that'll help them to think so—so don't you lose no time, Jim, but just shove off for the big water as fast as ever you can."

I never felt easy till the raft was two mile below there and out in the middle of the Mississippi. Then we hung up our signal lantern, and judged that we was free and safe once more. I hadn't had a bite to eat since yesterday; so Jim he got out some corn-dodgers and buttermilk, and pork and cabbage, and greens—there ain't nothing in the world so good, when it's cooked right—and whilst I eat my supper we talked, and had a good time. I was powerful glad to get away from the feuds, and so was Jim to get away from the swamp. We said there warn't no home like a raft, after all. Other places do seem so cramped up and smothery, but a raft don't. You feel mighty free and easy and comfortable on a raft.

Chapter XIX

HIDING DAY-TIMES.

TWO OR THREE days and nights went by; I reckon I might say they swum by, they slid along so quiet and smooth and lovely. Here is the way we put in the time. It was a monstrous big river down there—sometimes a mile and a half wide; we run nights, and laid up and hid day-times; soon as night was most gone, we stopped navigating and tied up—nearly always in the dead water under a towhead; and then cut young cotton-woods and willows and hid the raft with them. Then we set out the lines. Next we slid into the river and had a swim, so as to freshen up and cool off; then we set down on the sandy bottom where the water was about knee deep, and watched the daylight come. Not a sound, any-wheres—perfectly still—just like the whole world was asleep, only sometimes the bull-frogs a-cluttering, maybe. The first thing to see, looking away over the water, was a kind of dull line—that was the woods on t'other side—you couldn't make nothing else out; then a pale place in the sky; then more paleness, spreading around; then the river softened up, away off, and warn't black any more, but gray; you could see little dark spots drifting along, ever so far away—trading scows, and such things; and long black streaks—rafts; sometimes you could hear a sweep screaking; or jumbled up voices, it was so still, and sounds come so far; and by and by you could see a streak on the water which you know by the look of the streak that there's a snag there in a swift current which breaks on it and makes that streak look that way; and you see the mist curl up off of the water, and the east reddens up, and the river, and you make out a log cabin in the edge of the woods, away on the bank on t'other side of the river, being a wood-yard, likely, and piled by them cheats so you can throw a dog through it anywheres; then the nice breeze springs up, and comes fanning you from over there, so cool and fresh, and sweet to smell, on account of the woods and the flowers; but sometimes not that way, because they've left dead fish laying around, gars, and such, and they do get pretty rank; and next you've got the full day, and everything smiling in the sun, and the song-birds just going it!

A little smoke couldn't be noticed, now, so we would take some fish off of the lines, and cook up a hot breakfast. And afterwards we would watch the lonesomeness of the river, and kind of lazy along, and by and by lazy off to sleep. Wake up, by and by, and look to see what done it, and maybe see a steamboat, coughing along up stream, so far off towards the other side you couldn't tell nothing about her only whether she was stern-wheel or side-wheel; then for about an hour there wouldn't be nothing to hear nor nothing to see—just solid lonesomeness. Next you'd see a raft sliding by, away off yonder, and maybe a galoot on it chopping, because they're most always doing it on a raft; you'd see the axe flash, and come down—you don't hear nothing; you see that axe go up again, and by the time it's above the man's head, then you hear the *k'chunk!*—it had took all that time to come over the water. So we would put in the day, lazying around, listening to the stillness. Once there was a thick fog, and the rafts and things that went by was beating tin pans so the steamboats wouldn't run over them. A scow or a raft went by so close we could hear them talking and cussing and laughing—heard them plain; but we couldn't see no sign of them; it made you feel crawly, it was like spirits carrying on that way in the air. Jim said he believed it was spirits; but I says:

"No, spirits wouldn't say, 'dern the dern fog.' "

Soon as it was night, out we shoved; when we got her out to about the middle, we let her alone, and let her float wherever the current wanted her to; then we lit the pipes, and dangled our legs in the water and talked about all kinds of things—we was always naked, day and night, whenever the mosquitoes would let us—the new clothes Buck's folks made for me was too good to be comfortable, and besides I didn't go much on clothes, nohow.

Sometimes we'd have that whole river all to ourselves for the longest time. Yonder was the banks and the islands, across the water; and maybe a spark—which was a candle in a cabin window— and sometimes on the water you could see a spark or two—on a raft or a scow, you know; and maybe you could hear a fiddle or a song coming over from one of them crafts. It's lovely to live on a raft. We had the sky, up there, all speckled with stars, and we used to lay on our backs and look up at them, and discuss about whether they was made, or only just happened—Jim he allowed they was made, but I allowed they happened; I judged it would have took too long to *make* so many. Jim said the moon could a *laid* them; well, that looked kind of reasonable, so I didn't say nothing against it, because I've seen a frog lay most as many, so of course it could be done. We used to watch the stars that fell, too, and see them streak down. Jim allowed they'd got spoiled and was hove out of the nest.

Once or twice of a night we would see a steamboat slipping along in the dark, and now and then she would belch a whole world of sparks up out of her chimbleys, and they would rain down in the river and look awful pretty; then she would turn a corner and her lights would wink out and her pow-wow shut off and leave the river still again; and by and by her waves would get to us, a long time after she was gone, and joggle the raft a bit, and after that you wouldn't hear nothing for you couldn't tell how long, except maybe frogs or something.

After midnight the people on shore went to bed, and then for two or three hours the shores was black—no more sparks in the cabin windows. These sparks was our clock—the first one that showed again meant morning was coming, so we hunted a place to hide and tie up, right away.

One morning about day-break, I found a canoe and crossed over a chute to the main shore—it was only two hundred yards—and paddled about a mile up a crick amongst the cypress woods, to see if I couldn't get some berries. Just as I was passing a place where a kind of a cow-path crossed the crick, here comes a couple of men tearing up the path as tight as they could foot it. I thought I was a goner, for whenever anybody was after anybody I judged it was *me*—

or maybe Jim. I was about to dig out from there in a hurry, but they was pretty close to me then, and sung out and begged me to save their lives—said they hadn't been doing nothing, and was being

"AND DOGS A-COMING."

chased for it—said there was men and dogs a-coming. They wanted to jump right in, but I says—

"Don't you do it. I don't hear the dogs and horses yet; you've got time to crowd through the brush and get up the crick a little ways; then you take to the water and wade down to me and get in—that'll throw the dogs off the scent."

They done it, and soon as they was aboard I lit out for our towhead, and in about five or ten minutes we heard the dogs and the men away off, shouting. We heard them come along towards the crick, but couldn't see them; they seemed to stop and fool around a while; then, as we got further and further away all the time, we couldn't hardly hear them at all; by the time we had left a mile of woods behind us and struck the river, everything was quiet, and we paddled over to the tow-head and hid in the cotton-woods and was safe.

One of these fellows was about seventy, or upwards, and had a bald head and very gray whiskers. He had an old battered-up slouch hat on, and a greasy blue woolen shirt, and ragged old blue jeans britches stuffed into his boot tops, and home-knit galluses—no, he only had one. He had an old long-tailed blue jeans coat with slick brass buttons, flung over his arm, and both of them had big fat ratty-looking carpet-bags.

The other fellow was about thirty and dressed about as ornery. After breakfast we all laid off and talked, and the first thing that come out was that these chaps didn't know one another.

"What got you into trouble?" says the baldhead to t'other chap.

"Well, I'd been selling an article to take the tartar off the teeth—and it does take it off, too, and generly the enamel along with it—but I staid about one night longer than I ought to, and was just in the act of sliding out when I ran across you on the trail this side of town, and you told me they were coming, and begged me to help you to get off. So I told you I was expecting trouble myself and would scatter out *with* you. That's the whole yarn—what's yourn?"

"Well, I'd ben a-runnin' a little temperance revival thar, 'bout a week, and was the pet of the women-folks, big and little, for I was makin' it mighty warm for the rummies, I *tell* you, and takin' as much as five or six dollars a night—ten cents a head, children and niggers free—and business a growin' all the time; when somehow or another a little report got around, last night, that I had a way of puttin' in my time with a private jug, on the sly. A nigger rousted me out this mornin', and told me the people was getherin' on the quiet, with their dogs and horses, and they'd be along pretty soon and give me 'bout half an hour's start, and then run me down, if they could; and if they got me they'd tar and feather me and ride me on a rail, sure. I didn't wait for no breakfast—I warn't hungry."

"Old man," says the young one, "I reckon we might double-team it together; what do you think?"

"I ain't undisposed. What's your line—mainly?"

"Jour printer, by trade; do a little in patent medicines; theatre-actor—tragedy, you know; take a turn at mesmerism and phrenology when there's a chance; teach singing-geography school for a change; sling a lecture, sometimes—oh, I do lots of things—most anything that comes handy, so it ain't work. What's your lay?"

"I've done considerble in the doctoring way in my time. Layin' on o' hands is my best holt—for cancer, and paralysis, and sich things; and I k'n tell a fortune pretty good, when I've got somebody along to find out the facts for me. Preachin's my line, too; and workin' camp-meetin's; and missionaryin' around."

Nobody never said anything for a while; then the young man hove a sigh and says—

"Alas!"

"What 're you alassin' about?" says the baldhead.

"To think I should have lived to be leading such a life, and be degraded down into such company." And he begun to wipe the corner of his eye with a rag.

"Dern your skin, ain't the company good enough for you?" says the baldhead, pretty pert and uppish.

"Yes, it *is* good enough for me; it's as good as I deserve; for who fetched me so low, when I was so high? *I* did myself. I don't blame *you*, gentlemen—far from it; I don't blame anybody. I deserve it all. Let the cold world do its worst; one thing I know—there's a grave somewhere for me. The world may go on just as it's always done, and take everything from me—loved ones, property, everything—but it can't take that. Some day I'll lie down in it and forget it all, and my poor broken heart will be at rest." He went on a-wiping.

"Drot your pore broken heart," says the baldhead; "what are you heaving your pore broken heart at *us* f'r? *We* hain't done nothing."

"No, I know you haven't. I ain't blaming you, gentlemen. I brought myself down—yes, I did it myself. It's right I should suffer—perfectly right—I don't make any moan."

"Brought you down from whar? Whar was you brought down from?"

"Ah, you would not believe me; the world never believes—let it pass—'tis no matter. The secret of my birth—"

"The secret of your birth? Do you mean to say—"

"Gentlemen," says the young man, very solemn, "I will reveal it to you, for I feel I may have confidence in you. By rights I am a duke!"

Jim's eyes bugged out when he heard that; and I reckon mine did, too. Then the baldhead says: "No! you can't mean it?"

"Yes. My great-grandfather, eldest son of the Duke of Bridgewater, fled to this country about the end of the last century, to breathe the pure air of freedom; married here, and died, leaving a son, his own father dying about the same time. The second son of the late duke seized the title and estates—the infant real duke was ignored. I am the lineal descendant of that infant—I am the rightful Duke of

"BY RIGHTS I AM A DUKE!"

Bridgewater; and here am I, forlorn, torn from my high estate, hunted of men, despised by the cold world, ragged, worn, heart-broken, and degraded to the companionship of felons on a raft!"

Jim pitied him ever so much, and so did I. We tried to comfort him, but he said it warn't much use, he couldn't be much comforted; said if we was a mind to acknowledge him, that would do him more good than most anything else; so we said we would, if he would tell us how. He said we ought to bow, when we spoke to him, and say "Your Grace," or "My Lord," or "Your Lordship"—and he wouldn't mind it if we called him plain "Bridgewater," which he said was a title, anyway, and not a name; and one of us ought to wait on him at dinner, and do any little thing for him he wanted done.

Well, that was all easy, so we done it. All through dinner Jim stood around and waited on him, and says, "Will yo' Grace have some o' dis, or some o' dat?" and so on, and a body could see it was mighty pleasing to him.

But the old man got pretty silent, by and by—didn't have much to say, and didn't look pretty comfortable over all that petting that was going on around that duke. He seemed to have something on his mind. So, along in the afternoon, he says:

"Looky here, Bilgewater," he says, "I'm nation sorry for you, but you ain't the only person that's had troubles like that."

"No?"

"No, you ain't. You ain't the only person that's ben snaked down wrongfully out'n a high place."

"Alas!"

"No, you ain't the only person that's had a secret of his birth." And by jings, *he* begins to cry.

"Hold! What do you mean?"

"Bilgewater, kin I trust you?" says the old man, still sort of sobbing.

"To the bitter death!" He took the old man by the hand and squeezed it, and says, "The secret of your being: speak!"

"Bilgewater, I am the late Dauphin!"

You bet you Jim and me stared, this time. Then the duke says:

"You are what?"

"Yes, my friend, it is too true—your eyes is lookin' at this very moment on the pore disappeared Dauphin, Looy the Seventeen, son of Looy the Sixteen and Marry Antonette."

"You! At your age! No! You mean you're the late Charlemagne; you must be six or seven hundred years old, at the very least."

"Trouble has done it, Bilgewater, trouble has done it; trouble has brung these gray hairs and this premature balditude. Yes, gentlemen, you see before you, in blue jeans and misery, the wanderin', exiled, trampled-on and sufferin' rightful King of France."

Well, he cried and took on so, that me and Jim didn't know hardly what to do, we was so sorry—and so glad and proud we'd got him with us, too. So we set in, like we done before with the duke, and tried to comfort *him*. But he said it warn't no use, nothing but to be dead and done with it all could do him any good; though he said it often made him feel easier and better for a while if people treated him according to his rights, and got down on one knee to speak to him, and always called him "Your Majesty," and waited on him first at meals, and didn't set down in his presence till he asked them. So Jim and me set to majestying him, and doing this and that and t'other for him, and standing up till he told us we might set down.

"I AM THE LATE DAUPHIN!"

This done him heaps of good, and so he got cheerful and comfortable. But the duke kind of soured on him, and didn't look a bit satisfied with the way things was going; still, the king acted real friendly towards him, and said the duke's great-grandfather and all the other Dukes of Bilgewater was a good deal thought of by *his* father and was allowed to come to the palace considerable; but the duke staid huffy a good while, till by and by the king says:

"Like as not we got to be together a blamed long time, on thish-yer raft, Bilgewater, and so what's the use o' your bein' sour? It'll only make things oncomfortable. It ain't my fault I warn't born a duke, it ain't your fault you warn't born a king—so what's the use to worry? Make the best o' things the way you find 'em, says I—

that's my motto. This ain't no bad thing that we've struck here—
plenty grub and an easy life—come, give us your hand, Duke, and
less all be friends."

The duke done it, and Jim and me was pretty glad to see it. It took
away all the uncomfortableness, and we felt mighty good over it,
because it would a been a miserable business to have any unfriendli-
ness on the raft; for what you want, above all things, on a raft, is for
everybody to be satisfied, and feel right and kind towards the others.

It didn't take me long to make up my mind that these liars warn't
no kings nor dukes, at all, but just low-down humbugs and frauds.
But I never said nothing, never let on; kept it to myself; it's the best
way; then you don't have no quarrels, and don't get into no trouble.
If they wanted us to call them kings and dukes, I hadn't no objections, long as it would keep peace in the family; and it warn't no use
to tell Jim, so I didn't tell him. If I never learnt nothing else out of
pap, I learnt that the best way to get along with his kind of people is
to let them have their own way.

Chapter XX

ON THE RAFT.

THEY ASKED US considerable many questions; wanted to know what we covered up the raft that way for, and laid by in the daytime instead of running—was Jim a runaway nigger? Says I—

"Goodness sakes, would a runaway nigger run *south?*"

No, they allowed he wouldn't. I had to account for things some way, so I says:

"My folks was living in Pike County, in Missouri, where I was born, and they all died off but me and pa and my brother Ike. Pa, he 'lowed he'd break up and go down and live with uncle Ben, who's got a little one-horse place on the river, forty-four mile below Orleans. Pa was pretty poor, and had some debts; so when he'd squared up there warn't nothing left but sixteen dollars and our nigger, Jim. That warn't enough to take us fourteen hundred mile, deck passage nor no other way. Well, when the river rose, pa had a streak of luck one day; he ketched this piece of a raft; so we reckoned we'd go down to Orleans on it. Pa's luck didn't hold out; a steamboat run over the forrard corner of the raft, one night, and we all went overboard and dove under the wheel; Jim and me come up, all right, but pa was drunk, and Ike was only four years old, so they never come up no more. Well, for the next day or two we had considerable trouble, because people was always coming out in skiffs and trying to take Jim away from me, saying they believed he was a runaway nigger. We don't run day-times no more, now; nights they don't bother us."

The duke says—

"Leave me alone to cipher out a way so we can run in the day-time if we want to. I'll think the thing over—I'll invent a plan that'll fix it. We'll let it alone for to-day, because of course we don't want to go by that town yonder in daylight—it mightn't be healthy."

Towards night it begun to darken up and look like rain; the heat lightning was squirting around, low down in the sky, and the leaves was beginning to shiver—it was going to be pretty ugly, it was easy to see that. So the duke and the king went to overhauling our wigwam, to see what the beds was like. My bed was a straw tick—better than Jim's, which was a corn-shuck tick; there's always cobs around about in a shuck tick, and they poke into you and hurt; and when you roll over, the dry shucks sound like you was rolling over in a pile of dead leaves; it makes such a rustling that you wake up. Well, the duke allowed he would take my bed; but the king allowed he wouldn't. He says—

"I should a reckoned the difference in rank would a sejested to you that a corn-shuck bed warn't just fitten for me to sleep on. Your Grace'll take the shuck bed yourself."

Jim and me was in a sweat again, for a minute, being afraid there was going to be some more trouble amongst them; so we was pretty glad when the duke says—

"'Tis my fate to be always ground into the mire under the iron heel of oppression. Misfortune has broken my once haughty spirit; I yield, I submit; 'tis my fate. I am alone in the world—let me suffer; I can bear it."

We got away as soon as it was good and dark. The king told us to stand well out towards the middle of the river, and not show a light till we got a long ways below the town. We come in sight of the little bunch of lights by and by—that was the town, you know—and slid by, about a half a mile out, all right. When we was three-quarters of a mile below, we hoisted up our signal lantern; and about ten o'clock it come on to rain and blow and thunder and lighten like everything; so the king told us to both stay on watch till the weather got better; then him and the duke crawled into the wigwam and turned in for the night. It was my watch below, till twelve, but I wouldn't a turned in, anyway, if I'd had a bed; because a body don't see such a storm as that every day in the week, not by a long sight. My souls, how the wind did scream along! And every second or two there'd

come a glare that lit up the white-caps for a half a mile around, and
you'd see the islands looking dusty through the rain, and the trees
thrashing around in the wind; then comes a *h-wack!*—bum! bum!
bumble-umble-um-bum-bum-bum-bum—and the thunder would
go rumbling and grumbling away, and quit—and then *rip* comes
another flash and another sockdolager. The waves most washed me
off the raft, sometimes, but I hadn't any clothes on, and didn't mind.
We didn't have no trouble about snags; the lightning was glaring
and flittering around so constant that we could see them plenty
soon enough to throw her head this way or that and miss them.

I had the middle watch, you know, but I was pretty sleepy by that
time, so Jim he said he would stand the first half of it for me; he was
always mighty good, that way, Jim was. I crawled into the wigwam,
but the king and the duke had their legs sprawled around so there
warn't no show for me; so I laid outside—I didn't mind the rain,
because it was warm, and the waves warn't running so high, now.
About two they come up again, though, and Jim was going to call
me, but he changed his mind because he reckoned they warn't high
enough yet to do any harm; but he was mistaken about that, for
pretty soon all of a sudden along comes a regular ripper, and washed
me overboard. It most killed Jim a-laughing. He was the easiest
nigger to laugh that ever was, anyway.

I took the watch, and Jim he laid down and snored away; and by
and by the storm let up for good and all; and the first cabin-light
that showed, I rousted him out and we slid the raft into hiding-
quarters for the day.

The king got out an old ratty deck of cards, after breakfast, and
him and the duke played seven-up a while, five cents a game. Then
they got tired of it, and allowed they would "lay out a campaign,"
as they called it. The duke went down into his carpet-bag and
fetched up a lot of little printed bills, and read them out loud. One
bill said "The celebrated Dr. Armand de Montalban of Paris," would
"lecture on the Science of Phrenology" at such and such a place, on
the blank day of blank, at ten cents admission, and "furnish charts
of character at twenty-five cents apiece." The duke said that was
him. In another bill he was the "world renowned Shaksperean
tragedian, Garrick the Younger, of Drury Lane, London." In other
bills he had a lot of other names and done other wonderful things,

like finding water and gold with a "divining rod," "dissipating witch-spells," and so on. By and by he says—

"But the histrionic muse is the darling. Have you ever trod the boards, Royalty?"

"No," says the king.

"You shall, then, before you're three days older, Fallen Grandeur," says the duke. "The first good town we come to, we'll hire a hall and do the sword-fight in Richard III. and the balcony scene in Romeo and Juliet. How does that strike you?"

"I'm in, up to the hub, for anything that will pay, Bilgewater, but you see I don't know nothing about play-actn', and hain't ever seen much of it. I was too small when pap used to have 'em at the palace. Do you reckon you can learn me?"

"Easy!"

"All right. I'm jist a-freezn' for something fresh, anyway. Less commence, right away."

So the duke he told him all about who Romeo was, and who Juliet was, and said he was used to being Romeo, so the king could be Juliet.

"But if Juliet's such a young gal, Duke, my peeled head and my white whiskers is goin' to look oncommon odd on her, maybe."

"No, don't you worry—these country jakes won't ever think of that. Besides, you know, you'll be in costume, and that makes all the difference in the world; Juliet's in a balcony, enjoying the moonlight before she

THE KING AS JULIET.

goes to bed, and she's got on her night-gown and her ruffled night-cap. Here are the costumes for the parts."

He got out two or three curtain-calico suits, which he said was meedyevil armor for Richard III. and t'other chap, and a long white cotton night-shirt and a ruffled night-cap to match. The king was satisfied; so the duke got out his book and read the parts over in the most splendid spread-eagle way, prancing around and acting at the same time, to show how it had got to be done; then he give the book to the king and told him to get his part by heart.

There was a little one-horse town about three mile down the bend, and after dinner the duke said he had ciphered out his idea about how to run in daylight without it being dangersome for Jim; so he allowed he would go down to the town and fix that thing. The king allowed he would go too, and see if he couldn't strike some-thing. We was out of coffee, so Jim said I better go along with them in the canoe and get some.

When we got there, there warn't nobody stirring; streets empty, and perfectly dead and still, like Sunday. We found a sick nigger sunning himself in a back yard, and he said everybody that warn't too young or too sick or too old, was gone to camp-meeting, about two mile back in the woods. The king got the directions, and allowed he'd go and work that camp-meeting for all it was worth, and I might go, too.

The duke said what he was after was a printing office. We found it; a little bit of a concern, up over a carpenter shop—carpenters and printers all gone to the meeting, and no doors locked. It was a dirty, littered-up place, and had ink marks, and handbills with pictures of horses and runaway niggers on them, all over the walls. The duke shed his coat and said he was all right, now. So me and the king lit out for the camp-meeting.

We got there in about a half an hour, fairly dripping, for it was a most awful hot day. There was as much as a thousand people there, from twenty mile around. The woods was full of teams and wagons, hitched everywheres, feeding out of the wagon troughs and stomp-ing to keep off the flies. There was sheds made out of poles and roofed over with branches, where they had lemonade and ginger-bread to sell, and piles of watermelons and green corn and such-like truck.

The preaching was going on under the same kinds of sheds, only they was bigger and held crowds of people. The benches was made out of outside slabs of logs, with holes bored in the round side to drive sticks into for legs. They didn't have no backs. The preachers had high platforms to stand on, at one end of the sheds. The women

"COURTING ON THE SLY."

had on sun-bonnets; and some had linsey-woolsey frocks, some gingham ones, and a few of the young ones had on calico. Some of the young men was barefooted, and some of the children didn't have on any clothes but just a tow-linen shirt. Some of the old women was knitting, and some of the young folks was courting on the sly.

The first shed we come to, the preacher was lining out a hymn. He lined out two lines, everybody sung it, and it was kind of grand to hear it, there was so many of them and they done it in such a rousing way; then he lined out two more for them to sing—and so on. The people woke up more and more, and sung louder and louder; and towards the end, some begun to groan, and some begun to shout.

Then the preacher begun to preach; and begun in earnest, too; and went weaving first to one side of the platform and then the other, and then a leaning down over the front of it, with his arms and his body going all the time, and shouting his words out with all his might; and every now and then he would hold up his Bible and spread it open, and kind of pass it around this way and that, shouting, "It's the brazen serpent in the wilderness! Look upon it and live!" And people would shout out, "Glory!—A-a-*men!*" And so he went on, and the people groaning and crying and saying amen:

"Oh, come to the mourners' bench! come, black with sin! (*amen!*) come, sick and sore! (*amen!*) come, lame and halt, and blind! (*amen!*) come, pore and needy, sunk in shame! (*a-a-men!*) come all that's worn, and soiled, and suffering!—come with a broken spirit! come with a contrite heart! come in your rags and sin and dirt! the waters that cleanse is free, the door of heaven stands open—oh, enter in and be at rest!" (*a-a-men! glory, glory hallelujah!*)

And so on. You couldn't make out what the preacher said, any more, on account of the shouting and crying. Folks got up, everywheres in the crowd, and worked their way, just by main strength, to the mourners' bench, with the tears running down their faces; and when all the mourners had got up there to the front benches in a crowd, they sung, and shouted, and flung themselves down on the straw, just crazy and wild.

Well, the first I knowed, the king got agoing; and you could hear him over everybody; and next he went a-charging up on to the platform and the preacher he begged him to speak to the people, and he done it. He told them he was a pirate—been a pirate for thirty years, out in the Indian Ocean, and his crew was thinned out considerable, last spring, in a fight, and he was home now, to take out some fresh men, and thanks to goodness he'd been robbed last night, and put ashore off of a steamboat without a cent, and he was glad of it, it was the blessedest thing that ever happened to him, because he was a changed man now, and happy for the first time in his life; and poor as he was, he was going to start right off and work his way back to the Indian Ocean and put in the rest of his life trying to turn the pirates into the true path; for he could do it better than anybody else, being acquainted with all the pirate crews in that ocean; and though it would take him a long time to get there, without money, he would get there anyway, and every time he convinced a pirate he would say to him, "Don't you thank me, don't you give me no credit, it all belongs to them dear people in Pokeville camp-meeting, natural brothers and benefactors of the race—and that dear preacher there, the truest friend a pirate ever had!"

"A PIRATE FOR THIRTY YEARS."

And then he busted into tears, and so did everybody. Then somebody sings out, "Take up a collection for him, take up a collection!" Well, a half a dozen made a jump to do it, but somebody sings out, "Let *him* pass the hat around!" Then everybody said it, the preacher too.

So the king went all through the crowd with his hat, swabbing his eyes, and blessing the people and praising them and thanking them for being so good to the poor pirates away off there; and every little while the prettiest kind of girls, with the tears running down their cheeks, would up and ask him would he let them kiss him, for to remember him by; and he always done it; and some of them he hugged and kissed as many as five or six times—and he was invited to stay a week; and everybody wanted him to live in their houses, and said they'd think it was an honor; but he said as this was the last day of the camp-meeting he couldn't do no good, and besides he was in a sweat to get to the Indian Ocean right off and go to work on the pirates.

When we got back to the raft and he come to count up, he found he had collected eighty-seven dollars and seventy-five cents. And then he had fetched away a three-gallon jug of whisky, too, that he found under a wagon when we was starting home through the woods. The king said, take it all around, it laid over any day he'd ever put in in the missionarying line. He said it warn't no use talking, heathens don't amount to shucks, alongside of pirates, to work a camp-meeting with.

The duke was thinking *he'd* been doing pretty well, till the king come to show up, but after that he didn't think so so much. He had set up and printed off two little jobs for farmers, in that printing office—horse bills—and took the money, four dollars. And he had got in ten dollars' worth of advertisements for the paper, which he said he would put in for four dollars if they would pay in advance—so they done it. The price of the paper was two dollars a year, but he took in three subscriptions for half a dollar apiece on condition of them paying him in advance; they were going to pay in cord-wood and onions, as usual, but he said he had just bought the concern and knocked down the price as low as he could afford it, and was going to run it for cash. He set up a little piece of poetry, which he made, himself, out of his own head—three verses—kind of sweet and saddish—the name of it was, "Yes, crush, cold world, this breaking heart"—and he left that all set up and ready to print in the paper and didn't charge nothing for it. Well, he took in nine dollars and a half, and said he'd done a pretty square day's work for it.

Then he showed us another little job he'd printed and hadn't charged for, because it was for us. It had a picture of a runaway nigger, with a bundle on a stick, over his shoulder, and "$200 reward" under it. The reading was all about Jim, and just described him to a dot. It said he run away from St. Jacques' plantation, forty mile below New Orleans, last winter, and likely went north, and whoever would catch him and send him back, he could have the reward and expenses.

ANOTHER LITTLE JOB.

"Now," says the duke, "after to-night we can run in the daytime if we want to. Whenever we see anybody coming, we can tie Jim hand and foot with a rope, and lay him in the wigwam and show this handbill and say we captured him up the river, and were too poor to travel on a steamboat, so we got this little raft on credit from our friends and are going down to get the reward. Handcuffs and chains would look still better on Jim, but it wouldn't go well with the story of us being so poor. Too much like jewelry. Ropes are the correct thing—we must preserve the unities, as we say on the boards."

We all said the duke was pretty smart, and there couldn't be no trouble about running daytimes. We judged we could make miles enough that night to get out of the reach of the pow-wow we reckoned the duke's work in the printing office was going to make in that little town—then we could boom right along, if we wanted to.

We laid low and kept still, and never shoved out till nearly ten o'clock; then we slid by, pretty wide away from the town, and didn't hoist our lantern till we was clear out of sight of it.

When Jim called me to take the watch at four in the morning, he says—

"Huck, does you reck'n we gwyne to run acrost any mo' kings on dis trip?"

"No," I says, "I reckon not."

"Well," says he, "dat's all right, den. I doan' mine one er two kings, but dat's enough. Dis one's powerful drunk, en de duke ain' much better."

I found Jim had been trying to get him to talk French, so he could hear what it was like; but he said he had been in this country so long, and had so much trouble, he'd forgot it.

Chapter XXI

PRACTICING.

IT was after sun-up, now, but we went right on, and didn't tie up. The king and the duke turned out, by and by, looking pretty rusty; but after they'd jumped overboard and took a swim, it chippered them up a good deal. After breakfast the king he took a seat on a corner of the raft, and pulled off his boots and rolled up his britches, and let his legs dangle in the water, so as to be comfortable, and lit his pipe, and went to getting his Romeo and Juliet by heart. When he had got it pretty good, him and the duke begun to practice it together. The duke had to learn him over and over again, how to say every speech; and he made him sigh, and put his hand on his heart, and after a while he said he done it pretty well; "only," he says, "you mustn't bellow out *Romeo!* that way, like a bull—you must say it soft, and sick, and languishy, so—R—o—o—meo! that is the idea; for Juliet's a dear sweet mere child of a girl, you know, and she don't bray like a jackass."

Well, next they got out a couple of long swords that the duke made out of oak laths, and begun to practice the sword-fight—the duke called himself Richard III.; and the way they laid on, and pranced around the raft was grand to see. But by and by the king tripped and fell overboard, and after that they took a rest, and had a talk about all kinds of adventures they'd had in other times along the river.

After dinner, the duke says:

"Well, Capet, we'll want to made this a first-class show, you know, so I guess we'll add a little more to it. We want a little something to answer encores with, anyway."

"What's onkores, Bilgewater?"

The duke told him, and then says:

"I'll answer by doing the Highland fling or the sailor's hornpipe; and you—well, let me see—oh, I've got it—you can do Hamlet's soliloquy."

"Hamlet's which?"

"Hamlet's soliloquy, you know; the most celebrated thing in Shakespeare. Ah, it's sublime, sublime! Always fetches the house. I haven't got it in the book—I've only got one volume—but I reckon I can piece it out from memory. I'll just walk up and down a minute, and see if I can call it back from recollection's vaults."

So he went to marching up and down, thinking, and frowning horrible every now and then; then he would hoist up his eye-brows; next he would squeeze his hand on his forehead and stagger back

HAMLET'S SOLILOQUY.

and kind of moan; next he would sigh, and next he'd let on to drop a tear. It was beautiful to see him. By and by he got it. He told us to give attention. Then he strikes a most noble attitude, with one leg shoved forwards, and his arms stretched away up, and his head tilted back, looking up at the sky; and then he begins to rip and rave and grit his teeth; and after that, all through his speech he howled, and spread around, and swelled up his chest, and just knocked the spots out of any acting ever *I* see before. This is the speech—I learned it, easy enough, while he was learning it to the king:

> To be, or not to be; that is the bare bodkin
> That makes calamity of so long life;
> For who would fardels bear, till Birnam Wood do come to Dun-
> sinane,
> But that the fear of something after death
> Murders the innocent sleep,
> Great nature's second course,
> And makes us rather sling the arrows of outrageous fortune
> Than fly to others that we know not of.
> There's the respect must give us pause:
> Wake Duncan with thy knocking! I would thou couldst;
> For who would bear the whips and scorns of time,
> The oppressor's wrong, the proud man's contumely,
> The law's delay, and the quietus which his pangs might take,
> In the dead waste and middle of the night, when churchyards
> yawn
> In customary suits of solemn black,
> But that the undiscovered country from whose bourne no trav-
> eler returns,
> Breathes forth contagion on the world,
> And thus the native hue of resolution, like the poor cat i' the
> adage,
> Is sicklied o'er with care,
> And all the clouds that lowered o'er our housetops,
> With this regard their currents turn awry,
> And lose the name of action.
> 'Tis a consummation devoutly to be wished. But soft you, the
> fair Ophelia:
> Ope not thy ponderous and marble jaws,
> But get thee to a nunnery—go!

Well, the old man he liked that speech, and he mighty soon got it so he could do it first rate. It seemed like he was just born for it; and

when he had his hand in and was excited, it was perfectly lovely the
way he would rip and tear and rair up behind when he was getting it
off.

The first chance we got, the duke he had some show bills printed;
and after that, for two or three days as we floated along, the raft was
a most uncommon lively place, for there warn't nothing but sword-
fighting and rehearsing—as the duke called it—going on all the
time. One morning, when we was pretty well down the State of
Arkansaw, we come in sight of a little one-horse town in a big bend;
so we tied up about three-quarters of a mile above it, in the mouth
of a crick which was shut in like a tunnel by the cypress trees, and
all of us but Jim took the canoe and went down there to see if there
was any chance in that place for our show.

We struck it mighty lucky; there was going to be a circus there
that afternoon, and the country people was already beginning to
come in, in all kinds of old shackly wagons, and on horses. The
circus would leave before night, so our show would have a pretty
good chance. The duke he hired the court house, and we went
around and stuck up our bills. They read like this:

Shaksperean Revival!!!
Wonderful Attraction!
For One Night Only!
The world renowned tragedians,
David Garrick the younger, of Drury Lane Theatre, London,
and
Edmund Kean the elder, of the Royal Haymarket Theatre, White-
chapel, Pudding Lane, Piccadilly, London, and the
Royal Continental Theatres, in their sublime
Shaksperean Spectacle entitled
The Balcony Scene
in
Romeo and Juliet!!!

Romeo... Mr. Garrick.
Juliet.. Mr. Kean.

Assisted by the whole strength of the company!
New costumes, new scenery, new appointments!
Also:
The thrilling, masterly, and blood-curdling
Broad-sword conflict
In Richard III.!!!

Richard III. .... Mr. Garrick.
Richmond...................................... Mr. Kean.

also:
(by special request,)
Hamlet's Immortal Soliloquy!!
By the Illustrious Kean!
Done by him 300 consecutive nights in Paris!
For One Night Only,
On account of imperative European engagements!
Admission 25 cents; children and servants, 10 cents.

Then we went loafing around the town. The stores and houses was most all old shackly dried-up frame concerns that hadn't ever been painted; they was set up three or four foot above ground on stilts, so as to be out of reach of the water when the river was overflowed. The houses had little gardens around them, but they didn't seem to raise hardly anything in them but jimpson weeds, and sunflowers, and ash-piles, and old curled-up boots and shoes, and pieces of bottles, and rags, and played-out tin-ware. The fences was made of different kinds of boards, nailed on at different times; and they leaned every which-way, and had gates that didn't generly have but one hinge—a leather one. Some of the fences had been whitewashed, some time or another, but the duke said it was in Clumbus's time, like enough. There was generly hogs in the garden, and people driving them out.

All the stores was along one street. They had white-domestic awnings in front, and the country people hitched their horses to the awning-posts. There was empty dry-goods boxes under the awnings, and loafers roosting on them all day long, whittling them with their Barlow knives; and chawing tobacco, and gaping and yawning and stretching—a mighty ornery lot. They generly had on yellow straw hats most as wide as an umbrella, but didn't wear no coats nor waistcoats; they called one another Bill, and Buck, and Hank, and Joe, and Andy, and talked lazy and drawly, and used considerable many cuss-words. There was as many as one loafer leaning up against every awning-post, and he most always had his hands in his britches pockets, except when he fetched them out to lend a chaw of tobacco or scratch. What a body was hearing amongst them, all the time was—

"Gimme a chaw 'v tobacker, Hank."

"Cain't—I hain't got but one chaw left. Ask Bill."

Maybe Bill he gives him a chaw; maybe he lies and says he ain't got none. Some of them kinds of loafers never has a cent in the world, nor a chaw of tobacco of their own. They get all their chawing by borrowing—they say to a fellow, "I wisht you'd len' me a chaw, Jack, I jist this minute give Ben Thompson the last chaw I had"— which is a lie, pretty much every time; it don't fool nobody but a stranger; but Jack ain't no stranger, so he says—

"GIMME A CHAW."

"*You* give him a chaw, did you? so did your sister's cat's grand-mother. You pay me back the chaws you've awready borry'd off 'n me, Lafe Buckner, then I'll loan you one or two ton of it, and won't charge you no back intrust, nuther."

"Well, I *did* pay you back some of it wunst."

"Yes, you did—'bout six chaws. You borry'd store tobacker and paid back nigger-head."

Store tobacco is flat black plug, but these fellows mostly chaws the natural leaf twisted. When they borrow a chaw, they don't generly cut it off with a knife, but they set the plug in between their teeth, and gnaw with their teeth and tug at the plug with their hands till they get it in two—then sometimes the one that owns the tobacco looks mournful at it when it's handed back, and says, sarcastic—

"Here, gimme the *chaw*, and you take the *plug*."

All the streets and lanes was just mud, they warn't nothing else *but* mud—mud as black as tar, and nigh about a foot deep in some places; and two or three inches deep in *all* the places. The hogs loafed and grunted around, everywheres. You'd see a muddy sow and a litter of pigs come lazying along the street and whollop herself right down in the way, where folks had to walk around her, and she'd stretch out, and shut her eyes, and wave her ears, whilst the pigs was milking her, and look as happy as if she was on salary. And pretty soon you'd hear a loafer sing out, "Hi! *so* boy! sick him, Tige!" and away the sow would go, squealing most horrible, with a dog or two swinging to each ear, and three or four dozen more a-coming; and then you would see all the loafers get up and watch the thing out of sight, and laugh at the fun and look grateful for the noise. Then they'd settle back again till there was a dog-fight. There couldn't anything wake them up all over, and make them happy all over, like a dog-fight—unless it might be putting turpentine on a stray dog and setting fire to him, or tying a tin pan to his tail and see him run himself to death.

On the river front some of the houses was sticking out over the bank, and they was bowed and bent, and about ready to tumble in. The people had moved out of them. The bank was caved away under one corner of some others, and that corner was hanging over. People lived in them yet, but it was dangersome, because sometimes a strip of land as wide as a house caves in at a time. Sometimes a belt of land a quarter of a mile deep will start in and cave along and cave along till it all caves into the river in one summer. Such a town as that has to be always moving back, and back, and back, because the river's always gnawing at it.

The nearer it got to noon that day, the thicker and thicker was the wagons and horses in the streets, and more coming all the time. Families fetched their dinners with them, from the country, and eat them in the wagons. There was considerable whisky drinking going on, and I seen three fights. By and by somebody sings out—

"Here comes old Boggs!—in from the country for his little old monthly drunk—here he comes, boys!"

All the loafers looked glad—I reckoned they was used to having fun out of Boggs. One of them says—

"Wonder who he's a gwyne to chaw up this time. If he'd a chawed up all the men he's ben a gwyne to chaw up in the last twenty year, he'd have considerble ruputation, now."

Another one says, "I wisht old Boggs 'd threaten me, 'cuz then I'd know I warn't gwyne to die for a thousan' year."

Boggs comes a-tearing along on his horse, whooping and yelling like an Injun, and singing out—

"Cler the track, thar. I'm on the waw-path, and the price uv coffins is a gwyne to raise."

He was drunk, and weaving about in his saddle; he was over fifty year old, and had a very red face. Everybody yelled at him, and laughed at him, and sassed him, and he sassed back, and said he'd attend to them and lay them out in their regular turns, but he couldn't wait now, because he'd come to town to kill old Colonel Sherburn, and his motto was, "meat first, and spoon vittles to top off on."

He see me, and rode up and says—

"Whar'd you come f'm, boy? You prepared to die?"

Then he rode on. I was scared; but a man says—

"He don't mean nothing; he's always a carryin' on like that, when he's drunk. He's the best-naturedest old fool in Arkansaw—never hurt nobody, drunk nor sober."

Boggs rode up before the biggest store in town and bent his head down so he could see under the curtain of the awning, and yells—

"Come out here, Sherburn! Come out and meet the man you've swindled. You're the houn' I'm after, and I'm a gwyne to have you, too!"

And so he went on, calling Sherburn everything he could lay his tongue to, and the whole street packed with people listening and laughing and going on. By and by a proud-looking man about fifty-five—and he was a heap the best dressed man in that town, too—steps out of the store, and the crowd drops back on each side to let him come. He says to Boggs, mighty ca'm and slow—he says:

"I'm tired of this; but I'll endure it till one o'clock. Till one o'clock, mind—no longer. If you open your mouth against me only once, after that time, you can't travel so far but I will find you."

A LITTLE MONTHLY DRUNK.

Then he turns and goes in. The crowd looked mighty sober; nobody stirred, and there warn't no more laughing. Boggs rode off blackguarding Sherburn as loud as he could yell, all down the street; and pretty soon back he comes and stops before the store, still keeping it up. Some men crowded around him and tried to get him to shut up, but he wouldn't; they told him it would be one o'clock in about fifteen minutes, and so he *must* go home—he must go right away. But it didn't do no good. He cussed away, with all his might, and throwed his hat down in the mud and rode over it, and pretty soon away he went a-raging down the street again, with his gray hair a-flying. Everybody that could get a chance at him tried their best to coax him off of his horse so they could lock him up and get him sober; but it warn't no use—up the street he would tear again, and give Sherburn another cussing. By and by somebody says—

"Go for his daughter!—quick, go for his daughter; sometimes he'll listen to her. If anybody can persuade him, she can."

So somebody started on a run. I walked down street a ways, and stopped. In about five or ten minutes, here comes Boggs again—but not on his horse. He was a-reeling across the street towards me, bareheaded, with a friend on both sides of him aholt of his arms and hurrying him along. He was quiet, and looked uneasy; and he warn't hanging back any, but was doing some of the hurrying himself. Somebody sings out—

"Boggs!"

I looked over there to see who said it, and it was that Colonel Sherburn. He was standing perfectly still, in the street, and had a pistol raised in his right hand—not aiming it, but holding it out with the barrel tilted up towards the sky. The same second I see a young girl coming on the run, and two men with her. Boggs and the men turned round, to see who called him, and when they see the pistol the men jumped to one side, and the pistol barrel come down slow and steady to a level—both barrels cocked. Boggs throws up both of his hands, and says, "O Lord, don't shoot!" Bang! goes the first shot, and he staggers back clawing at the air—bang! goes the second one, and he tumbles backwards onto the ground, heavy and solid, with his arms spread out. That young girl screamed out, and comes rushing, and down she throws herself on her father, crying, and saying, "Oh, he's killed him, he's killed him!" The crowd closed up around them, and shouldered and jammed one another, with

THE DEATH OF BOGGS.

their necks stretched, trying to see, and people on the inside trying to shove them back, and shouting, "Back, back! give him air, give him air!"

Colonel Sherburn he tossed his pistol onto the ground, and turned around on his heels and walked off.

They took Boggs to a little drug store, the crowd pressing around, just the same, and the whole town following, and I rushed and got a good place at the window, where I was close to him and could see in. They laid him on the floor, and put one large Bible under his head, and opened another one and spread it on his breast—but they tore open his shirt first, and I seen where one of the bullets went in. He made about a dozen long gasps, his breast lifting the Bible up when he drawed in his breath, and letting it down again when he breathed it out—and after that he laid still; he was dead. Then they pulled his daughter away from him, screaming and crying, and took her off. She was about sixteen, and very sweet and gentle-looking, but awful pale and scared.

Well, pretty soon the whole town was there, squirming and scrouging and pushing and shoving to get at the window and have a look, but people that had the places wouldn't give them up, and folks behind them was saying all the time, "Say, now, you've looked enough, you fellows; 'taint right and 'taint fair, for you to stay thar all the time, and never give nobody a chance; other folks has their rights as well as you."

There was considerable jawing back, so I slid out, thinking maybe there was going to be trouble. The streets was full, and everybody was excited. Everybody that seen the shooting was telling how it happened, and there was a big crowd packed around each one of these fellows, stretching their necks and listening. One long lanky man, with long hair and a big white fur stove-pipe hat on the back of his head, and a crooked-handled cane, marked out the places on the ground where Boggs stood, and where Sherburn stood, and the people following him around from one place to t'other and watching everything he done, and bobbing their heads to show they understood, and stooping a little and resting their hands on their thighs to watch him mark the places on the ground with his cane; and then he stood up straight and stiff where Sherburn had stood, frowning and having his hat-brim down over his eyes, and sung out, "Boggs!"

and then fetched his cane down slow to a level, and says "Bang!" staggered backwards, says "Bang!" again, and fell down flat on his back. The people that had seen the thing said he done it perfect; said it was just exactly the way it all happened. Then as much as a dozen people got out their bottles and treated him.

Well, by and by somebody said Sherburn ought to be lynched. In about a minute everybody was saying it; so away they went, mad and yelling, and snatching down every clothes-line they come to, to do the hanging with.

Chapter XXII.

SHERBURN STEPS OUT.

They swarmed up the street, towards Sherburn's house, a-whooping and yelling and raging like Injuns, and everything had to clear the way or get run over and tromped to mush, and it was awful to see. Children was heeling it ahead of the mob, screaming and trying to get out of the way; and every window along the road was full of women's heads, and there was nigger boys in every tree, and bucks and wenches looking over every fence; and as soon as the mob would get nearly to them they would break and skaddle back out of reach. Lots of the women and girls was crying and taking on, scared most to death.

They swarmed up in front of Sherburn's palings as thick as they could jam together, and you couldn't hear yourself think for the noise. It was a little twenty-foot yard. Some sung out, "Tear down the fence! tear down the fence!" Then there was a racket of ripping and tearing and smashing, and down she goes, and the front wall of the crowd begins to roll in like a wave.

Just then Sherburn steps out onto the roof of his little front porch, with a double-barrel gun in his hand, and takes his stand, perfectly ca'm and deliberate, not saying a word. The racket stopped, and the wave sucked back.

Sherburn never said a word—just stood there, looking down. The stillness was awful creepy and uncomfortable. Sherburn run his eye slow along the crowd; and wherever it struck, the people tried a little to outgaze him, but they couldn't; they dropped their eyes and looked sneaky. Then pretty soon Sherburn sort of laughed; not the pleasant kind, but the kind that makes you feel like when you are eating bread that's got sand in it.

Then he says, slow and scornful:

"The idea of *you* lynching anybody! It's amusing. The idea of you thinking you had pluck enough to lynch a *man!* Because you're brave enough to tar and feather poor friendless cast-out women that come along here, did that make you think you had grit enough to lay your hands on a *man?* Why, a *man's* safe in the hands of ten thousand of your kind—as long as it's daytime and you're not behind him.

"Do I know you? I know you clear through. I was born and raised in the south, and I've lived in the north; so I know the average all around. The average man's a coward. In the north he lets anybody walk over him that wants to, and goes home and prays for a humble spirit to bear it. In the south one man, all by himself, has stopped a stage full of men, in the day-time, and robbed the lot. Your newspapers call you a brave people so much that you think you *are* braver than any other people—whereas you're just *as* brave, and no braver. Why don't your juries hang murderers? Because they're afraid the man's friends will shoot them in the back, in the dark—and it's just what they *would* do.

"So they always acquit; and then a *man* goes in the night, with a hundred masked cowards at his back, and lynches the rascal. Your mistake is, that you didn't bring a man with you; that's one mistake, and the other is that you didn't come in the dark, and fetch your masks. You brought *part* of a man—Buck Harkness, there—and if you hadn't had him to start you, you'd a taken it out in blowing.

"You didn't want to come. The average man don't like trouble and danger. *You* don't like trouble and danger. But if only *half* a man—like Buck Harkness, there—shouts 'Lynch him, lynch him!' you're afraid to back down—afraid you'll be found out to be what you are—*cowards*—and so you raise a yell, and hang yourselves onto that half-a-man's coat tail, and come raging up here, swearing what big things you're going to do. The pitifulest thing out is a mob;

that's what an army is—a mob; they don't fight with courage that's
born in them, but with courage that's borrowed from their mass,
and from their officers. But a mob without any *man* at the head of
it, is *beneath* pitifulness. Now the thing for *you* to do, is to droop
your tails and go home and crawl in a hole. If any real lynching's
going to be done, it will be done in the dark, southern fashion; and
when they come, they'll bring their masks, and fetch a *man* along.
Now *leave*—and take your half-a-man with you"—tossing his gun
up across his left arm and cocking it, when he says this.

The crowd washed back sudden, and then broke all apart and
went tearing off every which way, and Buck Harkness he heeled it
after them, looking tolerable cheap. I could a staid, if I'd a wanted
to, but I didn't want to.

I went to the circus, and loafed around the back side till the
watchman went by, and then dived in under the tent. I had my

A DEAD HEAD.

twenty-dollar gold piece and some other money, but I reckoned I
better save it, because there ain't no telling how soon you are going
to need it, away from home and amongst strangers, that way. You
can't be too careful. I ain't opposed to spending money on circuses,
when there ain't no other way, but there ain't no use in *wasting* it
on them.

It was a real bully circus. It was the splendidest sight that ever
was, when they all come riding in, two and two, a gentleman and

lady, side by side, the men just in their drawers and undershirts, and
no shoes nor stirrups, and resting their hands on their thighs, easy
and comfortable,—there must a been twenty of them—and every
lady with a lovely complexion, and perfectly beautiful, and looking
just like a gang of real sure-enough queens, and dressed in clothes
that cost millions of dollars, and just littered with dimonds. It was
a powerful fine sight; I never see anything so lovely. And then one
by one they got up and stood, and went a-weaving around the ring
so gentle, and wavy and graceful, the men looking ever so tall and
airy and straight, with their heads bobbing and skimming along,
away up there under the tent-roof, and every lady's rose-leafy dress
flapping soft and silky around her hips, and she looking like the
most loveliest parasol.

And then faster and faster they went, all of them dancing, first
one foot stuck out in the air and then the other, the horses leaning
more and more, and the ring-master going round and round the
centre-pole, cracking his whip and shouting "Hi!—hi!" and the
clown cracking jokes behind him; and by and by, all hands dropped
the reins, and every lady put her knuckles on her hips and every
gentleman folded his arms, and then how the horses did lean over
and hump themselves! And so, one after the other they all skipped
off into the ring, and made the sweetest bow I ever see, and then
scampered out, and everybody clapped their hands and went just
about wild.

Well, all through the circus they done the most astonishing
things; and all the time, that clown carried on so it most killed the
people. The ring-master couldn't ever say a word to him but he was
back at him quick as a wink with the funniest things a body ever
said; and how he ever *could* think of so many of them, and so sudden
and so pat, was what I couldn't no way understand. Why, I couldn't
a thought of them in a year. And by and by a drunk man tried to get
into the ring—said he wanted to ride; said he could ride as well as
anybody that ever was. They argued and tried to keep him out, but
he wouldn't listen, and the whole show come to a standstill. Then
the people begun to holler at him and make fun of him, and that
made him mad, and he begun to rip and tear; so that stirred up the
people, and a lot of men begun to pile down off of the benches and
swarm towards the ring, saying, "Knock him down! throw him
out!" and one or two women begun to scream. So, then, the ring-

master he made a little speech, and said he hoped there wouldn't be no disturbance, and if the man would promise he wouldn't make no more trouble, he would let him ride, if he thought he could stay on the horse. So everybody laughed and said all right, and the man got on. The minute he was on, the horse begun to rip and tear and jump, and cavort around, with two circus men hanging on to his bridle trying to hold him, and the drunk man hanging onto his neck, and his heels flying in the air every jump, and the whole crowd of people standing up shouting and laughing till the tears rolled down. And at last, sure enough, all the circus men could do, the horse broke loose, and away he went like the very nation, round and round the ring, with that sot laying down on him and hanging to his neck, with first one leg hanging most to the ground on one side, and then t'other one on t'other side, and the people just crazy. It warn't funny to me, though; I was all of a tremble to see his danger. But pretty soon he struggled up astraddle and grabbed the bridle, a-reeling this way and that; and the next minute he sprung up and dropped the

HE SHED SEVENTEEN SUITS.

bridle and stood! and the horse agoing like a house afire, too. He just stood up there, a-sailing around as easy and comfortable as if he warn't ever drunk in his life—and then he begun to pull off his clothes and fling them. He shed them so thick they kind of clogged up the air, and altogether he shed seventeen suits. And then, there he was, slim and handsome, and dressed the gaudiest and prettiest you ever saw, and he lit into that horse with his whip and made him fairly hum—and finally skipped off, and made his bow and danced off to the dressing room, and everybody just a-howling with pleasure and astonishment.

Then the ring-master he see how he had been fooled, and he *was* the sickest ring-master you ever see, I reckon. Why, it was one of his own men! He had got up that joke all out of his own head, and never let on to nobody. Well, I felt sheepish enough, to be took in so, but I wouldn't a been in that ring-master's place, not for a thousand dollars. I don't know; there may be bullier circuses than what that one was, but I never struck them yet. Anyways it was plenty good enough for *me;* and wherever I run across it, it can have all of *my* custom, every time.

Well, that night we had *our* show, but there warn't only about twelve people there; just enough to pay expenses. And they laughed all the time, and that made the duke mad; and everybody left, anyway, before the show was over, but one boy which was asleep. So the duke said these Arkansaw lunkheads couldn't come up to Shakspeare: what they wanted was low comedy—and maybe something ruther worse than low comedy, he reckoned. He said he could size their style. So next morning he got some big sheets of wrapping paper and some black paint, and drawed off some handbills and stuck them up all over the village. The bills said:

AT THE COURT HOUSE!
FOR 3 NIGHTS ONLY!
The World-Renowned Tragedians
DAVID GARRICK THE YOUNGER!
AND
EDMUND KEAN THE ELDER!
*Of the London and Continental
Theatres,*

In their Thrilling Tragedy of
THE KING'S CAMELOPARD
OR
THE ROYAL NONESUCH!!!
Admission 50 cents.

Then at the bottom was the biggest line of all—which said:

LADIES AND CHILDREN NOT ADMITTED.

"There," says he, "if that line don't fetch them, I don't know Arkansaw!"

Chapter XXIII

TRAGEDY.

Well, all day him and the king was hard at it, rigging up a stage, and a curtain, and a row of candles for footlights; and that night the house was jam full of men in no time. When the place couldn't hold no more, the duke he quit tending door and went around the back way and come onto the stage and stood up before the curtain, and made a little speech, and praised up this tragedy, and said it was the most thrillingest one that ever was; and so he went on, a-bragging about the tragedy, and about Edmund Kean the Elder, which was to play the main principal part in it; and at last when he'd got everybody's expectations up high enough, he rolled up the curtain, and the next minute the king come a-prancing out on all fours, naked; and he was painted, all over, ring-streaked-and-striped, all sorts of colors, as splendid as a rain-bow. And—but never mind the rest of his outfit, it was just wild, but it was awful funny. The people most killed themselves laughing; and when the king got done capering, and capered off behind the scenes, they roared and clapped and stormed and haw-hawed till he come back and done it over again; and after that, they made him do it another time. Well, it would a made a cow laugh, to see the shines that old idiot cut.

Then the duke he lets the curtain down, and bows to the people, and says the great tragedy will be performed only two nights more, on accounts of pressing London engagements, where the seats is all

sold aready for it in Drury Lane; and then he makes them another
bow, and says if he has succeeded in pleasing them and instructing
them, he will be deeply obleeged if they will mention it to their
friends and get them to come and see it.

Twenty people sings out:

"What, is it over? Is that *all?*"

The duke says yes. Then there was a fine time. Everybody sings
out "Sold!" and rose up mad, and was agoing for that stage and them
tragedians. But a big fine looking man jumps up on a bench and
shouts:

"Hold on! Just a word, gentlemen." They stopped to listen. "We
are sold—mighty badly sold. But we don't want to be the laughing-
stock of this whole town, I reckon, and never hear the last of this
thing as long as we live. *No.* What we want, is to go out of here quiet,
and talk this show up, and sell the *rest* of the town! Then we'll all
be in the same boat. Ain't that
sensible?" ["You bet it is!—
the jedge is right!" everybody
sings out.] "All right, then—
not a word about any sell. Go
along home, and advise
everybody to come and see
the tragedy."

Next day you couldn't hear
nothing around that town but
how splendid that show was.
House was jammed again,
that night, and we sold this
crowd the same way. When
me and the king and the duke
got home to the raft, we all
had a supper; and by and by,
about midnight, they made
Jim and me back her out and
float her down the middle of
the river and fetch her in and
hide her about two mile below town.

THEIR POCKETS BULGED.

The third night the house was crammed again—and they warn't newcomers, this time, but people that was at the show the other two nights. I stood by the duke at the door, and I see that every man that went in had his pockets bulging, or something muffled up under his coat—and I see it warn't no perfumery, neither, not by a long sight. I smelt sickly eggs by the barrel, and rotten cabbages, and such things; and if I know the signs of a dead cat being around, and I bet I do, there was sixty-four of them went in. I shoved in there for a minute, but it was too various for me, I couldn't stand it. Well, when the place couldn't hold no more people, the duke he give a fellow a quarter and told him to tend door for him a minute, and then he started around for the stage door, I after him; but the minute we turned the corner and was in the dark, he says:

"Walk fast, now, till you get away from the houses, and then shin for the raft like the dickens was after you!"

I done it, and he done the same. We struck the raft at the same time, and in less than two seconds we was gliding down stream, all dark and still, and edging towards the middle of the river, nobody saying a word. I reckoned the poor king was in for a gaudy time of it with the audience; but nothing of the sort: pretty soon he crawls out from under the wigwam, and says:

"Well, how'd the old thing pan out this time, duke?"

He hadn't been up town at all.

We never showed a light till we was about ten mile below that village. Then we lit up and had a supper, and the king and the duke fairly laughed their bones loose over the way they'd served them people. The duke says:

"Greenhorns, flatheads! *I* knew the first house would keep mum and let the rest of the town get roped in; and I knew they'd lay for us the third night, and consider it was *their* turn now. Well, it *is* their turn, and I'd give something to know how much they'd take for it. I *would* just like to know how they're putting in their opportunity. They can turn it into a picnic, if they want to—they brought plenty provisions."

Them rapscallions took in four hundred and sixty-five dollars in that three nights. I never see money hauled in by the wagon load like that, before.

By and by, when they was asleep and snoring, Jim says:

"Don't it sprise you, de way dem kings carries on, Huck?"

"No," I says, "it don't."

"Why don't it, Huck?"

"Well, it don't, because it's in the breed. I reckon they're all alike."

"But Huck, dese kings o' ourn is reglar rapscallions; dat's jist what dey is; dey's reglar rapscallions."

"Well, that's what I'm a-saying; all kings is mostly rapscallions, as fur as I can make out."

"Is dat so?"

"You read about them once—you'll see. Look at Henry the Eight; this'n 's a Sunday School superintendent to *him*. And look at Charles Second, and Louis Fourteen, and Louis Fifteen, and James Second, and Edward Second, and Richard Third, and forty more; besides all them Saxon heptarchies that used to rip around so in old times and raise Cain. My, you ought to seen old Henry the Eight when he was in bloom. He *was* a blossom. He used to marry a new wife every day, and chop off her head next morning. And he would do it just as indifferent as if he was ordering up eggs. 'Fetch up Nell Gwynn,' he says. They fetch her up. Next morning, 'Chop off her head!' And they chop it off. 'Fetch up Jane Shore,' he says; and up she comes. Next morning, 'Chop off her head'—and they chop it off. 'Ring up Fair Rosamun.' Fair Rosamun answers the bell. Next morning, 'Chop off her head.' And he made every one of them tell him a tale every night; and he kept that up till he had hogged a thousand and one tales that way, and then he put them all in a book, and called it Domesday Book—which was a good name, and stated the case. You don't know kings, Jim, but I know them; and this old rip of ourn is one of the cleanest I've struck in history. Well, Henry he takes a notion he wants to get up some trouble with this country. How does he go at it—give notice?—give the country a show? No. All of a sudden he heaves all the tea in Boston harbor overboard, and whacks out a declaration of independence, and dares them to come on. That was *his* style—he never give anybody a chance. He had suspicions of his father, the duke of Wellington. Well, what did he do?—ask him to show up? No—drownded him a butt of mamsey, like a cat. Spose people left money laying around where he was—what did he do? He collared it. Spose he contracted to do a thing; and you paid

him, and didn't set down there and see that he done it—what did he
do? He always done the other thing. Spose he opened his mouth—
what then? If he didn't shut it up powerful quick, he'd lose a lie,
every time. That's the kind of a bug Henry was; and if we'd a had
him along stead of our kings, he'd a fooled that town a heap worse

HENRY THE EIGHTH IN BOSTON HARBOR.

than ourn done. I don't say that ourn is lambs, because they ain't,
when you come right down to the cold facts; but they ain't nothing
to *that* old ram, anyway. All I say, is, kings is kings, and you got to
make allowances. Take them all around, they're a mighty ornery
lot. It's the way they're raised."

"But dis one do *smell* so like de nation, Huck."

"Well, they all do, Jim. *We* can't help the way a king smells;
history don't tell no way."

"Now de duke, he's a tolerble likely man, in some ways."

"Yes, a duke's different. But not very different. This one's a
middling hard lot,—for a duke. When he's drunk, there ain't no
near-sighted man could tell him from a king."

"Well, anyways, I doan hanker for no mo' un um, Huck. Dese is
all I kin stan'."

"It's the way I feel, too, Jim. But we've got them on our hands, and we got to remember what they are, and make allowances. Sometimes I wish we could hear of a country that's out of kings."

What was the use to tell Jim these warn't real kings and dukes? It wouldn't a done no good; and besides, it was just as I said; you couldn't tell them from the real kind.

I went to sleep, and Jim didn't call me when it was my turn. He often done that. When I waked up, just at daybreak, he was setting there with his head down betwixt his knees, moaning and mourning to himself. I didn't take notice, nor let on. I knowed what it was about. He was thinking about his wife and his children, away up yonder, and he was low and homesick; because he hadn't ever been away from home before in his life; and I do believe he cared just as much for his people as white folks does for their'n. It don't seem natural, but I reckon it's so. He was often moaning and mourning, that way, nights, when he judged I was asleep, and saying "Po' little 'Lizabeth! po' little Johnny! it mighty hard; I spec' I ain't ever gwyne to see you no mo', no mo'!" He was a mighty good nigger, Jim was.

But this time I somehow got to talking to him about his wife and young ones; and by and by he says:

"What make me feel so bad dis time, 'uz bekase I hear sumpn over yonder on de bank like a whack, er a slam, while ago, en it mine me er de time I treat my little 'Lizabeth so ornery. She warn't on'y 'bout fo' year ole, en she tuck de sk'yarlet fever, en had a powful rough spell; but she got well, en one day she was a-stannin' aroun', en I says to her, I says:

" 'Shet de do'.'

"She never done it; jis' stood dah, kiner smilin' up at me. It make me mad; en I says agin, mighty loud, I says:

" 'Doan you hear me?—shet de do'!'

"She jis' stood de same way, kiner smilin' up. I was a-bilin'! I says:

" 'I lay I *make* you mine!'

"En wid dat I fetch' her a slap side de head dat sont her a-sprawlin'. Den I went into de yuther room, en 'uz gone 'bout ten minutes; en when I come back, dah was dat do' a-stannin' open *yit*, en dat chile stannin' mos' right in it, a-lookin' down en mournin', en de tears runnin' down. My, but I *wuz* mad. I was agwyne for de chile, but jis' den—it was a do' dat open' innerds—jis' den, 'long come de wind en slam it to, behine de chile, ker-*blam!*—en my lan', de chile never move'! My breff mos' hop outer me; en I feel so—so—I doan know *how* I feel. I crope out, all a-tremblin', en crope aroun' en open de do' easy en slow, en poke my head in behine de chile, sof' en still, en all uv a sudden I says *pow!* jis' as loud as I could yell. *She never budge!* O, Huck, I bust out a-cryin', en grab her up in my arms en say, 'O de po' little thing! de Lord God Amighty fogive po' ole Jim, kaze he never gwyne to fogive hisseff as long's he live!' O, she was plumb deef en dumb, Huck, plumb deef en dumb—en I'd ben a treat'n her so!"

Chapter XXIV

Sick Arab — but harmless when not out of his head

HARMLESS.

Next day, towards night, we laid up under a little willow towhead out in the middle, where there was a village on each side of the river, and the duke and the king begun to lay out a plan for working them towns. Jim he spoke to the duke, and said he hoped it wouldn't take but a few hours, because it got mighty heavy and tiresome to him when he had to lay all day in the wigwam tied with the rope. You see, when we left him all alone we had to tie him, because if anybody happened on him all by himself and not tied, it wouldn't look much like he was a runaway nigger, you know. So the duke said it *was* kind of hard to have to lay roped all day, and he'd cipher out some way to get around it.

He was uncommon bright, the duke was, and he soon struck it. He dressed Jim up in King Leer's outfit—it was a long curtain-calico gown, and a white horse-hair wig and whiskers; and then he took his theatre-paint and painted Jim's face and hands and ears and neck all over a dead dull solid blue, like a man that's been drownded nine days. Blamed if he warn't the horriblest looking outrage I ever see. Then the duke took and wrote out a sign on a shingle, so—

Sick Arab—but harmless when not out of his head.

And he nailed that shingle to a lath, and stood the lath up four or five foot in front of the wigwam. Jim was satisfied. He said it was a sight better than laying tied a couple of years every day and trembling all over every time there was a sound. The duke told him to make himself free and easy, and if anybody ever come meddling around, he must hop out of the wigwam, and carry on a little, and fetch a howl or two like a wild beast, and he reckoned they would light out and leave him alone. Which was sound enough judgment; but you take the average man, and he wouldn't wait for him to howl. Why, he didn't only look like he was dead, he looked considerable more than that.

These rapscallions wanted to try the Nonesuch again, because there was so much money in it, but they judged it wouldn't be safe, because maybe the news might a worked along down by this time. They couldn't hit no project that suited, exactly; so at last the duke said he reckoned he'd lay off and work his brains an hour or two and see if he couldn't put up something on the Arkansaw village; and the king he allowed he would drop over to t'other village, without any plan, but just trust in Providence to lead him the profitable way—meaning the devil, I reckon. We had all bought store clothes where we stopped last; and now the king put his'n on, and he told me to put mine on. I done it, of course. The king's duds was all black, and he did look real swell and starchy. I never knowed how clothes could change a body before. Why, before, he looked like the orneriest old rip that ever was; but now, when he'd take off his new white beaver and make a bow and do a smile, he looked that grand and good and pious that you'd say he had walked right out of the ark, and maybe was old Leviticus himself. Jim cleaned up the canoe, and I got my paddle ready. There was a big steamboat laying at the shore away up under the point, about three mile above town—been there a couple of hours—taking on freight. Says the king:

"Seein' how I'm dressed, I reckon maybe I better arrive down from St. Louis or Cincinnati, or some other big place. Go for the steamboat, Huckleberry; we'll come down to the village on her."

I didn't have to be ordered twice, to go and take a steamboat ride. I fetched the shore a half a mile above the village, and then went scooting along the bluff bank in the easy water. Pretty soon we come to a nice innocent looking young country jake setting on a log swabbing the sweat off of his face, for it was powerful warm weather; and he had a couple of big carpet bags by him.

"Run her nose in shore," says the king. I done it. "Wher' you bound for, young man?"

"For the steamboat; going to Orleans."

"Git aboard," says the king. "Hold on a minute, my servant 'll he'p you with them bags. Jump out and he'p the gentleman, Adolphus"—meaning me, I see.

I done so, and then we all three started on again. The young chap was mighty thankful; said it was tough work toting his baggage

ADOLPHUS.

such weather. He asked the king where he was going, and the king told him he'd come down the river and landed at the other village this morning, and now he was going up a few mile to see an old friend on a farm up there. The young fellow says:

"When I first see you, I says to myself, 'It's Mr. Wilks, sure, and he come mighty near getting here in time.' But then I says, again, 'No, I reckon it ain't him, or else he wouldn't be paddling up the river.' You *ain't* him, are you?"

"No, my name's Blodgett—Elexander Blodgett—*Reverend* Elexander Blodgett, I spose I must say, as I'm one o' the Lord's poor servants. But still I'm jest as able to be sorry for Mr. Wilks for not arriving in time, all the same, if he's missed anything by it—which I hope he hasn't."

"Well, he don't miss any property by it, because he'll get that, all right; but he's missed seeing his brother Peter die—which he mayn't mind, nobody can tell, as to that—but his brother would a give anything in this world to see *him* before he died; never talked about nothing else all these three weeks; hadn't seen him since they was boys together—and hadn't ever seen his brother William, at all— that's the deef and dumb one—William ain't more than thirty or thirty-five. Peter and George was the only ones that come out here; George was the married brother; him and his wife both died last year. Harvey and William's the only ones that's left, now; and as I was saying, they haven't got here in time."

"Did anybody send 'em word?"

"O, yes; a month or two ago, when Peter was first took; because Peter said, then, that he sorter felt like he warn't going to get well this time. You see, he was pretty old, and George's g'yirls was too young to be much company for him, except Mary Jane the red-headed one; and so he was kinder lonesome after George and his wife died, and didn't seem to care much to live. He most desperately wanted to see Harvey—and William too, for that matter—because he was one of them kind that can't bear to make a will. He left a letter behind, for Harvey, and said he'd told in it where his money was hid, and how he wanted the rest of the property divided up so George's g'yirls would be all right—for George didn't leave nothing. And that letter was all they could get him to put a pen to."

"Why do you reckon Harvey don't come? Wher' does he live?"

"O, he lives in England—Sheffield—preaches there—hasn't ever been in this country. He hasn't had any too much time—and besides he mightn't a got the letter at all, you know."

"Too bad, too bad he couldn't a lived to see his brothers, poor soul. You going to Orleans, you say?"

"Yes, but that ain't only a part of it. I'm going in a ship, next Wednesday, for Ryo Janeero, where my uncle lives."

"It's a pretty long journey. But it'll be lovely; I wisht I was agoing. Is Mary Jane the oldest? How old is the others?"

"Mary Jane's nineteen, Susan's fifteen, and Joanna's about fourteen—that's the one that gives herself to good works and has a hare-lip."

"Poor things! to be left alone in the cold world, so."

"Well, they could be worse off. Old Peter had friends, and they ain't going to let them come to no harm. There's Hobson, the Babtis' preacher; and deacon Lot Hovey, and Ben Rucker, and Abner Shackleford; and Levi Bell, the lawyer; and Dr. Robinson; and their wives; and the widow Bartley, and—well, there's a lot of them; but these are the ones that Peter was thickest with, and used to write about, sometimes, when he wrote home; so Harvey'll know where to look for friends when he gets here."

Well, the old man he went on asking questions till he just fairly emptied that young fellow. Blamed if he didn't inquire about everybody and every thing in that blessed town, and all about all the Wilkses; and about Peter's business—which was a tanner; and about George's—which was a carpenter; and about Harvey's— which was a dissentering minister; and so on, and so on. Then he says:

"What did you want to walk all the way up to the steamboat, for?"

"Because she's a big Orleans boat, and I was afeard she mightn't stop there. When they're deep they won't stop for a hail. A Cincinnati boat will, but this is a St. Louis one."

"Was Peter Wilks well off?"

HE FAIRLY EMPTIED THAT YOUNG FELLOW.

"O, yes, pretty well off. He had houses and land, and it's reckoned he left three or four thousand in cash hid up som'ers."

"When did you say he died?"

"I didn't say; but it was last night."

"Funeral to-morrow, likely?"

"Yes, 'bout the middle of the day."

"Well, it's all terrible sad; but we've all got to go, one time or another. So what we want to do is to be prepared; then we're all right."

"Yes, sir, it's the best way. Ma used to always say that."

When we struck the boat, she was about done loading, and pretty soon she got off. The king never said nothing about going aboard, so I lost my ride, after all. When the boat was gone, the king made me paddle up another mile, to a lonesome place, and then he got ashore and says:

"Now hustle back, right off, and fetch the duke up here, and the new carpet-bags. And if he's gone over to t'other side, go over there and git him. And tell him to git himself up regardless. Shove along, now."

I see what *he* was up to; but I never said nothing, of course. When I got back with the duke, we hid the canoe, and then they set down on a log, and the king told him everything, just like the young fellow had said it—every last word of it. And all the time he was a doing it, he tried to talk like an Englishman; and he done it pretty well, too, for a slouch. I can't imitate him, and so I ain't agoing to try to; but he really done it pretty good. Then he says:

"How are you on the deef and dumb, Bilgewater?"

The duke said, leave him alone for that; said he had played a deef and dumb person on the histrionic boards. So then they waited for a steamboat.

About the middle of the afternoon a couple of little boats come along, but they didn't come from high enough up the river; but at last there was a big one, and they hailed her. She sent out her yawl, and we went aboard, and she was from Cincinnati; and when they found we only wanted to go four or five mile, they was booming mad, and give us a cussing, and said they wouldn't land us. But the king was ca'm. He says:

"If gentlemen kin afford to pay a dollar a mile, apiece, to be took on and put off in a yawl, a steamboat kin afford to carry 'em, can't it?''

So they softened down and said it was all right; and when we got to the village, they yawled us ashore. About two dozen men flocked down, when they see the yawl a coming; and when the king says—

"Kin any of you gentlemen tell me wher' Mr. Peter Wilks lives?'' they give a glance at one another, and nodded their heads, as much as to say, "What d' I tell you?'' Then one of them says, kind of soft and gentle:

"I'm sorry, sir, but the best we can do is to tell you where he *did* live, yesterday evening.''

Sudden as winking, the ornery old cretur went all to smash, and fell up against the man, and put his chin on his shoulder, and cried down his back, and says:

"Alas, alas, our poor brother—gone, and we never got to see him; oh, it's too, *too* hard!''

Then he turns around, blubbering, and makes a lot of idiotic signs to the duke on his hands, and blamed if *he* didn't drop a carpet-bag

"ALAS, OUR POOR BROTHER.''

and bust out a-crying. If they warn't the beatenest lot, them two frauds, that ever I struck.

Well, the men gethered around, and sympathized with them, and said all sorts of kind things to them, and carried their carpet bags up the hill for them, and let them lean on them and cry, and told the king all about his brother's last moments, and the king he told it all over again on his hands to the duke, and both of them took on about that dead tanner like they'd lost the twelve disciples. Well, if ever I struck anything like it, I'm a nigger. It was enough to make a body ashamed of the human race.

Chapter XXV

"YOU BET IT IS."

The news was all over town in two minutes, and you could see the people tearing down on the run, from every which way, some of them putting on their coats as they come. Pretty soon we was in the middle of a crowd, and the noise of the tramping was like a soldier-march. The windows and door-yards was full; and every minute somebody would say, over a fence:

"Is it *them?*"

And somebody trotting along with the gang would answer back and say:

"You bet it is."

When we got to the house, the street in front of it was packed, and the three girls was standing in the door. Mary Jane *was* red-headed, but that don't make no difference, she was most awful beautiful, and her face and her eyes was all lit up like glory, she was so glad her uncles was come. The king he spread his arms, and Mary Jane she jumped for them, and the hare-lip jumped for the duke, and there they *had* it! Everybody, most, leastways women, cried for joy to see them meet at last and have such good times.

Then the king he hunched the duke, private—I see him do it—and then he looked around and see the coffin, over in the corner on two chairs; so then, him and the duke, with a hand across each other's shoulder, and t'other hand to their eyes, walked slow and solemn over there, everybody dropping back to give them room, and all the talk and noise stopping, people saying "Sh!" and all the men taking their hats off and drooping their heads, so you could a heard a pin fall. And when they got there, they bent over and looked in the coffin, and took one sight, and then they bust out a crying so you could a heard them to Orleans, most; and then they put their arms around each other's necks, and hung their chins over each other's shoulders; and then for three minutes, or maybe four, I never see two men leak the way they done. And mind you, everybody was doing the same; and the place was that damp I never see anything like it. Then one of them got on one side of the coffin, and t'other on t'other side, and they kneeled down and rested their foreheads on the coffin, and let on to pray, all to their selves. Well, when it come to that, it worked the crowd like you never see anything like it, and so everybody broke down and went to sobbing right out loud—the poor girls, too; and every woman, nearly, went up to the girls, without saying a word, and kissed them, solemn, on the forehead, and then put their hand on their head, and looked up towards the sky, with the tears running down, and then busted out and went off sobbing and swabbing, and give the next woman a show. I never see anything so disgusting.

Well, by and by the king he gets up and comes forward a little,

LEAKING.

and works himself up and slobbers out a speech, all full of tears and flapdoodle about its being a sore trial for him and his poor brother to lose the diseased, and to miss seeing diseased alive, after the long journey of four thousand mile, but it's a trial that's sweetened and sanctified to us by this dear sympathy and these holy tears, and so he thanks them out of his heart and out of his brother's heart, because out of their mouths they can't, words being too weak and cold, and all that kind of rot and slush, till it was just sickening; and then he blubbers out a pious goody-goody Amen, and turns himself loose and goes to crying fit to bust.

And the minute the words was out of his mouth somebody over in the crowd struck up the doxolojer, and everybody joined in with all their might, and it just warmed you up and made you feel as good as church letting out. Music *is* a good thing; and after all that soul-butter and hogwash, I never see it freshen up things so, and sound so honest and bully.

Then the king begins to work his jaw again, and says how him and his nieces would be glad if a few of the main principal friends of the family would take supper here with them this evening, and help set up with the ashes of the diseased; and says if his poor brother laying yonder could speak, he knows who he would name, for they was names that was very dear to him, and mentioned often in his letters; and so he will name the same, to-wit, as follows, vizz:—Rev. Mr. Hobson, and deacon Lot Hovey, and Mr. Ben Rucker, and Abner Shackleford, and Levi Bell, and Dr. Robinson, and their wives, and the widow Bartley.

Rev. Hobson and Dr. Robinson was down to the end of the town, a-hunting together; that is, I mean the doctor was shipping a sick man to t'other world, and the preacher was pinting him right. Lawyer Bell was away up to Louisville on some business. But the rest was on hand, and so they all come and shook hands with the king and thanked him and talked to him; and then they shook hands with the duke, and didn't say nothing, but just kept a-smiling and bobbing their heads like a passel of sapheads whilst he made all sorts of signs with his hands and said "Goo-goo—goo-goo-goo," all the time, like a baby that can't talk.

So the king he blatted along, and managed to inquire about pretty much everybody and dog in town, by his name, and mentioned all sorts of little things that happened one time or another in the town, or to George's family, or to Peter; and he always let on that Peter wrote him the things, but that was a lie, he got every blessed one of them out of that young flathead that we canoed up to the steamboat.

Then Mary Jane she fetched the letter her uncle left behind, and the king he read it out loud and cried over it. It give the dwelling house and three thousand dollars, gold, to the girls; and it give the tanyard, (which was doing a good business,) along with some other houses and land (worth about seven thousand,) and three thousand dollars in gold, to Harvey and William, and told where the six thousand cash was hid, down cellar. So these two frauds said they'd go and fetch it up, and have everything square and aboveboard; and told me to come with a candle. We shut the cellar door behind us, and when they found the bag they spilt it out on the floor, and it was a lovely sight, all them yaller-boys. My, the way the king's eyes did shine! He slaps the duke on the shoulder, and says:

"O, *this* ain't bully nor noth'n! O, no, I reckon not! Why, Biljy, it beats the Nonesuch, *don't* it!"

The duke allowed it did. They pawed the yaller-boys, and sifted them through their fingers and let them jingle down on the floor; and the king says:

"It ain't no use talkin': bein' brothers to a rich dead man, and representatives of furrin heirs that's got left, is the line for you and me, Bilge. Thish-yer comes of trust'n to Providence. It's the best way, in the long run. I've tried 'em all, and ther' ain't no better way."

Most everybody would a been satisfied with the pile, and took it on trust; but no, they must count it. So they counts it, and it comes out four hundred and fifteen dollars short. Says the king:

"Dern him, I wonder what he done with that four hunderd and fifteen dollars?"

They worried over that, a while, and ransacked all around for it. Then the duke says:

"Well, he was a pretty sick man, and likely he made a mistake— I reckon that's the way of it. The best way's to let it go, and keep still about it. We can spare it."

"Oh, shucks, yes, we can *spare* it. I don't k'yer noth'n 'bout that— it's the *count* I'm thinkin' about. We want to be awful square and open and aboveboard, here, you know. We want to lug thish-yer

money up stairs and count it before everybody—then ther' ain't
noth'n suspicious. But when the dead man says ther's six thous'n
dollars, you know, we don't want to—"

"Hold on," says the duke. "Less make up the deffisit"—and he
begun to haul out yaller-boys out of his pocket.

MAKING UP THE "DEFFISIT."

"It's a most amaz'n' good idea, duke—you *have* got a rattlin'
clever head on you," says the king. "Blest if the old Nonesuch ain't
a heppin' us out agin"—and *he* begun to haul out yaller-jackets and
stack them up.

It most busted them, but they made up the six thousand clean
and clear.

"Say," says the duke, "I got another idea. Le's go up stairs and
count this money, and then take and *give it to the girls.*"

"Good land, duke, lemme hug you! It's the most dazzling idea 'at
ever a man struck. You have cert'nly got the most astonishin' head
I ever see. O, this is the boss dodge, ther' ain't no mistake 'bout it.

Let 'em fetch along their suspicions, now, if they want to—this 'll lay 'em out.''

When we got up stairs, everybody gethered around the table, and the king he counted it and stacked it up, three hundred dollars in a pile—twenty elegant little piles. Everybody looked hungry at it, and licked their chops. Then they raked it into the bag again, and I see the king begin to swell himself up for another speech. He says:

"Friends all, my poor brother that lays yonder, has done generous by them that's left behind in the vale of sorrers. He has done generous by these-yer poor little lambs that he loved and sheltered, and that's left fatherless and motherless. Yes, and we that knowed him, knows that he would a done *more* generous by 'em if he hadn't ben afeard o' woundin' his dear William and me. Now, *wouldn't* he? Ther' ain't no question 'bout it, in *my* mind. Well, then—what kind o' brothers would it be, that 'd stand in his way at sech a time? And what kind o' uncles would it be that 'd rob—yes, *rob*—sech poor sweet lambs as these 'at he loved so, at sech a time? If I know William—and I *think* I do—he—well, I'll jest ask him." He turns around and begins to make a lot of signs to the duke with his hands; and the duke he looks at him stupid and leatherheaded a while, then all of a sudden he seems to catch his meaning, and jumps for the king goo-gooing with all his might for joy, and hugs him about fifteen times before he lets up. Then the king says, "I knowed it; I reckon *that*'ll convince anybody the way *he* feels about it. Here, Mary Jane, Susan, Joanner, take the money—take it *all*. It's the gift of him that lays yonder, cold but joyful."

Mary Jane she went for him, Susan and the hare-lip went for the duke, and then such another hugging and kissing I never see yet. And everybody crowded up, with the tears in their eyes, and most shook the hands off of them frauds, saying all the time:

"You *dear* good souls!—how *lovely!*—how *could* you!"

Well, then, pretty soon all hands got to talking about the diseased again, and how good he was, and what a loss he was, and all that; and before long a big iron-jawed man worked himself in there from outside, and stood a-listening and looking, and not saying anything; and nobody saying anything to him, either, because the king was talking and they was all busy listening. The king was saying—in the middle of something he'd started in on—

"—they bein' partickler friends o' the diseased. That's why they're invited here this evenin'; but to-morrow we want *all* to come—everybody; for he respected everybody, he liked everybody, and so it's fitten that his funeral orgies sh'd be public."

GOING FOR HIM.

And so he went a-mooning on and on, liking to hear himself talk, and every little while he fetched in his funeral orgies again, till the duke he couldn't stand it no more; so he writes on a little scrap of paper, "*obsequies*, you old fool," and folds it up and goes to goo-gooing and reaching it over people's heads to him. The king he reads it, and puts it in his pocket, and says:

"Poor William, afflicted as he is, his *heart's* aluz right. Asks me to invite everybody to come to the funeral—wants me to make 'em all welcome. But he needn't a worried—it was jest what I was at."

Then he weaves along, again, perfectly ca'm, and goes to dropping in his funeral orgies again every now and then, just like he done before. And when he done it the third time, he says:

"I say orgies, not because it's the common term, because it ain't—

obsequies bein' the common term—but because orgies is the right term. Obsequies ain't used in England no more, now—it's gone out. We say orgies, now, in England. Orgies is better, because it means the thing you're after, more exact. It's a word that's made up out'n the Greek *orgo*, outside, open, abroad; and the Hebrew *jeesum*, to plant, cover up; hence in*ter*. So, you see, funeral orgies is an open er public funeral."

He was the *worst* I ever struck. Well, the iron-jawed man he

THE DOCTOR.

laughed right in his face. Everybody was shocked. Everybody says, "Why *doctor!*" and Abner Shackleford says:

"Why, Robinson, hain't you heard the news? This is Harvey Wilks."

The king he smiled, eager, and shoved out his flapper, and says:

"*Is* it my poor brother's dear good friend and physician? I—"

"Keep your hands off of me!" says the doctor. "*You* talk like an Englishman—*don't* you? It's the worst imitation I ever heard. *You* Peter Wilks's brother. You're a fraud, that's what you are!"

Well, how they all took on! They crowded around the doctor, and tried to quiet him down, and tried to explain to him, and tell him how Harvey'd showed in forty ways that he *was* Harvey, and knowed everybody by name, and the names of the very dogs, and begged and *begged* him not to hurt Harvey's feelings and the poor girls' feelings, and all that; but it warn't no use, he stormed right along, and said any man that pretended to be an Englishman and couldn't imitate the lingo no better than what he did, was a fraud and a liar. The poor girls was hanging to the king and crying; and all of a sudden the doctor ups and turns on *them*. He says:

"I was your father's friend, and I'm your friend; and I warn you *as* a friend, and an honest one, that wants to protect you and keep you out of harm and trouble, to turn your backs on that scoundrel, and have nothing to do with him, the ignorant tramp, with his idiotic Greek and Hebrew as he calls it. He is the thinnest kind of an imposter—has come here with a lot of empty names and facts which he has picked up somewhere, and you take them for *proofs*, and are helped to fool yourselves by these foolish friends here, who ought to know better. Mary Jane Wilks, you know me for your friend, and for your unselfish friend, too. Now listen to me; turn this pitiful rascal out—I *beg* you to do it. Will you?"

Mary Jane straightened herself up, and my, but she was handsome! She says:

"*Here* is my answer." She hove up the bag of money, and put it in the king's hands, and says, "Take this six thousand dollars, and invest for me and my sisters any way you want to, and don't give us no receipt for it."

Then she put her arm around the king on one side, and Susan and the hare-lip done the same on the other. Everybody clapped their hands and stomped on the floor like a perfect storm, whilst the king held up his head and smiled proud. The doctor says:

"All right, I wash *my* hands of the matter. But I warn you all that a time's coming when you're going to feel sick whenever you think of this day"—and away he went.

"All right, doctor" says the king, kinder mocking him, "we'll try and git 'em to send for you"—which made them all laugh, and they said it was a prime good hit.

THE BAG OF MONEY.

Chapter XXVI

THE CUBBY.

Well, when they was all gone, the king he asks Mary Jane how they was off for spare rooms, and she said she had one spare room, which would do for uncle William, and she'd give her own room to uncle Harvey, which was a little bigger, and she would turn into the room with her sisters and sleep on a cot; and up garret was a little cubby, with a pallet in it. The king said the cubby would do for his valley—meaning me.

So Mary Jane took us up, and she showed them their rooms, which was plain but nice. She said she'd have her frocks and a lot of other traps took out of her room if they was in uncle Harvey's way, but he said they warn't. The frocks was hung along the wall, and before them was a curtain made out of calico that hung down to the floor. There was an old hair trunk in one corner, and a guitar box in another, and all sorts of little knick-knacks and jimcracks around, like girls brisken up a room with. The king said it was all the more homely and more pleasanter for these fixings, and so don't disturb them. The duke's room was pretty small, but plenty good enough, and so was my cubby.

That night they had a big supper, and all them men and women was there, and I stood behind the king and the duke's chairs and waited on them, and the niggers waited on the rest. Mary Jane she set at the head of the table, with Susan alongside of her, and said how bad the biscuits was, and how mean the preserves was, and how ornery and tough the fried chickens was,—and all that kind of rot, the way women always do for to force out compliments; and the people all knowed everything was tip-top, and said so—said "How *do* you get biscuits to brown so nice?" and "Where, for the land's sake *did* you get these amaz'n pickles?" and all that kind of humbug talky-talk, just the way people always does at a supper, you know.

And when it was all done, me and the hare-lip had supper in the kitchen off of the leavings, whilst the others was helping the niggers clean up the things. The hare-lip she got to pumping me about England, and blest if I didn't think the ice was getting mighty thin, sometimes. She says:

"Did you ever see the king?"

"Who? William Fourth? Well, I bet I have—he goes to our church." I knowed he was dead years ago, but I never let on. So when I says he goes to our church, she says:

"What—regular?"

"Yes—regular. His pew's right over opposite ourn—on t'other side the pulpit."

SUPPER WITH THE HARE-LIP.

"I thought he lived in London?"

"Well, he does. Where *would* he live?"

"But I thought *you* lived in Sheffield?"

I see I was up a stump. I had to let on to get choked with a chicken bone, so as to get time to think how to get down again. Then I says:

"I mean he goes to our church regular when he's in Sheffield. That's only in the summer time, when he comes there to take the sea baths."

"Why, how you talk—Sheffield ain't on the sea."

"Well, who said it was?"

"Why, you did."

"I *didn't*, nuther."

"You did!"

"I didn't."

"You did."

"I never said nothing of the kind."

"Well, what *did* you say, then?"

"Said he come to take the sea *baths*—that's what I said."

"Well, then!—how's he going to take the sea baths if it ain't on the sea?"

"Looky here," I says; "did you ever see any Congress-water?"

"Yes."

"Well, did you have to go to Congress to get it?"

"Why, no."

"Well, neither does William Fourth have to go to the sea to get a sea bath."

"How does he get it, then?"

"Gets it the way people down here gets Congress-water—in barrels. There in the palace at Sheffield they've got furnaces, and he wants his water hot. They can't bile that amount of water away off there at the sea. They haven't got no conveniences for it."

"O, I see, now. You might a said that in the first place, and saved time."

When she said that, I see I was out of the woods again, and so I was comfortable and glad. Next, she says:

"Do you go to church, too?"

"Yes—regular."

"Where do you set?"

"Why, in our pew."

"*Whose* pew?"

"Why, *ourn*—your uncle Harvey's."

"His'n? What does *he* want with a pew?"

"Wants it to set in. What did you *reckon* he wanted with it?"

"Why, I thought he'd be in the pulpit."

Rot him, I forgot he was a preacher. I see I was up a stump again; so I played another chicken bone and got another think. Then I says:

"Blame it, do you suppose there ain't but one preacher to a church?"

"Why, what do they want with more?"

"What!—to preach before a king? I never see such a girl as you. They don't have no less than seventeen."

"Seventeen! My land! Why, I wouldn't set out such a string as that, not if I *never* got to glory. It must take 'em a week."

"Shucks, they don't *all* of 'em preach the same day—only *one* of 'em."

"Well, then, what does the rest of 'em do?"

"Oh, nothing much. Loll around, pass the plate—and one thing or another. But mainly they don't do nothing."

"Well, then, what are they *for?*"

"Why, they're for *style*. Don't you know nothing?"

"Well, I don't *want* to know no such foolishness as that. How is servants treated in England? Do they treat 'em better'n we treat our niggers?"

"*No!* A servant ain't nobody, there. They treat them worse than dogs."

"Don't they give 'em holidays, the way we do, Christmas, and New Year's week, and fourth of July?"

"Oh, just listen! A body could tell *you* hain't ever been to England, by that. Why, Hare-l—why, Joanna, they never see a holiday from year's end to year's end; never go to the circus, nor theatre, nor nigger shows, nor nowheres."

"Nor church?"

"Nor church."

"But *you* always went to church."

Well, I was gone up again. I forgot I was the old man's servant. But next minute I whirled in on a kind of an explanation how a valley was different from a common servant, and *had* to go to church whether he wanted to or not, and set with the family, on account of it's being the law. But I didn't do it pretty good, and when I got done I see she warn't satisfied. She says:

"Honest injun, now, hain't you been telling me a lot of lies?"

"Honest injun," says I.

"None of it at all?"

"None of it at all. Not a lie in it," says I.

"Lay your hand on this book and say it."

"HONEST INJUN."

I see it warn't nothing but a dictionary, so I laid my hand on it and said it. So then she looked a little better satisfied, and says:

"Well, then, I'll believe some of it; but I hope to gracious if I'll believe the rest."

"What is it you won't believe, Joe?" says Mary Jane, stepping in, with Susan behind her. "It ain't right nor kind for you to talk so to him, and him a stranger and so far from his people. How would you like to be treated so?"

"That's always your way, Maim—always sailing in to help somebody before they're hurt. I hain't done nothing to him. He's told some stretchers, I reckon; and I said I wouldn't swallow it all; and that's every bit and grain I *did* say. I reckon he can stand a little thing like that, can't he?"

"I don't care whether 'twas little or whether 'twas big, he's here in our house and a stranger, and it wasn't good of you to say it. If you was in his place, it would make you feel ashamed; and so you oughtn't to say a thing to another person that will make *them* feel ashamed."

"Why, Maim, he said—"

"It don't make no difference what he *said*—that ain't the thing. The thing is for you to treat him *kind*, and not be saying things to make him remember he ain't in his own country and amongst his own folks."

I says to myself, *This* is a girl that I'm letting that old reptle rob her of her money!

Then Susan *she* waltzed in; and if you'll believe me, she did give Hare-Lip hark from the tomb!

Says I to myself, And this is *another* one that I'm letting him rob her of her money!

Then Mary Jane she took another inning, and went in sweet and lovely again—which was her way—but when she got done there warn't hardly anything left o' poor Hare-Lip. So she hollered.

"All right, then," says the other girls, "you just ask his pardon."

She done it, too. And she done it beautiful. She done it so beautiful it was good to hear; and I wished I could tell her a thousand lies, so she could do it again.

I says to myself, This is *another* one that I'm letting him rob her of her money. And when she got through, they all jest laid theirselves out to make me feel at home and know I was amongst friends. I felt so ornery and low down and mean, that I says to myself, My mind's made up; I'll hive that money for them or bust.

So then I lit out—for bed, I said, meaning some time or another. When I got by myself, I went to thinking the thing over. I says to myself, Shall I go to that doctor, private, and blow on these frauds? No—that won't do. He might tell who told him; then the king and the duke would make it warm for me. Shall I go, private, and tell Mary Jane? No—I dasn't do it. Her face would give them a hint, sure; they've got the money, and they'd slide right out and get away with it. If she was to fetch in help, I'd get mixed up in the business, before it was done with, I judge. No, there ain't no good way but one: I got to steal that money, somehow; and I got to steal it some way that they won't suspicion that I done it. They've got a good thing, here; and they ain't agoing to leave till they've played this family and this town for all they're worth, so I'll find a chance time enough. I'll steal it, and hide it; and by and by, when I'm away down the river, I'll write a letter and tell Mary Jane where it's hid. But I better hive it to-night, if I can, because the doctor maybe hasn't let up as much as he lets on he has; he might scare them out of here, yet.

So, thinks I, I'll go and search them rooms. Up stairs the hall was dark, but I found the duke's room, and started to paw around it with my hands; but I recollected it wouldn't be much like the king to let anybody else take care of that money but his own self; so then I went to his room and begun to paw around there. But I see I couldn't do nothing without a candle, and I dasn't light one, of course. So I judged I'd got to do the other thing—lay for them, and eavesdrop. About that time, I hears their footsteps coming, and was going to skip under the bed; I reached for it, but it wasn't where I thought it would be; but I touched the curtain that hid Mary Jane's frocks, so I jumped in behind that and snuggled in amongst the gowns, and stood there perfectly still.

They come in and shut the door; and the first thing the duke done was to get down and look under the bed. Then I was glad I hadn't found the bed when I wanted it. And yet you know it's kind of natural to hide under the bed when you are up to anything private. They sets down, then, and the king says:

"Well, what is it? And cut it middlin' short, because it's better for us to be down there a whoopin'-up the mournin', than up here givin' 'em a chance to talk us over."

"Well, this is it, Capet. I ain't easy; I ain't comfortable. That doctor lays on my mind. I wanted to know your plans. I've got a notion, and I think it's a sound one."

"What is it, duke?"

"That we better glide out of this, before three in the morning, and clip it down the river with what we've got. Specially, seeing we

THE DUKE LOOKS UNDER THE BED.

got it so easy—*given* back to us, flung at our heads, as you may say, when of course we allowed to have to steal it back. I'm for knocking off and lighting out.''

That made me feel pretty bad. About an hour or two ago, it would a been a little different, but now it made me feel bad and disappointed. The king rips out and says:

''What! And not sell out the rest o' the property? March off like a passel o' fools and leave eight or nine thous'n' dollars' worth o' property layin' around jest sufferin' to be scooped in?—and all good saleable stuff, too.''

The duke he grumbled; said the bag of gold was enough, and he didn't want to go no deeper—didn't want to rob a lot of orphans of *everything* they had.

''Why, how you talk!'' says the king. ''We shan't rob 'em of nothing at all but jest this money. The people that *buys* the property is the suff'rers; because as soon's it's found out 'at we didn't own it—which won't be long after we've slid—the sale won't be valid, and it'll all go back to the estate. These-yer orphans 'll git their house back agin, and that's enough for *them*: they're young, and spry, and k'n easy earn a livin'. *They* ain't agoing to suffer. Why, jest think—there's thous'n's and thous'n's that ain't nigh so well off. Bless you, *they* ain't got noth'n to complain of."

Well, the king he talked him blind; so at last he give in, and said all right, but said he believed it was blame' foolishness to stay, and that doctor hanging over them. But the king says:

"Cuss the doctor! What do we k'yer for *him?* Hain't we got all the fools in town on our side? and ain't that a big enough majority in any town?"

So they got ready to go down stairs again. The duke says:

"I don't think we put that money in a good place."

That cheered me up. I'd begun to think I warn't going to get a hint of no kind to help me. The king says:

"Why?"

"Because Mary Jane'll be in mourning from this out; and first you know the nigger that does up the rooms will get an order to box these duds up and put 'em away; and do you reckon a nigger can run across money and not borrow some of it?"

"Your head's level, agin, duke," says the king; and he come a fumbling under the curtain two or three foot from where I was. I stuck tight to the wall, and kept mighty still, though quivery; and I wondered what them fellows would say to me if they catched me; and I tried to think what I'd better do if they did catch me. But the king he got the bag before I could think more than about a half a thought, and he never suspicioned I was around. They took and shoved the bag through a rip in the straw tick that was under the feather bed, and crammed it in a foot or two amongst the straw, and said it was all right, now, because a nigger only makes up the feather bed, and don't turn over the straw tick only about twice a year, and so it warn't in no danger of getting stole, now.

But I knowed better. I had it out of there before they was half way down stairs. I groped along up to my cubby, and hid it there till I could get a chance to do better. I judged I better hide it outside of the house somewheres, because if they missed it they would give the house a good ransacking, I knowed that very well. Then I turned in, with my clothes all on; but I couldn't a gone to sleep, if I'd a wanted to, I was in such a sweat to get through with the business. By and by I heard the king and the duke come up; so I rolled off of my pallet and laid with my chin at the top of my ladder and waited to see if anything was going to happen. But nothing did.

So I held on till all the late sounds had quit and the early ones hadn't begun, yet; and then I slipped down the ladder.

HUCK TAKES THE MONEY.

Chapter XXVI.

A CRACK IN THE
DINING ROOM DOOR.

I crept to their doors and listened; they was snoring, so I tip-toed along, and got down stairs all right. There warn't a sound anywheres. I peeped through a crack of the dining room door, and see the men that was watching the corpse all sound asleep on their chairs. The door was open into the parlor, where the corpse was laying, and there was a candle in both rooms. I passed along, and the parlor door was open; but I see there warn't nobody in there but the remainders of Peter; so I shoved on by; but the front door was locked, and the key wasn't there. Just then I heard somebody coming down the stairs, back behind me. I run in the parlor, and took a swift look around, and the only place I see to hide the bag, was in the coffin. The lid was shoved along about a foot, showing the dead man's face down in there, with a wet cloth over it, and his shroud on. I tucked the money bag in under the lid, just down beyond where his hands was crossed, which made me creep, they was so cold, and then I run back across the room and in behind the door.

The person coming was Mary Jane. She went to the coffin, very soft, and kneeled down and looked in; then she put up her handkerchief and I see she begun to cry, though I couldn't hear her, and her back was to me. I slid out, and as I passed the dining room I thought I'd make sure them watchers hadn't seen me; so I looked through the crack and everything was all right. They hadn't stirred.

I slipped up to bed, feeling ruther blue, on accounts of the thing
playing out that way after I had took so much trouble and run so
much resk about it. Says I, if it could stay where it is, all right;
because when we get down the river a hundred mile or two, I could
write back to Mary Jane, and she could dig him up again and get it;
but that ain't the thing that's going to happen; the thing that's going
to happen, is, the money'll be found when they come to screw on
the lid. Then the king 'll get it again, and it'll be a long day before he
gives anybody another chance to smouch it from him. Of course I
wanted to slide down and get it out of there, but I dasn't try it. Every
minute it was getting earlier, now, and pretty soon some of them
watchers would begin to stir, and I might get catched—catched
with six thousand dollars in my hands that nobody hadn't hired me
to take care of. I don't wish to be mixed up in no such business as
that, I says to myself.

When I got down stairs in the morning, the parlor was shut up,
and the watchers was gone. There warn't nobody around but the
family and the widow Bartley and our tribe. I watched their faces to
see if anything had been happening, but
I couldn't tell.

Towards the middle of the day the
undertaker come, with his man, and
they set the coffin in the middle of the
room on a couple of chairs, and then set
all our chairs in rows, and borrowed
more from the neighbors till the hall
and the parlor and the dining room was
full. I see the coffin lid was the way it
was before, but I dasn't go to look in
under it, with folks around.

Then the people begun to flock in,
and the beats and the girls took seats in
the front row at the head of the coffin,
and for a half an hour the people filed
around slow, in single rank, and looked
down at the dead man's face a minute,
and some dropped in a tear, and it was
all very still and solemn, only the girls

THE UNDERTAKER.

and the beats holding handkerchiefs to their eyes and keeping their heads bent, and sobbing a little. There warn't no other sound but the scraping of the feet on the floor, and blowing noses—because people always blows them more at a funeral than they do at other places except church.

When the place was packed full, the undertaker he slid around in his black gloves with his softy soothering ways, putting on the last touches, and getting people and things all ship-shape and comfortable, and making no more sound than a cat. He never spoke; he moved people around, he squeezed in late ones, he opened up passage-ways, and done it all with nods, and signs with his hands. Then he took his place over against the wall. He was the softest, glidingest, stealthiest man I ever see; and there warn't no more smile to him than there is to a ham.

They had borrowed a melodeum—a sick one; and when everything was ready, a young woman set down and worked it, and it was pretty skreeky and colicky, and everybody joined in and sung, and Peter was the only one that had a good thing, according to my notion. Then the Reverend Hobson opened up, slow and solemn, and begun to talk; and straight off the most outrageous row busted out in the cellar a body ever heard; it was only one dog, but he made a most powerful racket, and he kept it up, right along; the parson he had to stand there, over the coffin, and wait—you couldn't hear yourself think. It was right down awkward, and nobody didn't seem to know what to do. But pretty soon they see that long-legged undertaker make a sign to the preacher as much as to say, "Don't you worry—just depend on me." Then he stooped down and begun to glide along the wall, just his shoulders showing over the people's heads. So he glided along, and the pow-wow and racket getting more and more outrageous all the time; and at last, when he had gone around two sides of the room, he disappears down cellar. Then, in about two seconds we heard a whack, and the dog he finished up with a most amazing howl or two and then everything was dead still, and the parson begun his solemn talk where he left off. In a minute or two here comes this undertaker's back and shoulders gliding along the wall again; and so he glided, and glided, around three sides of the room, and then rose up, and shaded his mouth with his hands, and stretched his neck out towards the preacher, over the people's heads, and says, in a kind of a coarse whisper, *"He had a rat!"* Then he drooped down and glided along the wall again, to his place. You could see it was a great satisfaction to the people, because naturally they wanted to know. A little thing like that don't cost nothing, and it's just the little things that makes a man to be looked up to and liked. There warn't no more popular man in town than what that undertaker was.

"HE HAD A RAT!"

Well, the funeral sermon was very good, but pison-long and tiresome; and then the king he shoved in and got off some of his usual rubbage, and at last the job was through, and the undertaker begun to sneak up on the coffin with his screw-driver. I was in a sweat, then, and watched him pretty keen. But he never meddled at all; just slid the lid along, as soft as mush, and screwed it down tight and fast. So there I was! I didn't know whether the money was in there or not. So, says I, spose somebody has hogged that bag, on the sly?—now how do *I* know whether to write to Mary Jane or not? Spose she dug him up and didn't find nothing—what would she think of me? Blame it, I says, I might get hunted up and jailed; I'd better lay low and keep dark, and not write at all; the thing's awful mixed, now; trying to better it, I've worsened it a hundred times, and I wish to goodness I'd just let it alone, dad fetch the whole business!

They buried him, and we come back home, and I went to watching faces again—I couldn't help it, and I couldn't rest easy. But nothing come of it; the faces didn't tell me nothing.

The king he visited around, in the evening, and sweetened everybody up, and made himself ever so friendly; and he give out the idea that his congregation over in England would be in a sweat about him, so he must hurry and settle up the estate right away, and leave for home. He was very sorry he was so pushed, and so was everybody; they wished he could stay longer, but they said they could see it couldn't be done. And he said of course him and William would take the girls home with them; and that pleased everybody too, because then the girls would be well fixed, and amongst their own relations; and it pleased the girls, too—tickled them so they clean forgot they ever had a trouble in the world; and told him to sell out as quick as he wanted to, they would be ready. Them poor things was that glad and happy it made my heart ache to see them getting fooled and lied to, so, but I didn't see no safe way for me to chip in and change the general tune.

Well, blamed if the king didn't bill the house and the niggers and all the property for auction straight off—sale two days after the funeral; but anybody could buy private beforehand if they wanted to.

So the next day after the funeral, along about noontime, the girls' joy got the first jolt: a couple of nigger traders come along, and the king sold them the niggers reasonable, for three-day drafts as they called it, and away they went—the two sons up the river to Memphis, and their mother down the river to Orleans. I thought them poor girls and them niggers would break their hearts for grief; they cried around each other, and took on so it most made me down sick to see it. The girls said they hadn't ever dreamed of seeing the family separated or sold away from the town. I can't ever get it out of my memory, the sight of them poor miserable girls and niggers hanging around each other's necks and crying; and I reckon I couldn't a stood it all but would a had to bust out and tell on our gang if I hadn't knowed the sale warn't no account and the niggers would be back home in a week or two.

The thing made a big stir in the town, too, and a good many come out flatfooted and said it was scandalous to separate the mother and the children that way. It injured the frauds some, but the old fool he bulled right along, spite of all the duke could say or do, and I tell you the duke was powerful uneasy.

Next day was auction day. About broad-day in the morning, the king and the duke come up in the garret and woke me up, and I see by their look that there was trouble. The king says:

"Was you in my room night before last?"

"No, your majesty"—which was the way I always called him when nobody but our gang warn't around.

"WAS YOU IN MY ROOM?"

"Was you in there yesterday er last night?"

"No, your majesty."

"Honor bright, now—no lies."

"Honor bright, your majesty, I'm telling you the truth. I hain't been anear your room since Miss Mary Jane took you and the duke and showed it to you."

The duke says:

"Have you seen anybody else go in there?"

"No, your grace, not as I remember, I believe."

"Stop and think."

I studied a while, and see my chance; then I says:

"Well, I see the niggers go in there several times."

Both of them give a little jump; and looked like they hadn't ever expected it, and then like they *had*. Then the duke says:

"What, *all* of them?"

"No—leastways not all at once. That is, I don't think I ever see them all come *out* at once but just one time."

"Hello—when was that?"

"It was the day we had the funeral. In the morning. It warn't early, because I overslept. I was just starting down the ladder, and I see them."

"Well, go on, *go* on—what did they do? how'd they act?"

"They didn't do nothing. And they didn't act anyway, much, as fur as I see. They tip-toed away; so, I seen, easy enough, that they'd shoved in there to do up your majesty's room, or something, sposing you was up; and found you *warn't* up, and so they was hoping to slide out of the way of trouble without waking you up, if they hadn't already waked you up."

"Great guns, *this* is a go!" says the king; and both of them looked pretty sick, and tolerable silly. They stood there a thinking and scratching their heads, a minute, and then the duke he bust into a kind of a little raspy chuckle, and says:

"It does beat all, how neat the niggers played their hand. They let on to be *sorry* they was going out of this region! and I believed they *was* sorry. And so did you, and so did everybody. Don't ever tell *me*, any more, that a nigger ain't got any histrionic talent. Why, the way they played that thing, it would fool *anybody*. In my opinion, there's a fortune in 'em. If I had capital and a theatre, I wouldn't want a better layout than that—and here we've gone and sold 'em for a song. Yes, and ain't privileged to sing the song, yet. Say, where *is* that song?—that draft."

"In the bank for to be collected. Where *would* it be?"

"Well, *that's* all right, then, thank goodness."

Says I, kind of timid-like:

"Is something gone wrong?"

The king whirls on me and rips out:

"None o' your business! You keep your head shet, and mind y'r own affairs—if you got any. Long as you're in this town, don't you forgit *that*, you hear?" Then he says to the duke, "We got to jest swaller it, and say noth'n: mum's the word, for *us*."

As they was starting down the ladder, the duke he chuckles again, and says:

"Quick sales *and* small profits! It's a good business—yes."

The king snarls around on him and says:

"I was trying to do for the best, in sellin' 'm out so quick. If the profits has turned out to be none, lackin' considable, and none to carry, is it my fault any more'n it's yourn?"

"Well, *they*'d be in this house yet, and we *wouldn't*, if I could a got my advice listened to."

The king sassed back, as much as was safe for him, and then swapped around and lit into *me* again. He give me down the banks for not coming and *telling* him I see the niggers come out of his room acting that way—said any fool would a *knowed* something was up. And then waltzed in and cussed *himself* a while; and said it all come of him not laying late and taking his natural rest that morning, and he'd be blamed if he'd ever do it again. So they went off a-jawing; and I felt dreadful glad I'd worked it all off onto the niggers and yet hadn't done the niggers no harm by it.

JAWING.

Chapter XXVIII

IN TROUBLE.

By and by it was getting-up time; so I come down the ladder and started for down stairs, but as I come to the girls' room, the door was open, and I see Mary Jane setting by her old hair trunk, which was open and she'd been packing things in it—getting ready to go to England. But she had stopped, now, with a folded gown in her lap, and had her face in her hands, crying. I felt awful bad to see it; of course anybody would. I went in there, and says:

"Miss Mary Jane, you can't abear to see people in trouble, and I can't—most always. Tell me about it."

So she done it. And it was the niggers—I just expected it. She said the beautiful trip to England was most about spoiled for her; she didn't know *how* she was ever going to be happy there, knowing the mother and the children warn't ever going to see each other no more—and then busted out bitterer than ever, and flung up her hands and says:

"O, dear, dear, to think they ain't *ever* going to see each other any more!"

"But they *will*—and inside of two weeks—and I *know* it!" says I.

Laws, it was out before I could think!—and before I could budge, she throws her arms around my neck, and told me to say it *again*, say it *again*, say it *again*!

I see I had spoke too sudden, and said too much, and was in a close place. I asked her to let me think, a minute; and she set there, very impatient and excited and handsome, but looking kind of happy and eased-up, like a person that's had a tooth pulled out. So I went to studying it out. I says to myself, I reckon a body that ups and tells the truth when he is in a tight place, is taking considerable many resks; though I ain't had no experience, and can't say for certain; but it looks so to me, anyway; and yet here's a case where I'm blest if it don't look to me like the truth is better, and actuly *safer*, than a lie. I must lay it by in my mind, and think it over some time or other, it's so kind of strange and unregular. I never see nothing like it. Well, I says to myself, at last, I'm agoing to chance it; I'll up and tell the truth this time, though it does seem most like setting down on a kag of powder and touching it off, just to see where you'll go to. Then I says:

"Miss Mary Jane, is there any place, out of town a little ways, where you could go and stay three or four days?"

"Yes—Mr. Lothrop's. Why?"

"Never mind why, yet. If I'll tell you how I know the niggers will see each other again—inside of two weeks—here in this house—and *prove* how I know it—will you go to Mr. Lothrop's and stay four days?"

"Four days!" she says; "I'll stay a year!"

"All right," I says, "I don't want nothing more out of *you* than just your word—I druther have it than another man's kiss-the-Bible." She smiled, and reddened up very sweet, and I says, "if you don't mind it, I'll shut the door—and bolt it."

Then I come back and set down again, and says:

"Don't you holler. Just set still, and take it like a man. I got to tell the truth, and you want to brace up, Miss Mary, because it's a bad kind, and going to be hard to take, but there ain't no help for it. These uncles of yourn ain't no uncles at all—they're a couple of frauds—regular dead-beats. There, now, we're over the worst of it—you can stand the rest middling easy."

It jolted her up, like everything, of course; but I was over the shoal water, now, so I went right along,—her eyes a-blazing higher and higher all the time—and told her every blame thing, from where we first struck that young fool going up to the steamboat, clear

through to where she flung herself onto the king's breast at the front
door and he kissed her sixteen or seventeen times—and then up she
jumps, with her face afire like sunset, and says:

"The brute! Come—don't waste a minute—not a *second*—we'll
have them tarred and feathered, and flung in the river!"

Says I:

"Cert'nly. But do you mean, *before* you go to Mr. Lothrop's,
or—"

Kemble

INDIGNATION.

"O," she says, "what am I *thinking*
about!" she says, and set right down
again. "Don't mind what I said—
please don't—you *won't*, now, *will*
you?" laying her silky hand on mine
in that kind of a way that I said I would
die first. "I never thought, I was so
stirred up," she says; "now go on, and
I won't do so any more. You tell me
what to do, and whatever you say, I'll
do it."

"Well," I says, "it's a rough gang,
them two frauds, and I'm fixed so I got
to travel with them a while longer,
whether I want to or not—I druther
not tell you why—and if you was to
blow on them this town would get me
out of their claws, and I'd be all right,
but there'd be another person that you
don't know about who'd be in big trouble. Well, we got to save *him*
hain't we? Of course. Well then, we won't blow on them."

Saying them words put a good idea in my head. I see how maybe
I could get me and Jim rid of the frauds: get them jailed, here, and
then leave. But I didn't want to run the raft in daytime, without
anybody aboard to answer questions but me; so I didn't want the
plan to begin working till pretty late to-night. I says:

"Miss Mary Jane, I'll tell you what we'll do—and you won't have
to stay at Mr. Lothrop's so long, nuther. How fur is it?"

"A little short of four miles—right out in the country, back here."

"Well, that'll answer. Now you go along out there, and lay low till nine or half-past, to-night, and then get them to fetch you home again—tell them you've thought of something. If you get here before eleven, put a candle in this window, and if I don't turn up, wait *till* eleven, and *then* if I don't turn up, it means I'm gone, and out of the way, and safe. Then you come out and spread the news around, and get these beats jailed."

"Good," she says, "I'll do it."

"And if it just happens so that I don't get away, but get took up, along with them, you must up and say I told you the whole thing beforehand, and you must stand by me all you can."

"Stand by you, indeed I will. They shan't touch a hair of your head!" she says, and I see her nostrils spread and her eyes snap when she said it, too.

"If I get away, I shan't be here," I says, "to prove these rapscallions ain't your uncles, and I couldn't do it if I *was* here. I could swear they was beats and bummers, that's all; though that's worth something. Well, there's others can do that, better than what I can—and they're people that ain't going to be doubted as quick as I'd be. I'll tell you how to find them. Gimme a pencil and a piece of paper. There—'*Royal Nonesuch, Bricksville.*' Put it away, and don't lose it. When the court wants to find out something about these two, let them send up to Bricksville and say they've got the men that played the Royal Nonesuch, and ask for some witnesses—why, you'll have that entire town down here before you can hardly wink, Miss Mary. And they'll come a-biling, too."

HOW TO FIND THEM.

I judged we had got everything fixed about right, now. So I says:

"Just let the auction go right along, and don't worry. Nobody don't have to pay for the things they buy till a whole day after the auction, on accounts of the short notice, and they ain't going out of this till they get that money—and the way we've fixed it the sale ain't going to count, and they ain't going to *get* no money. It's just like the way it was with the niggers—it warn't no sale, and the niggers will be back before long. Why, they can't collect the money for the *niggers*, yet—they're in the worst kind of a fix, Miss Mary."

"Well," she says, "I'll run down to breakfast, now, and then I'll start straight for Mr. Lothrop's."

"'Deed, *that* ain't the ticket, Miss Mary Jane," I says, "by no manner of means; go *before* breakfast."

"Why?"

"What did you reckon I wanted you to go at all, for, Miss Mary?"

"Well, I never thought—and come to think, I don't know. What was it?"

"Why, it's because you ain't one of these leather-face people. I don't want no better book than what your face is. A body can set down and read it off like coarse print. Do you reckon you can go and face your uncles, when they come to kiss you good-morning, and never—"

"There, there, don't! Yes, I'll go before breakfast—I'll be glad to. And leave my sisters with them?"

"Yes—never mind about them. They've got to stand it yet awhile. They might suspicion something if all of you was to go. I don't want you to see them, nor your sisters, nor nobody in this town—if a neighbor was to ask how is your uncles this morning, your face would tell something. No, you go right along, Miss Mary Jane, and I'll fix it with all of them. I'll tell Miss Susan to give your love to your uncles and say you've went away for a few hours for to get a little rest and change, or to see a friend, and you'll be back to-night or early in the morning."

"Gone to see a friend is all right, but I won't have my love given to them."

"Well, then, it shan't be." It was well enough to tell *her* so—no harm in it. It was only a little thing to do, and no trouble; and it's the little things that smoothes people's roads the most, down here below; it would make Mary Jane comfortable, and it wouldn't cost nothing. Then I says: "There's one more thing—that bag of money."

"Well, they've got that; and it makes me feel pretty silly to think *how* they got it."

"No, you're out, there. They hain't got it."

"Why, who's got it?"

"I wish I knowed, but I don't. I *had* it, because I stole it from them; and I stole it to give to you; and I know where I hid it, but I'm afraid it ain't there no more. I'm awful sorry, Miss Mary Jane, I'm just as sorry as I can be; but I done the best I could; I did, honest. I come nigh getting caught, and I had to shove it into the first place I come to, and run—and it warn't a good place."

"O, stop blaming yourself—it's too bad to do it, and I won't allow it—you couldn't help it; it wasn't your fault. Where did you hide it?"

I didn't want to set her to thinking about her troubles again; and I couldn't seem to get my mouth to tell her what would make her see that corpse laying in the coffin with that bag of money on his stomach. So, for a minute I didn't say nothing—then I says:

"I'd rather not *tell* you where I put it, Miss Mary Jane, if you don't mind letting me off; but I'll write it for you on a piece of paper, and you can read it along the road to Mr. Lothrop's, if you want to. Do you reckon that'll do?"

"O, yes."

HE WROTE.

So I wrote: "I put it in the coffin. It was in there when you was crying there, away in the night. I was behind the door, and I was mighty sorry for you, Miss Mary Jane."

It made my eyes water a little, to remember her crying there all by herself in the night, and them devils laying there right under her own roof, shaming her and robbing her; and when I folded it up and give it to her, I see the water come into her eyes, too; and she shook me by the hand, hard, and says:

"*Good*-bye—I'm going to do everything just as you've told me; and if I don't ever see you again, I shan't ever forget you, and I'll think of you a many and a many a time, and I'll *pray* for you, too!"— and she was gone.

Pray for me! I reckoned if she knowed me she'd take a job that was more nearer her size. But I bet she done it, just the same—she was just that kind. She had the grit to pray for Judus if she took the notion—there warn't no back-down to her, I judge. You may say what you want to, but in my opinion she had more sand in her than any girl I ever see; in my opinion she was just full of sand. It sounds like flattery, but it ain't no flattery. And when it comes to beauty— and goodness too—she lays over them all. I hain't ever seen her since that time that I see her go out of that door; no, I hain't ever seen her since; but I reckon I've thought of her a many and a many a million times, and of her saying she would pray for me; and if ever I'd a thought it would do any good for me to pray for *her*, blamed if I wouldn't a done it or bust.

Well, Mary Jane she lit out the back way, I reckon, because nobody see her go. When I struck Susan and the hare-lip, I says:

"What's the name of them people over on t'other side of the river that you-all goes to see sometimes?"

They says:

"There's several; but it's the Proctors, mainly."

"That's the name," I says; "I most forgot it. Well, Miss Mary Jane she told me to tell you she's gone over there in a dreadful hurry— one of them's sick."

"Which one?"

"I don't know; leastways I kinder forget; but I think it's—"

"Sakes alive, I hope it ain't *Hanner*?"

"I'm sorry to say it," I says, "but Hanner's the very one."

"My goodness—and she so well only last week! Is she took bad?"

"It ain't no name for it. They set up with her all night, Miss Mary Jane said, and they don't think she'll last many hours."

"Only think of that, now! What's the matter with her?"

I couldn't think of anything reasonable, right off that way, so I says:

"Mumps."

"Mumps your granny!—they don't set up with people that's got the mumps."

"They don't, don't they? You better bet they do with *these* mumps. These mumps is different. It's a new kind, Miss Mary Jane said."

HANNER WITH THE MUMPS.

"How's it a new kind?"

"Because it's mixed up with other things."

"What other things?"

"Well, measles, and whooping cough, and erysiplas, and consumption, and yaller janders, and brain fever, and I don't know what all."

"My land! And they call it the *mumps!*"

"That's what Miss Mary Jane said."

"Well, what in the nation do they call it the *mumps* for?"

"Why, because it *is* the mumps. That's what it starts with."

"Well, ther' ain't no sense in it. A body might stump his toe, and take pison, and fall down the well, and break his neck, and bust his brains out, and somebody come along and ask what killed him, and

some numskull up and say, 'Why, he stumped his *toe*.' Would ther'
be any sense in that? *No.* And ther' ain't no sense in *this*, nuther. Is
it ketching?"

"Is it *ketching?* Why, how you talk. Is a *harrow* catching?—in the
dark? If you don't hitch onto one tooth, you're bound to on another,
ain't you? And you can't get away with that tooth without fetching
the whole harrow along, can you? Well,these kind of mumps is a
kind of a harrow, as you may say—and it ain't no slouch of a harrow,
nuther, you come to get it hitched on good."

"Well, it's awful, *I* think," says the hare-lip. "I'll go to uncle
Harvey and—"

"O, yes," I says, "I *would*. Of *course* I would. I wouldn't lose no
time."

"Well, why wouldn't you?"

"Just look at it a minute, and maybe you can see. Hain't your
uncles obleeged to get along home to England as fast as they can?
And do you reckon they 'd be mean enough to go off and leave you
to go all that journey by yourselves? *You* know they'll wait for you.
So fur, so good. Your uncle Harvey's a preacher, ain't he? Very well,
then; is a *preacher* going to deceive a steamboat clerk? is he going
to deceive a *ship clerk?*—so as to get them to let Miss Mary Jane go
aboard? Now *you* know he ain't. What *will* he do, then? Why, he'll
say, 'It's a great pity, but my church matters has got to get along the
best way they can; for my niece has been exposed to the dreadful
pluribus-unum mumps, and so it's my bounden duty to set down
here and wait the three months it takes to show on her if she's
got it.' But never mind, if you think it's best to tell your uncle
Harvey—"

"Shucks, and stay fooling around here when we could all be
having good times in England whilst we was waiting to find out
whether Mary Jane's got it or not? Why, you talk like a muggins."

"Well, anyway, maybe you better tell some of the neighbors."

"Listen at that, now. You do beat all, for natural stupidness. Can't
you *see* that *they*'d go and tell? Ther' ain't no way but just to not tell
anybody at *all*."

"Well, maybe you're right—yes, I judge you *are* right."

"But I reckon we ought to tell uncle Harvey she's gone out a
while, anyway, so he won't be uneasy about her?"

"Yes, Miss Mary Jane she wanted you to do that. She says, 'Tell them to give uncle Harvey and William my love and a kiss, and say I've run over the river to see Mr.—Mr.'—what *is* the name of that rich family your uncle Peter used to think so much of?—I mean the one that—"

"Why, you must mean the Apthorps, ain't it?"

"Of course; bother them kind of names, a body can't ever seem to remember them, half the time, somehow. Yes, she said, say she has run over for to ask the Apthorps to be sure and come to the auction and buy this house, because she allowed her uncle Peter would ruther they had it than anybody else; and she's going to stick

THE AUCTION.

to them till they say they'll come; and then if she ain't too tired, she's coming home; and if she is, she'll be home in the morning, anyway. She said, don't say nothing about the Proctors, but only about the Apthorps—which'll be perfectly true, because she *is* going there to speak about their buying the house; I know it, because she told me so, herself."

"All right," they said, and cleared out to lay for their uncles, and give them the love and the kisses, and tell them the message.

Everything was all right, now. The girls wouldn't say nothing, because they wanted to go to England; and the king and the duke would ruther Mary Jane was off working for the auction than around in reach of doctor Robinson. I felt very good; I judged I had done it pretty neat—I reckoned Tom Sawyer couldn't a done it no neater, himself. Of course he would a throwed more style into it, but I can't do that very handy, not being brung up to it.

Well, they held the auction, in the public square, along towards the end of the afternoon, and it strung along, and strung along, and the old man he was on hand and looking his level piousest, up there longside of the auctioneer, and chipping in a little Scripture, now and then, or a little goody-goody saying, of some kind, and the duke he was around goo-gooing for sympathy all he knowed how, and just spreading himself generly.

But by and by the thing dragged through, and everything was sold. Everything but a little old trifling lot in the graveyard. So they'd got to work *that* off—I never see such a girafft as the king was for wanting to swallow *everything*. Well, whilst they was at it, a steamboat landed, and in about two minutes, up comes a crowd a whooping and yelling and laughing and carrying on, and singing out:

"*Here's* your opposition line! Here's your two sets o' heirs to old Peter Wilks—and you pays your money and you takes your choice!"

Chapter XXIX

THE TRUE BROTHERS.

They was fetching a very nice looking old gentleman along, and a nice looking younger one, with his right arm in a sling. And my souls, how the people yelled, and laughed, and kept it up. But I didn't see no joke about it, and I judged it would strain the duke and the king some, to see any. I reckoned they'd turn pale. But no, nary a pale did *they* turn. The duke he never let on he suspicioned what was up, but just went a goo-gooing around, happy and satisfied, like a jug that's googling out buttermilk; and as for the king, he just gazed and gazed down sorrowful on them newcomers like it give him the stomach-ache in his very heart to think there could be such frauds and rascals in the world. O, he done it admirable. Lots of the principal people gethered around the king, to let him see they was on his side. That old gentleman that had just come, looked all puzzled to death. Pretty soon he begun to speak, and I see, straight off, he pronounced *like* an Englishman; not the king's way, though the king's *was* pretty good, for an imitation. I can't give the old gent's words, nor I can't imitate him; but he turned around to the crowd, and says, about like this:

"This is a surprise to me which I wasn't looking for; and I'll acknowledge, candid and frank, I ain't very well fixed to meet it and answer it; for my brother and me has had misfortunes: he's broke his arm, and our baggage got put off at a town above here, last night in the night, by a mistake. I am Peter Wilks's brother Harvey, and this is his brother William, which can't hear nor speak—and can't even make signs to amount to much, now 't he's only got one hand to work them with. We are who we say we are; and in a day or two, when I get the baggage, I can prove it. But, up till then, I won't say nothing more, but go to the hotel and wait."

So him and the new dummy started off; and the king he laughs, and blethers out:

"Broke his arm—*very* likely, *ain't* it?—and very convenient, too, for a fraud that's got to make signs, and hain't learnt how. Lost their baggage! That's *mighty* good!—and mighty ingenious—under the *circumstances!*"

So he laughed again; and so did everybody else, except three or four, or maybe half a dozen. One of these was that doctor; another one was a sharp looking gentleman, with a carpet bag of the old-fashioned kind made out of carpet-stuff, that had just come off of the steamboat and was talking to him in a low voice, and glancing towards the king now and then and nodding their heads—it was Levi Bell, the lawyer that was gone up to Louisville; and another one was a big rough husky that come along and listened to all the old gentleman said, and was listening to the king, now. And when the king got done, this husky up and says:

"Say, looky-here; if you are Harvey Wilks, when'd you come to this town?"

"The day before the funeral, friend," says the king.

"But what time o' day?"

"In the evenin'—'bout an hour er two before sundown."

"*How'd* you come?"

"I come down on the Susan Powell, from Cincinnati."

"Well, then, how'd you come to be up at the Pint in the *mornin'*—in a canoe?"

"I warn't up at the Pint in the mornin'."

"It's a lie."

Several of them jumped for him and begged him not to talk that way to an old man and a preacher.

"Preacher be hanged, he's a fraud and a liar. He was up at the Pint that mornin'. I live up there, don't I? Well, I was up there, and he was up there. I *see* him there. He come in a canoe, along with Tim Collins and a boy."

The doctor he up and says:

"Would you know the boy again if you was to see him, Hines?"

"I reckon I would, but I don't know. Why, yonder he is, now. I know him perfectly easy."

It was me he pointed at. The doctor says:

"Neighbors, I don't know whether the new couple is frauds or not; but if *these* two ain't frauds, I am an idiot, that's all. I think it's our duty to see that they don't get away from here till we've looked into this thing. Come along, Hines; come along, the rest of you. We'll take these fellows to the tavern and affront them with t'other couple, and I reckon we'll find out *something* before we get through."

THE DOCTOR LEADS HUCK.

It was nuts for the crowd, though maybe not for the king's friends; so we all started. It was about sundown. The doctor he led me along by the hand, and was plenty kind enough, but he never let *go* my hand.

We all got in a big room in the hotel, and lit up some candles, and fetched in the new couple.

First, the doctor says:

"I don't wish to be too hard on these two men, but *I* think they're frauds, and they may have complices that we don't know nothing about. If they have, won't the complices get away with that bag of gold Peter Wilks left? It ain't unlikely. If these men ain't frauds, they won't object to sending for that money and letting us keep it till they prove they're all right—ain't that so?"

Everybody agreed to that. So I judged they had our gang in a pretty tight place, right at the outstart. But the king he only looked sorrowful, and says:

"Gentlemen, I wish the money was there, for I ain't got no disposition to throw anything in the way of a fair, open, out-and-out investigation o' this misable business; but alas, the money ain't there; you k'n send and see, if you want to."

"Where is it, then?"

"Well, when my niece give it to me to keep for her, I took and hid it inside o' the straw tick o' my bed, not wishin' to bank it for the few days we'd be here, and considerin' the bed a safe place, we not bein' used to niggers, and suppos'n' 'em honest, like servants in England. The niggers stole it the very next mornin', after I had went down stairs; and when I sold 'em, I hadn't missed the money yit, so they got clean away with it. My servant here k'n tell you 'bout it, gentlemen."

The doctor and several said "Shucks!" and I see nobody didn't altogether believe him. One man asked me if I see the niggers steal it. I said no, but I see them sneaking out of the room and hustling away, and I never thought nothing, only I reckoned they was afraid they had waked up my master and was trying to get away before he made trouble with them. That was all they asked me. Then the doctor whirls on me and says:

"Are *you* English, too?"

I says yes; and him and some others laughed, and said, "Stuff!"

Well, then they sailed in on the general investigation, and there we had it, up and down, hour in, hour out, and nobody never said a word about supper, nor ever seemed to think about it—and so they kept it up, and kept it up; and it *was* the worst mixed-up thing you ever see. They made the king tell his yarn, and they made the old gentleman tell his'n; and anybody but a lot of prejudiced chuckleheads would a *seen* that the old gentleman was spinning truth and t'other one lies. And by and by they had me up to tell what I knowed. The king he give me a left-handed look out of the corner of his eye, and so I knowed enough to talk on the right side. I begun to tell about Sheffield, and how we lived there, and all about the English Wilkses, and so on; but I didn't get pretty fur till the doctor begun to laugh; and Levi Bell, the lawyer, says:

"Set down, my boy, I wouldn't strain myself, if I was you. I reckon you ain't used to lying, it don't seem to come handy; what you want is practice. You do it pretty awkward."

I didn't care nothing for the compliment, but I was glad to be let off, any way.

The doctor he started to say something, and turns and says:

"If you'd been in town at first, Levi Bell—"

The king broke in and reached out his hand and says:

"Why, is this my poor dead brother's old friend that he's wrote so often about?"

The lawyer and him shook hands, and the lawyer smiled, and looked pleased, and they talked right along, a while, and then got to one side and talked low; and at last the lawyer speaks up and says:

"That'll fix it. I'll take the order and send it, along with your brother's, and then they'll know it's all right."

So they got some paper and a pen, and the king he set down and twisted his head to one side, and chawed his tongue, and scrawled off something; and then they give the pen to the duke—and then for the first time, the duke looked sick. But he took the pen and wrote. So then the lawyer turns to the new old gentleman and says:

THE DUKE WROTE.

"You and your brother please write a line or two and sign your names."

The old gentleman wrote, but nobody couldn't read it. The lawyer looked powerful astonished, and says:

"Well, it beats *me*"—and snaked a lot of old letters out of his pocket, and examined them, and then examined the old man's writing, and then *them* again; and then says: "These old letters is from Harvey Wilks; and here's *these* two's handwritings, and anybody can see *they* didn't write them" (the king and the duke looked sold and foolish, I tell you, to see how the lawyer had took them in), "and here's *this* old gentleman's handwriting, and anybody can tell, easy enough, *he* didn't write them—fact is, the scratches he makes ain't properly *writing*, at all. Now here's some letters from—"

The new old gentleman says:

"If you please, let me explain. Nobody can read my hand but my brother there—so he copies for me. It's *his* hand you've got there, not mine."

"*Well!*" says the lawyer, "this *is* a state of things. I've got some of William's letters, too; so if you'll get him to write a line or so we can com—"

"He *can't* write with his left hand," says the old gentleman. "If he could use his right hand, you would see that he wrote his own letters and mine too. Look at both, please—they're by the same hand."

The lawyer done it, and says:

"I believe it's so—and if it ain't so there's a heap stronger resemblance than I'd noticed before, anyway. Well, well, well! I thought we was right on the track of a slution, but it's gone to grass, partly. But anyway, *one* thing is proved—*these* two ain't either of 'em Wilkses"—and he wagged his head towards the king and the duke.

Well, what do you think?—that muleheaded old fool wouldn't give in *then!* Indeed he wouldn't. Said it warn't no fair test. Said his brother William was the cussedest joker in the world, and hadn't *tried* to write—*he* see William was going to play one of his jokes the minute he put the pen to paper. And so he warmed up and went warbling and warbling right along, till he was actuly beginning to believe what he was saying, *himself*—but pretty soon the new old gentleman broke in and says:

"I've thought of something. Is there anybody here that helped to lay out my br—helped to lay out the late Peter Wilks for burying?"

"Yes" says somebody, "me and Ab Turner done it. We're both here."

Then the old man turns towards the king and says:

"Peraps this gentleman can tell me what was tattooed on his breast?"

Blamed if the king didn't have to brace up mighty quick, or he'd a squshed down like a bluff bank that the river has cut under, it took him so sudden—and mind you it was a thing that was calculated to make most *anybody* sqush, to get fetched such a solid one as that without any notice—because how was *he* going to know what was tattooed on the man? He whitened a little; he couldn't help it; and it was mighty still, in there, and everybody bending a little forward and gazing at him. Says I to myself, *Now* he'll throw up the sponge—there ain't no more use. Well, did he? A body can't hardly believe it, but he didn't. I reckon he thought he'd keep the thing up till he tired them people out, so they'd thin out and him and the duke could break loose and get away. Anyway, he set there, and pretty soon he begun to smile, and says:

"Mf! It's a *very* tough question, *ain't* it! *Yes*, sir, I k'n tell you what's tattooed on his breast. It's jest a small, thin, blue arrow—that's what it is; and if you don't look clost, you can't see it. *Now* what do you say—hey?"

Well, *I* never see anything like that old blister, for clean out-and-out cheek.

The new old gentleman turns brisk towards Ab Turner and his pard, and his eye lights up like he judged he'd got the king *this* time, and says:

"There—you've heard what he said! Was there any such mark on Peter Wilks's breast?"

Both of them spoke up and says:

"We didn't see no such mark."

"Good!" says the old gentleman. "Now what you *did* see on his breast was a small dim P, and a B, (which is an initial he dropped when he was young,) and a W, with dashes between them, so: P—B—W"—and he marked them that way on a piece of paper. "Come—ain't that what you saw?"

Both of them spoke up again, and says:

"No, we *didn't*. We never seen any marks, at all."

Well, everybody *was* in a state of mind, now; and they sings out:

"The whole *bilin'* of 'm 's frauds! Le's duck 'em! le's drown 'em! le's ride 'em on a rail!" and everybody was whooping at once, and there was a rattling pow-pow. But the lawyer he jumps on the table and yells, and says:

"Gentlemen—gentle*men!* Hear me just a word—just a *single* word—if you PLEASE! There's one way, yet—let's go and dig up the corpse and look."

That took them.

"GENTLEMEN—GENTLE*MEN!*"

"Hooray!" they all shouted, and was starting right off; but the lawyer and the doctor sung out:

"Hold on, hold on! Collar all these four men and the boy, and fetch *them* along, too!"

"We'll do it!" they all shouted; "and if we don't find them marks, we'll lynch the whole gang!"

I *was* scared, now, I tell you. But there warn't no getting away, you know. They gripped us all, and marched us right along, straight for the graveyard, which was a mile and a half down the river, and the whole town at our heels, for we made noise enough, and it was only nine in the evening.

As we went by our house I wished I hadn't sent Mary Jane out of town; because now if I could tip her the wink, she'd light out and save me, and blow on our dead-beats.

Well, we swarmed along down the river road, just carrying on like wild-cats; and to make it more scary, the sky was darking up, and the lightning beginning to wink and flitter, and the wind to shiver amongst the leaves. This was the most awful trouble and most dangersome I ever was in; and I was kinder stunned, everything was going so different from what I had allowed for: 'stead of being fixed so I could take my own time, if I wanted to, and see all the fun, and have Mary Jane at my back to save me and set me free when the close-fit come, here was nothing in the world betwixt me and sudden death but just them tattoo-marks. If they didn't find them—

I couldn't bear to think about it; and yet, somehow, I couldn't think about nothing else. It got darker and darker, and it was a beautiful time to give the crowd the slip; but that big husky had me by the wrist—Hines—and a body might as well try to give Goliar the slip. He dragged me right along, he was so excited; and I had to run to keep up.

When they got there they swarmed into the graveyard, and washed over it like an overflow. And when they got to the grave, they found they had about a hundred times as many shovels as they wanted, but nobody hadn't thought to fetch a lantern. But they sailed into digging, anyway, by the flicker of the lightning, and sent a man to the nearest house a half a mile off, to borrow one.

So they dug and dug, like everything; and it got awful dark, and the rain started, and the wind swished and swushed along, and the lightning come brisker and brisker, and the thunder boomed; but them people never took no notice of it, they was so full of this business; and one minute you could see every thing and every face in that big crowd, and the shovelfuls of dirt sailing up out of the grave, and the next second the dark wiped it all out, and you couldn't see nothing at all.

At last they got out the coffin, and begun to unscrew the lid, and then such another crowding, and shouldering and shoving as there was, to scrouge in and get a sight, you never see; and in the dark, that way, it was awful. Hines he hurt my wrist dreadful, pulling and tugging so, and I reckon he clean forgot I was in the world, he was so excited and panting.

All of a sudden the lightning let go a perfect sluice of white glare, and somebody sings out:

"By the living jingo, here's the bag of gold on his breast!"

Hines let out a whoop, like everybody else, and dropped my wrist and give a big surge to bust his way in and get a look, and the way I lit out and shinned for the road in the dark, there ain't nobody can tell.

I had the road all to myself, and I fairly flew—leastways I had it all to myself except the solid dark, and the now-and-then glares, and the buzzing of the rain, and the thrashing of the wind, and the splitting of the thunder; and sure as you are born I did clip it along!

When I struck the town, I see there warn't nobody out in the storm, so I never hunted for no back steets, but humped it straight through the main one; and when I begun to get towards our house I aimed my eye and set it. No light there; the house all dark—which made me feel sorry and disappointed, I didn't know why. But at last, just as I was sailing by, *flash* comes the light in Mary Jane's window! and my heart swelled up sudden, like to bust, and the same second the house and all was behind me in the dark, and wasn't ever going to be before me no more in this world. She *was* the best girl I ever see, and had the most sand.

The minute I was far enough above the town to see I could make the towhead, I begun to look sharp for a boat to borrow; and the first time the lightning showed me one that wasn't chained, I snatched it and shoved. It was a canoe, and warn't fastened with nothing but a rope. The towhead was a rattling big distance off, away out there in the middle of the river, but I didn't lose no time; and when I struck the raft at last, I was so fagged I would a just laid down to blow and gasp if I could afforded it. But I didn't. As I sprung aboard I sung out:

"Out with you Jim, and set her loose! Glory be to goodness, we're shut of them!"

Jim lit out, and was a coming for me with both arms spread, he was so full of joy, but when I glimpsed him in the lightning, my heart shot up in my mouth, and I went overboard backwards; for I forgot he was old King Leer and a drownded A-rab all in one, and it

"JIM LIT OUT."

most scared the livers and lights out of me. But Jim fished me out, and was going to hug me and bless me, and so on, he was so glad I was back and we was shut of the king and the duke, but I says:

"Not now—have it for breakfast, have it for breakfast! Cut loose and let her slide!"

So, in two seconds, away we went, a sliding down the river, and it *did* seem so good to be free again and all by ourselves on the big river and nobody to bother us. I had to skip around a bit, and jump up and crack my heels a few times, I couldn't help it; but about the third crack, I noticed a sound that I knowed mighty well,—and held my breath, and listened and waited—and sure enough, when the next flash busted out over the water, here they come!—and just a laying to their oars and making their skiff hum! It was the king and the duke.

So I wilted right down onto the planks, then, and give up; and it was all I could do to keep from crying.

Chapter XXX

THE KING SHAKES HUCK.

When they got aboard, the king went for me, and shook me by the collar, and says:

"Tryin' to give us the slip, was ye, you pup! Tired of our company—hey?"

I says:

"No, your majesty, we warn't —*please* don't, your majesty!"

"Quick, then, and tell us what *was* your idea, or I'll shake the insides out o' you!"

"Honest, I'll tell you everything, just as it happened, your majesty. The man that had aholt of me was very good to me, and kept saying he had a boy about as big as me, that died last year, and he was sorry to see a boy in such a dangerous fix; and when they was all took by surprise by finding the gold, and made a rush for the coffin, he lets go of me and whispers, 'Heel it, now, or they'll hang ye, sure!' and I lit out. It didn't seem no good for *me* to stay—*I* couldn't do nothing, and I didn't want to be hung if I could get away. So I never stopped running till I found the canoe; and when I got here I told Jim to hurry, or they'd catch me and hang me, yet, and said I was afeard you and the duke wasn't alive, now, and I was awful sorry, and so was Jim, and was awful glad when we see you coming, you may ask Jim if I didn't."

Jim said it was so; and the king told him to shut up, and said, "O, yes, it's *mighty* likely!" and shook me up again, and said he reckoned he'd drownd me. But the duke says:

"Leggo the boy, you old idiot! Would *you* a done any different? Did you inquire around for *him*, when you got loose? *I* don't remember it."

So the king let go of me, and begun to cuss that town, and everybody in it. But the duke says:

"You better a blame sight give *yourself* a good cussing, for you're the one that's entitled to it most. You hain't done a thing, from the start, that had any sense in it, except coming out so cool and cheeky with that imaginary blue-arrow mark. That *was* bright—it was right down bully; and it was the thing that saved us. For if it hadn't been for that, they'd a jailed us till them Englishmen's baggage come, and then—the penitentiary, you bet! But that trick took 'em to the graveyard, and the gold done us a still bigger kindness; for if the excited fools hadn't let go all holts and made that rush to get a look, we'd a slept in our cravats to-night—cravats warranted to *wear*, too—longer than *we'd* need 'em."

They was still a minute—thinking—then the king says, kind of absent-minded like:

"Mf! And we reckoned the *niggers* stole it!"

That made me squirm!

"Yes," says the duke, kinder slow, and deliberate, and sarcastic. "*We* did."

After about a half a minute, the king drawls out:

"Leastways—*I* did."

The duke says, the same way:

"On the contrary—*I* did."

The king kind of ruffles up, and says:

"Looky here, Bilgewater, what'r you referrin' to?"

The duke says, pretty brisk:

"When it comes to that, maybe you'll let me ask, what was *you* referring to?"

"Shucks!" says the king, very sarcastic; "but *I* don't know—maybe you was asleep, and didn't know what you was about."

The duke bristles right up, now, and says:

"O, let *up* on this cussed nonsense—do you take me for a blame' fool? Don't you reckon *I* know who hid that money in that coffin?"

"*Yes* sir! I know you *do* know—because you done it yourself!"

"It's a lie!"—and the duke went for him. The king sings out:

THE DUKE WENT FOR HIM.

"Take y'r hands off!—leggo my throat!—I take it all back!"

The duke says:

"Well, you just own up, first, that you *did* hide that money there, intending to give me the slip one of these days, and come back and dig it up, and have it all to yourself."

"Wait jest a minute, duke—answer me this one question, honest and fair: if you didn't put the money there, say it, and I'll b'lieve you, and take back everything I said."

"You old scoundrel, I didn't, and you know I didn't. There, now!"

"Well then, I b'lieve you. But answer me only jest this one more—now *don't* git mad: didn't you have it in your *mind* to hook the money and hide it?"

The duke never said nothing for a little bit; then he says:

"Well—I don't care if I *did*, I didn't *do* it, anyway. But you not only had it in mind to do it, but you *done* it."

"I wisht I may never die if I done it, duke, and that's honest. I won't say I warn't *goin'* to do it, because I *was*; but you—I mean somebody—got in ahead o' me."

"It's a lie! You done it, and you got to *say* you done it, or—"

The king begun to gurgle, and then he gasps out:

" 'Nough!—*I own up!*"

I was very glad to hear him say that, it made me feel much more easier than what I was feeling before. So the duke took his hands off, and says:

"If you ever deny it again, I'll drown you. It's *well* for you to set there and blubber like a baby—it's fitten for you, after the way you've acted. I never see such an old ostrich for wanting to gobble everything—and I a trusting you all the time, like you was my own father. You ought to been ashamed of yourself to stand by and hear it saddled onto a lot of poor niggers and you never say a word for 'em. It makes me feel ridiculous to think I was soft enough to *believe* that rubbage. Cuss you, I can see, now, why you was so anxious to make up the deffesit—you wanted to get what money I'd got out of the Nonesuch and one thing or another, and scoop it *all!*"

The king says, timid, and still a snuffling:

"Why, duke, it was you that said make up the deffersit, it warn't me."

"Dry up! I don't want to hear no more *out* of you!" says the duke. "And *now* you see what you *got* by it. They've got all their own money back, and all of *ourn* but a shekel or two, *besides*. G'long to bed—and don't you deffersit *me* no more deffersits, long's *you* live!"

So the king sneaked into the wigwam, and took to his bottle for comfort; and before long the duke tackled *his* bottle; and so in about a half an hour they was as thick as thieves again, and the tighter they got the lovinger they got; and went off a-snoring in each other's arms. They both got powerful mellow, but I noticed the king didn't get mellow enough to forget to remember to not deny about hiding the money-bag, again. That made me feel easy and satisfied. Of course when they got to snoring, we had a long gabble, and I told Jim everything.

Chapter XXXI.

SPANISH MOSS.

We dasn't stop again at any town, for days and days; kept right along down the river. We was down south in the warm weather, now, and a mighty long ways from home. We begun to come to trees with Spanish moss on them, hanging down from the limbs like long gray beards. It was the first I ever see it growing, and it made the woods look solemn and dismal. So now the frauds reckoned they was out of danger, and they begun to work the villages again.

First they done a lecture on temperance; but they didn't make enough for them both to get drunk on. Then in another village they started a dancing school; but they didn't know no more how to dance than a kangaroo does; so the first prance they made, the general public jumped in and pranced them out of town. Another time they tried a go at yellocution; but they didn't yellocute long till the audience got up and give them a solid good cussing and made them skip out. They tackled missionarying, and mesmerizering, and doctoring, and telling fortunes, and a little of everything; but they couldn't seem to have no luck. So at last they got just about dead broke, and laid around the raft, as she floated along, thinking, and thinking, and never saying nothing, by the half a day at a time, and dreadful blue and desperate.

And at last they took a change and begun to lay their heads together in the wigwam and talk low and confidential two or three hours at a time. Jim and me got uneasy. We didn't like the look of it.

We judged they was studying up some kind of worse deviltry than ever. We turned it over and over, and at last we made up our minds they was going to break into somebody's house or store, or was going into the counterfeit money business, or something. So then we was pretty scared, and made up an agreement that we wouldn't have nothing in the world to do with such actions, and if we ever got the least show we would give them the cold shake, and clear out and leave them behind. Well, early one morning we hid the raft in a good safe place about two mile below a little bit of a shabby village, named Pikesville, and the king he went ashore, and told us all to stay hid whilst he went up to town and smelt around to see if anybody had got any wind of the Royal Nonesuch there yet. ("House to rob, you *mean*," says I to myself; "and when you get through robbing it you'll come back here and wonder what's become of me and Jim and the raft—and you'll have to take it out in wondering.") And he said if he warn't back by midday, the duke and me would know it was all right, and we was to come along.

So we staid where we was. The duke he fretted and sweated around, and was in a mighty sour way. He scolded us for everything, and we couldn't seem to do nothing right; he found fault with every little thing. Something was a-brewing, sure. I was good and glad when midday come and no king; we could have a change, anyway— and maybe a chance for *the* change, on top of it. So me and the duke went up to the village, and hunted around there for the king, and by and by we found him in the back room of a little low doggery, very tight, and a lot of loafers bullyragging him for sport, and he a cussing and threatening with all his might, and so tight he couldn't walk, and couldn't do nothing to them. The duke he begun to abuse him for an old fool, and the king begun to sass back; and the minute they was fairly at it, I lit out, and shook the reefs out of my hind legs, and spun down the river road like a deer—for I see our chance; and I made up my mind that it would be a long day before they ever see me and Jim again. I got down there all out of breath but loaded up with joy, and sung out—

"Set her loose, Jim, we're all right, now!"

But there warn't no answer, and nobody come out of the wigwam. Jim was gone! I set up a shout,—and then another—and then another one; and run this way and that in the woods, whooping and screeching; but it warn't no use—old Jim was gone. Then I set down and cried; I couldn't help it. But I couldn't set still long. Pretty soon I went out on the road, trying to think what I better do, and I run across a boy walking, and asked him if he'd seen a strange nigger, dressed so and so, and he says:

"Yes."

"Wherebouts?" says I.

"Down to Silas Phelps's place, two mile below here. He's a runaway nigger, and they've got him. Was you looking for him?"

"You bet I ain't! I run across him in the woods about an hour or two ago, and he said if I hollered he'd cut my livers out—and told me to lay down and stay where I was; and I done it. Been there ever since; afeard to come out."

"Well," he says, "you needn't be afeard no more, becuz they've got him. He run off f'm down south, som'ers."

"It's a good job they got him."

"Well, I *reckon!* There's two hunderd dollars reward on him. It's like picking up money out'n the road."

"Yes, it is—and *I* could a had it if I'd been big enough: I see him *first*. Who nailed him?"

"WHO NAILED HIM?"

"It was an old fellow—a stranger—and he sold out his chance in him for forty dollars, becuz he's got to go up the river and can't wait. Think o' that, now! You bet *I*'d wait, if it was seven year."

"That's me, every time," says I. "But maybe his chance ain't worth no more than that, if he'll sell it so cheap. Maybe there's something ain't straight about it."

"But it *is*, though—straight as a string. I see the handbill myself. It tells all about him, to a dot—paints him like a picture, and tells the plantation he's frum, below Newr*leans*. No-sir-ree-*bob*, they ain't no trouble 'bout *that* speculation, you bet you. Say, gimme a chaw tobacker, won't ye?"

I didn't have none, so he left. I went to the raft, and set down in the wigwam to think. But I couldn't come to nothing. I thought, till I wore my head sore, but I couldn't see no way out of the trouble. After all this long journey, and after all we'd done for them scoundrels, here was it all come to nothing, everything all busted up and ruined, because they could have the heart to serve Jim such a trick as that, and make him a slave again all his life, and amongst strangers, too, for forty dirty dollars.

Once I said to myself it would be a thousand times better for Jim to be a slave at home where his family was, as long as he'd *got* to be a slave, and so I'd better write a letter to Tom Sawyer and tell him to tell Miss Watson where he was. But I soon give up that notion, for two things: she'd be mad and disgusted at his rascality and ungratefulness for leaving her, and so she'd sell him straight down the river again; and if she didn't, everybody naturally despises an ungrateful nigger, and they'd make Jim feel it all the time, and so he'd feel ornery and disgraced. And then think of *me!* It would get all around, that Huck Finn helped a nigger to get his freedom; and if I was to ever see anybody from that town again, I'd be ready to get down and lick his boots for shame. That's just the way: a person does a low-down thing, and then he don't want to take no consequences of it. Thinks as long as he can hide it, it ain't no disgrace. That was my fix exactly. The more I studied about this, the more my conscience went to grinding me, and the more wicked, and low-down and ornery I got to feeling. And at last, when it hit me all of a sudden that here was the plain hand of Providence slapping me in the face and letting me know my wickedness was being watched all the time from up there in heaven, whilst I was stealing a poor old woman's nigger that hadn't ever done me no harm, and now was showing me there's One that's always on the lookout, and ain't agoing to allow no such miserable doings to go only just so fur and no further, I most dropped in my tracks I was so scared. Well, I tried the best I could to kinder soften it up somehow for myself, by saying I was brung up wicked, and so I warn't so much to blame; but something inside of me kept saying, "There was the Sunday School, you could a gone to it; and if you'd a done it they'd a learnt you, there, that people that acts as I'd been acting about that nigger goes to everlasting fire."

It made me shiver. And I about made up my mind to pray; and see if I couldn't try to quit being the kind of a boy I was, and be better. So I kneeled down. But the words wouldn't come. Why wouldn't they? It warn't no use to try and hide it from Him. Nor from *me*, neither. I knowed very well why they wouldn't come. It was because my heart warn't right; it was because I warn't square; it was because I was playing double. I was letting *on* to give up sin, but away inside of me I was holding on to the biggest one of all. I was trying to make my mouth *say* I would do the right thing and the clean thing, and go and write to that nigger's owner and tell where he was; but deep down in me I knowed it was a lie—and He knowed it. You can't pray a lie—I found that out.

So I was full of trouble, full as I could be; and didn't know what to do. At last I had an idea; and I says, I'll go and write the letter— and *then* see if I can pray. Why, it was astonishing, the way I felt as light as a feather, right straight off, and my troubles all gone. So I got a piece of paper and a pencil, all glad and excited, and set down and wrote:

Miss Watson your runaway nigger Jim is down here two mile below Pikesville and Mr. Phelps has got him and he will give him up for the reward if you send. HUCK FINN.

I felt good and all washed clean of sin for the first time I had ever felt so in my life, and I knowed I could pray, now. But I didn't do it straight off, but laid the paper down and set there thinking; thinking how good it was all this happened so, and how near I come to being lost and going to hell. And went on thinking. And got to thinking over our trip down the river; and I see Jim before me, all the time, in the day, and in the night-time, sometimes moonlight, sometimes storms, and we a floating along, talking, and singing, and laughing. But somehow I couldn't seem to strike no places to harden me against him, but only the other kind. I'd see him standing my watch on top of his'n, stead of calling me—so I could go on sleeping; and see him how glad he was when I come back out of the fog; and when

THINKING.

I come to him again in the swamp, up there where the feud was; and such-like times; and would always call me honey, and pet me, and do everything he could think of for me, and how good he always was; and at last I struck the time I saved him by telling the men we had small-pox aboard, and he was so grateful, and said I was the best friend old Jim ever had in the world, and the *only* one he's got now; and then I happened to look around, and see that paper.

It was a close place. I took it up, and held it in my hand. I was a trembling, because I'd got to decide, forever, betwixt two things, and I knowed it. I studied a minute, sort of holding my breath, and then says to myself:

"All right, then, I'll *go* to hell"—and tore it up.

It was awful thoughts, and awful words, but they was said. And I let them stay said; and never thought no more about reforming. I shoved the whole thing out of my head; and said I would take up wickedness again, which was in my line, being brung up to it, and the other warn't. And for a starter, I would go to work and steal Jim out of slavery again; and if I could think up anything worse, I would do that, too; because as long as I was in, and in for good, I might as well go the whole hog.

Then I set to thinking over how to get at it, and turned over considerable many ways in my mind; and at last fixed up a plan that suited me. So then I took the bearings of a woody island that was down the river a piece, and as soon as it was fairly dark I crept out with my raft and went for it, and hid it there, and then turned in. I slept the night through, and got up before it was light, and had my breakfast, and put on my store clothes, and tied up some others and one thing or another in a bundle, and took the canoe and cleared for shore. I landed below where I judged was Phelps's place, and hid my bundle in the woods, and then filled up the canoe with water, and loaded rocks into her and sunk her where I could find her again when I wanted her, about a quarter of a mile below a little steam sawmill that was on the bank.

Then I struck up the road, and when I passed the mill I see a sign on it, "Phelps's Sawmill," and when I come to the farm houses, two or three hundred yards further along, I kept my eyes peeled, but didn't see nobody around, though it was good daylight, now. But I didn't mind, because I didn't want to see nobody just yet—I only wanted to get the lay of the land. According to my plan, I was going to turn up there from the village, not from below. So I just took a look, and shoved along, straight for town. Well, the very first man I see, when I got there, was the duke. He was sticking up a bill for the Royal Nonesuch—three-night performance, like that other time. *They* had the cheek, them frauds! I was right on him, before I could shirk. He looked astonished, and says:

"Hel-*lo!* Where'd *you* come from?" Then he says, kind of glad, and eager, "Where's the raft?—got her in a good place?"

I says:

"Why, that's just what I was agoing to ask your grace."

Then he didn't look so joyful—and says:

"What was your idea for asking *me?*" he says.

"Well," I says, "when I see the king in that doggery, yesterday, I says to myself, we can't get him home for hours, till he's soberer; so I went a loafing around town to put in the time, and wait. A man up and offered me ten cents to help him pull a skiff over the river and back to fetch a sheep, and so I went along; but when we was dragging him to the boat, and the man left me aholt of the rope and went behind him to shove him along, he was too strong for me, and jerked loose and run, and we after him. We didn't have no dog, and so we had to chase him all over the country till we tired him out. We never got him till dark, then we fetched him over, and I started down for the raft. When I got there and see it was gone, I says to myself, 'They've got into trouble and had to leave; and they've took my nigger, which is the only nigger I've got in the world, and now I'm in a strange country, and ain't got no property no more, nor nothing, and no way to make my living;' so I set down and cried. I slept in the woods all night. But what *did* become of the raft, then?—and Jim, poor Jim!"

"Blamed if *I* know—that is, what's become of the raft. That old fool had made a trade and got forty dollars, and when we found him in the doggery, the loafers had matched half dollars with him and got every cent but what he'd spent for whisky; and when I got him home late last night and found the raft gone, we said, 'That little rascal has stole our raft and shook us, and run off down the river.' "

"I wouldn't shake my *nigger*, would I?—the only nigger I had in the world, and the only property."

"We never thought of that. Fact is, I reckon we'd come to consider him *our* nigger; yes, we did consider him so—goodness knows we had trouble enough for him. So, when we see the raft was gone, and we flat broke, there warn't anything for it but to try the Royal Nonesuch another shake. And I've pegged along ever since, dry as a powder horn. Where's that ten cents? Give it here."

I had considerable money, so I give him ten cents, but begged him to spend it for something to eat, and give me some, because it was all the money I had, and I hadn't had nothing to eat since yesterday. He never said nothing. The next minute he whirls on me and says:

"Do you reckon that nigger would blow on us? We'd skin him if he done that!"

"How can he blow? Hain't he run off?"

"No! That old fool sold him, and never divided with me, and the money's gone."

"*Sold* him?" I says, and begun to cry: "Why, he was *my* nigger, and that was my money. Where is he?—I want my nigger."

HE GAVE HIM TEN CENTS.

"Well, you can't *get* your nigger, that's all—so dry up your blubbering. Looky-here—do you think *you'd* venture to blow on us? Blamed if I think I'd trust you. Why, if you *was* to blow on us—"

He stopped, but I never see the duke look so ugly out of his eyes before. I went on a-whimpering, and says:

"I don't want to blow on nobody; and I ain't got no time to blow, nohow. I got to turn out and find my nigger."

He looked kinder bothered, and stood there with his bills fluttering on his arm, thinking, and wrinkling up his forehead. At last he says:

"I'll tell you something. We got to be here three days. If you'll promise you won't blow, and won't let the nigger blow, I'll tell you where to find him."

So I promised, and he says:

"A farmer by the name of Silas Ph—" and then he stopped. You see, he started to tell me the truth; but when he stopped, that way, and begun to study and think, again, I reckoned he was changing his mind. And so he was. He wouldn't trust me; he wanted to make sure of having me out of the way the whole three days. So pretty soon he says:

"The man that bought him is named Abram Foster—Abram G. Foster—and he lives forty mile back here in the country, on the road to Lafayette."

"All right," I says, "I can walk it in three days. And I'll start this very afternoon."

"No you won't, you'll start *now*; and don't you lose any time about it, neither, nor do any gabbling by the way. Just keep a tight tongue in your head and move right along, and then you won't get into trouble with *us*, d'ye hear?"

That was the order I wanted, and that was the one I played for. I wanted to be left free to work my plans.

"So clear out," he says; "and you can tell Mr. Foster whatever you want to. Maybe you can get him to believe that Jim *is* your nigger—some idiots don't require documents—leastways I've heard there's such down South here. And when you tell him the handbill and the reward's bogus, maybe he'll believe you when you explain to him what the idea was for getting 'em out. Go 'long, now, and tell him anything you want to; but mind you don't work your jaw any *between* here and there."

So I left, and struck for the back country. I didn't look around, but I kinder felt like he was watching me. But I knowed I could tire him out at that. I went straight out in the country as much as a mile, before I stopped; then I doubled back through the woods towards Phelps's. I reckoned I better start in on my plan straight off, without fooling around, because I wanted to stop Jim's mouth till these fellows could get away. I didn't want no trouble with their kind. I'd seen all I wanted to of them, and wanted to get entirely shut of them.

STRIKING FOR THE BACK COUNTRY.

Chapter XXXII

STILL AND SUNDAY-LIKE.

When I got there it was all still and Sunday-like, and hot and sun-shiny—the hands was gone to the fields; and there was them kind of faint dronings of bugs and flies in the air that makes it seem so lonesome and like everybody's dead and gone; and if a breeze fans along and quivers the leaves, it makes you feel mournful, because you feel like it's spirits whis-pering—spirits that's been dead ever so many years—and you always think they're talk-ing about *you*. As a general thing, it makes a body wish *he* was dead, too, and done with it all.

Phelps's was one of these little one-horse cotton plantations; and they all look alike. A rail fence round a two-acre yard; a stile, made out of logs sawed off and up-ended, in steps, like barrels of a different length, to climb over the fence with, and for the women to stand on when they are going to jump onto a horse; some sickly grass-patches in the big yard, but mostly it was bare and smooth, like an old hat with the nap rubbed off; big double log house for the white folks,— hewed logs, with the chinks stopped up with mud or mortar, and these mud-stripes been whitewashed some time or another; round-log kitchen, with a big broad, open, but roofed passage, joining it to the house; log smoke-house back of the kitchen; three little log nigger-cabins in a row t'other side the smoke-house; one little hut all by itself, away down against the back fence, and some out-buildings down a piece the other side; ash-hopper, and big kettle to bile soap in, by the little hut; bench by the kitchen door, with bucket of water and a gourd; hound asleep there, in the sun; more hounds asleep, round about; about three shade trees, away off in a corner; some currant bushes and gooseberry bushes in one place by the fence; outside of the fence, a garden and a watermelon patch; then the cotton fields begins; and after the fields, the woods.

I went around and clumb over the back stile by the ash-hopper, and started for the kitchen. When I got a little ways, I heard the dim hum of a spinning wheel wailing along up and sinking along down again: and then I knowed for certain I wished I was dead—for that *is* the lonesomest sound in the whole world.

I went right along, not fixing up any particular plan, but just trusting to Providence to put the right words in my mouth when the time come; for I'd noticed that Providence always did put the right words in my mouth, if I left it alone.

When I got half way, first one hound and then another got up and went for me, and of course I stopped, and faced them, and kept still. And such another pow-wow as they made! in a quarter of a minute I was a kind of a hub of a wheel, as you may say—spokes made out of dogs—circle of fifteen of them packed together around me, with their necks and noses stretched up towards me, a-barking and howling; and more a-coming; you could see them sailing over fences and around corners, from everywheres.

A nigger woman come tearing out of the kitchen, with a rolling-pin in her hand, singing out, "Begone! *you* Tige! you Spot! bedone, sah!" and she fetched first one and then another of them a clip and sent him howling, and then the rest followed; and the next second, half of them come back, wagging their tails around me and making friends with me. There ain't no harm in a hound, nohow.

And behind the woman comes a little nigger girl and two little nigger boys, without anything on but tow-linen shirts, and they hung onto their mother's gown, and peeped out from behind her at me, bashful, the way they always do. And here comes the white woman running from the house, about forty-five or fifty year old, bareheaded, and her spinning-stick in her hand; and behind her comes her little white children, acting the same way the little niggers was doing. She was smiling all over so she could hardly stand—and says:

"It's *you*, at last!—*ain't* it?"

I out with a "Yes'm," before I thought.

She grabbed me and hugged me tight; and then gripped me by both hands, and shook and shook; and the tears come in her eyes, and run down over; and she couldn't seem to hug and shake enough, and kept saying, "You don't look as much like your mother as I reckoned you would, but law sakes, I don't care for that, I'm *so* glad to see you! Dear, dear, it does seem like I could eat you up! Childern, it's your cousin Tom!—tell him howdy."

SHE HUGGED HIM TIGHT.

But they ducked their heads, and put their fingers in their mouths, and hid behind her. So she run on:

"Lize, hurry up and get him a hot breakfast, right away—or did you get your breakfast on the boat?"

I said I had got it on the boat. So then she started for the house, leading me by the hand, and the children tagging after. When we got there, she set me down in a split-bottomed chair, and set herself down on a little low stool in front of me, holding both of my hands, and says:

"Now I can have a *good* look at you; and laws-a-me, I've been hungry for it a many and a many a time, all these long years, and it's come at last! We been expecting you a couple of days and more. What's kep' you?—boat get aground?"

"Yes'm—she—"

"Don't say yes'm—say Aunt Sally. Where'd she get aground?"

I didn't rightly know what to say, because I didn't know whether the boat would be coming up the river, or down. But I go a good deal on instinct; and my instinct said she would be coming up—from down towards Orleans. That didn't help me much, though; for I didn't know the names of bars down that way. I see I'd got to invent a bar, or forget the name of the one we got aground on—or—. Now I struck an idea, and fetched it out:

"It warn't the grounding—that didn't keep us back but a little. We blowed out a cylinder-head."

"Good gracious! anybody hurt?"

"No'm. Killed a nigger."

"Well, it's lucky; because sometimes people do get hurt. Two years ago last Christmas, your uncle Silas was coming up from Newrleans on the old Lally Rook, and she blowed out a cylinder-head and crippled a man. And I think he died, afterwards. He was a Babtist. Your uncle Silas knowed a family in Baton Rouge that knowed his people very well. Yes, I remember, now, he *did* die. Mortification set in, and they had to amputate him. But it didn't save him. Yes, it was mortification—that was it. He turned blue all over, and died in the hope of a glorious resurrection. They say he was a sight to look at. Your uncle's been up to the town every day to fetch you. And he's gone again, not more'n an hour ago; he'll be back any minute, now. You must a met him on the road, didn't you?—oldish man, with a—"

"No, I didn't see nobody, aunt Sally. The boat landed just at daylight, and I left my baggage on the wharfboat and went looking around the town and out a piece in the country, to put in the time and not get here too soon; and so I come down the back way."

"Who'd you give the baggage to?"

"Nobody."

"Why, child, it'll be stole!"

"Not where *I* hid it I reckon it won't," I says.

"How'd you get your breakfast so early on the boat?"

It was kinder thin ice, but I says:

"The captain see me standing around, and told me I better have something to eat before I went ashore; so he took me in the texas to the officers' lunch, and give me all I wanted."

I was getting so uneasy I couldn't listen good. I had my mind on the children all the time; I wanted to get them out to one side, and pump them a little, and find out who I was. But I couldn't get no show, Mrs. Phelps kept it up and run on so. Pretty soon she made the cold chills streak all down my back; because she says:

"But here we're a running on, this way, and you hain't told me a word about Sis, nor any of them. Now I'll rest my works a little, and you start-up yourn; just tell me *everything*—tell me all about 'm all—every one of 'm; and how they are, and what they're doing, and what they told you to tell me; and every last thing you can think of."

Well, I see I was up a stump—and up it good. Providence had stood by me this fur, all right, but I was hard and tight aground, now. I see it warn't a bit of use to try to go ahead—I'd *got* to throw up my hand. So I says to myself, here's another place where I got to resk the truth. I opened my mouth to begin; but she grabbed me and hustled me in behind the bed, and says:

"Here he comes! Stick your head down lower—there, that'll do; you can't be seen, now. Don't you let on you're here: I'll play a joke on him. Childern, don't you say a word."

I see I was in a fix, now. But it warn't no use to worry; there warn't nothing to do but just hold still, and try and be ready to stand from under when the lightning struck.

I had just one little glimpse of the old gentleman when he come in,—then the bed hid him. Mrs. Phelps she jumps for him and says:

"Has he come?"

"No," says her husband.

"Good-*ness* gracious!" she says, "what in the world *can* have become of him?"

"I can't imagine," says the old gentleman; "and I must say, it makes me dreadful uneasy."

"Uneasy!" she says, "I'm ready to go distracted! He *must* a come; and you've missed him along the road. I *know* it's so—something *tells* me so."

"Why Sally, I *couldn't* miss him along the road—*you* know that."

"But oh, dear, dear, what *will* Sis say! He must a come! You must a missed him. He—"

"Oh, don't distress me any more'n I'm already distressed. I don't know what in the world to make of it. I'm at my wit's end, and I don't mind acknowledging 't I'm right down scared. But there's no hope that he's come; for he *couldn't* come and me miss him. Sally it's terrible—just terrible—something's happened to the boat, sure!"

"Why, Silas! Look yonder!—up the road!—ain't that somebody coming?"

He sprung to the window at the head of the bed, and that give Mrs. Phelps the chance she wanted. She stooped down quick, at the foot of the bed, and give me a pull, and out I come; and when he turned back from the window, there she stood, a-beaming and a-smiling like a house afire, and I standing pretty meek and sweaty alongside. The old gentleman stared, and says:

"Why, who's that?"

"Who do you reckon 't is?"

"WHO DO YOU RECKON 'T IS?"

"I hain't no idea. Who *is* it?"

"It's *Tom Sawyer!*"

By jings, I most slumped through the floor. But there warn't no time to swap knives: the old man grabbed me by the hand and shook, and kept on shaking; and all the time, how the woman did dance around and laugh and cry; and then how they both did fire off questions about Sid, and Mary, and the rest of the tribe.

But if they was joyful, it warn't nothing to what I was; for it was like being born again, I was so glad to find out who I was. Well, they froze to me for two hours; and at last when my chin was so tired it couldn't hardly go, any more, I had told them more about my family—I mean the Sawyer family—than ever happened to any six Sawyer families. And I explained all about how we blowed out a cylinder head at the mouth of White river and it took us three days to fix it. Which was all right, and worked first-rate; because *they* didn't know but what it would take three days to fix it. If I'd a called it a bolt-head it would a done just as well.

Now I was feeling pretty comfortable all down one side, and pretty uncomfortable all up the other. Being Tom Sawyer was easy and comfortable; and it staid easy and comfortable till by and by I hear a steamboat coughing along down the river—then I says to myself, spose Tom Sawyer come down on that boat?—and spose he steps in here, any minute, and sings out my name before I can throw him a wink to keep quiet? Well, I couldn't *have* it that way—it wouldn't do, at all. I must go up the road and waylay him. So I told the folks I reckoned I would go up to the town and fetch down my baggage. The old gentleman was for going along with me, but I said no, I could drive the horse myself, and I druther he wouldn't take no trouble about me.

Chapter XXXIII.

"IT WAS TOM SAWYER."

So I started for town, in the wagon, and when I was half way I see a wagon coming, and sure enough it was Tom Sawyer, and I stopped and waited till he come along. I says "Hold on!" and it stopped alongside, and his mouth opened up like a trunk, and staid so; and he swallowed two or three times, like a person that's got a dry throat, and then says:

"I hain't ever done you no harm. You know that. So then, what you want to come back and ha'nt *me*, for?"

I says:

"I hain't come back—I hain't been *gone*."

When he heard my voice, it righted him up, some, but he warn't quite satisfied, yet. He says:

"Don't you play nothing on me, because I wouldn't on you. Honest injun, now, you ain't a ghost?"

"Honest injun, I ain't," I says.

"Well—I—I—well, that ought to settle it, of course; but I can't somehow seem to understand it, no way. Lookyhere, warn't you ever murdered *at all?*"

"No. I warn't ever murdered at all—I played it on them. You come in here and feel of me if you don't believe me."

So he done it; and it satisfied him; and he was that glad to see me again, he didn't know what to do. And he wanted to know all about it, right off; because it was a grand adventure, and mysterious, and so it hit him where he lived. But I said, leave it alone till by and by;

and told his driver to wait, and we drove off a little piece, and I told
him the kind of a fix I was in, and what did he reckon we better do?
He said, let him alone a minute, and don't disturb him. So he
thought and thought, and pretty soon he says:

"It's all right, I've got it. Take my trunk in your wagon, and let on
it's your'n; and you turn back and fool along slow, so as to get to the
house about the time you ought to; and I'll go towards town a piece,
and take a fresh start, and get there a quarter or a half an hour after
you; and you needn't let on to know me, at first."

I says:

"All right; but wait a minute. There's one more thing—a thing
that *nobody* don't know but me. And that is, there's a nigger here
that I'm a trying to steal out of slavery—and his name is *Jim*—old
Miss Watson's Jim."

He says:

"What! Why Jim is—"

He stopped, and went to studying. I says:

"*I* know what you'll say. You'll say it's dirty low-down business;
but what if it is?—*I'm* low-down; and I'm agoing to steal him, and I
want you to keep mum and not let on. Will you?"

His eye lit up, and he says:

"I'll *help* you steal him!"

Well, I let go all holts, then, like I was shot. It was the most
astonishing speech I ever heard—and I'm bound to say Tom Sawyer
fell, considerable, in my estimation. Only I couldn't believe it. Tom
Sawyer a *nigger stealer!*

"Oh, shucks," I says, "you're joking."

"I ain't joking, either."

"Well, then," I says, "joking or no joking, if you hear anything
said about a runaway nigger, don't forget to remember that *you*
don't know nothing about him, and *I* don't know nothing about
him."

Then we took the trunk and put it in my wagon, and he drove off
his way, and I drove mine. But of course I forgot all about driving
slow, on accounts of being glad and full of thinking; so I got home a
heap too quick for that length of a trip. The old gentleman was at
the door, and he says:

"Why, this is wonderful. Who ever would a thought it was in that mare to do it. I wish we'd a timed her. And she hain't sweated a hair—not a hair. It's wonderful. Why, I wouldn't take a hunderd dollars for that horse now; I wouldn't, honest; and yet I'd a sold her for fifteen, before, and thought 'twas all she was worth."

That's all he said. He was the innocentest best old soul I ever see. But it warn't surprising; because he warn't only just a farmer, he was a preacher, too, and had a little one-horse log church down back of the plantation, which he built it himself at his own expense, for a church and school house, and never charged nothing for his preaching, and it was worth it, too. There was plenty other farmer-preachers like that, and done the same way, down South.

In about half an hour Tom's wagon drove up to the front stile, and aunt Sally she see it through the window—because it was only about fifty yards—and says:

"Why, there's somebody come! I wonder who 'tis? Why, I do believe it's a stranger. Jimmy," (that's one of the children,) "run and tell Lize to put on another plate for dinner."

Everybody made a rush for the front door—because, of course, a stranger don't come *every* year, and so he lays over the yaller fever, for interest, when he does come. Tom was over the stile and starting for the house; the wagon was spinning up the road for the village, and we was all bunched in the front door. Tom had his store clothes on, and an audience—and that was always nuts for Tom Sawyer. In them circumstances it warn't no trouble to him to throw in an amount of style that was suitable. He warn't a boy to meeky along up that yard like a sheep; no, he come ca'm and important, like the ram. When he got afront of us, he lifts his hat ever so gracious and dainty, like it was the lid of a box that had butterflies asleep in it and he didn't want to disturb them, and says:

"Mr. Archibald Nichols, I presume?"

"No, my boy," says the old gentleman, "I'm sorry to say 't your driver has deceived you; Nichols's place is down a matter of three mile more. Come in, come in."

Tom he took a look back over his shoulder, and says, "Too late— he's out of sight."

"Yes, he's gone, my son, and you must come in and eat your dinner with us; and then we'll hitch up and take you down to Nichols's."

"MR. ARCHIBALD NICHOLS, I PRESUME?"

"Oh, I *can't* make you so much trouble, I couldn't think of it. I'll walk—I don't mind the distance."

"But we won't *let* you walk—it wouldn't be southern hospitality to do it. Come right in."

"Oh, *do,*" says aunt Sally; "it ain't a bit of trouble to us, not a bit in the world. You *must* stay. It's a long, dusty three mile, and we *can't* let you walk. And besides, I've already told 'em to put on another plate, when I see you coming; so you mustn't disappoint us. Come right in, and make yourself at home."

So Tom he thanked them very hearty and handsome, and let himself be persuaded, and come in; and when he was in, he said he was a stranger from Hicksville, Ohio, and his name was William Thompson—and he made another bow.

Well, he run on, and on, and on, making up stuff about Hicksville and everybody in it he could invent, and I getting a little nervous, and wondering how this was going to help me out of my scrape; and at last, still talking along, he reached over and kissed aunt Sally right on the mouth, and then settled back again, in his chair, comfortable, and was going on talking; but she jumped up and wiped it off with the back of her hand, and says:

"You owdacious puppy!"

He looked kind of hurt, and says:

"I'm surprised at you, m'am."

"You're s'rp— Why, what do you reckon *I* am? I've a good notion to take and—say, what do you mean by kissing me?"

He looked kind of humble, and says:

"I didn't mean nothing, m'am. I didn't mean no harm. I—I—thought you'd like it."

"Why, you born fool!" She took up the spinning-stick, and it looked like it was all she could do to keep from giving him a crack with it. "What made you think I'd like it?"

"Well, I don't know. Only, they—they—told me you would."

"*They* told you I would. Whoever told you, 's *another* lunatic. I never heard the beat of it. Who's *they?*"

"Why—everybody. They all said so, m'am."

It was all she could do to hold in; and her eyes snapped, and her fingers worked like she wanted to scratch him; and she says:

"Who's 'everybody?' Out with their names—or ther'll be an idiot short."

He got up and looked distressed, and fumbled his hat, and says:

"I'm sorry, and I warn't expecting it. They told me to. They all told me to. They all said kiss her; and said, she'll like it. They all said it—every one of them. But I'm sorry, m'am, and I won't do it no more—I won't, honest."

"You won't, won't you? Well, I sh'd *reckon* you won't!"

"No'm, I'm honest about it; I won't ever do it again. Till you ask me."

"Till I *ask* you! Well, I never see the beat of it in my born days! I lay you'll be the Methusalem-numskull of creation before ever *I* ask you—or the likes of you."

"Well," he says, "it does surprise me so. I can't make it out, somehow. They said you would, and I thought you would. But—" He stopped, and looked around slow, like he wished he could run across a friendly eye, somewheres; and fetched up on the old gentleman's, and says, "Didn't *you* think she'd like me to kiss her, sir?"

"Why, no, I—I—well, no, I b'lieve I didn't."

Then he looks on around, the same way, to me—and says:

"Tom, didn't *you* think aunt Sally 'd open out her arms and say, 'Sid Sawyer'—"

"My land!" she says, breaking in and jumping for him, "you impudent young rascal, to fool a body so—" and was going to hug him, but he fended her off, and says:

"No, not till you've asked me, first."

So she didn't lose no time, but asked him; and hugged him and kissed him, over and over again, and then turned him over to the old man, and he took what was left. And after they got a little quiet again, she says:

"Why dear me, I never see such a surprise. We warn't looking for *you*, at all, but only Tom. Sis never wrote to me about anybody coming but him."

"It's because it warn't *intended* for any of us to come but Tom," he says; "but I begged and begged, and at the last minute she let me come, too; so, coming down the river, me and Tom thought it would be a first rate surprise for him to come here to the house first, and for me to by and by tag along and drop in and let on to be a stranger. But it was a mistake, aunt Sally. This ain't no healthy place for a stranger to come."

"No—not impudent whelps, Sid. You ought to had your jaws boxed; I hain't been so put out since I don't know when. But I don't care, I don't mind the terms—I'd be willing to stand a thousand such jokes to have you here. Well, to think of that performance! I don't deny it, I was most putrefied with astonishment when you give me that smack."

We had dinner out in that broad open passage betwixt the house and the kitchen; and there was things enough on that table for seven families—and all hot, too; none of your flabby tough meat that's laid in a cupboard in a damp cellar all night and tastes like a hunk of old cold cannibal in the morning. Uncle Silas he asked a pretty long blessing over it, but it was worth it; and it didn't cool it a bit, neither, the way I've seen them kind of interruptions do, lots of times.

There was a considerable good deal of talk, all the afternoon, and me and Tom was on the lookout all the time, but it warn't no use,

they didn't happen to say nothing about any runaway nigger, and
we was afraid to try to work up to it. But at supper, at night, one of
the little boys says:

"Pa, mayn't Tom and Sid and me go to the show?"

"No," says the old man, "I reckon there ain't going to be any; and
you couldn't go if there was; because the runaway nigger told Burton

A PRETTY LONG BLESSING.

and me all about that scandalous show, and Burton said he would
tell the people; so I reckon they've drove the owdacious loafers out
of town before this time."

So there it was!—but *I* couldn't help it. Tom and me was to sleep
in the same room and bed; so, being tired, we bid good night and
went up to bed, right after supper, and clumb out of the window and
down the lightning rod, and shoved for the town; for I didn't believe
anybody was going to give the king and the duke a hint, and so if I
didn't hurry up and give them one they'd get into trouble, sure.

On the road Tom he told me all about how it was reckoned I was
murdered, and how pap disappeared, pretty soon, and didn't come
back no more, and what a stir there was when Jim run away; and I
told Tom all about our Royal Nonesuch rapscallions, and as much
of the raft-voyage as I had time to; and as we struck into the town
and up through the middle of it—it was as much as half after eight,

then—here comes a raging rush of people, with torches, and an awful whooping and yelling, and banging tin pans and blowing horns; and we jumped to one side to let them go by; and as they went by, I see they had the king and the duke astraddle of a rail—that is, I knowed it *was* the king and the duke, though they was all over tar and feathers, and didn't look like nothing in the world that was human—just looked like a couple of monstrous big soldier-plumes. Well, it made me sick to see it; and I was sorry for them poor pitiful rascals, it seemed like I couldn't ever feel any hardness against them any more in the world. It was a dreadful thing to see. Human beings *can* be awful cruel to one another.

We see we was too late—couldn't do no good. We asked some stragglers about it, and they said everybody went to the show looking very innocent; and laid low and kept dark till the poor old king was in the middle of his cavortings on the stage; then somebody give a signal, and the house rose up and went for them.

So we poked along back home, and I warn't feeling so brash as I was before, but kind of ornery, and humble, and to blame, somehow—though *I* hadn't done nothing. But that's always the way: it don't make no difference whether you do right or wrong, a person's conscience ain't got no sense, and just goes for him *anyway*. If I had a yaller dog that didn't know no more than a person's conscience does, I would pison him. It takes up more room than all the rest of a person's insides, and yet ain't no good, nohow. Tom Sawyer he says the same.

TRAVELING BY RAIL.

Chapter XXXIV.

VITTLES.

We stopped talking, and got to thinking. By and by, Tom says:

"Looky-here, Huck, what fools we are, to not think of it before! I bet I know where Jim is."

"No! Where?"

"In that hut down by the ash-hopper. Why, looky-here. When we was at dinner, didn't you see a nigger man go in there with some vittles?"

"Yes."

"What did you think the vittles was for?"

"For a dog."

"So'd I. Well, it warn't for a dog."

"Why?"

"Because part of it was watermelon."

"So it was—I noticed it. Well, it does beat all, that I never thought about a dog not eating watermelon. It shows how a body can see and don't see, at the same time."

"Well, the nigger unlocked the padlock when he went in, and he locked it again when he come out. He fetched uncle a key, about the time we got up from table—same key, I bet. Watermelon shows man, lock shows prisoner; and it ain't likely there's two prisoners on such a little plantation, and where the people's all so kind and good. Jim's the prisoner. All right—I'm glad we found it out detective fashion; I wouldn't give shucks for any other way. Now you work your mind and study out a plan to steal Jim, and I will study out one, too; and we'll take the one we like the best."

What a head for just a boy to have! If I had Tom Sawyer's head, I wouldn't trade it off to be a duke, nor mate of a steamboat, nor clown in a circus, nor nothing I can think of. I went to thinking out a plan, but only just to be doing something: I knowed very well where the right plan was going to come from. Pretty soon, Tom says:

"Ready?"

"Yes," I says.

"All right,—bring it out."

"My plan is this," I says. "We can easy find out if it's Jim in there. Then get up my canoe to-morrow night, and fetch my raft over from the island. Then the first dark night that comes, steal the key out of the old man's britches, after he goes to bed, and shove off down the river on the raft, with Jim, hiding daytimes and running nights, the way me and Jim used to do before. Wouldn't that plan work?"

"*Work?* Why cert'nly, it would work, like rats a-fighting. But it's too blame' simple; there ain't nothing *to* it. What's the good of a plan that ain't no more trouble than that? It's as mild as goose-milk. Why, Huck, it wouldn't make no more talk than breaking into a soap factory."

I never said nothing, because I warn't expecting nothing different; but I knowed mighty well that whenever he got *his* plan ready it wouldn't have none of them objections to it.

And it didn't. He told me what it was, and I see in a minute it was worth fifteen of mine, for style, and would make Jim just as free a man as mine would, and maybe get us all killed, besides. So I was satisfied, and said we would waltz in on it. I needn't tell what it was, here, because I knowed it wouldn't stay the way it was. I knowed he would be changing it around, every which way, as we went along, and heaving in new bullinesses wherever he got a chance. And that is what he done.

Well, one thing was dead sure; and that was, that Tom Sawyer was in earnest, and was actuly going to help steal that nigger out of slavery. That was the thing that was too many for me. Here was a boy that was respectable, and well brung up; and had a character to lose; and folks at home that had characters; and he was bright and not leatherheaded; and knowing, and not ignorant; and not mean, but kind; and yet here he was, without any more pride, or rightness, or feeling, than to stoop to this business, and make himself a shame, and his family a shame, before everybody. I *couldn't* understand it, no way at all. It was outrageous, and I knowed I ought to just up and tell him so; and so be his true friend, and let him quit the thing right where he was, and save himself. And I *did* start to tell him; but he shut me up, and says:

"Don't you reckon I know what I'm about? Don't I generly know what I'm about?"

"Yes."

"Didn't I *say* I was going to help steal the nigger?"

"Yes."

"*Well*, then."

That's all he said, and that's all I said. It warn't no use to say any more; because when he said he'd do a thing, he always done it. But *I* couldn't make out how he was willing to go into this thing; so I just let it go, and never bothered no more about it. If he was bound to have it so, *I* couldn't help it.

When we got home, the house was all dark and still; so we went on down to the hut by the ash-hopper, for to examine it. We went through the yard, so as to see what the hounds would do. They knowed us, and didn't make no more noise than country dogs is always doing when anything comes by in the night. When we got to the cabin, we took a look at the front and the two sides; and on the side I warn't acquainted with—which was the north side—we found a square window-hole, up tolerable high, with just one stout board nailed across it. I says:

"Here's the ticket. This hole's big enough for Jim to get through, if we wrench off the board."

Tom says:

"It's as simple as tit-tat-toe, three-in-a-row, and as easy as playing hookey. I should *hope* we can find a way that's a little more compli-cated than *that*, Huck Finn."

"Well, then," I says, "how'll it do to saw him out, the way I done before I was murdered, that time?"

"That's more *like*," he says. "It's real mysterious, and trouble-some, and good," he says; "but I bet we can find a way that's twice as long. There ain't no hurry; le's keep on looking around."

Betwixt the hut and the fence, on the backside, was a lean-to, that joined the hut at the eaves, and was made out of plank. It was as long as the hut, but narrow—only about six foot wide. The door

A SIMPLE JOB.

to it was at the south end, and was padlocked. Tom he went to the soap kettle, and searched around and fetched back the iron thing they lift the lid with; so he took it and prized out one of the staples. The chain fell down, and we opened the door and went in, and shut it and struck a match, and see the shed was only built against the cabin and hadn't no connection with it; and there warn't no floor to the shed, nor nothing in it but some old rusty played-out hoes, and spades, and picks and a crippled plow. The match went out, and so did we, and shoved in the staple again, and the door was locked as good as ever. Tom was joyful. He says:

"Now we're all right. We'll *dig* him out. It'll take about a week!"

Then we started for the house, and I went in the back door—you only have to pull a buckskin latch-string, they don't fasten the doors—but that warn't romantical enough for Tom Sawyer: no way would do him but he must climb up the lightning rod. But after he got up half way about three times, and missed fire and fell every

time, and the last time most busted his brains out, he thought he'd
got to give it up; but after he was rested, he allowed he would give
her one more turn for luck, and this time he made the trip.

In the morning we was up at break of day, and down to the nigger
cabins to pet the dogs and make friends with the nigger that fed
Jim—if it *was* Jim that was being fed. The niggers was just getting
through breakfast and starting for the fields; and Jim's nigger was
piling up a tin pan with bread and meat and things; and whilst the
others was leaving, the key come from the house.

This nigger had a good-natured chuckleheaded face, and his wool
was all tied up in little bunches with thread. That was to keep
witches off. He said the witches was pestering him awful, these
nights, and making him see all kinds of strange things, and hear all
kinds of strange words and noises, and he didn't believe he was ever
witched so long, before, in his life. He got so worked up, and got to
running on so, about his troubles, he forgot all about what he'd been
agoing to do. So Tom says:

"What's the vittles for? Going to feed the dogs?"

The nigger kind of smiled around gradully over his face like when
you heave a brickbat in a mud puddle, and he says:

"Yes, mars Sid, *a* dog. Cur'us dog, too. Does you want to go en
look at 'im?"

"Yes."

I hunched Tom, and whispers:

"You going, right here in the daybreak? *That* warn't the plan."

"No, it warn't—but it's the plan *now*."

So, drat him, we went along, but I didn't like it much. When we
got in, we couldn't hardly see anything, it was so dark; but Jim was
there, sure enough, and could see us; and he sings out:

"Why *Huck!* En good *lan'!* ain' dat Misto Tom?"

I just knowed how it would be; I just expected it. *I* didn't know
nothing to do; and if I had, I couldn't a done it; because that nigger
busted in and says:

"Why, de gracious sakes! do he know you genlmen?"

We could see pretty well, now. Tom he looked at the nigger,
steady and kind of wondering, and says:

"Does *who* know us?"

"Why, dish-yer runaway nigger."

"I don't reckon he does; but what put that into your head?"

"What *put* it dar? Didn' he jis' dis minute sing out like he knowed you?"

Tom says, in a puzzled-up kind of way:

"Well, that's mighty curious. *Who* sung out? *When* did he sing out? *What* did he sing out?" And turns to me, perfectly ca'm, and says, "Did *you* hear anybody sing out?"

Of course there warn't nothing to be said but the one thing; so I says:

"No; *I* ain't heard nobody say nothing."

Then he turns to Jim, and looks him over like he never see him before; and says:

"Did you sing out?"

"No, sah," says Jim, "*I* hain't said nothing, sah."

"Not a word?"

"No, sah, I hain't said a word."

"Did you ever see us before?"

"No, sah; not as *I* knows on."

So Tom turns to the nigger, which was looking wild and dis-tressed, and says, kind of se-vere:

WITCHES.

"What do you reckon's the matter with you, anyway? What made you think some-body sung out?"

"O, it's de dad-blame' witches, sah, en I wisht I was dead, I do. Dey's awluz at it, sah, en dey do mos' kill me, dey sk'yers me so. Please to don't tell nobody 'bout it, sah, er ole mars Silas he'll scole me; 'kase he say dey *ain'* no witches. I jis' wish to good-ness he was heah now—*den* what would he say! I jis' bet he couldn' fine no way to git aroun' it *dis* time. But it's awluz jis' so: people dat's *sot,* stays sot; dey won't look into noth'n en fine it out f'r deyselves, en when *you* fine it out en tell um 'bout it, dey doan b'lieve you."

Tom give him a dime, and said we wouldn't tell nobody; and told him to buy some more thread to tie up his wool with; and then looks at Jim and says:

"I wonder if uncle Silas is going to hang this nigger. If I was to catch a nigger that was ungrateful enough to run away, *I* wouldn't give him up, I'd hang him." And whilst the nigger stepped to the door to look at the dime and bite it to see if it was good, he whispers to Jim, and says:

"Don't ever let on to know us. And if you hear any digging going on, nights, it's us: we're going to set you free."

Jim only had time to grab us by the hand and squeeze it, then the nigger come back, and we said we'd come again some time if the nigger wanted us to; and he said he would, more particular if it was dark, because the witches went for him mostly in the dark, and it was good to have folks around, then.

Chapter XXXV.

GETTING WOOD.

It would be most an hour, yet, till breakfast, so we left, and struck down into the woods; because Tom said we got to have *some* light to see how to dig by, and a lantern makes too much, and might get us into trouble; what we must have was a lot of them rotten chunks that's called fox-fire, and just makes a soft kind of a glow when you lay them in a dark place. We fetched an armful and hid it in the weeds, and set down to rest, and Tom says, kind of dissatisfied:

"Blame it, this whole thing is just as easy and awkard as it can be. And so it makes it so rotten difficult to get up a difficult plan. There ain't no watchman to be drugged—now there *ought* to be a watchman. There ain't even a dog, to give a sleeping-mixture to. And there's Jim chained by one leg, with a ten-foot chain, to the leg of his bed: why, all you got to do is to lift up the bedstead and slip off the chain. And uncle Silas he trusts everybody; sends the key to the punkinheaded nigger, and don't send nobody to watch the nigger. Jim could a got out of that window-hole, before this, only there wouldn't be no use trying to travel with a ten-foot chain on his leg. Why, drat it, Huck, it's the stupidest arrangement I ever see: You got to invent *all* the difficulties. Well, we can't help it, we got to do the best we can with the materials we've got. Anyhow, there's one thing—there's more honor in getting him out through a lot of difficulties and dangers, where there warn't one of them furnished to you by the people who it was their duty to furnish them, and you had to contrive them all out of your own head. Now look at just that one thing of the lantern. When you come down to the cold facts, we simply got to *let on* that a lantern's resky. Why, we could work with a torchlight procession if we wanted to, *I* believe. Now whilst I think of it, we got to hunt up something to make a saw out of, the first chance we get."

"What do we want of a saw?"

"What do we *want* of it? Hain't we got to saw the leg of Jim's bed off, so as to get the chain loose?"

"Why, you just said a body could lift up the bedstead and slip the chain off."

"Well, if that ain't just like you, Huck Finn. You *can* get up the infant-schooliest ways of going at a thing. Why, hain't you ever read any books at all?—Baron Trenck, nor Casanova, nor Benvenuto Chelleeny, nor Henri IV, nor none of them heroes? Whoever heard of getting a prisoner loose in such an old-maidy way as that? No; the way all the best authorities does, is to saw the bed-leg in two, and leave it just so, and swallow the sawdust, so it can't be found, and put some dirt and grease around the sawed place so the very keenest seneskal can't see no sign of its being sawed, and thinks the bed-leg is perfectly sound. Then, the night you're ready, fetch the leg a kick, down she goes; slip off your chain, and there you are: nothing to do but hitch your rope-ladder to the battlements, shin down it, break your leg in the moat—because a rope-ladder is nineteen foot too short, you know—and there's your horses and your trusty vassles, and they scoop you up and fling you across a saddle and away you go, to your native Langudoc, or Navarre, or wherever it is. It's gaudy, Huck. I wish there was a moat to this cabin. If we get time, the night of the escape, we'll dig one."

I says:

"What do we want of a moat, when we're going to snake him out from under the cabin?"

But he never heard me. He had forgot me and everything else. He had his chin in his hand, thinking. Pretty soon, he sighs, and shakes his head; then sighs again, and says:

"No, it wouldn't do—there ain't necessity enough for it."

"For what?" I says.

"Why, to saw Jim's leg off," he says.

"Good land!" I says, "Why, there ain't *no* necessity for it. And what would you want to saw his leg off, for, anyway?"

"Well, some of the best authorities has done it. They couldn't get the chain off, so they just cut their hand off, and shoved. And a leg would be better still. But we got to let that go. There ain't necessity

ONE OF THE BEST AUTHORITIES.

enough in this case; and besides, Jim's a nigger and wouldn't understand the reasons for it, and how it's the custom in Europe; so we'll let it go. But there's one thing—he can have a rope ladder; we can tear up our sheets and make him a rope ladder easy enough. And we can send it to him in a pie; it's mostly done that way. And I've et worse pies."

"Why, Tom Sawyer, how you talk," I says; "Jim ain't got no use for a rope ladder."

"He *has* got use for it. How *you* talk, you better say: you don't know nothing about it. He's *got* to have a rope ladder: they all do."

"What in the nation can he *do* with it?"

"*Do* with it? He can hide it in his bed, can't he? That's what they all do; and *he's* got to, too. Huck, you don't ever seem to want to do anything that's regular: you want to be starting something fresh all the time. Spose he *don't* do nothing with it? ain't it there in his bed, for a clew, after he's gone? and don't you reckon they'll want clews? Of course they will. And you wouldn't leave them any? That would be a *pretty* howdy-do, *wouldn't* it! I never heard of such a thing."

"Well," I says, "if it's in the regulations, and he's got to have it, all right, let him have it; because I don't wish to go back on no regulations; but there's one thing, Tom Sawyer—if we go to tearing up our sheets to make Jim a rope ladder, we're going to get into trouble with aunt Sally, just as sure as you're born. Now the way I look at it, a hickry bark ladder don't cost nothing, and don't waste nothing, and is just as good to load up a pie with, and hide in a straw tick, as any rag-ladder you can start; and as for Jim, he ain't had no experience, and so *he* don't care what kind of a—"

"O shucks, Huck Finn, if I was as ignorant as you, I'd keep still— that's what *I'd* do. Who ever heard of a state prisoner escaping by a hickry bark ladder? Why, it's perfectly ridiculous."

"Well, all right, Tom, fix it your own way; but if you'll take my advice, you'll let me borrow a sheet off of the clothes line."

He said that would do. And that give him another idea, and he says:

"Borrow a shirt, too."

"What do we want of a shirt, Tom?"

"Want it for Jim to keep a journal on."

"Journal your granny—*Jim* can't write."

"Spose he *can't* write—he can make marks on the shirt, can't he, if we make him a pen out of an old pewter spoon or a piece of an old iron barrel-hoop?"

"Why, Tom, we can pull a feather out of a goose and make him a better one; and quicker, too."

"*Prisoners* don't have geese running around the donjon-keep to pull pens out of, you muggins. They *always* make their pens out of the hardest, toughest, troublesomest piece of old brass candlestick or something like that they can get their hands on; and it takes them weeks and weeks, and months and months to file it out, too, because they've got to do it by rubbing it on the wall. *They* wouldn't use a goose-quill if they had it. It ain't regular."

"Well, then, what'll we make him the ink out of?"

"Many makes it out of iron-rust and tears; but that's the common sort and women; the best authorities uses their own blood. Jim can do that; and when he wants to send any little common ordinary mysterious message to let the world know where he's captivated, he can write it on the bottom of a tin plate with a fork and throw it out of the window. The Iron Mask always done that, and it's a blame' good way, too."

"Jim ain't got no tin plates. They feed him in a pan."

"That ain't anything; we can get him some."

"Can't nobody *read* his plates."

"That ain't got nothing to *do* with it, Huck Finn. All *he*'s got to do is to write on the plate and throw it out. You don't *have* to be able to read it. Why, half the time you can't read anything a prisoner writes on a tin plate, or anywhere else."

"Well, then, what's the sense in wasting the plates?"

"Why, blame it all, it ain't the *prisoner's* plates."

"But it's *somebody's* plates, ain't it?"

THE BREAKFAST HORN.

"Well, spos'n it is? What does the *prisoner* care whose—"

He broke off there, because we heard the breakfast horn blowing. So we cleared out for the house.

Along during that morning I borrowed a sheet and a white shirt off of the clothes line; and I found an old sack and put them in it, and we went down and got the fox-fire, and put that in, too. I called it borrowing, because that was what pap always called it; but Tom said it warn't borrowing, it was stealing. He said we was representing prisoners; and prisoners don't care how they get a thing so they get it, and nobody don't blame them for it, either. It ain't no crime in a prisoner to steal the thing he needs to get away with, Tom said; it's his right; and so, as long as we was representing a prisoner, we had a perfect right to steal anything on this place we had the least use for, to get ourselves out of prison with. He said if we warn't prisoners it would be a very different thing, and nobody but a mean ornery person would steal when he warn't a prisoner. So we allowed we would steal everything there was that come handy. And yet he made a mighty fuss, one day, after that, when I stole a watermelon out of the nigger patch and eat it; and he made me go and give the niggers a dime, without telling them what it was for. Tom said that what he meant was, we could steal anything we *needed*. Well, I says, I needed the watermelon. But he said I didn't need it to get out of prison with, there's where the difference was. He said if I'd a wanted it to hide a knife in, and smuggle it to Jim to kill the seneskal with, it would a been all right. So I let it go at that, though I couldn't see no advantage in my representing a prisoner, if I got to set down and chaw over a lot of gold-leaf distinctions like that, every time I see a chance to hog a watermelon.

Well, as I was saying, we waited, that morning, till everybody was settled down to business, and nobody in sight around the yard; then Tom he carried the sack into the lean-to whilst I stood off a piece to keep watch. By and by he come out, and we went and set down on the woodpile, to talk. He says:

"Everything's all right, now, except tools; and that's easy fixed."

"Tools?" I says.

"Yes."

"Tools for what?"

"Why, to dig with. We ain't agoing to *gnaw* him out, are we?"

"Ain't them old crippled picks and things in there good enough to dig a nigger out with?" I says.

He turns on me looking pitying enough to make a body cry; and says:

"Huck Finn, did you *ever* hear of a prisoner having picks and shovels and all the modern conveniences in his wardrobe to dig himself out with? Now I want to ask you—if you got any reasonableness in you at all—what kind of a show would *that* give him to be a hero? Why they might as well lend him the key, and done with it. Picks and shovels—why they wouldn't furnish 'em to a king."

"Well, then," I says, "if we don't want the picks and shovels, what do we want?"

"A couple of caseknives."

"To dig the foundations out from under that cabin with?"

"Yes."

"Consound it, it's foolish, Tom."

"It don't make no difference how foolish it is, it's the *right* way—and it's the regular way. And there ain't no *other* way, that ever *I* heard of; and I've read all the books that gives any information about these things. They always dig out with a caseknife—and not through dirt, mind you; generly it's through solid rock. And it takes them weeks and weeks and weeks, and forever and ever. Why, look at one of them prisoners in the bottom dungeon of the Castle Deef, in the harbor of Marseilles, that dug himself out that way: how long was *he* at it, you reckon?"

"I don't know."

"Well, guess."

"I don't know. A month and a half?"

"*Thirty-seven year*—and he come out in China. *That's* the kind. I wish the bottom of *this* fortress was solid rock."

"*Jim* don't know nobody in China."

"What's *that* got to do with it? Neither did that other fellow. But you're always a-wandering off on a side issue. Why can't you stick to the main point?"

"All right—*I* don't care where he comes out, so he *comes* out; and Jim don't, either, I reckon. But there's one thing, anyway—Jim's too old to be dug out with a caseknife. He won't last."

"Yes he will *last*, too. You don't reckon it's going to take thirty-seven years to dig out through a *dirt* foundation, do you?"

"How long will it take, Tom?"

"Well, we can't resk being as long as we ought to, because it mayn't take very long for uncle Silas to hear from down there by New Orleans. He'll hear Jim ain't from there. Then his next move will be to advertise Jim, or something like that. So we can't resk being as long digging him out as we ought to. By rights I reckon we ought to be a couple of years; but we can't. Things being so uncertain, what I recommend is this: that we really dig right in, as quick as we can; and after that, we can *let on*, to ourselves, that we was at it thirty-seven years. Then we can snatch him out and rush him away the first time there's an alarm. Yes, I reckon that'll be the best way."

"Now there's *sense* in that," I says. "Letting-on don't cost nothing; letting-on ain't no trouble; and if it's any object, I don't mind letting on we was at it a hundred and fifty year. It wouldn't strain me none, after I got my hand in. So I'll mosey along, now, and smouch a couple of case-knives."

"Smouch three," he says; "we want one to make a saw out of."

"Tom, if it ain't unregular and irreligious to sejest it," I says, "there's an old rusty

SMOUCHING THE KNIVES.

saw-blade around yonder sticking under the weatherboarding behind the smokehouse."

He looked kind of weary and discouraged-like, and says:

"It ain't no use to try to learn you nothing, Huck. Run along and smouch the knives—three of them." So I done it.

Chapter XXXVI ·

GOING DOWN
THE LIGHTNING ROD.

As soon as we reckoned everybody was asleep, that night, we went down the lightning rod, and shut ourselves up in the lean-to, and got out our pile of fox-fire, and went to work. We cleared everything out of the way, about four or five foot along the middle of the bottom log. Tom said we was right behind Jim's bed, now, and we'd dig in under it, and when we got through, there couldn't nobody in the cabin ever know there was any hole there, because Jim's counterpin hung down most to the ground, and you'd have to raise it up and look under, to see the hole. So we dug and dug, with the caseknives, till most midnight; and then we was dog-tired, and our hands was blistered, and yet you couldn't see we'd done anything, hardly. At last I says:

"This ain't no thirty-seven year job, this is a thirty-eight year job, Tom Sawyer."

He never said nothing. But he sighed, and pretty soon he stopped digging, and then for a good little while I knowed he was thinking. Then he says:

"It ain't no use, Huck, it ain't agoing to work. If we was prisoners, it would, because then we'd have as many years as we wanted, and no hurry; and we wouldn't get but a few minutes to dig, every day, while they was changing watches, and so our hands wouldn't get blistered, and we could keep it up right along, year in and year out, and do it right and the way it ought to be done. But *we* can't fool along, we got to rush; we ain't got no time to spare. If we was to put in another night this way, we'd have to knock off for a week to let our hands get well—couldn't touch a caseknife with them sooner."

"Well, then, what we going to do, Tom?"

"I'll tell you. It ain't right, and it ain't moral, and I wouldn't like it to get out—but there ain't only just the one way: we got to dig him out with the picks, and *let on* it's case-knives."

"*Now* you're *talking!*" I says; "your head gets leveler and leveler all the time, Tom Sawyer," I says. "Picks is the thing, moral or no moral; and as for me, I don't care shucks for the morality of it, nohow. When I start in to steal a nigger, or a watermelon, or a Sunday school book, I ain't no ways particular how it's done, so it's done. What I want is my nigger; or what I want is my watermelon; or what I want is my Sunday school book: and if a pick's the handiest thing, that's the thing I'm agoing to dig that nigger or that watermelon or that Sunday school book out with; and I don't give a dead rat what the authorities thinks about it, nuther."

"Well," he says, "there's excuse for picks and letting-on, in a case like this; if it warn't so, I wouldn't approve of it, nor I wouldn't stand by and see the rules broke—because right is right, and wrong is wrong, and a body ain't got no business doing wrong when he ain't ignorant and knows better. It might answer for *you* to dig Jim out with a pick, *without* any letting-on, because you don't know no better; but it wouldn't for me, because I do know better. Gimme a caseknife."

He had his own by him, but I handed him mine. He flung it down, and says:

"Gimme a *caseknife.*"

I didn't know just what to do—but then I thought. I scratched around amongst the old tools, and got a pick-axe and give it to him, and he took it and went to work, and never said a word.

He was always just that particular. Full of principle.

So then I got a shovel, and then we picked and shoveled, turn about, and made the fur fly. We stuck to it about a half an hour, which was as long as we could stand up; but we had a good deal of a hole to show for it. When I got up stairs, I looked out at the window and see Tom doing his level best with the lightning rod, but he couldn't come it, his hands was so sore. At last he says:

"It ain't no use, it can't be done. What you reckon I better do? Can't you think up no way?"

"Yes," I says, "but I reckon it ain't regular. Come up the stairs, and let on it's a lightning rod."

So he done it.

Next day Tom stole a pewter spoon and a brass candlestick in the house, for to make some pens for Jim out of, and six tallow candles; and I hung around the nigger cabins, and laid for a chance, and stole

STEALING SPOONS.

three tin plates. Tom said it wasn't enough; but I said nobody wouldn't ever see the plates that Jim throwed out, because they'd fall in the dog-fennel and jimpson weeds under the window-hole— then we could tote them back and he could use them over again. So Tom was satisfied. Then he says:

"Now, the thing to study out, is, how to get the things to Jim."

"Take them in through the hole," I says, "when we get it done."

He only just looked scornful, and said something about nobody ever heard of such an idiotic idea, and then he went to studying. By and by he said he had ciphered out two or three ways, but there warn't no need to decide on any of them, yet. Said we'd got to post Jim, first.

That night we went down the lightning rod a little after ten, and took one of the candles along, and listened under the window-hole, and heard Jim snoring; so we pitched it in, and it didn't wake him. Then we whirled in with the pick and shovel, and in about two hours and a half the job was done. We crept in under Jim's bed and into the cabin, and pawed around and found the candle and lit it, and stood over Jim awhile, and found him looking hearty and healthy, and then we woke him up, gentle and gradual. He was so glad to see us he most cried; and called us honey, and all the pet names he could think of; and was for having us hunt up a cold chisel to cut the chain off of his leg with, right away, and clearing out without losing any time. But Tom he showed him how unregular it would be, and set down and told him all about our plans, and how we could alter them in a minute any time there was an alarm; and not to be the least afraid, because we would see he got away, *sure*. So Jim he said it was all right, and we set there and talked over old times a while, and then Tom asked a lot of questions, and when Jim told him uncle Silas come in every day or two to pray with him, and aunt Sally come in to see if he was comfortable and had plenty to eat, and both of them was kind as they could be, Tom says:

"*Now* I know how to fix it. We'll send you some things by them."

I said, "Don't do nothing of the kind; it's one of the most jackass ideas I ever struck;" but he never paid no attention to me; went right on. It was his way when he'd got his plans set.

So he told Jim how we'd have to smuggle in the rope-ladder pie, and other large things, by Nat, the nigger that fed him, and he must be on the lookout, and not be surprised, and not let Nat see him open them; and we would put small things in uncle's coat pockets and he must steal them out; and we would tie things to aunt's apron strings or put them in her apron pocket, if we got a chance; and told him what they would be and what they was for. And told him how to keep a journal on the shirt with his blood, and all that. He told him everything. Jim he couldn't see no sense in the most of it, but he allowed we was white folks and knowed better than him; so he was satisfied and said he would do it all just as Tom said.

Jim had plenty corn-cob pipes and tobacco; so we had a right down good sociable time; then we crawled out through the hole, and so home to bed, with hands that looked like they'd been chawed by a dog. Tom was in high spirits. He said it was the best fun he ever had in his life, and the most intellectural; and said if he only could see his way to it we would keep it up all the rest of our lives and leave Jim to our children to get out; for he believed Jim would come to like it better and better the more he got used to it. He said that in that way it could be strung out to as much as eighty year, and would be the best time on record. And he said it would make us all celebrated that had a hand in it.

In the morning we went out to the woodpile and chopped up the brass candlestick into handy sizes, and Tom put them and the pewter spoon in his pocket. Then we went to the nigger cabins, and while I got Nat's notice off, Tom shoved a piece of candlestick into the middle of a corn-pone that was in Jim's pan, and we went along with Nat to see how it would work, and it just worked noble: when Jim bit into it it most mashed all his teeth out; and there warn't ever anything could a worked better. Tom said so himself. Jim he never let on but what it was only just a piece of rock or something like that that's always getting into bread, you know, but after that he never bit into nothing but what he jabbed his fork into it in three or four places, first.

And whilst we was a standing there in the dimmish light, here comes a couple of the hounds bulging in, from under Jim's bed; and they kept on piling in till there was eleven of them, and there warn't hardly room in there to get your breath. By jings we forgot to fasten that lean-to door. The nigger Nat he only just hollered "witches!" once, and keeled over onto the floor amongst the dogs and begun to groan like he was dying. Tom jerked the door open and flung out a slab of Jim's meat, and the dogs went for it; and in two seconds he was out himself and back again and shut the door, and I knowed he'd fixed the other door, too. Then he went to work on the nigger, coaxing him and petting him, and asking him if he'd been imagining he saw something again. He raised up, and blinked his eyes around, and says:

"Mars Sid, you'll say I's a fool, but if I didn't b'lieve I see most a million dogs, er devils, er some'n, I wisht I may die right heah in dese tracks. I did, mos' sholy. Mars Sid, I *felt* um—I *felt* um, sah; dey was all over me. Dad fetch it, I jis' wisht I could git my han's on one er dem witches jis' wunst—on'y jis' wunst—it's all *I*'d ast. But mos'ly I wisht dey'd lemme 'lone, I does.''

Tom says:

''Well, I tell you what *I* think. What makes them come here just at this runaway nigger's breakfast time? It's because they're hungry; that's the reason. You make them a witch pie; that's the thing for *you* to do.''

TOM ADVISES A WITCH PIE.

''But my lan', mars Sid, how's *I* gwyne to make 'm a witch pie? I doan know how to make it. I hain't ever hearn er sich a thing b'fo'.''

''Well, then, I'll have to make it myself.''

''Will you do it, honey?—will you? I'll wusshup de groun' und' yo' foot, I will!''

''All right, I'll do it, seeing it's you, and you've been good to us and showed us the runaway nigger. But you got to be mighty careful. When we come around, you turn your back; and then whatever we've put in the pan, don't you let on you see it at all. And don't you look, when Jim unloads the pan—something might happen, I don't know what. And above all, don't you *handle* the witch-things."

"*Hannel* 'm, mars Sid? What *is* you a talkin' 'bout? I wouldn' lay de weight er my finger on um, not f'r ten hund'd thous'n' billion dollars, I wouldn't."

Chapter XXXVII

THE RUBBAGE PILE.

That was all fixed. So then we went away, and went to the rubbage pile in the back yard where they keep the old boots, and rags, and pieces of bottles, and wore-out tin things, and all such truck, and scratched around and found an old tin washpan and stopped up the holes as well as we could, to bake the pie in, and took it down cellar and stole it full of flour, and started for breakfast, and found a couple of shingle nails that Tom said would be handy for a prisoner to scrabble his name and sorrows on the dungeon walls with, and dropped one of them in aunt Sally's apron pocket which was hanging on a chair, and t'other we stuck in the band of uncle Silas's hat, which was on the bureau, because we heard the children say their pa and ma was going to the runaway nigger's house this morning, and then went to breakfast, and Tom dropped the pewter spoon in uncle Silas's coat pocket, and aunt Sally wasn't come yet, so we had to wait a little while.

And when she come she was hot, and red, and cross, and couldn't hardly wait for the blessing, and then she went to sluicing out coffee with one hand and cracking the handiest child's head with her thimble with the other, and says:

"I've hunted high, and I've hunted low, and it does beat all, what *has* become of your other shirt."

My heart fell down amongst my lungs and livers and things, and a hard piece of corn-crust started down my throat after it and got met on the road with a cough and was shot across the table and took one of the children in the eye and curled him up like a fishing-worm, and let a cry out of him the size of a war-whoop, and Tom he turned kinder blue around the gills, and it all amounted to a considerable state of things for about a quarter of a minute or as much as that, and I would a sold out for half price if there was a bidder. But after that, we was all right again—it was the sudden surprise of it that knocked us so kind of cold. Uncle Silas he says:

"It's most uncommon curious, I can't understand it. I know perfectly well I took it *off*, because—"

"Because you hain't got but one *on*. Just *listen* at the man! *I* know you took it off, and know it by a better way than your wool-gethering memory, too, because it was on the clo'es line yesterday—I see it there myself. But it's gone—that's the long and the short of it, and you'll just have to change to a red flann'l one till I can get time to make a new one. And it'll be the third I've made in two years; it just keeps a body on the jump to keep you in shirts; and whatever you do manage to *do* with 'm all, is more'n *I* can make out. A body'd think you *would* learn to take some sort of care of 'em, at your time of life."

"I know it, Sally, and I do try, all I can. But it oughtn't to be altogether my fault, because you know I don't see them nor have nothing to do with them except when they're on me; and I don't believe I've ever lost one of them *off* of me."

"Well, it ain't *your* fault if you haven't, Silas—you'd a done it if you could, I reckon. And the shirt ain't all that's gone, nuther. Ther's a spoon gone; and *that* ain't all. There was ten, and now ther's only nine. The calf got the shirt, I reckon, but the calf never took the spoon, *that's* certain."

"Why, what else is gone, Sally?"

"Ther's six *candles* gone—that's what. The rats could a got the candles, and I reckon they did; I wonder they don't walk off with the whole place, the way you're always going to stop their holes and don't do it; and if they warn't fools they'd sleep in your hair, Silas— *you*'d never find it out; but you can't lay the *spoon* on the rats, and that I *know*."

"Well, Sally, I'm in fault, and I acknowledge it; I've been remiss; but I won't let to-morrow go by without stopping up them holes."

"O, I wouldn't hurry, next year'll do. Matilda Angelina Araminta *Phelps!*"

Whack comes the thimble, and the child snatches her claws out of the sugar bowl without fooling around any. Just then, the nigger woman steps onto the passage, and says:

"Missus, dey's a sheet gone."

"A *sheet* gone! Well, for the land's sake!"

"I'll stop up them holes *to-day*," says uncle Silas, looking sorrowful.

"O, *do* shet up!—Spose the rats took the *sheet? Where's* it gone, Lize?"

"Clah to goodness I hain't no notion, Miss Sally. She wuz on de clo's line yistiddy, but she done gone; she ain' dah no mo', now."

"I reckon the world *is* coming to an end. I *never* see the beat of it, in all my born days. A shirt, and a sheet, and a spoon, and six can—"

"Missus," comes a young yaller wench, "dey's a brass cannelstick miss'n."

"Cler out from here, you hussy, er I'll take a skillet to ye!"

Well, she was just a biling. I begun to lay for a chance; I reckoned I would sneak out and go for the woods till the weather moderated. She kept a-raging right along, running her insurrection all by herself, and everybody else mighty meek and quiet; and at

"MISSUS, DEY'S A SHEET GONE."

last uncle Silas, looking kind of foolish, fishes up that spoon out of his pocket. She stopped, with her mouth open and her hands up; and as for me, I wished I was in Jeruslem or somewheres. But not long; because she says:

"It's *just* as I expected. So you had it in your pocket all the time; and like as not you've got the other things there, too. How'd it get there?"

"I reely don't know, Sally," he says, kind of apologizing, "or you know I would tell. I was a-studying over my text in Acts seventeen, before breakfast, and I reckon I put it in there, not noticing, meaning to put my Testament in, and it must be so, because my Testament ain't in, but I'll go and see, and if the Testament is where I had it, I'll know I didn't put it in, and that will show that I laid the Testament down and took up the spoon, and—"

"O, for the land's sake! Give a body a rest! Go 'long, now, the whole kit and biling of ye; and don't come nigh me again till I've got back my peace of mind."

I'd a heard her, if she'd a said it to herself, let alone speaking it out; and I'd a got up and obeyed her, if I'd a been dead. As we was passing through the setting room, the old man he took up his hat, and the shingle nail fell out on the floor, and he just merely picked it up and laid it on the mantel shelf, and never said nothing, and went out. Tom see him do it, and remembered about the spoon, and says:

"Well, it ain't no use to send things by *him* no more, he ain't reliable." Then he says: "But he done us a good turn with the spoon, anyway, without knowing it, and so we'll go and do him one without *him* knowing it—stop up his rat holes."

There was a noble good lot of them, down cellar, and it took us a whole hour, but we done the job tight and good, and ship-shape. Then we heard steps on the stairs, and blowed out our light, and hid; and here comes the old man, with a candle in one hand and a bundle of stuff in t'other, looking as absent-minded as year before last. He went a mooning around, first to one rat hole and then another, till he'd been to them all. Then he stood about five minutes, picking tallow-drip off of his candle and thinking. Then he turns off slow and dreamy towards the stairs, saying:

"Well, for the life of me I can't remember when I done it. I could show her, now, that I warn't to blame on account of the rats. But never mind—let it go. I reckon it wouldn't do no good."

And so he went on a-mumbling up stairs, and then we left. He was a mighty nice old man. And always is.

Tom was a good deal bothered about what to do for a spoon, but he said we'd got to have it; so he took a think. When he had ciphered it out, he told me how we was to do; then we went and waited around the spoon-basket till we see aunt Sally coming, and then

Tom went to counting the spoons and laying them out to one side, and I slid one of them up my sleeve, and Tom says:

"Why, aunt Sally, there ain't but nine spoons, *yet*."

She says:

"Go 'long to your play, and don't bother me. I know better, I counted 'm myself."

"Well, I've counted them twice, aunty, and *I* can't make but nine."

She looked out of all patience, but of course she come to count—anybody would.

"I declare to gracious ther' *ain't* but nine!" she says. "Why, what in the world—plague *take* the things, I'll count 'm again."

So I slipped back the one I had, and when she got done counting, she says:

"Hang the troublesome rubbage, ther's *ten*, now!" and she looked huffy and bothered both. But Tom says:

"Why, aunty, *I* don't think there's ten."

"You numscull, didn't you see me *count* 'm?"

IN A TEARING WAY.

"I know, but—"

"Well, I'll count 'm *again*."

So I smouched one, and they come out nine, same as the other time. Well, she *was* in a tearing way—just a trembling all over, she was so mad. But she counted, and counted, till she got that addled she'd start to count-in the *basket* for a spoon, sometimes: and so, three times they come out right, and three times they come out wrong. Then she grabbed up the basket and slammed it across the house and knocked the cat galley-west; and she said "cle'r out and let her have some peace, and if we come bothering around her again betwixt that and dinner, she'd skin us." So we had the odd spoon; and dropped it in her apron pocket whilst she was a-giving us our sailing-orders, and Jim got it, all right, along with her shingle-nail, before noon. We was very well satisfied with this business, and Tom allowed it was worth twice the trouble it took, because he said *now* she couldn't ever count them spoons twice alike again to save her life; and wouldn't believe she'd counted them right, if she *did*; and said that after she'd about counted her head off, for the next three days, he judged she'd give it up and offer to kill anybody that wanted her to ever count them any more.

So we put the sheet back on the line, that night, and stole one out of her closet; and kept on putting it back and stealing it again, for a couple of days, till she didn't know how many sheets she had, any more, and said she didn't *care*, and warn't agoing to bullyrag the rest of her soul out about it, and wouldn't count them again not to save her life, she druther die first.

So we was all right, now, as to the shirt and the sheet and the spoon and the candles, by the help of the calf and the rats and the mixed-up counting; and as to the candlestick, it warn't no consequence, it would blow over by and by.

But that pie was a job; we had no end of trouble with that pie. We fixed it up away down in the woods, and cooked it there; and we got it done, at last, and very satisfactory, too; but not all in one day; and we had to use up three washpans full of flour, before we got through, and we got burnt pretty much all over, in places, and eyes put out with the smoke; because, you see, we didn't want nothing but a crust, and we couldn't prop it up, right, and she would always cave in. But of course we thought of the right way at last; which was, to cook the ladder, too, in the pie. So then we laid in with Jim, the second night, and tore up the sheet all in little strings, and twisted them together, and long before daylight we had a lovely rope, that you could a hung a person with. We let on it took nine months to make it.

And in the forenoon we took it down to the woods, but it wouldn't go in the pie. Being made of a whole sheet, that way, there was rope enough for forty pies, if we'd a wanted them, and plenty left over for soup, or sausage, or anything you choose. We could a had a whole dinner.

But we didn't need it. All we needed was just enough for the pie, and so we throwed the rest away. We didn't cook none of the pies in the washpan, afraid the solder would melt; but uncle Silas he had a noble brass warming pan which he thought considerable of, because it belonged to one of his ancestors with a long wooden handle that come over from England with William the Conqueror in the Mayflower or one of them early ships and was hid away up garret with a lot of other old pots and things that was valuable, not on account of being any account, because they warn't, but on account of them being relicts, you know, and we snaked her out, private, and took her down there, but she failed on the first pies, because we didn't know how, but she come up smiling on the last one. We took and lined her with dough, and set her in the coals, and loaded her up with rag-rope, and put on a dough roof, and shut down the lid, and

ONE OF HIS ANCESTORS.

put hot embers on top, and stood off five foot, with the long handle, cool and comfortable, and in fifteen minutes she turned out a pie that was a satisfaction to look at. But the person that et it would want to fetch a couple of kags of toothpicks along, for if that rope ladder wouldn't cramp him down to business, I don't know nothing what I'm talking about, and lay him in enough stomach-ache to last him till next time, too.

Nat didn't look, when we put the witch-pie in Jim's pan; and we put the three tin plates in the bottom of the pan under the vittles; and so Jim got everything all right, and as soon as he was by himself he busted into the pie and hid the rope ladder inside of his straw tick, and scratched some marks on a tin plate and throwed it out of the window-hole.

Chapter XXXVIII

JIM'S COAT OF ARMS.

Making them pens was a distressid tough job, and so was the saw; and Jim allowed the inscription was going to be the toughest of all. That's the one which the prisoner has to scrabble on the wall. But we had to have it; Tom said we'd *got* to: there warn't no case of a state prisoner not scrabbling his inscription to leave behind, and his coat of arms.

"Look at lady Jane Grey," he says; "look at Gilford Dudley; look at old Northumberland! Why, Huck, spose it *is* considerble trouble?—what you going to do?—how you going to get around it? Jim's *got* to do his inscription and coat of arms. They all do."

Jim says:

"Why, mars Tom, I hain't got no coat o' arms; I hain't got nuffn but dish-yer ole shirt, en you knows I got to keep de journal on dat."

"O, you don't understand, Jim; a coat of arms is very different."

"Well," I says, "Jim's right, anyway, when he says he hain't got no coat of arms, because he hain't."

"I reckon *I* knowed that," Tom says, "but you bet he'll have one before he goes out of this—because he's going out *right*, and there ain't going to be no flaws in his record."

So whilst me and Jim filed away at the pens on a brickbat apiece, Jim a making his'n out of the brass and I making mine out of the spoon, Tom set to work to think out the coat of arms. By and by he said he'd struck so many good ones he didn't hardly know which to take, but there was one which he reckoned he'd decide on. He says:

"On the scutcheon we'll have a bend *or* in the dexter base, a saltire *murrey* in the fess, with a dog, couchant, for common charge, and under his foot a chain embattled, for slavery, with a chevron *vert* in a chief engrailed, and three invected lines on a field *azure*, with the nombril points rampant on a dancette indented; crest, a runaway nigger, *sable*, with his bundle over his shoulder on a bar sinister; and a couple of gules for supporters, which is you and me; motto, *Maggiore fretta, minore atto*. Got it out of a book—means, the more haste, the less speed."

"Geewhillikins," I says, "but what does the rest of it mean?"

"We ain't got no time to bother over that," he says, "we got to dig in like all git-out."

"Well, anyway," I says, "what's *some* of it? What's a fess?"

"A fess—a fess is—*you* don't need to know what a fess is: I'll show him how to make it when he gets to it."

"Shucks, Tom," I says, "I think you might tell a person. What's a bar sinister?"

"Oh, *I* don't know. But he's got to have it. All the nobility does."

That was just his way. If it didn't suit him to explain a thing to you, he wouldn't do it. You might pump at him a week, it wouldn't make no difference.

He'd got all that coat of arms business fixed, so now he started in to finish up the rest of that part of the work, which was to plan out a mournful inscription—said Jim got to have one, like they all done. He made up a lot, and wrote them out on a paper, and read them off, so:

1. *Here a captive heart busted.*

2. *Here a poor prisoner, forsook by the world and friends, fretted out his sorrowful life.*

3. *Here a lonely heart broke, and a worn spirit went to its rest, after thirty seven years of solitary captivity.*

4. *Here, homeless and friendless, after thirty-seven years of bitter captivity, perished a noble stranger, natural son of Louis XIV.*

Tom's voice trembled, whilst he was reading them, and he most broke down. When he got done, he couldn't no way make up his mind which one for Jim to scrabble onto the wall, they was all so good; but at last he allowed he would let him scrabble them all on. Jim said it would take him a year to scrabble such a lot of truck onto the logs with a nail, and he didn't know how to make letters, besides; but Tom said he would block them out for him, and then he wouldn't have nothing to do but just follow the lines. Then pretty soon he says:

"Come to think, the logs ain't agoing to do; they don't have log walls in a dungeon: we got to dig the inscriptions into a rock. We'll fetch a rock."

Jim said the rock was worse than the logs; he said it would take him such a pison long time to dig them into a rock, he wouldn't ever get out. But Tom said he would let me help him do it. Then he took a look to see how me and Jim was getting along with the pens. It was most pesky tedious hard work and slow, and didn't give my hands no show to get well of the sores, and we didn't seem to make no headway, hardly. So Tom says:

"I know how to fix it. We got to have a rock for the coat of arms and mournful inscriptions, and we can kill two birds with that same rock. There's a gaudy big grindstone down at the mill, and we'll smouch it, and carve the things on it, and file out the pens and the saw on it, too."

It warn't no slouch of an idea; and it warn't no slouch of a grindstone, nuther; but we allowed we'd tackle it. It warn't quite midnight, yet, so we cleared out for the mill, leaving Jim at work. We smouched the grindstone, and set out to roll her home, but it was a most nation tough job. Sometimes, do what we could, we couldn't keep her from falling over, and she come mighty near mashing us, every time. Tom said she was going to get one of us, sure, before we got through. We got her half way; and then we was plumb played out, and most drowned with sweat. We see it warn't no use, we got to go and fetch Jim. So he raised up his bed and slid the chain off of the bed-leg, and wrapt it round and round his neck, and we crawled out through our hole and down there, and Jim and me laid into that grindstone and walked her along like nothing; and Tom superintended. He could out-superintend any boy I ever see. He knowed how to do everything.

A TOUGH JOB.

Our hole was pretty big, but it warn't big enough to get the grindstone through; but Jim he took the pick and soon made it big enough. Then Tom marked out them things on it with the nail, and set Jim to work on them, with the nail for a chisel and an iron bolt from the rubbage in the lean-to for a hammer, and told him to work till the rest of his candle quit on him, and then he could go to bed, and hide the grindstone under his straw tick and sleep on it. Then we helped him fix his chain back, on the bedleg, and was ready for bed ourselves. But Tom thought of something, and says:

"You got any spiders in here, Jim?"

"No, sah, thanks to goodness I hain't, mars Tom."

"All right, we'll get you some."

"But bless you, honey, I doan *want* none. I's afeard un um. I jis' 's soon have rattlesnakes aroun'."

Tom thought a minute or two, and says:

"It's a good idea. And I reckon it's been done. It *must* a been done: it stands to reason. Yes, it's a prime good idea. Where could you keep it?"

"Keep what, mars Tom?"

"Why, a rattlesnake."

"De goodness gracious alive, mars Tom! Why, if dey was a rattle-snake to come in heah, I'd take en bust right out thoo dat log wall, I would, wid my head."

"Why, Jim, you wouldn't be afraid of it, after a little. You could tame it."

"*Tame* it!"

"Yes—easy enough. Every animal is grateful for kindness and petting, and they wouldn't *think* of hurting a person that pets them. Any book will tell you that. You try—that's all I ask; just try for two or three days. Why, you can get him so, in a little while, that he'll love you; and sleep with you; and won't stay away from you a minute; and will let you wrap him round your neck and put his head in your mouth."

"*Please*, mars Tom—*doan'* talk so! I can't *stan'* it! He'd *let* me shove his head in my mouf—fer a favor, hain't it? I lay he'd wait a pow'ful long time 'fo' I *ast* him. En mo' en dat, I doan' *want* him to sleep wid me."

"Jim, don't act so foolish. A prisoner's *got* to have some kind of a dumb pet, and if a rattlesnake hain't ever been tried, why there's more glory to be gained in your being the first to ever try it than any other way you could ever think of to save your life."

"Why, mars Tom, I doan' *want* no sich glory. Snake take 'n bite Jim's chin off, den *whah* is de glory? No, sah, I doan' want no sich doin's."

"Blame it, can't you *try?* I only *want* you to try—you needn't keep it up if it don't work."

"But de trouble all *done*, ef de snake bite me while I's a-tryin' him. Mars Tom, I's willin' to tackle mos' anything 'at ain't onrea-sonable, but ef you en Huck fetches a rattlesnake in heah for me to tame, I's gwyne to *leave*, dat's *shore*."

"Well, then, let it go, let it go, if you're so bullheaded about it. We can get you some garter-snakes and you can tie some buttons on their tails, and let on they're rattlesnakes, and I reckon that'll have to do."

"I k'n stan' *dem*, mars Tom, but blame' 'f I couldn' git along widout um, I tell you dat. I never knowed, b'fo', 't was so much bother and trouble to be a prisoner."

BUTTONS ON THEIR TAILS.

"Well, it *always* is, when it's done right. You got any rats around here?"

"No, sah, I hain't seed none."

"Well, we'll get you some rats."

"Why, mars Tom, I doan *want* no rats. Dey's de dad-blamedest creturs to 'sturb a body, en rustle roun' over 'im, en bite his feet, when he's tryin' to sleep, I ever see. No, sah, gimme g'yarter snakes, 'f I's got to have 'm, but doan' gimme no rats, I ain' got no use f'r um, skasely."

"But Jim, you *got* to have 'em,—they all do. So don't make no more fuss about it. Prisoners ain't ever without rats. There ain't no instance of it. And they train them, and pet them, and learn them tricks, and they get to be as sociable as flies. But you got to play music to them. You got anything to play music on?"

"I ain' got nuffn but a coase comb en a piece o' paper, en a juice-harp; but I reck'n dey wouldn' take no stock in a juice-harp."

"Yes they would. *They* don't care what kind of music 'tis. A jewsharp's plenty good enough for a rat. All animals likes music—in a prison; they dote on it. Specially, painful music; and you can't get no other kind out of a jewsharp. It always interests them; they come out to see what's the matter with you. Yes, you're all right; you're fixed very well. You want to set on your bed, nights, before you go to sleep, and early in the mornings, and play your jewsharp; play The Last Link is Broken—that's the thing that'll scoop a rat,

quicker'n anything else: and when you've played about two minutes, you'll see all the rats, and the snakes, and spiders, and things
begin to feel worried about you, and come. And they'll just fairly
swarm over you, and have a noble good time."

"Yes, *dey* will, I reck'n, mars Tom, but what kine er time is *Jim*
havin'? Blest if I kin see de pint. But I'll do it, ef I got to. I reck'n I
better keep de animals satisfied, en not have no trouble in de house."

Tom waited to think over, and see if there wasn't nothing else;
and pretty soon he says:

"Oh—there's one thing I forgot. Could you raise a flower here,
do you reckon?"

"I doan' know but maybe I could, mars Tom; but it's tolable dark
in heah, en I ain' got no use f'r no flower, nohow, en she'd be a powful
sight o' trouble."

"Well, you try it, anyway. Some other prisoners has done it."

"One er dem big cat-tail-lookin' mullen-stalks would grow in
heah, mars Tom, I reck'n, but she wouldn' be wuth half de trouble
she'd coss."

"Don't you believe it. We'll fetch you a little one, and you plant
it in the corner, over there, and raise it. And don't call it mullen, call
it Pitchiola—that's its right name, when it's in a prison. And you
want to water it with your tears."

"Why, I got plenty spring water, mars Tom."

"You don't *want* spring water; you want to water it with your
tears. It's the way they always do."

IRRIGATION.

"Why mars Tom, I lay I kin raise one er dem mullen-stalks twyste wid spring water whiles another man's a *start*'n one wid tears."

"That ain't the idea. You *got* to do it with tears."

"She'll die on my han's, mars Tom, she sholy will; kase I doan' skasely ever cry."

So Tom was stumped. But he studied it over, and then said Jim would have to worry along the best he could with an onion. He promised he would go to the nigger cabins and drop one, private, in Jim's coffee pot, in the morning. Jim said he would "jis' 's soon have tobacker in his coffee"; and found so much fault with it, and with the work and bother of raising the mullen, and jewsharping the rats, and petting and flattering up the snakes and spiders and things, on top of all the other work he had to do on pens, and inscriptions, and journals, and things, which made it more trouble and worry and responsibility to be a prisoner than anything he ever undertook, that Tom most lost all patience with him; and said he was just loadened down with more gaudier chances than a prisoner ever had in the world to make a name for himself, and yet he didn't know enough to appreciate them, and they was just about wasted on him. So Jim he was sorry, and said he wouldn't behave so no more, and then me and Tom shoved for bed.

Ϛhapter XXXIX

KEEPING OFF DULL TIMES.

In the morning we went up to the village and bought a wire rat trap and fetched it down, and unstopped the best rat hole, and in about an hour we had fifteen of the bulliest kind of ones; and then we took it and put it in a safe place under aunt Sally's bed. But while we was gone for spiders, little Thomas Franklin Benjamin Jefferson Elexander Phelps found it there, and opened the door of it to see if the rats would come out, and they did; and aunt Sally she come in, and when we got back she was a standing on top of the bed raising Cain, and the rats was doing what they could to keep off the dull times for her. So she took and dusted us both with the hickry, and we was as much as two hours catching another fifteen or sixteen, drat that meddlesome cub, and they warn't the likeliest, nuther, because the first haul was the pick of the flock. I never see a likelier lot of rats than what that first haul was.

We got a splendid stock of sorted spiders, and bugs, and frogs, and caterpillars, and one thing or another; and we like-to got a hornet's nest, but we didn't. The family was at home. We didn't give it right up, but staid with them as long as we could; because we allowed we'd tire them out or they'd got to tire us out, and they done it. Then we got allycumpain and rubbed on the places, and was pretty near all right, again, but couldn't set down convenient. And so we went for the snakes, and grabbed a couple of dozen garters and house-snakes, and put them in a bag, and put it in our room, and by that time it was supper time, and a rattling good honest day's work; and hungry?—oh, no, I reckon not! And there warn't a blessed snake up there, when we went back—we didn't half tie the sack, and they worked out, somehow, and left. But it didn't matter much, because they was still on the premises somewheres. So we judged we could get some of them again. No, there warn't no real scarcity of snakes about the house for a considerble spell. You'd see them dripping from the rafters and places, every now and then; and they generly landed in your plate, or down the back of your neck, and most of the time where you didn't want them. Well, they was handsome, and striped, and there warn't no harm in a million of them; but that never made no difference to aunt Sally, she despised snakes, be the breed what they might, and she couldn't stand them, no way you could fix it; and every time one of them flopped down on her, it didn't make no difference what she was doing, she would just lay that work down and light out. I never see such a woman. And you could hear her whoop to Jericho. You couldn't get her to take aholt of one of them with the tongs. And if she turned over and found one in bed, she would scramble out and lift a howl that you would think the house was afire. She disturbed the old man so, that he said he could most wish there hadn't ever been no snakes created. Why, after every last snake had been gone clear out of the house for as much as a week, aunt Sally warn't over it yet; she warn't near over it; when she was setting thinking about something, you could touch her on the back of her neck with a feather and she would jump right out of her stockings. It was very curious. But Tom said all women was just so. He said they was made that way; for some reason or other.

We got a licking every time one of our snakes come in her way; and she allowed these lickings warn't nothing to what she would do if we ever loaded up the place again with them. I didn't mind the lickings, because they didn't amount to nothing; but I minded the trouble we had, to lay in another lot. But we got them laid in, and all the other things; and you never see a cabin as blithesome as Jim's was when they'd all swarm out for music and go for him. Jim didn't like the spiders, and the spiders didn't like Jim; and so they'd lay for him and make it mighty warm for him. And he said that between the rats, and the snakes, and the grindstone, there warn't no room in bed for him, skasely; and when there was, a body couldn't sleep, it was so lively, and it was always lively, he said, because *they* never all slept at one time, but took turn about, so when the snakes was asleep the rats was on deck, and when the rats turned in the snakes come on watch, so he always had one gang under him, in his way, and t'other gang having a circus over him, and if he got up to hunt a new place, the spiders would take a chance at him as he crossed over. He said if he ever got out, this time, he wouldn't ever be a prisoner again, not for a salary.

Well, by the end of three weeks, everything was in pretty good shape. The shirt was sent in early, in a pie, and every time a rat bit

SAWDUST DIET.

Jim he would get up and write a little in his journal, whilst the ink was fresh; the pens was made, the inscriptions and so-on was all carved on the grindstone; the bed-leg was sawed in two, and we had et up the sawdust, and it give us a most amazing stomach-ache. We reckoned we was all going to die, but didn't. It was the most undigestible sawdust I ever see; and Tom said the same. But as I was saying, we'd got all the work done, now, at last; and we was all pretty much fagged out, too, but mainly Jim. The old man had wrote a couple of times to the plantation below Orleans to come and get their runaway nigger, but hadn't got no answer, because there warn't no such plantation; so he allowed he would advertise Jim in the St. Louis and New Orleans papers; and when he mentioned the St. Louis ones, it give me the cold shivers, and I see we hadn't no time to lose. So Tom said, now for the nonnamous letters.

"What's them?" I says.

"Warnings to the people that something is up. Sometimes it's done one way, sometimes another. But there's always somebody spying around, that gives notice to the governor of the castle. When Louis XVI was going to light out of the Tooleries, a servant girl done it. It's a very good way, and so is the nonnamous letters. We'll use them both. And it's usual for the prisoner's mother to change clothes with him, and she stays in, and he slides out in her clothes. We'll do that, too."

"But lookyhere, Tom, what do we want to *warn* anybody for, that something's up? Let them find it out for themselves—it's their lookout."

"Yes, I know; but you can't depend on them. It's the way they've acted from the very start—left us to do *everything*. They're so confiding and mullet-headed they don't take notice of nothing at all. So if we don't *give* them notice, there won't be nobody nor nothing to interfere with us, and so after all our hard work and trouble this escape 'll go off perfectly flat: won't amount to nothing—won't be nothing *to* it."

"Well, as for me, Tom, that's the way I'd like."

"Shucks," he says, and looked disgusted. So I says:

"But I ain't going to make no complaint. Any way that suits you suits me. What you going to do about the servant girl?"

"You'll be her. You slide in, in the middle of the night, and hook that yaller girl's frock."

"Why, Tom, that'll make trouble, next morning, because of course she prob'ly hain't got any but that one."

"I know; but you don't want it but fifteen minutes, to carry the nonnamous letter and shove it under the front door."

"All right, then, I'll do it; but I could carry it just as handy in my own togs."

"You wouldn't look like a servant girl *then*, would you?"

"No, but there won't be nobody to see what I look like, *anyway*."

"That ain't got nothing to do with it. The thing for us to do, is just to do our *duty*, and not worry about whether anybody *sees* us do it or not. Hain't you got no principle at all?"

"All right, I ain't saying nothing: I'm the servant girl. Who's Jim's mother?"

"I'm his mother. I'll hook a gown from aunt Sally."

"Well, then, you'll have to stay in the cabin when me and Jim leaves."

"Not much. I'll stuff Jim's clothes full of straw and lay it on his bed to represent his mother in disguise, and Jim 'll take aunt Sally's gown off of me and wear it, and we'll all evade together. When a prisoner of style escapes, it's called an evasion. It's always called so when a king escapes, frinstance. And the same with a king's son; it don't make no difference whether he's a natural one or an unnatural one."

So Tom he wrote the nonnamous letter, and I smouched the yaller wench's frock, that night, and put it on, and shoved it under the front door, the way Tom told me to. It said:

TROUBLE IS BREWING.

Beware. Trouble is brewing. Keep a sharp lookout. UNKNOWN
FRIEND.

Next night, we stuck a picture which Tom drawed in blood, of a
skull and crossbones, on the front door; and next night another one
of a coffin, on the back door. I never see a family in such a sweat.
They couldn't a been worse scared if the place had a been full of
ghosts laying for them behind everything and under the beds and
shivering through the air. If a door banged, aunt Sally she jumped,
and said "ouch!" if anything fell, she jumped and said "ouch!" if
you happened to touch her, when she warn't noticing, she done the
same; she couldn't face noway and be satisfied, because she allowed
there was something behind her every time—so she was always a
whirling around, sudden, and saying "ouch," and before she'd get
two-thirds around, she'd whirl back again, and say it again; and she
was afraid to go to bed, but she dasn't set up. So the thing was
working very well, Tom said; he said he never see a thing work more
satisfactory. He said it showed it was done right.

So he said, now for the grand bulge! So the very next morning at
the streak of dawn we got another letter ready, and was wondering
what we better do with it, because we heard them say at supper they
was going to have a nigger on watch at both doors all night. Tom he
went down the lightning rod to spy around; and the nigger at the
back door was asleep, and he stuck it in the back of his neck and
come back. This letter said:

*Don't betray me, I wish to be your friend. There is a desprate
gang of cutthroats from over in the Ingean Territory going to steal
your runaway nigger to-night, and they have been trying to scare
you so as you will stay in the house and not bother them. I am one
of the gang, but have got religgion and wish to quit it and lead a
honest life again, and will betray the helish design. They will sneak
down from northards, along the fence, at midnight exact, with a
false key, and go in the nigger's cabin to get him. I am to be off a
piece and blow a tin horn if I see any danger; but stead of that, I
will* BA *like a sheep soon as they get in and not blow at all; then
whilst they are getting his chains loose, you slip there and lock
them in, and can kill them at your leasure. Don't do anything but
just the way I am telling you, if you do they will suspicion something and raise whoopjamboreehoo. I do not wish any reward but
to know I have done the right thing.* UNKNOWN FRIEND.

Chapter XL

KEMBLE

FISHING.

We was feeling pretty good, after breakfast, and took my canoe and went over the river a-fishing, with a lunch, and had a good time, and took a look at the raft and found her all right, and got home late to supper, and found them in such a sweat and worry they didn't know which end they was standing on, and made us go right off to bed the minute we was done supper, and wouldn't tell us what the trouble was, and never let on a word about the new letter, but didn't need to, because we knowed as much about it as anybody did, and as soon as we was half up stairs and her back was turned, we slid for the cellar cubboard and loaded up a good lunch and took it up to our room and went to bed, and got up about half past eleven, and Tom put on aunt Sally's dress that he stole and was going to start with the lunch, but says:

"Where's the butter?"

"I laid out a hunk of it," I says, "on a piece of a corn-pone."

"Well, you *left* it laid out, then—it ain't here."

"We can get along without it," I says.

"We can get along *with* it, too," he says; "just you slide down cellar and fetch it. And then mosey right down the lightning rod and come along. I'll go and stuff the straw into Jim's clothes to represent his mother in disguise, and be ready to *ba* like a sheep and shove, soon as you get there."

So out he went, and down cellar went I. The hunk of butter, big

as a person's fist, was where I had left it, so I took up the slab of corn-
pone with it on, and blowed out my light, and started up stairs, very
stealthy, and got up to the main floor all right, but here comes aunt
Sally with a candle, and I clapped the truck in my hat, and clapped
my hat on my head, and the next second she see me; and she says:

"You been down cellar?"

"Yes'm."

"What you been doing down there?"

"Noth'n."

"*Noth'n!*"

"No'm."

"Well, then, what possessed you to go down there, this time of
night?"

"I don't know'm."

"You don't *know?* Don't answer me that way, Tom, I want to
know what you been *doing* down there?"

"I hain't been doing a single thing, aunt Sally, I hope to gracious
if I have."

I reckoned she'd let me go, now, and as a generl thing she would;
but I spose there was so many strange things going on she was just
in a sweat about every little thing that warn't yard-stick straight;
so she says, very decided:

"You just march into that setting-room and stay there till I come.
You been up to something you no business to, and I lay I'll find out
what it is before *I'm* done with you."

So she went away as I opened the door and walked into the setting
room. My, but there was a crowd there! Fifteen farmers, and every
one of them had a gun. I was most powerful sick, and slunk to a
chair and set down. They was setting around, some of them talking
a little, in a low voice, and all of them fidgety and uneasy, but trying
to look like they warn't; but I knowed they was, because they was
always taking off their hats, and putting them on, and scratching
their heads, and changing their seats, and fumbling with their
buttons. I warn't easy, myself, but I didn't take my hat off, all the
same.

I did wish aunt Sally would come, and get done with me, and lick
me, if she wanted to, and let me get away and tell Tom how we'd
overdone this thing, and what a thundering hornet's nest we'd got

ourselves into, so we could stop fooling around, straight off, and clear out with Jim before these rips got out of patience and come for us.

At last she come, and begun to ask me questions, but I *couldn't* answer them straight, I didn't know which end of me was up; because these men was in such a fidget, now, that some was wanting to start right *now* and lay for them desperadoes, and saying it warn't but a few minutes to midnight; and others was trying to get them to hold on and wait for the sheep-signal; and here was aunty pegging away at the questions, and me a shaking all over and ready to sink

EVERY ONE HAD A GUN.

down in my tracks I was that scared; and the place getting hotter and hotter, and the butter beginning to melt and run down my neck and behind my ears; and pretty soon, when one of them says, "*I*'m for going and getting in the cabin *first*, and right *now*, and catching them when they come," I most dropped; and a streak of butter come a trickling down my forehead, and aunt Sally she see it, and turns white as a sheet, and says:

"For the land's sake what *is* the matter with the child!—he's got the brain fever as shore as you're born, and they're oozing out!"

And everybody runs to see, and she snatches off my hat, and out comes the bread, and what was left of the butter, and she grabbed me, and hugged me, and says:

"Oh, what a turn you did give me! and how glad and grateful I am it ain't no worse; for luck's against us, and it never rains but it pours, and when I see that truck I thought we'd lost you, for I knowed by the color and all, it was just like your brains would be if— Dear, dear, whydn't you *tell* me that was what you'd been down there for, *I* wouldn't a cared. Now cler out to bed, and don't lemme see no more of you till morning!''

I was up stairs in a second, and down the lightning rod in another one, and shinning through the dark for the lean-to. I couldn't hardly get my words out, I was so anxious; but I told Tom as quick as I could, we must jump for it, now, and not a minute to lose—the house full of men, yonder, with guns!

His eyes just blazed; and he says:

"No!—is that so? *Ain't* it bully! Why, Huck, if it was to do over again, I bet I could fetch two hundred! If we could put it off till—"

"Hurry! *hurry!*" I says; "where's Jim?"

"Right at your elbow; if you reach out your arm you can touch him. He's dressed, and everything's ready. Now we'll slide out and give the sheep-signal."

But then we heard the tramp of men, coming to the door, and heard them begin to fumble with the padlock; and heard a man say:

"I *told* you we'd be too soon; they haven't come—the door is locked. Here—I'll lock some of you into the cabin and you lay for 'em in the dark and kill 'em when they come; and the rest scatter around a piece, and listen if you can hear 'em coming."

So in they come, but couldn't see us in the dark, and most trod on us whilst we was hustling to get under the bed. But we got under, all right, and out through the hole, swift but soft—Jim first, me next, and Tom last, which was according to Tom's orders. Now we was in the lean-to, and heard trampings close by, outside. So we crept to the door, and Tom stopped us there and put his eye to the crack, but couldn't make out nothing, it was so dark; and whispered and said he would listen for the steps to get further, and when he nudged us Jim must glide out first, and him last. So he set his ear to the crack and listened, and listened, and listened, and the steps a scraping around, out there, all the time; and at last he nudged us, and we slid out, and stooped down, not breathing, and not making the least noise, and slipped stealthy towards the fence, in Injun file, and got to it, all right, and me and Jim over it; but Tom's britches catched fast on a splinter on the top rail, and then he hear the steps coming, so he had to pull loose, which snapped the splinter and made a noise; and as he dropped in our tracks and started, somebody sings out:

"Who's that? Answer, or I'll shoot!"

But we didn't answer; we just unfurled our heels and shoved.

TOM CAUGHT ON A SPLINTER.

Then there was a rush, and a *bang, bang, bang!* and the bullets fairly whizzed around us! We heard them sing out:

"Here they are! They've broke for the river! after 'em, boys! And turn loose the dogs!"

So here they come, full tilt. We could hear them, because they wore boots, and yelled, but we didn't wear no boots, and didn't yell. We was in the path to the mill; and when they got pretty close onto us, we dodged into the bush and let them go by, and then dropped in behind them. They'd had all the dogs shut up, so they wouldn't scare off the robbers; but by this time somebody had let them loose, and here they come, making pow-wow enough for a million; but they was our dogs; so we stopped in our tracks till they catched up; and when they see it warn't nobody but us, and no excitement to offer them, they only just said howdy, and tore right ahead towards the shouting and clattering; and then we up steam again and whizzed along after them till we was nearly to the mill, and then struck up through the bush to where my canoe was tied, and hopped in and pulled for dear life towards the middle of the river, but didn't make no more noise than we was obleeged to. Then we struck out, easy and comfortable, for the island where my raft was; and we could hear them yelling and barking at each other all up and down the bank, till we was so far away the sounds got dim and died out. And when we stepped onto the raft, I says:

"*Now*, old Jim, you're a free man *again*, and I bet you won't ever be a slave no more."

"En a mighty good job it wuz, too, Huck. It 'uz planned beautiful, en it 'uz *done* beautiful; en dey ain't *nobody* kin git up a plan dat's mo' mixed-up en splendid den what dat one wuz."

We was all as glad as we could be, but Tom was the gladdest of all, because he had a bullet in the calf of his leg.

When me and Jim heard that, we didn't feel so brash as what we did before. It was hurting him considerble, and bleeding; so we laid him in the wigwam and tore up one of the duke's shirts for to bandage him; but he says:

"Gimme the rags, I can do it myself. Don't stop, now; don't fool around here, and the evasion booming along so handsome: man the sweeps, and set her loose! Boys, we done it elegant!—'deed we did. I wish *we*'d a had the handling of Louis XVI, there wouldn't a been no 'Son of Saint Louis, ascend to heaven!' wrote down in *his* biography: no, sir, we'd a whooped him over the *border*—that's what we'd a done with *him*—and done it just as slick as nothing at all, too. Man the sweeps—man the sweeps!"

But me and Jim was consulting—and thinking. And after we'd thought a minute, I says:

"Say it, Jim."

So he says:

"Well, den, dis is de way it look to me, Huck. Ef it wuz *him* dat 'uz bein' sot free, en one er de boys wuz to git shot, would he say, 'Go on en save me, nemmine 'bout a doctor f'r to save dis one?' Is

dat like mars Tom Sawyer? Would he say dat? You *bet* he wouldn't!
Well den—is *Jim* gwyne to say it? No, sah—I doan' budge a step
out'n dis place, 'dout a *doctor;* not ef it's forty year!''

I knowed he was white inside, and I reckoned he'd say what he
did say—so it was all right, now, and I told Tom I was agoing for a

JIM ADVISES A DOCTOR.

doctor. He raised considerble row about it, but me and Jim stuck to
it and wouldn't budge; so he was for crawling out and setting the
raft loose himself; but we wouldn't let him. Then he give us a piece
of his mind—but it didn't do no good.

So when he see me getting the canoe ready, he says:

"Well, then, if you're bound to go, I'll tell you the way to do, when
you get to the village. Shut the door, and blindfold the doctor tight
and fast, and make him swear to be silent as the grave, and put a
purse full of gold in his hand, and then take and lead him all around
the back alleys and everywheres, in the dark, and then fetch him
here in the canoe, in a roundabout way amongst the islands, and

search him and take his chalk away from him, and don't give it back to him till you get him back to the village, or else he will chalk this raft so he can find it again. It's the way they all do."

So I said I would, and left, and Jim was to hide in the woods when he see the doctor coming, till he was gone again.

Chapter XLI

THE DOCTOR.

The doctor was an old man; a very nice, kind looking old man, when I got him up. I told him me and my brother was over on Spanish island hunting, yesterday after noon, and camped on a piece of a raft we found, and about midnight he must a kicked his gun in his dreams, for it went off and shot him in the leg; and we wanted him to go over there and fix it and not say nothing about it, nor let anybody know, because we wanted to come home this evening, and surprise the folks.

"Who is your folks?" he says.

"The Phelpses, down yonder."

"Oh," he says. And after a minute, he says: "How'd you say he got shot?"

"He had a dream," I says, "and it shot him."

"Singular dream," he says.

So he lit up his lantern, and got his saddlebags, and we started. But when he see the canoe, he didn't like the look of her—said she was big enough for one, but didn't look pretty safe for two. I says:

"O, you needn't be afeard, sir, she carried the three of us, easy enough."

"What three?"

"Why, me and Sid, and—and—and *the guns;* that's what I mean."

"Oh," he says.

But he put his foot on the gunnel, and rocked her; and shook his head, and said he reckoned he'd look around for a bigger one. But they was all locked and chained; so he took my canoe, and said for me to wait till he come back, or I could hunt around further, or maybe I better go down home and get them ready for the surprise, if I wanted to. But I said I didn't; so I told him just how to find the raft, and then he started.

I struck an idea, pretty soon. I says to myself, spos'n he can't fix that leg just in three shakes of a sheep's tail, as the saying is? spos'n it takes him three or four days? What are we going to do?—lay around there till he lets the cat out of the bag? No, sir, I know what *I'll* do: I'll wait, and when he comes back, if he says he's got to go any more, I'll get down there, too, if I swim; and we'll take and tie him, and keep him, and shove out down the river; and when Tom's done with him, we'll give him what it's worth, or all we got, and then let him get ashore.

So then I crept into a lumber pile to get some sleep; and next time I waked up the sun was away up over my head! I shot out and went for the doctor's house, but they told me he'd gone away in the night, some time or other, and warn't back yet. Well, thinks I, that looks

UNCLE SILAS IN DANGER.

powerful bad for Tom, and I'll dig out for the island, right off. So
away I shoved, and turned the corner, and nearly rammed my head
into uncle Silas's stomach! He says:

"Why, *Tom!* Where you been, all this time, you rascal?"

"*I* hain't been nowheres," I says, "only just hunting for the runaway nigger—me and Sid."

"Why, where ever did you go?" he says. "Your aunt's been mighty
uneasy."

"She needn't," I says, "because we was all right. We followed the
men and the dogs, but they outrun us, and we lost them; but we
thought we heard them on the water, so we got a canoe and took out
after them, and crossed over, but couldn't find nothing of them; so
we cruised along up shore till we got kind of tired and beat out; and
tied up the canoe and went to sleep, and never waked up till about
an hour ago, then we paddled over here to hear the news, and Sid's
at the postoffice to see what he can hear, and I'm a-branching out to
get something to eat for us, and then we're going home."

So then we went to the postoffice to get 'Sid'; but, just as I
suspicioned, he warn't there; so the old man he got a letter out of
the office, and we waited a while longer, but Sid didn't come; so the
old man said come along, let Sid foot it home, or canoe-it, when he
got done fooling around—but we would ride. I couldn't get him to
let me stay and wait for Sid; and he said there warn't no use in it,
and I must come along, and let aunt Sally see we was all right.

When we got home, aunt Sally was that glad to see me she laughed
and cried both, and hugged me, and give me one of them lickings of
hern that don't amount to shucks, and said she'd serve Sid the same
when he come.

And the place was plumb full of farmers and farmers' wives, to
dinner; and such another clack a body never heard. Old Mrs. Hotchkiss was the worst; her tongue was agoing all the time. She says:

"Well, sister Phelps, I've ransacked that-air cabin over, an' I
b'lieve the nigger was crazy. I says so to sister Damrell—didn't I,
sister Damrell?—s'I, he's crazy, s'I—them's the very words I said.
You all hearn me: he's crazy, s'I; everything shows it, s'I. Look at
that-air grindstone, s'I: want to tell *me* 't any cretur 'ts in his right
mind 's agoin' to scrabble all them crazy things onto a grindstone,
s'I? Here sich 'n' sich a person busted his heart; 'n' here so 'n' so

pegged along for thirty-seven year, 'n' all that—natcherl son o' Louis somebody, 'n' sich everlast'n rubbage. He's plumb crazy, s'I; it's what I says in the fust place, it's what I says in the middle, 'n' it's what I says last 'n' all the time—the nigger's crazy—crazy 's Nebo-koodneezer, s'I."

"An' look at that-air ladder made out'n rags, sister Hotchkiss," says old Mrs. Damrell, "what in the name o' goodness *could* he ever want of—"

OLD MRS. HOTCHKISS.

"The very words I was a-sayin' no longer ago th'n this minute to sister Utterback, 'n' she'll tell you so herself. Sh-she, look at that-air rag ladder, sh-she; 'n' s'I, yes, *look* at it, s'I—what *could* he a wanted of it, s'I. Sh-she, sister Hotchkiss, sh-she—"

"But how in the nation'd they ever *git* that grindstone *in* there, *any*way? 'n' who dug that-air *hole?* 'n' who—"

"My very *words*, Brer Penrod! I was a-sayin'—pass that-air sasser o' m'lasses, won't ye?—I was a-sayin' to sister Dunlap, jist this minute, how *did* they git that grindstone in there, s'I. Without *help*, mind you—'thout *help! Thar's* wher' 'tis. Don't tell *me*, s'I; there *wuz* help, s'I; 'n' ther' wuz a *plenty* help, too, s'I; ther's ben a *dozen* a-helpin' that nigger, 'n' I lay I'd skin every last nigger on this place, but *I'd* find out who done it, s'I; 'n' moreover, s'I—"

"A *dozen*, says you!—*forty* couldn't a done everything that's been done. Look at them caseknife saws and things, how tedious they've been made; look at that bed-leg sawed off with 'm, a week's work for six men; look at that nigger made out'n straw on the bed; and look at—"

"You may *well* say it, Brer Hightower! It's jist as I was a-sayin' to Brer Phelps, his own self. S'e, what do *you* think of it, sister Hotchkiss, s'e? think o' what, Brer Phelps, s'I? think o' that bed-leg sawed off that a way, s'e? *think* of it, s'I? I lay it never sawed *itself* off, s'I—somebody *sawed* it, s'I; that's my opinion, take it or leave it, it mayn't be no 'count, s'I, but sich as 't is, it's my opinion, s'I, 'n' if anybody k'n start a better one, s'I, let him *do* it, s'I, that's all. I says to sister Dunlap, s'I—"

"Why, dog my cats, they must a ben a house-full o' niggers in there every night for four weeks, to a done all that work, sister Phelps. Look at that shirt—every last inch of it kivered over with secret African writ'n, done with blood! Must a ben a raft uv 'm at it right along, all the time, amost. Why, I'd give two dollars to have it read to me; 'n' as for the niggers that wrote it, I 'low I'd take 'n' lash 'm t'll—"

"People to *help* him, Brother Marples! Well, I reckon you'd *think* so, if you'd a been in this house for a while back. Why, they've stole everything they could lay their hands on—and we a watching, all the time, mind you. They stole that shirt right off o' the line! and as for that sheet they made the rag ladder out of, ther' ain't no telling how many times they *didn't* steal that; and flour, and candles, and candlesticks, and spoons, and the old warming pan, and most a thousand things that I disremember, now, and my new calico dress; and me, and Silas, and my Sid and Tom on the constant watch day *and* night, as I was a-telling you, and not a one of us could catch hide nor hair, nor sight nor sound of them; and here at the last minute, lo and behold you, they slides right in under our noses, and fools us, and not only fools *us* but the Injun Territory robbers too, and actly gets *away* with that nigger, safe and sound, and that with sixteen men and twenty-two dogs right on their very heels at that very time! I tell you, it just bangs anything I ever *heard* of. Why, *sperits* couldn't a done better, and been no smarter. And I reckon they must a *been* sperits—because, *you* know our dogs, and ther' ain't no better: well, them dogs never even got on the *track* of 'm, once! You explain *that* to me, if you can!—*any* of you!"

"Well, it does beat—"

"Land alive, I never—"

"So help me, I wouldn't a be—"

"*House*-thieves as well as—"

"Goodnessgracioussakes, I'd a ben afeard to *live* in sich a—"

" 'Fraid to *live!*—why, I was that scared I dasn't hardly go to bed, or get up, or lay down, or *set* down, sister Ridgeway. Why, they'd steal the very—why, goodness sakes, you can guess what kind of a fluster *I* was in by the time midnight come, last night: I hope to gracious if I warn't afraid they'd steal some o' the family! I was just to that pass, I didn't have no reasoning faculties no more. It looks foolish enough, *now*, in the daytime; but I says to myself, there's my two poor boys asleep, 'way up stairs in that lonesome room, and I declare to goodness I was that uneasy 't I crep' up there and locked 'em in! I *did*. And anybody would. Because, you know, when you get scared, that way, and it keeps running on, and getting worse and worse, all the time, and your wits gets to addling, and you get to doing all sorts o' wild things, and by and by you think to yourself, spos'n *I* was a boy, and was away up there, and the door ain't locked, and you—" She stopped, looking kind of wondering, and then she turned her head around slow, and when her eye lit on me—I got up and took a walk.

Says I to myself, I can explain better how we come to not be in that room this morning, if I go out to one side and study over it a little. So I done it. But I dasn't go fur, or she'd a sent for me. And when it was late in the day, the people all went, and then I come in and told her the noise and shooting waked up me and 'Sid,' and the door was locked, and we wanted to see the fun, so we went down the lightning rod, and both of us got hurt a little, and we didn't never want to try *that* no more. And then I went on and told her all what I told uncle Silas before; and then she said she'd forgive us, and maybe it was all right enough, anyway, and about what a body might expect of boys, for all boys was a pretty harum-scarum lot, as fur as she could see; and so, as long as no harm hadn't come of it, she judged she better put in her time being grateful we was alive and well and she had us still, stead of fretting over what was past and done. So then she kissed me, and patted me on the head, and dropped into a kind of a brown study; and pretty soon jumps up and says:

"Why, lawsamercy, it's most night, and Sid not come yet! What *has* become of that boy?"

I see my chance; so I skips up and says:

"I'll run right up to town and get him," I says.

"No you won't," she says. "You'll stay right wher' you are; *one's* enough to be lost at a time. If he ain't here to supper, your uncle 'll go."

Well, he warn't there to supper; so right after supper, uncle went.

He come back about ten, a little bit uneasy; hadn't run across Tom's track. Aunt Sally was a good *deal* uneasy; but uncle Silas he said there warn't no occasion to be—boys will be boys, he said, and you'll see this one turn up in the morning, all sound and right. So she had to be satisfied. But she said she'd set up for him a while, anyway, and keep a light burning, so he could see it.

And then when I went up to bed, she come up with me, and fetched her candle, and tucked me in, and mothered me so good I felt mean and like I couldn't look her in the face; and she set down on the bed and talked with me a long time, and said what a splendid boy Sid was, and didn't seem to want to ever stop talking about him; and kept asking me every now and then, if I reckoned he could a got lost, or hurt, or maybe drownded, and might be laying at this minute, somewheres, suffering or dead, and she not by him to help him; and

AUNT SALLY TALKS TO HUCK.

so the tears would drip down, silent, and I would tell her that Sid was all right, and would be home in the morning, sure; and she would squeeze my hand, or maybe kiss me, and tell me to say it again, and keep on saying it, because it done her good, and she was in so much trouble. And when she was going away, she looked down in my eyes, so steady and gentle, and says:

"The door ain't going to be locked, Tom; and there's the window and the rod; but you'll be good, *won't* you? And you won't go? For *my* sake."

Laws knows I *wanted* to go, bad enough, to see about Tom, and was all intending to go; but after that, I wouldn't a went, not for kingdoms.

But she was on my mind, and Tom was on my mind; so I slept very restless. And twice I went down the rod, away in the night, and slipped around front, and see her setting there by her candle in the window with her eyes towards the road and the tears in them; and I wished I could do something for her, but I couldn't, only to swear that I wouldn't never do nothing to grieve her any more. And the third time, I waked up at dawn, and slid down, and she was there yet, and her candle was most out, and her old gray head was resting on her hand, and she was asleep.

TOM SAWYER WOUNDED.

The old man was up town again, before breakfast, but couldn't get no track of Tom; and both of them set at the table, thinking, and not saying nothing, and looking mournful, and their coffee getting cold, and not eating anything. And by and by the old man says:

"Did I give you the letter?"

"What letter?"

"The one I got yesterday, out of the postoffice."

"No, you didn't give me no letter."

"Well, I must a forgot it."

So he rummaged his pockets, and then went off somewheres where he had laid it down, and fetched it, and give it to her. She says:

"Why, it's from St. Petersburg—it's from Sis."

I allowed another walk would do me good; but I couldn't stir. But before she could break it open, she dropped it and run—for she see something. And so did I. It was Tom Sawyer on a mattrass; and that old doctor; and Jim, in *her* calico dress, with his hands tied behind him; and a lot of people. I hid the letter behind the first thing that come handy, and rushed. She flung herself at Tom, crying, and says:

"O, he's dead, he's dead, I know he's dead!"

And Tom he turned his head a little, and muttered something or other, which showed he warn't in his right mind; then she flung up her hands, and says:

"He's alive, thank God! And that's enough!" and she snatched a kiss of him, and flew for the house, to get the bed ready, and scattering orders right and left at the niggers and everybody else, as fast as her tongue could go, every jump of the way.

I followed the men to see what they was going to do with Jim; and the old doctor and uncle Silas followed after Tom into the house. The men was very huffy, and some of them wanted to hang Jim, for an example to all the other niggers around there, so they wouldn't be trying to run away, like Jim done, and making such a raft of trouble, and keeping a whole family scared most to death for days and nights. But the others said, don't do it, it wouldn't answer at all, he ain't our nigger, and his owner would turn up and make us pay for him, sure. So that cooled them down a little, because the people that's always the most anxious for to hang a nigger that hain't done just right, is always the very ones that ain't the most anxious to pay for him when they've got their satisfaction out of him.

They cussed Jim considerble, though, and give him a cuff or two, side the head, once in a while, but Jim never said nothing, and he never let on to know me, and they took him to the same cabin, and put his own clothes on him, and chained him again, and not to no bed-leg, this time, but to a big staple drove into the bottom log, and chained his hands, too, and both legs, and said he warn't to have nothing but bread and water to eat, after this, till his owner come or he was sold at auction, because he didn't come in a certain length of time, and filled up our hole, and said a couple of farmers with guns must stand watch around about the cabin every night, and a bulldog tied to the door in the daytime, and about this time they was through with the job and was tapering off with a kind of generl goodbye cussing, and then the old doctor comes, and takes a look, and says:

"Don't be no rougher on him than you're obleeged to, because he ain't a bad nigger. When I got to where I found the boy, I see I couldn't cut the bullet out without some help, and he warn't in no condition for me to leave, to go and get help; and he got a little worse and a little worse, and after a long time he went out of his head, and wouldn't let me come anigh him, any more, and said if I chalked his raft he'd kill me, and no end of wild foolishness like that, and I see I couldn't do anything at all with him; so I says, I got to have *help*, somehow; and the minute I says it, out crawls this nigger from

somewheres, and says he'll help; and he done it, too, and done it
very well. Of course I judged he must be a runaway nigger, and there
I *was!* and there I had to stick, right straight along, all the rest of the
day, and all night. It was a fix, I tell you! I had a couple of patients
with the chills, and of course I'd of liked to run up to town and see
them, but I dasn't, because the nigger might get away, and then I'd
be to blame; and yet never a skiff come close enough for me to hail.

THE DOCTOR SPEAKS FOR JIM.

So there I had to stick, plumb till daylight this morning; and I never
see a nigger that was a better nuss or faithfuller, and yet he was
resking his freedom to do it, and was all tired out, too, and I see plain
enough he'd been worked main hard, lately. I liked the nigger for
that; I tell you, gentlemen, a nigger like that is worth a thousand
dollars—and kind treatment, too. I had everything I needed, and the
boy was doing as well there as he would a done at home—better,
maybe, because it was so quiet; but there I *was*, with both of 'm on
my hands; and there I had to stick, till about dawn this morning;
then some men in a skiff come by, and as good luck would have it,
the nigger was setting by the pallet with his head propped on his

knees, sound asleep; so I motioned them in, quiet, and they slipped up on him and grabbed him and tied him before he knowed what he was about, and we never had no trouble. And the boy being in a kind of a flighty sleep, too, we muffled the oars and hitched the raft on, and towed her over very nice and quiet, and the nigger never made the least row nor said a word, from the start. He ain't no bad nigger, gentlemen; that's what I think about him."

Somebody says:

"Well, it sounds very good, doctor, I'm obleeged to say."

Then the others softened up a little, too, and I was mighty thankful to that old doctor for doing Jim that good turn; and I was glad it was according to my judgement of him, too; because I thought he had a good heart in him and was a good man, the first time I see him. Then they all agreed that Jim had acted very well, and was deserving to have some notice took of it, and reward. So every one of them promised, right out and hearty, that they wouldn't cuss him no more.

Then they come out and locked him up. I hoped they was going to say he could have one or two of the chains took off, because they was rotten heavy, or could have meat and greens with his bread and water, but they didn't think of it, and I reckoned it warn't best for me to mix in, but I judged I'd get the doctor's yarn to aunt Sally, somehow or other, as soon as I'd got through the breakers that was laying just ahead of me. Explanations, I mean, of how I forgot to mention about 'Sid' being shot, when I was telling how him and me put in that dratted night paddling around hunting the runaway nigger.

But I had plenty time. Aunt Sally she stuck to the sick room all day and all night; and every time I see uncle Silas mooning around, I dodged him.

Next morning I heard Tom was a good deal better, and they said aunt Sally was gone to get a nap. So I slips to the sick room and if I found him awake I reckoned we could put up a yarn for the family that would wash. But he was sleeping, and sleeping very peaceful, too; and pale, not fire-faced the way he was when he come. So I set down and laid for him to wake. In about a half an hour, aunt Sally comes gliding in, and there I was, up a stump again! She motioned me to be still, and set down by me, and begun to whisper, and said we could all be joyful, now, because all the symptoms was first rate, and he'd been sleeping like that for ever so long, and looking better and peacefuller all the time, and ten to one he'd wake up in his right mind.

So we set there watching, and by and by, he stirs a bit, and opens his eyes very natural, and takes a look, and says:

"Hello, why I'm at *home!* How's that? Where's the raft?"

"It's all right," I says.

"And *Jim?*"

"The same," I says, but couldn't say it pretty brash. But he never noticed, but says:

"Good! Splendid! *Now* we're all right and safe! Did you tell aunty?"

I was going to say yes; but she chipped in and says:

"About what, Sid?"

"Why, about the way the whole thing was done."

"What whole thing?"

"Why, *the* whole thing—there ain't but one: how we set the runaway nigger free—me and Tom."

"Good land! Set the run— What *is* the child talking about! Dear, dear, out of his head again!"

"*No* I ain't out of my HEAD, I know all what I'm talking about. We *did* set him free—me and Tom. We laid out to do it and we *done* it. And we done it elegant, too." He'd got a start, and she never checked him up, just set and stared and stared, and let him clip along, and I see it warn't no use for *me* to put in. "Why, aunty, it cost us a power of work—weeks of it—hours and hours, every night, whilst you was all asleep. And we had to steal candles, and the sheet and the shirt, and your dress, and spoons, and tin plates, and case-knives, and the warming pan, and the grindstone, and flour, and just no end of things, and you can't think what work it was, to make the saws, and pens, and inscriptions, and one thing or another, and you can't think *half* the fun it was. And we had to make up the pictures of coffins and things, and nonnamous letters from the robbers, and get up and down the lightning rod, and dig the hole into the cabin, and make the rope-ladder and send it in, cooked up in a pie, and send in spoons and things to work with, in your apron pocket"—

"Mercy sakes!"

—"and load up the cabin with rats and snakes and so-on, for company for Jim; and then you kept Tom here so long with the butter in his hat that you come near spiling the whole business, because the men come before we was out of the cabin, and we had to rush, and they heard us and let drive at us, and I got my share, and we dodged out of the path and let them go by, and when the dogs come they warn't interested in us, but went for the most noise, and we got our canoe, and made for the raft, and was all safe, and Jim was a free man, and we done it all by ourselves, and *wasn't* it bully, aunty!"

"Well, I never heard the likes of it in all my born days! So it was *you*, you little rapscallions, that's been making all this trouble, and turned everybody's wits clean inside out and scared us all most to death. I've as good a notion as ever I had in my life, to take it out o' you this very minute. To think, here I've been, night after night, a— *you* just get well, once, you young scamp, and I lay I'll tan the Old Harry out o' both o' ye!"

But Tom, he *was* so proud and joyful, he just *couldn't* hold in, and his tongue just *went* it—she a-chipping in, and spitting fire all along, and both of them going it at once, like a cat-convention; and she says:

"*Well*, you get all the enjoyment you can out of it *now*, for mind I tell you if I catch you meddling with him again—"

"Meddling with *who*?" Tom says, dropping his smile and looking surprised.

"With *who*? Why, the runaway nigger, of course. Who'd you reckon?"

Tom looks at me very grave, and says:

"Tom, didn't you just tell me he was all right? Hasn't he got away?"

"*Him*?" says aunt Sally; "the runaway nigger? 'Deed he hasn't. They've got him back, safe and sound, and he's in that cabin again, on bread and water, and loaded down with chains, till he's claimed or sold!"

Tom rose square up in bed, with his eye hot, and his nostrils opening and shutting like gills, and sings out to me:

"They hain't no *right* to shut him up! *Shove!*—and don't you lose a minute. Turn him loose! he ain't no slave, he's as free as any cretur that walks this earth!"

"What *does* the child mean!"

"I mean every word I *say*, aunt Sally, and if somebody don't go, *I*'ll go. I've knowed him all his life, and so has Tom, there. Old Miss Watson died two months ago, and she was ashamed she ever was going to sell him down the river, and *said* so; and she set him free in her will."

TOM ROSE SQUARE UP IN BED.

"Then what on earth did *you* want to set him free for, seeing he was already free?"

"Well that *is* a question, I must say; and *just* like women! Why, I wanted the *adventure* of it; and I'd a waded neck-deep in blood to— goodness alive, AUNT POLLY!"

If she warn't standing right there, just inside the door, looking as sweet and contented as an angel half-full of pie, I wish I may never!

Aunt Sally jumped for her, and most hugged the head off of her, and cried over her, and I found a good enough place for me under the bed, for it was getting pretty sultry for *us*, seemed to me. And I peeped out, and in a little while Tom's aunt Polly shook herself loose and stood there looking across at Tom over her spectacles— kind of grinding him into the earth, you know. And then she says:

"Yes, you *better* turn y'r head away—I would if I was you, Tom."

"Oh, deary me!" says aunt Sally, "*is* he changed so? Why, that ain't *Tom*, it's Sid; Tom's—Tom's—why, where is Tom? He was here a minute ago."

"You mean where's Huck *Finn*—that's what you mean! I reckon I hain't raised such a scamp as my Tom all these years, not to know him when I *see* him. That *would* be a pretty howdy-do. Come out from under that bed, Huck Finn."

So I done it. But not feeling brash.

Aunt Sally she was one of the mixed-upest looking persons I ever see; except one, and that was uncle Silas, when he come in, and they told it all to him. It kind of made him drunk, as you may say, and he didn't know nothing at all the rest of the day, and preached a prayer meeting sermon that night that give him a rattling ruputation, because the oldest man in the world couldn't a understood it. So Tom's aunt Polly she told all about who I was, and what; and I had to up and tell how I was in such a tight place that when Mrs. Phelps took me for Tom Sawyer—she chipped in and says, "O, go on and call me aunt Sally, I'm used to it, now, and 't ain't no need to change"—that when aunt Sally took me for Tom Sawyer, I had to stand it—there warn't no other way, and I knowed he wouldn't mind, because it would be nuts for him, being a mystery, and he'd make an adventure out of it and be perfectly satisfied. And so it turned out, and he let on to be Sid, and made things as soft as he could for me.

And his aunt Polly she said Tom was right about old Miss Watson setting Jim free in her will; and so, sure enough, Tom Sawyer had gone and took all that trouble and bother to set a free nigger free! and I couldn't ever understand, before, until that minute and that talk, how he *could* help a body set a nigger free, with his bringing-up.

Well, aunt Polly she said that when aunt Sally wrote to her that Tom and *Sid* had come, all right and safe, she says to herself:

"Look at that, now! I might have expected it, letting him go off that way without anybody to watch him. So now I got to go and trapse all the way down the river eleven hundred mile, and find out what that cretur's up to, *this* time; as long as I couldn't seem to get any answer out of *you* about it."

"Why, I never heard nothing from you," says aunt Sally.

"Well, I wonder! Why, I wrote to you twice, to ask you what you could mean by Sid being here."

"Well, I never got 'em, Sis."

Aunt Polly she turns around slow and severe, and says:

"You, Tom!"

"Well—*what?*" he says, kind of pettish.

"Don't you what *me*, you impudent thing—hand out them letters."

"What letters?"

"*Them* letters. I be bound, if I have to take aholt of you I'll—"

"They're in the trunk. There, now. And they're just the same as they was when I got them out of the office. I hain't looked into them, I hain't touched them. But I knowed they'd make trouble, and I thought if you warn't in no hurry, I'd—"

"Well, you *do* need skinning, there ain't no mistake about it. And I wrote another one to tell you I was coming; and I spose he—"

"No, it come yesterday; I hain't read it yet, but *it's* all right, I've got that one."

"HAND OUT THEM LETTERS."

I wanted to offer to bet two dollars she hadn't, but I reckoned maybe it was just as safe to not to. So I never said nothing.

Chapter the last

OUT OF BONDAGE.

The first time I catched Tom, private, I asked him what was his idea, time of the evasion?—what it was he'd planned to do if the evasion worked all right and he managed to set a nigger free that was already free before? And he said, what he had planned in his head, from the start, if we got Jim out, all safe, was for us to run him down the river, on the raft, and have adventures plumb to the mouth of the river, and then tell him about his being free, and take him back up home on a steamboat, in style, and pay him for his lost time, and write word ahead, and get out all the niggers around, and have them waltz him into town with a torchlight procession, and a brass band, and then he would be a hero, and so would we. But I reckoned it was about as well the way it was.

We had Jim out of the chains in no time, and when aunt Polly and uncle Silas and aunt Sally found out how good he helped the doctor nurse Tom, they made a heap of fuss over him, and fixed him up prime, and give him all he wanted to eat, and a good time, and nothing to do. And we had him up to the sick room; and had a high talk; and Tom give Jim forty dollars for being prisoner for us so patient, and doing it up so good, and Jim was pleased most to death, and busted out, and says:

"*Dah*, now, Huck, what I tell you?—what I tell you up dah on Jackson islan'? I *tole* you I got a hairy breas', en what's de sign un it;

en I *tole* you I ben rich wunst, en gwineter be rich *agin*; en it's come true; en heah she *is*! *Dah*, now! doan' talk to *me*—signs is *signs*, mine I tell you; en I knowed jis' 's well 'at I 'uz gwineter be rich agin as I's a stannin' heah dis minute!"

And then Tom he talked along, and talked along, and says, le's all three slide out of here, one of these nights, and get an outfit, and go for howling adventures amongst the Injuns, over in the Territory, for a couple of weeks or two; and I says, all right, that suits me, but I ain't got no money for to buy the outfit, and I reckon I couldn't get none from home, because it's likely pap's been back before now, and got it all away from Judge Thatcher and drunk it up.

"No he hain't," Tom says; "it's all there, yet—six thousand dollars and more; and your pap hain't ever been back since. Hadn't when I come away, anyhow."

Jim says, kind of solemn:

"He ain't a comin' back no mo', Huck."

I says:

"Why, Jim?"

"Nemmine why, Huck—but he ain't comin' back no mo'."

But I kept at him; so at last he says:

"Doan' you 'member de house dat was float'n down de river, en dey wuz a man in dah, kivered up, en I went in en unkivered him en

TOM'S LIBERALITY.

didn' let you come in? Well, den, you k'n git yo' money when you wants it; kase dat wuz him.''

Tom's most well, now, and got his bullet around his neck on a watch-guard for a watch, and is always seeing what time it is, and so there ain't nothing more to write about, and I am rotten glad of it, because if I'd a knowed what a trouble it was to make a book I wouldn't a tackled it and ain't agoing to no more. But I reckon I got to light out for the Territory ahead of the rest, because aunt Sally she's going to adopt me and sivilize me and I can't stand it. I been there before.

THE END, YOURS TRULY HUCK FINN.

REFERENCE
MATERIAL

MAPS

Mark Twain's title page for *Huckleberry Finn* announced that his story took place in the Mississippi Valley "forty to fifty years ago," or between about 1835 and 1845, when Clemens would have been, at most, ten years old. The geography of St. Petersburg does in fact depend on the author's boyhood memory of Hannibal, which he left in 1853 at the age of seventeen. But his knowledge of the rest of the river valley dates primarily from the years 1857 to 1861, when he worked as a pilot on steamboats plying between St. Louis and New Orleans.

The five maps that follow here are intended to represent some of the real geography on which Mark Twain relied in writing his story. When Mark Twain used a fictional name for a real place, it appears within parentheses and in capitals and small capitals below the real name: for example, "Hannibal | (ST. PETERSBURG)". Not every fictional place is so readily equated with a real one. When the link is more tentative, the fictional name is preceded by "VICINITY OF," still within parentheses, and the rationale for the identification is discussed in the explanatory notes.

Map Sources

■ *Mississippi River Valley, ca. 1840.* Based on the frontispiece from *Mighty Mississippi* (Childs), this map also draws on plates 19 and 20 of the *Century Atlas* (Smith 1902), and an 1849 map of the river in *Appletons' Hand-Book* (Hall, following page 428). (The system of citation used here is discussed at the beginning of the explanatory notes.)

■ *Hannibal, ca. 1845.* This map is based on the following: "Plat of Original Town of Hannibal," dated 1836 (photofacsimile in CU-MARK), which provides the configuration of the town proper; "Map of the Mississippi River from the Falls of St. Anthony to the Junction of the Illinois River" (U.S. Army Corps of Engineers, 1887–88, DLC), which provides the Missouri and Illinois shorelines. No precisely scaled map has been found that shows Glasscock's Island at the time Clemens knew it, and later maps demonstrate no consensus about its size and location. This map, therefore, relies on Mark Twain's description of the island in chapters 7–9 of *Huck-*

leberry Finn and the virtually identical description, adjusted for the June rise of the river, in *Tom Sawyer*, chapters 13–15.

■ *Thebes, Ill., to Commerce, Mo., ca. 1857 (Vicinity of* Walter Scott *Wreck)*. Based on a contemporary river guide (James, 25, 27), this map also draws on "Map of the Alluvial Valley of the Upper Mississippi River from the Falls of St. Anthony to the Mouth of the Ohio River" (Mississippi River Commission, 1899, CU-MAPS).

■ *Cairo, ca. 1857*. Based on maps provided in two contemporary river guides (Conclin, 65, 89, and James, 27).

■ *Compromise, ca. 1878*. Based on "Map of a Reconnaissance of the Mississippi River from Cairo, Ill's. to New Orleans, La." (U.S. Army Corps of Engineers, 1878?, DLC); "Preliminary Map of the Lower Mississippi River, from the Mouth of the Ohio River to the Head of the Passes" (Mississippi River Commission, 1881–85, DLC); and "The Mississippi River from St. Louis to the Sea" (J. A. Ockerson, assisted by Charles W. Stewart, 1892, DLC).

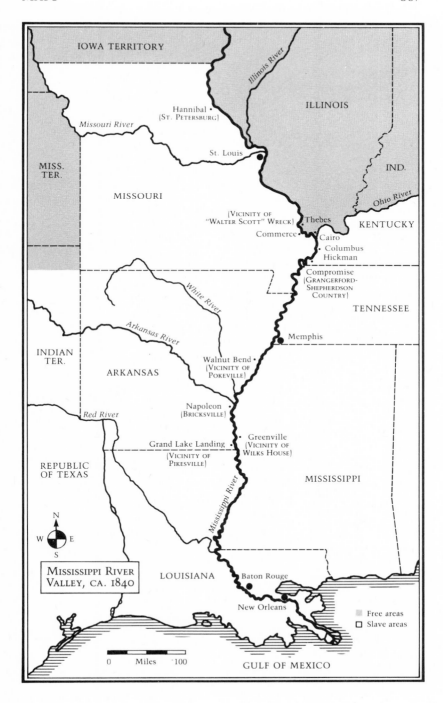

IOWA TERRITORY

ILLINOIS

Illinois River

Hannibal •
(ST. PETERSBURG)

Missouri River

St. Louis

MISS.
TER.

IND.

Ohio River

MISSOURI

(VICINITY OF
"WALTER SCOTT" WRECK)   Thebes

KENTUCKY

Commerce •

• Cairo
• Columbus
Hickman

Compromise
(GRANGERFORD-
SHEPHERDSON
COUNTRY)

TENNESSEE

White River

Arkansas River

Memphis

INDIAN
TER.

ARKANSAS

Walnut Bend •
(VICINITY OF
POKEVILLE)

Red River

Napoleon •
(BRICKSVILLE)

Grand Lake Landing •
(VICINITY OF
PIKESVILLE)

• Greenville
(VICINITY OF
WILKS HOUSE)

REPUBLIC
OF TEXAS

MISSISSIPPI

Mississippi River

N
W   E
S

MISSISSIPPI RIVER
VALLEY, CA. 1840

LOUISIANA

• Baton Rouge

New Orleans

■ Free areas
□ Slave areas

0   Miles   100

GULF OF MEXICO

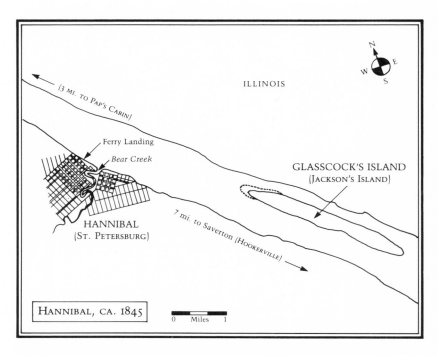

ILLINOIS

(3 MI. TO PAP'S CABIN)

Ferry Landing

Bear Creek

GLASSCOCK'S ISLAND
(JACKSON'S ISLAND)

7 mi. to Saverton (HOOKERVILLE)

HANNIBAL
(ST. PETERSBURG)

HANNIBAL, CA. 1845

0   Miles   1

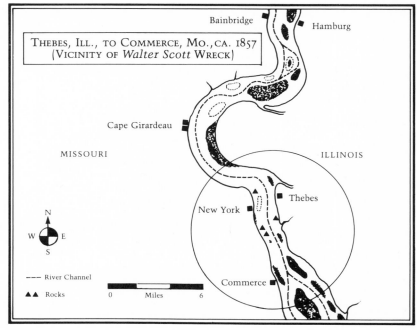

Bainbridge

Hamburg

THEBES, ILL., TO COMMERCE, MO., CA. 1857
(VICINITY OF *Walter Scott* WRECK)

Cape Girardeau

MISSOURI

ILLINOIS

New York

Thebes

- - - River Channel

▲▲ Rocks

0   Miles   6

Commerce

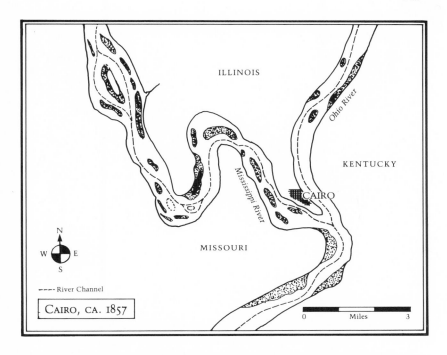

CAIRO, CA. 1857

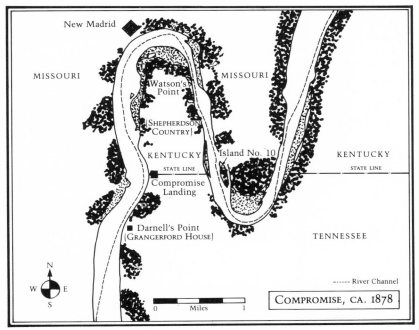

COMPROMISE, CA. 1878

EXPLANATORY NOTES

In 1895 Mark Twain told an interviewer, "I don't believe an author, good, bad or indifferent, ever lived, who created a character. It was always drawn from his recollection of someone he had known. Sometimes, like a composite photograph, an author's presentation of a character may possibly be from the blending of . . . two or more real characters in his recollection. But, even when he is making no attempt to draw his character from life, . . . he is yet unconsciously drawing from memory" (Pease, 10). These notes identify people, places, and incidents that served this literary purpose for *Adventures of Huckleberry Finn*. In addition, they selectively discuss literary allusions and topical references, and provide historical background.

Huck frequently alludes to folk beliefs and superstitions that, as Mark Twain said, were "prevalent among children and slaves" in the old Southwest during his own childhood (*ATS*, xvii). The author drew upon his recollections—especially of informal instruction he received as a boy from the slaves on his uncle John Quarles's farm near Florida, Missouri—for Huck's descriptions of various omens, magical rituals, and methods of prophecy. Wherever possible, independent evidence of such beliefs, which were usually localized versions of ancient European traditions, is cited.

Notes are keyed to the text by page and line: thus, 3.10 means page 3, line 10. Unless *title* is part of this cue, chapter titles, section headings, and picture captions are not counted. Works existing in many different editions may, for convenience, be cited only by chapter number (or equivalents, such as book, canto, act, etc.). Frequently cited works have been assigned an abbreviation, always italicized, which is followed by the page (or page and volume) number: (*MTBus*, 21) or (*MTL*, 1:456–57). Most works, however, are cited by author's last name: (Abbott, 16–17) or (Gribben, 2:571–72). If more than one work by an author is cited in this way, the date of publication is used to distinguish them: (Budd 1985, 21) or (Budd 1962, 34–76). All works cited are fully listed in References, alphabetically under the author's name or the designated abbreviation. Quotations are made to correspond exactly with the original documents quoted, and are cited by repository, which is given in the standard Library of Congress abbreviation or by last name of the owner, both defined in References. If the quoted words have been previously published in another work, whether accurate or not, it is cited after the repository: (Clemens to Bliss, 6 Feb 71, NN-B, in *MTBus*, 122). Previously unpublished words by Mark Twain are cited by repository, modified by a dagger (†), and are © 1985 by Edward J. Willi and Manufacturers Hanover Trust Company as Trustees of the Mark Twain Foundation, which reserves all reproduction or dramatization rights in every medium.

v   *illustration*] In September 1884, late in the process of manufacturing his book, Clemens decided to "help sell" it by including his autograph and this photograph of a bust of himself sculpted by his protégé Karl Gerhardt (*MTBus*, 275–76). Since the author seldom included portraits of himself in his books, one critic has suggested a possible motive for doing so here: to give a strong sign of his presence behind a narrative that otherwise might appear to be "made" by an unlettered fourteen-year-old boy (Budd 1985, 34).

vi   *frontispiece*] On seeing the first sketches by the illustrator he had chosen for *Huckleberry Finn*, Edward Windsor Kemble (1861–1933), Clemens complained to his publisher that Huck's mouth was "a trifle more Irishy than necessary" and, later, that the frontispiece drawing had "the usual blemish—an ugly, ill-drawn face." He said Huck was "an exceedingly good-hearted boy, & should carry a good & good-looking face." Kemble may have modified the face before this drawing was reproduced in the first edition, and he evidently drew Huck's face more satisfactorily in subsequent illustrations, for the author called the pictures "rattling good" (*MTBus*, 253, 255–56, 260). Kemble recalled that his model for Huck, and indeed "for every character in the story," had been Courtland P. Morris, "a youngster . . . who tallied with my idea of Huck. He was a bit tall for the ideal boy, but I could jam him down a few pegs in my drawing and use him for the other characters. . . . He was always grinning, and one side of his cheek was usually well padded with a 'sour ball' or a huge wad of molasses taffy" (Kemble, 3).

vii.8   Time: Forty to Fifty Years Ago] That is, sometime between about 1835 and 1845. Originally Mark Twain had written "Time, forty years ago," but in July 1884, during production of the first edition, he altered the dating so that it accorded with a sequel he was calling "Huck Finn & Tom Sawyer among the Indians 40 or 50 years ago," possibly because he had set the sequel on the Oregon Trail prior to the great migration of the 1840s (*MTBus*, 271; *MTHL*, 1:496; *HH&T*, 81–140, 372–74; Clemens 1983, 1–2).

xxv.*title*–6   NOTICE . . . Per G. G., CHIEF OF ORDNANCE] Mark Twain may have intended "G. G." to invoke the authority of General

Ulysses S. Grant (1822–85), with whom he was on good terms and whose memoirs he would contract to publish soon after *Huckleberry Finn* was issued in February 1885. If so, the allusion must have been a private joke. Although Clemens occasionally referred to Grant by these initials (*N&J*3, 108, 128, 135, 156), Grant never signed himself in this way, nor was he ever chief of ordnance, the high-ranking officer responsible for the army's supplies and weaponry.

xxvii.*title*–12 EXPLANATORY . . . THE AUTHOR] Mark Twain was neither joking nor being deliberately obscure, despite the conclusions drawn by critics (see, among others, Rulon, and Buxbaum). David Carkeet has shown that, except for some inconsistencies overlooked during the long course of composition and revision, Mark Twain indeed made distinctions among "dialects," or kinds of nonstandard English (1979). The seven mentioned in this notice can be identified with the following speakers:

1. "the Missouri negro dialect":
    Jim and four other black characters (Jack, Lize, Nat, young "wench" at Phelps farm);

2. "the extremest form of the backwoods South-Western dialect":
    Arkansas gossips (Sister Hotchkiss and others, chapter 41);

3. "the ordinary 'Pike-County' dialect":
    Huck, Tom, Aunt Polly, Ben Rogers, Pap Finn, Judith Loftus, the duke, Buck Grangerford, the Wilks daughters, and the watchman on the *Walter Scott*;

4–7. "four modified varieties of this last":
    (a) thieves on the *Walter Scott*;
    (b) the king, Tim Collins;
    (c) the Bricksville loafers;
    (d) Aunt Sally and Uncle Silas Phelps, the Pikesville boy.

Mark Twain's authority on the subject was well recognized by his fellow practitioners: John Hay declared Mark Twain "the finest living delineator of the true Pike accent," and Melville D. Landon (Eli Perkins) expressed a preference for *Huckleberry Finn* over Mark Twain's other books "because it has the truest dialect" (Hay, 5; Landon, 76). Mark Twain himself once told an interviewer: "the only one of my own books that I can ever read with pleasure is . . . 'Huck Finn,' and partly because I know the dialect is true and good" (Blathwait, 26). Mark Twain knew, however, that in writing for print an author "follows forms which have but little resemblance to conversation, but they make the reader understand what the writer is trying to convey" (Clemens to Edward W. Bok, ca. 1888, in *MTL*, 2:504).

1.1–4   You don't know about me . . . "The Adventures of Tom Sawyer,"]
In *Tom Sawyer* (1876) Mark Twain had described Huck Finn as "the
juvenile pariah of the village . . . son of the town drunkard," adding that
he "was cordially hated and dreaded by all the mothers of the town,
because he was idle, and lawless, and vulgar and bad—and because all
their children admired him so, and delighted in his forbidden society"
(*ATS*, 47). On hearing this read aloud, Clemens's sister Pamela is reported to have said, "Why, that's Tom Blankenship!" (*MTBus*, 265).
Mark Twain had said in his preface that "Huck Finn is drawn from life"
(*ATS*, xvii), and he repeated the assertion in his autobiography:

> In "Huckleberry Finn" I have drawn Tom Blankenship exactly as he was. He
> was ignorant, unwashed, insufficiently fed; but he had as good a heart as ever any
> boy had. His liberties were totally unrestricted. He was the only really indepen-
> dent person—boy or man—in the community, and by consequence he was tran-
> quilly and continuously happy, and was envied by all the rest of us. We liked him;
> we enjoyed his society. And as his society was forbidden us by our parents, the
> prohibition trebled and quadrupled its value, and therefore we sought and got
> more of his society than of any other boy's. (*MTA*, 2:174–75)

[These statements of course ignore substantial deviation from "reality"
in the novel, where Huck runs away whenever he is restricted, and he is
by no means "tranquilly and continuously happy."] Another boyhood
friend later described Tom as " 'talented,' bold, kind, and just" (Ayres,
no page). One of eight children of Woodson and Mahala Blankenship,
Tom was four years older than Clemens (*Inds*, biographical directory).
Tom's father was "at one time Town Drunkard, an exceedingly well
defined and unofficial office of those days," but Huck's last name was
borrowed from another town drunkard—Jimmy Finn, the prototype for
Pap Finn (see the note at 10.10–12). The origin of Huck's first name is
less clear. Clemens did not see or taste huckleberries until 1868, while
on a visit to Hartford (Blair 1960a, 2), but he well may have known the
slang meaning for "huckleberry"—an inconsequential or unimportant
person—or the huckleberry's general connotation: a plain, common
fruit, not requiring cultivation in order to flourish, often signifying
something backward or rural (Colwell, 71).

1.4   Tom Sawyer] In his preface to *Tom Sawyer*, Mark Twain explained
that like Huck Finn, Tom Sawyer was "drawn from life," but not from
"an individual—he is a combination of the characteristics of three boys
whom I knew" (*ATS*, 33). Albert Bigelow Paine identified the three boys
as John Briggs, Will Bowen, and Clemens himself (*MTB*, 1:54–55). In
1895, Mark Twain reflected on his reasons for naming Tom Sawyer as
he did: " 'Tom Sawyer' and 'Huckleberry Finn' were both real characters, but 'Tom Sawyer' was not the real name of the former, nor the name
of any person I knew, so far as I can remember, but that name was an
ordinary one—just the sort that seemed to fit the boy, someway, by its
sound, and so I used it" (Pease, 10).

1.12 aunt Polly] Clemens said that his mother, Jane Lampton Clemens, was the prototype for Tom Sawyer's aunt Polly: "I fitted her out with a dialect, & tried to think up other improvements for her, but did not find any" (*MTA*, 1:102). Aunt Polly bears a striking resemblance, however, to B. P. Shillaber's character Mrs. Partington, who is also a tender-hearted Calvinist widow charged with raising a mischievous nephew. Mark Twain had long been familiar with Shillaber's work when he published *Tom Sawyer* (Blair 1960a, 62–63).

1.13 Mary] Aunt Polly's daughter and Tom Sawyer's cousin. She was in some measure based upon Clemens's older sister, Pamela, who was known for her "amiable deportment and faithful application to her various studies" (*MTB*, 1:39).

1.15–16 the widow Douglas] In gratitude for Huck's rescuing her from the malevolent designs of Injun Joe, the widow adopted Huck in the last chapters of *Tom Sawyer*. Earlier in that book, Mark Twain had described her as "fair, smart and forty, a generous, good-hearted soul and well-to-do" (*ATS*, 37). Her Hannibal prototype was the twice-widowed Meliant S. (Mrs. Richard T.) Holliday, born ca. 1800, whom the author described in his 1897 "Villagers of 1840–3": "Lived on Holiday's Hill. Well off. Hospitable. Fond of having parties of young people. Widow. Old, but anxious to marry. Always consulting fortune-tellers; always managed to make them understand that she had been promised 3 [husbands] by the first fraud. . . . She finally died before the prophecies had a full chance" (*HH&T*, 30–31). She appears again as the "widow Guthrie" in Mark Twain's "Schoolhouse Hill" manuscript (*MSM*, 193).

1.22 Judge Thatcher] Father of Tom Sawyer's sweetheart, Becky Thatcher, he was described in *Tom Sawyer* as "a fine, portly, middle-aged gentleman with iron-gray hair" and as "a prodigious personage— no less a one than the county judge" (*ATS*, 32–33).

2.15–16 Moses and the Bulrushers] In 1861 when Clemens's eight-year-old niece, Annie Moffett, attempted to explain the story of Moses in Exodus 2:1–10 to him, "he just *couldn't* understand" (*MTBus*, 38–39; Clemens to Jane Clemens, 2 Apr 62, NPV, in Kruse, 210). In an 1866 sketch, Mark Twain published a letter from Annie which began, "Uncle Mark, if you was here I could tell you about Moses in the Bulrushers again, for I know it better, now" (Clemens 1866a, 1).

3.4–7 get down on a thing . . . that had some good in it] Huck's remarks bear more than a passing resemblance to Clemens's own response to similar disapproval from the Langdon family, just before his marriage to Olivia Langdon in 1870: "I cannot attach any weight to either the arguments or the evidence of those who know nothing about the matter personally & so must simply theorize. Theorizing has no effect on me. I have smoked habitually for 26 of my 34 years, & I am the only healthy member our family has. . . . There *is* no argument that can have even a feather's weight with me against smoking . . . for I *know*, & others merely *suppose*" (Clemens to Olivia Langdon, 13 Jan 70, CU-MARK, in *LLMT*, 135–36).

3.10   Miss Watson] This dour spinster's Hannibal prototype was Mary Ann Newcomb (1809–94), a schoolteacher of Clemens's who for a time boarded with his family. In "Villagers of 1840–3" Clemens described her as an "old maid and thin" (*HH&T*, 30). In "Autobiography of a Damned Fool" (1877), Mark Twain based the printer's wife on her: "Mrs. Bangs was three years older than her husband. She was a very thin, tall, Yankee person, who came west when she was thirty, taught school nine years in our town, and then married Mr. Bangs. . . . She had ringlets, and a long sharp nose, and thin, colorless lips, and you could not tell her breast from her back if she had her head up a stove-pipe hole looking for something in the attic. . . . She was a Calvinist and devotedly pious. . . . She had her share of vinegar" (*S&B*, 140, 163).

4.9–10   go around all day long with a harp and sing] Mark Twain had satirized this conventional vision of heaven in a story mapped out in 1869, worked on sporadically during the 1870s, and eventually published as *Extract from Captain Stormfield's Visit to Heaven*: "People take the figurative language of the Bible and the allegories for literal, and the first thing they ask for when they get here is a halo and a harp, and so on. . . . They go and sing and play just about one day, and that's the last you'll ever see them in the choir. They don't need anybody to tell them that that sort of thing wouldn't make a heaven—at least not a heaven that a sane man could stand a week and remain sane" (Clemens 1909, 40). Mark Twain returned to the subject in "Letters from the Earth," written in 1909 (*WIM*, 409).

4.15   niggers] This everyday term for black people in the South during the period of Huck's adventures was not Clemens's normal or customary word in writing or speaking. Public use of the word in 1884 was a sensitive matter, although partly as a matter of "good taste," and not necessarily for fear of offending black people. George Washington Cable advised Mark Twain not to label one of his readings from *Huck Finn* "Can't learn a nigger to argue": "When we consider that the programme is advertised & becomes cold-blooded newspaper reading I think we should avoid any risk of appearing—even to the most thin-skinned and super-sensative and hypercritical matrons and misses—the faintest bit gross. In the text, whether on the printed page or in the readers utterances the phrase is absolutely without a hint of grossness; but alone on a published programme, it invites discreditable conjectures of what the context may be, from that portion of our public who cannot live without aromatic vinegar" (Cable to Clemens, 25 Oct 84, CU-MARK, in Card-well, 105).

4.19–5.14   The stars . . . waiting for me.] Compare chapter 9 of *Tom Saw-yer*, which Mark Twain read in proof at about the time he composed the first chapters of *Huckleberry Finn* (Blair 1960a, 104–5).

4.21–22   an owl, . . . a whippowill and a dog crying] Folklore held that the cries of the owl, whippoorwill, and dog were signs or portents of death (Hyatt, items 14525, 14577–80, 14680–90, and Thomas and Thomas, items 3340–46, 3617, 3653; for descriptions of the traditions regarding death portents see Brand, 682–83, 693–94, and Hardwick, 245).

4.26–28   a ghost . . . can't rest easy in its grave] An ancient belief, dating from at least the tenth century. See, for example, *Hamlet*, 1.5.9–13.

4.30–31   a spider . . . lit in the candle] "If a spider is consumed through falling into a lamp, witches are near" (Thomas and Thomas, item 3808). This is apparently a variation of the widespread belief that killing a spider is unlucky (Hazlitt 1905, 2:559).

4.34–35   I . . . turned around in my tracks three times and crossed my breast every time] Two ancient gestures for warding off evil (see, for example, Hardwick, 248). Crossing one's breast is comparable to the Christian ritual of making the sign of the cross to invoke the protection of the Trinity.

4.35–36   I tied up a little lock of my hair] Closely tying one's hair was supposed to protect against the designs of witches, who braided the hair of victims at night in order to possess and ride them (Hoffman, 50; Hughes and Bontemps, 199–200). In 1866, Clemens recorded this super-stition in his notebook, and in 1897 he recalled his boyhood awe of an aged, "bed-ridden white-headed slave woman" on his uncle Quarles's farm: "Whenever witches were around she tied up the remnant of her wool in little tufts, with white thread, and this promptly made the witches impotent" (*N&J1*, 160; *MTA*, 1:99–100).

4.37–38   when you've lost a horse-shoe that you've found] Hanging a found horseshoe over a doorway was protection against witches: "Dey say de witch got to travel all over de road dat horseshoe been 'fo' she can git in de house" (Minor, 76; see also Thomas and Thomas, item 3435, and Hazlitt 1905, 1:330–31).

6.10   Jim] In 1897, recalling the summers he spent as a boy at his uncle John Quarles's farm, Mark Twain said:

> All the negroes were friends of ours, and with those of our own age we were in effect comrades. I say, in effect, using the phrase as a modification. We were comrades, and yet not comrades; color and condition interposed a subtle line

which both parties were conscious of, and which rendered complete fusion impossible. We had a faithful and affectionate good friend, ally and adviser in "Uncle Dan'l," a middle-aged slave whose head was the best one in the negro quarter, whose sympathies were wide and warm, and whose heart was honest and simple and knew no guile. He has served me well, these many, many years. I have not seen him for more than half a century, and yet spiritually I have had his welcome company a good part of that time, and have staged him in books under his own name and as "Jim," and carted him all around—to Hannibal, down the Mississippi on a raft, and even across the Desert of Sahara in a balloon [in *Tom Sawyer Abroad*]—and he has endured it all with the patience and friendliness and loyalty which were his birthright. It was on the farm that I got my strong liking for his race and my appreciation of certain of its fine qualities. This feeling and this estimate have stood the test of fifty years and have suffered no impairment. (*MTA*, 1:100–101)

For an argument that two other black men were important as prototypes for Jim—John Lewis, who worked on Quarry Farm, and George Griffin, the Clemens's family butler in Hartford—see Pettit, 95–106.

7.29–30   witches bewitched him . . . rode him all over the state] The belief that witches could commandeer people or animals to ride at night was common in European as well as American folklore (Hoffman, 50; Dorson, 238; Hughes and Bontemps, 199).

8.6–11   Jim always kept that five-center . . . fetch witches] Although wearing a coin around the neck was thought to bring good luck and protect the wearer against evil spirits and disease, Jim's particular beliefs about the coin's powers have not been found elsewhere (Hazlitt 1905, 1:6–7; Thomas and Thomas, item 3020).

8.27–28   village] As in *Tom Sawyer*, the village of St. Petersburg is modeled on Hannibal, Missouri, a busy river-port on the western bank of the Mississippi, where Clemens lived between the ages of three and seventeen (1839–53). In that time Hannibal nearly tripled its 1839 population of less than one thousand. "St. Petersburg" may be intended to suggest "St. Peter's town," or "heaven."

8.32   Jo Harper, and Ben Rogers] Mark Twain's working notes for "Tom Sawyer's Conspiracy" (1897) show that he based Harper on his best and closest friend, William Bowen (1836–93), and Rogers on another close friend, John B. Briggs (1836?–1907). Rogers first appears in chapter 2, and Harper in chapter 3 of *Tom Sawyer* (*HH&T*, 375, 383; *Inds*, biographical directory).

9.15   hacked a cross in their breasts] Tom appears to have read Robert Montgomery Bird's *Nick of the Woods; or, The Jibbenainosay* (1837), in which the murderous title character marks his victims with "a knife-cut, or a brace of 'em, over the ribs in the shape of a cross" (chapter 3). Mark Twain had probably read this book by the time he was twenty-three, for in his 1859 sketch "The Mysterious Murders in Risse" he portrayed an assassin who leaves his victim "bearing upon the centre of his forehead the form of a cross, apparently cut with a knife" (*ET&S1*, 134–41). In chapter 55 of *Life on the Mississippi*, written in 1882 or 1883, the author recalled hearing, as a young man, grisly confessions of murder that turned out to be fabrications inspired by *Nick of the Woods*.

10.10–12   a father . . . lay drunk with the hogs in the tanyard] The prototype for "Pap" Finn was the Hannibal town drunkard Jimmy Finn, although a few of Pap's qualities may have been adapted from two fellow drunkards (*MTA*, 2:174–75). Pap's bellicosity when drunk may derive from "General" Gaines, and his fatherhood clearly derives from Tom Blankenship's father, Woodson (see the note at 1.1–4). Nevertheless, Jimmy Finn's role as prototype is well established from Mark Twain's other descriptions of him: one in 1867 (reproduced in the note at 26.25–26); one in an 1870 letter to Will Bowen (Clemens to Bowen, 6 Feb 70, TxU, in *MTLBowen*, 18–19); one in the 1877 "Autobiography of a Damned Fool," where the character based on him is said to be "a monument of rags and dirt; he was the profanest man in town; . . . he slept with the hogs in an abandoned tan-yard" (*S&B*, 152, 164); another in chapter 23 of *A Tramp Abroad* (1880); and still another in chapter 56 of *Life on the Mississippi* (1883), where Finn is said to have died "in a tan vat, of a combination of delirium tremens and spontaneous combustion." He was buried a pauper in 1845, when Clemens was nine years old (Abbott, 16; Wecter, 150–51; see also *MTA*, 1:105; *Inds*, biographical directory).

13.8   she took me in the closet and prayed] Miss Watson follows literally the injunction of Matthew 6:6, "But thou, when thou prayest, enter into thy closet" (Marx, 21n).

13.10–11   whatever I asked for I would get it] Miss Watson's admonitions about prayer and Huck's disappointment in it derive from the author's recollection of his Hannibal schoolteacher Mrs. Elizabeth Horr (1790?–1873), described in a 1906 dictation as "a New England lady of middle-age, with New England ways and principles, and she always opened school with prayer and a chapter from the New Testament; also she explained the chapter with a brief talk. In one of these talks she dwelt upon the text 'Ask and ye shall receive,' and said that whosoever prayed for a thing with earnestness and strong desire need not doubt that his prayer would be answered." Dissatisfied with the result of his prayers, the young Clemens eventually decided the injunction was unsound (*MTE*, 108–9).

14.24–25   a drownded man don't float on his back, but on his face] Folklore held that one would "always find the body of a drowned woman floating face up; the body of a drowned man, face down. Although these positions are occasionally reversed in some sayings, this is the general belief— they are the normal positions in coitus" (Hyatt, item 15134). Mark

Twain may well have encountered a variant of this belief in one of his favorite books, W. E. H. Lecky's *History of European Morals from Augustus to Charlemagne*. Lecky quotes the Roman historian Pliny: "It was said that drowned men floated on their backs, and drowned women on their faces; and this, in the opinion of Roman naturalists, was due to the superior purity of the latter" (Lecky, 2:318). Dr. Alvin Tarlov of the University of Chicago Medical School, however, has compared reports by police in Norwalk and Westport, Connecticut, the New York City Harbor Squad, and the Marine Unit of the Chicago Police Department. All agreed with the findings of a veteran of the last unit: "I have been fishing bodies out of Lake Michigan for nine years running, about forty-four a year. . . . Men, women, boys and girls—they all float face down."

14.38   blazing stick, which he called a slogan] "Evidently, Tom has confused two passages from Sir Walter Scott. In *The Lay of the Last Minstrel* (Canto IV, xxvii), 'slogan' is used in its earlier sense to mean battle cry; in a well-known episode in *The Lady of the Lake* (Canto III), a 'fiery cross' is carried through the countryside to call the clans to battle" (Marx, 23n).

15.3   Cave Hollow] Mark Twain defined "hollow" as "Missourian for 'valley.' " Cave Hollow was the valley containing the entrance to McDowell's cave, south of Hannibal. In *Tom Sawyer*, Mark Twain described it as "a woody hollow" three miles below town, and in 1906, he remembered that "on the Saturday holidays in summertime we used to borrow skiffs whose owners were not present and go down the river three miles to the cave hollow" (Clemens 1907, 165; *ATS*, 204, 243; *MTA*, 2:215).

15.34–16.3   a book called "Don Quixote," . . . just out of spite] Tom refers to chapter 18 of part I of Cervantes's work, where "Don Quixote imagines that a herd of sheep, which he sees approaching, is really a motley army of Arabs, Spaniards, Christians and pagans. He attacks the sheep, and the shepherds repulse him, using their slings. Don Quixote explains that his enemy, the magician, has turned the armies into sheep, for spite." The relationship between Tom and Huck, and later between Huck and Jim, is in many ways similar to that between Don Quixote and Sancho Panza (Moore 1922, 327–28, 337–38).

16.13   they rub an old tin lamp] Aladdin does this, thereby conjuring up a genie, in "History of Aladdin, or the Wonderful Lamp," in *The Arabian Nights' Entertainments* (1839–41). In 1913, one of Clemens's boyhood friends recalled: "In those days, . . . we didn't have much to read. There was but one copy of the Arabian Nights in the village, and that volume was the property of Squire Clemens, Mark Twain's father. Sam knew all the stories. He could hire us, any day, to help him do his chores by merely a promise that as soon as we were done, he would give us the Forty Thieves or some other yarn" (Abbott, 17).

16.23   chewing gum] Indians taught the New England colonists to chew spruce-tree resins. Spruce gum was first commercially sold in the early 1800s.

18.3–6   I . . . could spell, and read, and write just a little] Some readers have questioned whether a boy so unschooled could have written this long novel (see, for example, O'Connor). In answer, one critic has suggested that Huck talked the book, addressing the "reader orally—for it is a *speaking* letter, dictated or tape-recorded as it were. . . . the absurdity of the form is glimpsed only momentarily" (Gibson, 102). Of course Huck's narrative conforms to a generally accepted, centuries-old literary convention of picaresque "autobiographies" (Blair 1979, 2).

18.28–30   turn over the salt-cellar . . . bad luck] A common superstition, recorded in Thomas and Thomas, items 1809, 1812, and in Hazlitt 1905, 2:532–33.

19.16   a cross in the left boot-heel] A cross was commonly invoked to ward off evil (see Hyatt, items 16508–13, and Hazlitt 1905, 1:156).

20.8   hair-ball] A dense, rounded mass of hair formed in the stomach of an animal. Jim's divination with the hair-ball of an ox is the only "voodoo belief . . . of incontestably African origin" in the book (Hoffman, 52).

24.5–6   You think you're better'n your father . . . because he can't] Mark Twain had read Dickens's *Our Mutual Friend* (1864–65) by 1867. There (book I, chapter 6) Gaffer Hexam likewise scolds his son after discovering that he has learned to read and write (Gardner, 155–56).

24.21–22   took up a book . . . something about General Washington and the wars] Anecdotes and praise of George Washington were frequent selections in the textbooks published by William H. McGuffey (1800–73), and used almost without exception in American schools at the time of the story. For instance, *The Eclectic Second Reader; Consisting of Progressive Lessons in Reading and Spelling* (1836) lists "Story about George Washington" and "More about George Washington," and *The Eclectic Fourth Reader: Containing Elegant Extracts in Prose and Poetry, from the Best American and English Writers* (1838) includes Daniel Webster's "Washington's Birth Day" (Westerhoff, 126, 148).

26.25–26   new judge said he was agoing to make a man of him] In 1867, having visited Hannibal for the first time in several years, Mark Twain recalled an incident from his youth when

Jimmy Finn, the town drunkard, reformed, and that broke up the only saloon in the village. But the temperance people liked it; they were willing enough to sacrifice public prosperity to public morality. And so they made much of Jimmy Finn—dressed him up in new clothes, and had him out to breakfast and to dinner, and so forth, and showed him off as a great living curiosity—a shining example of the power of temperance doctrines when earnestly and eloquently set forth. Which was all very well, you know, and sounded well, and looked well in print, but Jimmy Finn couldn't stand it. He got remorseful about the loss of his liberty; and then he got melancholy from thinking about it so much; and after that, he got drunk. He got awfully drunk in the chief citizen's house, and the next morning that house was as if the swine had tarried in it. That outraged the temperance people and delighted the opposite faction. The former rallied and reformed Jim once more, but in an evil hour temptation came upon him, and he sold his body to a doctor for a quart of whiskey, and that ended all his earthly troubles. He drank it all at one sitting, and his soul went to its long account and his body went to Dr. [Orville] Grant. (Clemens 1867, 1)

In 1877 Mark Twain attributed an effort to "reform" the town drunkard to the character based on his brother Orion in "Autobiography of a Damned Fool" (S&B, 152–54). In 1906, he would assert that his father had tried, and failed, to reform both Finn and Injun Joe (MTA, 2:175).

33.7   thought he was Adam, he was just all mud] In Genesis 2:7 God creates Adam "of the dust of the ground."

33.8–9   he most always went for the govment] Pap's favorite theme, like his prejudices against blacks and literates, would have been recognized by contemporary readers as typical of the southern whites who "served the South's reactionaries by opposing education, insisting on white supremacy, and lining up against 'governmental interference of any kind' " (Budd 1962, 96).

33.33–34.1   free nigger there, from Ohio . . . talk all kinds of languages] The learned black professor could hail from Ohio, because slavery had been banned there by the 1787 Northwest Ordinance long before Ohio became a state in 1803. Although Clemens's knowledge of him remains conjectural, there was in fact such a professor in the 1860s: John G. Mitchell (1827–1900), a light-skinned black, who earned his doctorate of divinity and became a professor of Greek, Latin, and mathematics at Wilberforce (Ohio) University. During the Civil War Mitchell raised funds for his university in Missouri (Baker, forthcoming). Clemens did know and greatly admire Frederick Douglass (1817?–95), whom he met in 1869. Born a slave, Douglass escaped to freedom in 1838. Although not a professor, he was an eloquent writer and lecturer against slavery.

34.2–3   he could *vote*, when he was at home] Actually, free blacks were not allowed to vote in Ohio. Like most states outside the Northeast, Ohio limited the "elective franchise to white male persons" (Hurd, 2:36, 37, 50, 51, 61, 116, 168).

34.13–14   he couldn't be sold till he'd been in the State six months] By the 1840s all slave states, including Missouri, absolutely prohibited immigration of free blacks. In Hannibal free blacks could be treated as runaways if they failed to satisfy stringent legal requirements. They needed to register with the state and have a certificate of freedom; and an 1843

Missouri law further required that they be licensed. One Hannibal ordinance made mandatory an annual fee of five dollars, a cash bond, and "evidence of good moral character and behavior" for such a license (Hurd, 2:168n, 169n, 170; Welsh, 38).

35.10–11   pap, looking wild and skipping around] The passage that follows is an accurate description of a delirium tremens attack; indeed, "many clinicians are inclined to think that [it is] the most artful account on record" (Roueché, 96). Mark Twain was certainly familiar with accounts of the horrors of alcohol addiction, which abounded in temperance literature and newspapers of the day (N&J1, 505; Branch 1983, 577–78). One famous contemporary temperance lecturer whom he knew, John Bartholomew Gough (1817–86), was noted for his dramatic recreations of alcoholic fits.

36.8   Tramp—tramp—tramp; that's the dead] "Tramp, tramp, tramp," a common nineteenth-century refrain, appears, for instance, in "The Dead March," a temperance song included in an 1882 collection that Clemens owned, *The Treasury of Song for the Home Circle: The Richest, Best-Loved Gems*. The lyrics read in part:

>Tramp, tramp, tramp, in the drunkard's way
>March the feet of a million men.
>If none shall pity and none shall save,
>Where will all this marching end?
>The young, the strong, and the old are there,
>In woeful ranks as they hurry past,
>With not a moment to think or care
>What the fate that comes at last.
>
>Tramp, tramp, tramp . . .
>They are rushing madly on,
>Tramp, tramp, tramp . . .
>What a fearful ghastly throng;
>Rouse, Christian rouse ere it be too late,
>Rescue these souls from the drunkard's fate.
>   (Morrison, 448–49; thanks to Paul
>   Baender for this discovery)

37.25   June rise] Mark Twain elsewhere specified that the action of his story took place at "high water and dead summer time" (*Life on the Mississippi*, chapter 3). In an 1875 installment of "Old Times on the Mississippi," written the year before he wrote this passage in *Huck Finn*, he had described the June rise from the perspective of a cub pilot: "we met a great rise coming down the river. The whole vast face of the stream was black with drifting dead logs, broken boughs, and great trees that had caved in and been washed away. It required the nicest steering to pick one's way through this rushing raft, even in the day-time" (Clemens 1875, 448).

39.33   matches] Described as "new-fangled things" in *Tom Sawyer* (chapter 33), phosphorus friction matches (sometimes called "lucifer" matches) had been patented in 1836 in the United States.

41.35   Jackson's Island] In *Tom Sawyer*, Joe Harper, Tom, and Huck use this island as their pirate refuge (chapters 13–16). Its geographical prototype was Glasscock's Island, near the Illinois shore and, according to Clemens, three miles long and three miles downstream from Hannibal in a mile-wide stretch of the Mississippi (see the map on page 368). Clemens once wrote Walter Besant about his "longing to go back to the seclusion of Jackson's island & give up the futilities of life. I suppose we all have a Jackson's island somewhere, & dream of it when we are tired" (Clemens to Besant, 22 Feb 98, NN-B†, cited by Hearn, 98).

45.1–16   The sun . . . very friendly] Mark Twain described comparable woodland scenes in *Tom Sawyer*, chapter 14, and *A Tramp Abroad*, chapter 2.

45.25–26   firing cannon over the water . . . carcass come to the top] A common and persistent superstition, both in Great Britain and the United States, was that "a gun fired over a corpse thought to be lying at the bottom of the sea, or a river, will by concussion break the gall bladder, and thus cause the body to float" (Radford and Radford, 87). A similar scene in *Tom Sawyer* (chapter 14), like this one, made use of a boyhood memory. In 1870 Clemens recalled the time "I jumped overboard from the ferry boat in the middle of the river that stormy day to get my hat, & swam two or three miles after it (& *got* it,) while all the town collected on the wharf & for an hour or so looked out across the angry waste of 'white-caps' toward where people said Sam. Clemens was last seen before he went down" (Clemens to William Bowen, 6 Feb 70, TxU, in *MTLBowen*, 19). In a late, undated note to himself, Clemens supplied one further detail of this incident: "fired cannon to raise drowned bodies of Clint Levering & me—when I escaped from ferry boat" (autobiographical notes, CU-MARK†).

46.3–4   quicksilver in loaves of bread . . . go right to the drownded carcass] Folklore stipulated: "to locate a drowned person, lay some quicksilver on the middle of a slice of bread and let the bread rest on the water where the person went down. The bread and quicksilver will float and stop above the submerged body" (Hyatt, item 15131). This superstition is "widely held in Britain. . . . A Biblical reference to quicksilver and life is probably the origin" (Radford and Radford, 46). An 1859 St. Louis *Missouri Democrat*, which Clemens might have seen, reports that after a long and fruitless search for the drowned body of a young man, a "loaf of *brown bread*" containing three ounces of quicksilver was thrown into the water and traveled "*against the wind*" to the very spot where the body had sunk (Branch 1983, 579).

47.17   Becky Thatcher] In *Tom Sawyer* Becky is Judge Thatcher's daughter
and of course Tom's sweetheart. She is based on Clemens's Hannibal
contemporary, Anna Laura Hawkins (1837–1928), generally known as
"Laura," who at one time lived across the street from the Clemenses.

47.18   Sid] Sid Sawyer is described in chapter 1 of *Tom Sawyer* as "Tom's
younger brother, (or rather, half-brother)." Clemens acknowledged elsewhere that Sid was based in part on his own younger brother, Henry
(1838–58), "but Sid was not Henry. Henry was a very much finer and
better boy than ever Sid was" (*MTA*, 2:92–93).

48.29–30   bounded right on to the ashes of a camp fire . . . still smoking]
A comparable scene occurs in Daniel Defoe's *Robinson Crusoe* (1719),
where Crusoe finds a footprint on the shore of his island. In chapter 2 of
Life on the Mississippi (1883), Mark Twain called the coming of Mar-
quette's party upon footprints "a Robinson Crusoe experience which
carries an electric shiver with it yet, when one stumbles on it in print."

52.39–53.1   People would call me a low down Ablitionist . . . for keeping
mum] In 1847, Tom Blankenship's older brother, Benson, had shunned
the fifty-dollar reward offered for a runaway slave he had found hiding
on Sny Island, near the Illinois shore. He "kept the runaway over there
in the marshes all summer. The negro would fish and Ben would carry
him scraps of other food" (*MTB*, 1:63–64; see also Wecter, 148). This
benevolence must have been the more impressive because Benson was
a member of the impoverished Blankenship family. "In those old slave-
holding days the whole community was agreed as to one thing," Mark
Twain wrote in 1895,

> the awful sacredness of slave property. To help steal a horse or a cow was a low
> crime, but to help a hunted slave, or feed him or shelter him, or hide him, or
> comfort him, in his troubles, his terrors, his despair, or hesitate to promptly
> betray him to the slave-catcher when opportunity offered was a much baser
> crime, & carried with it a stain, a moral smirch which nothing could wipe away.
> That this sentiment should exist among slave-owners is comprehensible—there
> were good commercial reasons for it—but that it should exist & did exist among
> the paupers, the loafers the tag-rag & bobtail of the community, & in a passionate
> & uncompromising form, is not in our remote day realizable. (Notebook 35, TS
> p. 35, CU-MARK, in Blair 1960a, 144)

53.6   sell me down to Orleans] For a slave, being sold "down the river" was
the worst of fates: not only would he be permanently separated from his
family, he would likely face a life of hard labor on a sugar or cotton
plantation in Louisiana. In 1890 or 1891, in an attempt to explain how
his "kind-hearted and compassionate" mother could tolerate slavery,
Mark Twain wrote that

> there was nothing about the slavery of the Hannibal region to rouse one's dozing
> humane instincts to activity. It was the mild domestic slavery, not the brutal
> plantation article. Cruelties were very rare, and exceedingly and wholesomely
> unpopular. To separate and sell the members of a slave family to different masters

was a thing not well liked by the people, and so it was not often done, except in the settling of estates. . . . The "nigger trader" was loathed by everybody. He was regarded as a sort of human devil who bought and conveyed poor helpless creatures to hell—for to our whites and blacks alike the southern plantation was simply hell; no milder name could describe it. If the threat to sell an incorrigible slave "down the river" would not reform him, nothing would—his case was past cure. ("Jane Lampton Clemens," *HH&T*, 49)

53.10–11   eight hund'd dollars for me] A price of $800 for Jim is consistent with other selling prices on record for young male slaves in Missouri in the 1830s and 1840s (Trexler, 38–39; Harris [1904] 1969, 261).

54.9   swim asho' en take to de woods on de Illinoi side] Some readers have questioned whether Jim could not have gained his freedom simply by crossing the river into the free state of Illinois. The answer is that Illinois, though nominally free, would not have recognized him as a free man, and that southern Illinois was a particularly dangerous place for runaway slaves. In compliance with the Fugitive Slave Act of 1793, Illinois authorities arrested blacks who were unable to produce a certificate of freedom, holding them as indentured laborers until claimed by their owners (McDougall, 105–6; Hurd, 134–35). Substantial rewards offered for fugitive slaves made their capture and return profitable to local residents as well as professional bounty hunters. Although the law required blacks be given a certificate of freedom if not claimed within a year, they were always in danger of being kidnapped, as were all "unattached" or free blacks. Laws against kidnapping were not enforced, with the result that it "assumed the proportions of an established enterprise" (Harris [1904] 1969, 54). Mark Twain knew that Jim's best route to freedom would have been northeast, up the Ohio River (see the note to 99.2–9).

54.31–32   I was going to catch some . . . it was death] Similar superstitions about catching birds are recorded in Hyatt, items 630, 639, 1748, 1756, 1770, 1771, and Thomas and Thomas, items 1908, 3634, 3647, 3658.

54.35–36   you mustn't count . . . bad luck] "Counting victuals as an invitation to bad luck would seem a derivation of witch belief, since the witches suffered a fatal compulsion of counting everything in their way. Hence many charms for the avoidance of witches advised laying brooms, brushes, or bundles of faggots on the doorstep, since it would take the witches all night to count the hairs or strands" (Hoffman, 52).

54.37   shook the table-cloth after sundown] Another superstition of European origin (recorded in Hyatt, items 11691–92, and Thomas and Thomas, item 1657).

54.37–38   if . . . that man died, the bees must be told] This ancient, widely observed European custom apparently derived from the belief that the bees are messengers of the gods (Hoffman, 51; Hazlitt 1905, 1:39; Radford and Radford, 30–31; recorded in Thomas and Thomas, item 3669).

55.2   bees wouldn't sting idiots] The innocence of virgins, children, priests, and idiots was believed to protect them from bee stings. In 1881, four years after first composing this section of the book, Clemens noted to himself: "Gilbert White, bees & idiots." White gave an account of an idiot boy's obsession with bees and his lack of any "apprehensions from their stings" in letter 27 of *The Natural History and Antiquities of Selborne* (1789). Clemens owned an 1875 edition of this work (*N&J2*, 408).

55.11–12   got hairy arms . . . you's agwyne to be rich] This superstition is recorded in Hyatt, items 3584, 3591.

55.20   I tuck to specalat'n', en got busted out] Jim's account is like one in *History of the Big Bonanza* by William Wright (Dan De Quille), in which a Piute guide named "Capitan" Juan tells how he "was pretty well off once, . . . had *fifty dollars*," but was "burst all to smash" when he married a Spanish woman, "one *mucho* bad spectoolashe" (Wright, 272–73). Clemens, Wright's friend since they worked on the Virginia City *Territorial Enterprise*, had invited him to Hartford in 1875 to write his book and was instrumental in getting it published.

55.32–33   one-laigged nigger dat b'longs to ole Misto Bradish] Higgins, the "one legged mulatto, who belonged to Mr. Garth," was a familiar character in Hannibal (1889 clipping from the Hannibal *Journal*, enclosed in Ben Coontz to Clemens, 18 Apr 89, CU-MARK). Sixteen-year-old Clemens reported in the Hannibal *Western Union* that when a certain Miss Jemima walked through the town wearing the new "Bloomer costume," Higgins was one of her critics: "Higgins (everybody knows Higgins,) plied his single leg with amazing industry and perseverance, keeping up a running fire of comment not calculated to initiate him in the good graces of the person addressed. When the leg became tired, its owner would seat himself and recover a little breath, after which, the indomitable leg would drag off the persevering Higgins at an accelerated pace" (Clemens 1851). In 1870 Clemens recalled the time he and Will Bowen "taught that one-legged nigger, Higgins," to pester another Hannibal resident (Clemens to Bowen, 6 Feb 70, TxU, in *MTLBowen*, 19). See also *Inds*, biographical directory.

56.12   Balum's Ass] Balaam, an Old Testament prophet, was rebuked by the ass he was riding (Numbers, 22:21–33).

62.9–22   We got an old tin lantern . . . hunted all around] T. S. Eliot admired the "consistency and perfect adaptation of the writing" in *Huck Finn*, citing this paragraph as exemplary, partly because "in the details he remembers . . . Huck is true to himself." The paragraph "provides the right counterpoise to the horror of the wrecked house and the corpse; it has a grim precision which tells the reader all he needs to know about the way of life of the human derelicts who had used the house; and (especially the wooden leg, and the fruitless search for its mate) reminds us at the right moment of the kinship of mind and the sympathy between the boy outcast from society and the negro fugitive from injustice of society" (Eliot, x, xi).

63.25–26   worst bad luck . . . to touch a snakeskin] One of many superstitions linking snakes with bad luck (Thomas and Thomas, item 3723; Hyatt, item 1607). Clemens said that "Aunty" Rachel Cord, a former slave whom he knew by the early 1870s, believed that snakes were so unlucky they "must be killed on sight, even the harmless ones; & the discoverer of a sloughed snake-skin lying in the road was in for all kinds of calamities" (Pettit, 53–54).

64.10–11   Jim grabbed pap's whisky jug and begun to pour it down] For snakebite the 1867 *Gunn's New Family Physician* prescribed:

> Internally, give the patient *all the Whisky he can drink*. From a quart to a gallon should be drunk in six or eight hours. No fears need be entertained of making the patient drunk. You may fill him with Whisky, then let him swim in it, and it will not make him drunk, so long as the poison of the snake remains in the system. . . . It is a complete antidote for Snakebite, if taken freely, and may be relied on in any and all cases. It should be drunk like water for a few hours, and continued, at short intervals, until the patient gives signs of intoxication, when the quantity should gradually be diminished, as the disease is beginning to recede. Keep him "under the influence of liquor," however, until you are sure he is out of danger. (Gunn 1867, 515)

An 1861 St. Louis *Missouri Democrat*, which Clemens could have read, told of a snakebite victim cured by "a full quart of whisky and ninety drops of hartshorn" given in three doses at five-minute intervals ("Remarkable Case of a Rattlesnake Bite," 11 June 61, in Branch 1983, 578).

64.13–14   wherever you leave a dead snake its mate always comes] A folk belief and frequent observation of travelers: "The friends and relatives of a slain snake would wage war upon the slayer and the latter's friends and relatives" (Hyatt, item 1585; Masterson, 177).

65.20   see the new moon over his left shoulder] Another well-known cause of bad luck (Thomas and Thomas, item 2212; Hazlitt 1905, 2:417).

65.33–35   cat-fish that . . . weighed over two hundred pounds] In *Life on the Mississippi* Mark Twain said that he had "seen a Mississippi cat-fish that was more than six feet long, and weighed two hundred and fifty pounds" (chapter 2), and in a late autobiographical note to himself he associated such a fish with the person whose actions were in part the prototype for the Jackson's Island episode: "Big catfish. Bence Blankenship" (autobiographical notes, CCamarSJ†). See the note to 52.39–53.1.

68.11–12   Hookerville, seven mile below] In his working notes for "Tom Sawyer's Conspiracy" (1897), Mark Twain identified Hookerville as Saverton, Missouri, the first river town below Hannibal. In the story, the boys paddle "down the river seven miles in the dugout to Hookerville" (*HH&T*, 383, 180).

68.19   My mother's down sick] Introducing an excerpt from the novel in *Century Magazine*, Mark Twain wrote, "Readers who have met Huck Finn before (in 'Tom Sawyer') will not be surprised to note that whenever Huck is caught in a close place and is obliged to explain, the truth gets well crippled before he gets through" (Clemens 1884, 268). Actually, Huck did not show this skill in *Tom Sawyer*.

73.22–23   Goshen's ten mile further up the river] Goshen corresponds to Marion City, Missouri, ten miles upriver from Hannibal. After his 1882 visit, Mark Twain wrote in *Life on the Mississippi*: "When I first saw Marion City, thirty-five years ago, it contained one street, and nearly or quite six houses" (chapter 57).

75.6–7   a girl . . . throws her knees apart] A folk belief recorded in Norfolk, England (Baughman, item H1578.1.4.1). The test is also described in chapter 63 of Charles Reade's *The Cloister and the Hearth*, which Clemens had read and enjoyed in 1869 (Clemens to Olivia Langdon, 28 Nov 69, CU-MARK, in *LLMT*, 126; see Gribben, 2:571).

78.23–29   stick to hang the old lantern on . . . hunted easy water] In "Old Times on the Mississippi" Mark Twain had said that the "law required all such helpless traders to keep a light burning, but it was a law that was often broken" (Clemens 1875, 448). Like the raft, downstream boats followed the current in the river's natural channel, where water was fastest and safest. Since such boats operated under power, there was always some danger of their overtaking and colliding with the raft, especially at night. Upstream boats, on the other hand, at least during high water, deliberately avoided the resistance of the channel, seeking out "easy water" near the banks. Since the channel itself meandered from one side of the river to the other, in what were called "crossings," upstream boats were sometimes obliged to cross in the opposite direction to avoid it. Huck reasons that upstream boats posed a danger of collision only when their paths intersected the channel.

80.22–25   big straight river . . . steamboat that had killed herself on a rock] Mark Twain may have had in mind a specific location for this steamboat wreck. In *Life on the Mississippi* he mentioned "the Grand Chain" between Thebes, Illinois, and Commerce, Missouri—"a chain of sunken rocks admirably arranged to capture and kill steamboats on bad nights. A good many steamboat corpses lie buried there, out of sight" (chapter 25). Since the entire episode involving the wreck is a late addition (1883) to the story, and since Huck specifically mentions "a rock" as the cause of sinking, "the Grand Chain" seems a likely place. Details mentioned in the episode, however, also correspond to a stretch of river a few miles above Thebes, between Bainbridge and Cape Girardeau (Miller, 198–99). See the map, page 368.

80.28–29   chair by the big bell, with an old slouch hat hanging on the back of it] The "big bell" was used to signal arrivals and departures as well as various alarms. It was a standard fixture on the roof of the upper (hurricane) deck. The captain would routinely "come on the roof" and stand beside the three-foot fixed bell, briefly resuming command from his pilot until the boat was again under way (Bates, 67; Way 1943, 260–61, 264; *Life on the Mississippi*, chapter 14). The captain might also take up this post during any hazardous maneuver. Dickens recalled, however, that "when the nights are very dark, the look-out, stationed in the head of the boat, knows by the ripple of the water if any great impediment be at hand, and rings a bell beside him, which is the signal for the engine to be stopped" (Dickens 1842, 64). See the steamboat diagrams below.

81.20–28   fetched the starboard derrick . . . down through the texas hall we see a light!] Here and elsewhere (see pages 86–87) Huck's description of the steamboat is laced with precise river jargon. The steamboat is pointed upstream, listing to port, with only her hurricane deck, texas, and pilothouse above water: see the steamboat diagrams below. Huck and Jim tie the raft to "the starboard derrick," an upright pole that passes just in front of the hurricane deck, onto which they climb. They move across this sloping surface, fending off the chimney guy wires, toward the officers' cabin, or "texas." They first reach a slight upward step in the deck, the front end of the skylight roof (also called the texas deck). Climbing onto this roof, they find themselves in front of the "captain's door," at the head of the "texas hall," which bisects the cabin and gives access to the staterooms on either side of it.

86.19–21   scrabbled along forwards on the skylight . . . to the cross-hall door] That is, they scramble forward on the left side of the texas, walking on the narrow and sloping skylight roof (or texas deck), holding onto the stateroom shutters because the edge of this deck is "in the water." See the steamboat diagrams.

89.12   *Walter Scott*] Names such as *Walter Scott, Waverley*, and *Ivanhoe* were common for steamboats during the time of the story (Lytle, 92, 109, 166, 198, 200). In *Life on the Mississippi* Mark Twain had argued that the South still suffered from "the Walter Scott disease" because antebellum southerners had been influenced by Scott's popular medieval romances to emulate "decayed and degraded systems of government; . . . sham chivalries of a brainless and worthless long-vanished society" (chapter 46).

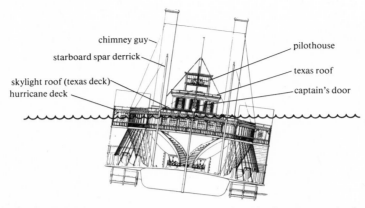

Bow view of the *Memphis*, a Mississippi steamboat built in 1860, tilted to suggest the position of the wrecked *Walter Scott*. Scale: ½ inch = 20.75 feet. (Reed, plate 14)

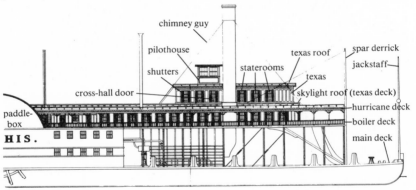

Side view of the *Memphis*. Scale: ½ inch = 20.75 feet. (Reed, plate 12)

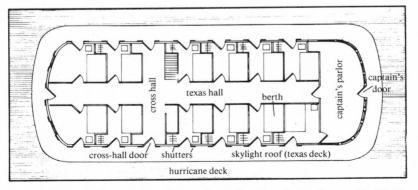

Plan of the texas of a Mississippi steamboat. (Based on Bates, figures 66, 69, 70, 71; Reed, plate 12; Hilton, Plummer, and Jobé, 88, 94; Way 1972, 24.)

91   *illustration*] On 25 June 1884, Clemens wrote to his publisher, Charles L. Webster, about the proof of this illustration: "It occurs to me, now, that on the pilot house of that steamboat-wreck the artist has put TEXAS—having been misled by some of Huck's remarks about the boat's 'texas'—a thing which is a part of *every* boat. That word had better be removed from that pilot house" (NPV, in *MTBus*, 262). Webster had the picture corrected before publication.

93.26–98.7   I read considerable to Jim about kings . . . I quit.] Mark Twain added this passage to the manuscript in 1883, having noted to himself: "Back yonder, Huck reads & tells about monarchies & kings &c. So Jim stares when he learns the rank of these 2" (*HF*, appendix A).

94.12   hawking and sp—] A venerable pun, found at least as early as 1639, but possibly suggested to Mark Twain by Scott's *The Fortunes of Nigel* (1822), a source for *The Prince and the Pauper*. Scott's Lord Dalgarno says to Dame Nelly, "you shall ride a hunting and hawking with a lord, instead of waiting upon an old ship-chandler, who could but hawk and spit" (Baetzhold, 94).

94.36   dat chile dat he 'uz gwyne to chop in two] See 1 Kings 3:16–28.

96.14–18   little boy the dolphin . . . come to America] Although Louis XVII (1785–95?), son of the guillotined Louis XVI, died in prison in France, he was widely believed to have escaped death and come to America (DeVoto, 318–19). In 1882 Clemens acquired Horace W. Fuller's *Noted French Trials: Impostors and Adventurers*, in which a chapter recounted the stories of "seven impostors [who] have claimed the name and the rights of the unhappy Louis XVII," some of whom visited the United States, and one of whom—Eleazar Williams—was born there (Fuller, 100, in Blair 1957, 27). Mark Twain's 1869 newspaper sketch, "The 'Wild Man,' " shows familiarity with Williams and the controversy surrounding his claims, and Clemens almost certainly had earlier knowledge of other such impostors: for instance, in 1853 the Hannibal *Journal* reprinted a story about the visit to a newspaper office of a Bourbon pretender calling himself "Aminidab Fitz-Louis Dolphin Borebon," whom the staff hailed as the "Dolphin" (Clemens 1869c, 1; Ashmead, 105–7).

97.3   Some of them gets on the police] Mark Twain remarks in *The Innocents Abroad* (chapter 13) that Napoleon III "kept his faithful watch and walked his weary beat a common policeman of London" (thanks to Henry Nash Smith for this suggestion). Napoleon III had joined a special constabulary formed in London in 1848 to prevent Chartist demonstrations (Simpson, 277–78).

97.3–4   some of them learns people how to talk French] In *A Tale of Two Cities*, Charles Darnay, a noble French emigrant, is "established in

England as a higher teacher of the French language" before the French Revolution. As Dickens comments, "Princes that had been, and Kings that were to be, were not yet of the teacher class" (book 2, chapter 10).

99.2–8   Cairo . . . was what we was after. We would . . . go way up the Ohio amongst the free States] One leg of Jim's intended flight to freedom was necessarily *south* on the Mississippi. Illinois would not have offered him a true refuge, as the note at 54.9 explains. In notes he made for his 1895–96 lecture tour, Mark Twain accounted for Huck's and Jim's southward journey as follows: "Night after night they kept a sharp lookout for Cairo, where the Ohio river comes in; for there they would land & try to escape far north & east away from the domain of slavery" (Clemens 1885b, 2:160†). Ohio had far more Underground Railroad operators than any other state, and most routes of this famed network began at the Ohio River and proceeded northward through eastern Indiana and Ohio (Siebert [1898] 1967, map facing 113, 119, appendix E; Siebert 1947, 77, 85, 89).

104.12–13   dog my cats ef it ain't de powerfullest dream I ever see] In chapter 72 of William Wright's *History of the Big Bonanza*, some miners fool a companion, Pike, leading him to believe that an Indian attack that they had staged to frighten him was only a dream. Pike remarks that his "dream" was as "plain" as an actual experience—"the doggonest plainest dream I ever did hev" (see the note at 55.20).

107.1–123.29   But you know . . . home again.] In 1883 Mark Twain had published this passage in *Life on the Mississippi* as "a chapter from a book which I have been working at, by fits and starts, during the past five or six years, and may possibly finish in the course of five or six more" (chapter 3). When he finished *Huckleberry Finn* and sent it to his publisher, the latter suggested that he shorten the text by omitting the passage. The author accepted the suggestion: no illustrations were prepared for the episode, and it never appeared in the novel during his lifetime. It is here restored because Mark Twain's agreement to omit it seems to have been solely for the practical convenience of his publisher. In the absence of Kemble illustrations, those by John Harley for *Life on the Mississippi* are included. Mark Twain had seen and approved these thirteen illustrations two years before publishing *Huckleberry Finn*.

108.1–8   "There was a woman in our towdn, . . . twyste as wed'l."] This folk-ballad, originally from the British Isles, was a particular favorite of Mark Twain's: he had already used it in 1865 in an unfinished play (S&B, 211), and in *The Prince and the Pauper* (1881). His niece remembered his singing it in the family's private railroad car during his wedding journey in 1870 (*MTBus*, 109), and he recalled his own rendition in an 1885 family parlor performance of *Prince*: "I was great in that song" (*MTS*, 72). Under various titles, among them "There Was an Old Woman in Ireland," "The Rich Old Lady," and "She Loved Her Husband Dearly," the song survives in Missouri and neighboring states (Wolford, 93; Sharp, 348–49; Moore 1964, 218–19; Belden, 238–39).

108.10–11   the tune the old cow died on] Although the old cow dies in a great many folk and minstrel songs, the only one found in which she is killed by the tune is a folk song, evidently of English or Irish origin:

> Farmer John from his work came home
> One summer's afternoon,
> And sat himself down by the maple grove
> And sang himself this tune.
> *Chorus*:
> Ri fol de ol, Di ri fol dal di
> Tune the old cow died on.
>   (Musick, 105–6; in Hearn, 366)

109.7–112.13   "Whoo-oop! I'm the old original . . . after-sweeps.] Bob and the Child of Calamity have as literary ancestors hosts of comic braggarts dating back at least to 405 B.C., when Aristophanes pictured one in *The Frogs*. Plautus (254?–184 B.C.) had fun with such characters in seven comedies, one of which, *Miles Gloriosus*, gave critics a name for the type that they would use for centuries. From the publication of Thomas Malory's *Morte D'Arthur* in 1485 to the present day, writers throughout the Western world depicted such characters in their plays and novels, many of which were very popular. In America, from the early nineteenth century on, hundreds of ring-tailed roarers bellowed boasts and fought rough-and-tumble in frontier humor, such as that about Mike Fink and Davy Crockett, whose exploits were familiar to young Clemens. Typical Old World swaggerers, however, had been bluffing cowards who ran away from fights, whereas most early American specimens were mighty men and heroic battlers whose exploits almost justified their imaginative threats. Beginning in the 1850s most American comic writers followed European patterns. Mark Twain did so in his 1852 sketch "The Dandy Frightening the Squatter" (*ET&S1*, 63–65), as well as in the present episode. (See Blair 1960a, 115–16; Blair 1960b, 29–31, 154; Blair and Hill, 128–51, 255–62, 314.)

110.7   Whoo-oop! bow your neck and spread] Mark Twain recalled that "old General Gaines used to say, 'Whoop! Bow your neck & spread!' " (Clemens to Bowen, 6 Feb 70, TxU, in *MTLBowen*, 18). Gaines, one of Hannibal's "prominent and very intemperate ne'er do wells," was the town's "first drunkard before Jimmy Finn got the place" (AD, 25 Mar 1909, CU-MARK†; *MTA*, 1:105). He appears in chapter 1 of "Huck Finn and Tom Sawyer among the Indians" (1884), and in the working notes for "Tom Sawyer's Conspiracy" (1897), which show that Mark Twain intended to base another fictional keelboatman, "Admiral Grimes," upon him (*HH&T*, 94, 383, 384).

112.18   another patted juba] In patting juba, adapted from African dances, slaves used their hands in rhythmic accompaniment to music. According to a former slave, one patted by "striking the hands on the knees, then striking the hands together, then striking the right shoulder with one hand, the left with the other—all the while keeping time with the feet, and singing" (Northup, 219). According to another account, "the position was usually a half-stoop or forward bend, with a slap of one hand on the left knee followed by the same stroke and noise on the right, and then a loud slap of the two palms together. . . . the left hand made two strokes in half-time to one for the right. . . . One of the best known . . . dance tunes was called 'Juba' " (Wyeth, 59, 62).

112.18–19   a regular old-fashioned keel-boat break-down] A breakdown was a boisterous, rapid, shuffling dance in the "Negro style," often danced competitively by dancers in succession, and sometimes accompanied by patting juba (Nathan, 92). Like the music that accompanied them, breakdowns were especially popular among white riverboatmen. An 1844 St. Louis newspaper reports the boatmen's fondness for "river yarns, boatman songs, and 'nigger break-downs,' interspersed with wrestling-matches, jumping, laugh, and yell" (Field, 180). But the dance had been observed among slaves as early as 1700: "The dancers brought along boards, called shingles, upon which they performed. These wooden planks were usually about five or six feet long and equally wide, and were kept in place during the dancing by four of their companions. Rarely in their deft 'turning and shying off' did they step from the boards" (Ottley and Weatherby, 25–26). Dickens described a breakdown dancer he saw in 1842: "Single shuffle, double shuffle, cut and crosscut: snapping his fingers, rolling his eyes, turning in his knees, presenting the backs of his legs in front, spinning about on his toes and heels . . . dancing with two left legs, two right legs, two wooden legs, two wire legs, two spring legs—all sorts of legs and no legs" (Dickens 1842, 36).

112.22   "jolly, jolly raftsman's the life for me,"] An 1844 minstrel song attributed to Daniel Emmett, with lyrics by Andrew Evans (entitled "The Raftsman," as sung by A. F. Winnemore of the Georgia Champions, and "The Jolly Raftsman," in *Old Dan Emmit's Original Banjo Melodies*, the latter in Nathan, 302–3).

> Chorus:
> My Raft is by the shore
> She's light and free
> To be a jolly Raftsman's the life for me
> And as we glide along
> Our song shall be
> Dearest Dine I love but thee.

112.30–32   the muddy Mississippi water was wholesomer to drink than the clear water of the Ohio] More than one nineteenth-century traveler reported hearing claims about the potability of Mississippi River water.

Charles Murray explained that "a stranger . . . cannot endure the dirty and muddy appearance of the water, although he is told (and with truth) that, when placed in a barrel, or any other vessel, and allowed to settle, it purifies very rapidly and becomes excellent drinking-water" (Murray, 1:233). Dickens in *American Notes* commented on the belief of natives that the water was wholesome (Dickens 1842, 65). And in 1849 Alexander Mackay noted that the "Mississippi water, turgid though it be, is not considered unwholesome, and those long accustomed to it prefer it to any other" (Mackay, 2:128).

113.8–11   Ohio water didn't like to mix with Mississippi water . . . for a hundred mile or more] Alexander Mackay reported that "in passing the Ohio, we were for a few minutes in clear and limpid water; quite a contrast, in this respect, to the turgid and muddy volume with which it mingled. . . . Opposite the northern bank of the Ohio, the line where the two currents mingle is distinctly traceable for some distance into the Mississippi" (Mackay, 2:128).

127.20   a twenty-dollar gold piece] A technical anachronism, since coins of this denomination did not begin to circulate until 1850 (Goodyear, 37).

127.33–34   a body that don't get *started* right when he's little, ain't got no show] This passage echoes an opinion Mark Twain held about the moral nature of mankind. According to Albert Bigelow Paine, "Among the books of his summer reading at Quarry Farm, as far back as 1874, there was a copy of [W. E. H.] Lecky's *History of European Morals*, a volume that made a deep impression upon Mark Twain and exerted no small influence upon his intellectual life" (Paine, ix). Lecky distinguished two opposing schools of morality:

> One of them is generally described as the stoical, the intuitive, the independent or the sentimental; the other as the epicurean, the inductive, the utilitarian, or the selfish. The moralists of the former school . . . believe that we have a natural power of perceiving that some qualities, such as benevolence, chastity, or veracity, are better than others. . . . The moralist of the opposite school denies that we have any such natural perception. He maintains that we have by nature absolutely no knowledge of merit and demerit, . . . and that we derive these notions solely from an observation of the course of life which is conducive to human happiness. (Lecky, 1:3)

Lecky favored "the former school," and Huck, in his instinctual desire to help Jim, seems to conform to this point of view. Nevertheless, his statement that he has failed to do the right thing because he didn't "get *started* right" when he was little, illustrates the position of "the opposite school," which held that environment determines morality. In a marginal comment written in his copy of Lecky, Clemens expressed his own belief that "all moral perceptions are acquired by the influences around us; these influences begin in infancy; we never get a chance to find out whether we have any that are innate or not" (Davis, 4; see Blair 1960a, 131–44).

129.31–33   the clear Ohio water in shore . . . So it was all up with Cairo]
For the two towns Huck and Jim have just mistaken for Cairo, Mark Twain may have had in mind Columbus and Hickman, Kentucky. Columbus was "away down in a left-hand bend" (129.6–7) twenty miles below Cairo, and Hickman was the next town on that shore, albeit on "high ground" (129.19). On his 1882 downriver trip, Mark Twain had remarked in a note that "Hickman looks about as it always did; and so does Columbus" (James, 27–30; Miller, 200–201; N&J2, 534). See the map on page 367. In the first edition of *Huckleberry Finn*, which omitted the "raft episode" and consequently the explanation of the difference between Ohio and Mississippi river water (112.30–32 and 113.8–13), the reader was left unintentionally perplexed as to why the contrasting colors meant "it was all up with Cairo," not to mention how Huck suddenly knew what he was clearly ignorant of just pages before (106.20–27; see Beidler, 13–14).

130.27–31   She aimed right for us . . . going to try to shave us] In "Old Times on the Mississippi" Mark Twain recalled that the timber rafts, coal barges, and little trading scows heading downstream during the June rise were regarded by steamboat pilots as an "intolerable nuisance." "Pilots bore a mortal hatred" to such "small-fry craft," because the latter often failed to keep a light burning and were difficult to see on a murky night (Clemens 1875, 448, 449; see also the note at 78.23–29).

131.1   I dived—and I aimed to find the bottom] In "Old Times on the Mississippi," Mark Twain told of a cub pilot who "plunged head-first into the river and dived under the wheel" and thus saved himself when his sounding boat was struck in the dark by the steamboat's paddlewheel (Clemens 1875, 570).

131.14–17   towards the left-hand shore . . . long, slanting, two-mile crossings] Huck finds himself in the crossing at New Madrid Bend, a notoriously dangerous part of the river. In an introduction for a public reading of this episode in 1895, Mark Twain wrote that "Huck swam to the Kentucky side" (Clemens 1885b, 2:174†). As the map on page 369 shows, when Huck follows the current toward the "left-hand shore," it carries him toward Kentucky, but finally lands him just over the line in Tennessee, near Darnell's Point, about two miles below Compromise Landing, Kentucky (Branch and Hirst, 75).

134.10–12   about as old as me—thirteen or fourteen or along there] Huck is never more specific about his age, probably because Mark Twain deliberately avoided the subject, much as he had "studiously avoided mentioning" the ages of his protagonists in *The Prince and the Pauper*

(Clemens to A. V. S. Anthony, 9 Mar 81, transcript in CU-MARK†). In 1895, however, preparing to read from his book, Mark Twain noted to himself that Huck was "a boy of 14" (Notebook 35, TS p. 35, CU-MARK, in Blair 1960a, 143).

136.15–17 hadn't seen no house . . . had so much style] The Grangerford property generally resembles that of John Quarles, Clemens's uncle, who lived in the country near Florida, Missouri, where Clemens recalled he spent "two or three months every year, from the fourth year we removed to Hannibal till I was eleven or twelve years old" (*MTA*, 1:96). In many of its furnishings, however, the Grangerford parlor resembles what Mark Twain described in *Life on the Mississippi* as the typical "residence of the principal citizen" of towns in the Mississippi Valley, "all the way from the suburbs of New Orleans to the edge of St. Louis" (chapter 38).

137.5–7 prettier than real ones . . . white chalk or whatever it was, underneath] In *Life on the Mississippi*, Mark Twain had scorned such decorative fruit, "all done in plaster, rudely, or in wax, and painted to resemble the originals—which they don't" (chapter 38). The Grangerfords' "apples and oranges and peaches and grapes" were perhaps manufactured by the daughters, acting on the sort of encouragement one could find in articles like "The Art of Making Wax Fruit and Flowers" in *Godey's Lady's Book and Magazine*: "So exact indeed are they, if well made, that the most practised eye cannot sometimes detect the real from the artificial" (Hale and Godey, 20).

137.12–13 "Pilgrim's Progress," about a man that left his family it didn't say why] John Bunyan's allegory, *The Pilgrim's Progress from This World, to That Which Is to Come* (1678). Clemens owned several copies, including a facsimile of the first edition, published in 1875 (Gribben, 1:111–12).

137.15–16 "Friendship's Offering," . . . but I didn't read the poetry] In *Life on the Mississippi*, Mark Twain had included *Friendship's Offering*, with its "sappy inanities illustrated in die-away mezzotints," among the books arranged "with cast-iron exactness" on the center table of the House Beautiful (chapter 38). First published in 1841 in Philadelphia, *Friendship's Offering* was typical of the annuals and gift books that flooded the market in the 1840s. It combined moralizing verse and prose with a dozen or so illustrative steel engravings. Its first editor, Miss Catharine H. Waterman, argued that such books "elevate the general standard of taste," and that the illustrations helped ensure that the contributions "will be read" (Waterman, iii–iv). But Mark Twain recognized that the books were, in fact, designed as much to be seen as read. When, several years later, he criticized the unnatural speech of certain characters in James Fenimore Cooper's novels, he likened their style to "an illustrated, gilt-edged, tree-calf, hand-tooled, seven-dollar Friendship's Offering" (Clemens 1895, 2, cited by Gribben, 1:246–47).

137.16–17 Henry Clay's Speeches] Probably *Speeches of the Honorable Henry Clay, in the Congress of the United States*, edited by Richard Chambers and published in 1842. Famous for his eloquence and his combativeness, Clay (1777–1852) was closely identified with Kentucky throughout his public career as congressman, senator, and secretary of state.

137.17–18 Dr. Gunn's Family Medicine . . . if a body was sick or dead] *Gunn's Domestic Medicine, or Poor Man's Friend, in the Hours of Affliction, Pain and Sickness*, first copyrighted by John C. Gunn in 1832. The title page of the eighth edition (1836) gives an account of the book's purpose: "This book points out, in plain language, free from doctors' terms, the diseases of men, women, and children, and the latest and most approved means used in their cure, and is intended expressly for the benefit of families in the western and southern states. It also contains descriptions of the medicinal roots and herbs of the western and southern country, and how they are to be used in the cure of diseases. Arranged on a new and simple plan, by which the practice of medicine is reduced to principles of common sense."

137.22–24 Washingtons and Lafayettes, and battles . . . "Signing the Declaration."] Engraved reproductions of George Washington and other Revolutionary War heroes, such as the Marquis de Lafayette, by John Trumbull (1756–1843), Emanuel Leutze (1816–68), and many others, were very popular in the early nineteenth century. Mark Twain mentioned an engraving of Leutze's "Washington Crossing the Delaware" and two of paintings by Trumbull in chapter 38 of *Life on the Mississippi*. "Signing the Declaration" was almost certainly a reproduction of Trumbull's most famous painting, "The Declaration of Independence, July 4, 1776," completed in 1820 (Cooper, 76).

137.23 Highland Marys] Widely circulated pictures of Mary Campbell, or "Highland Mary," whose early death in 1786 inspired several of Robert Burns's poems, and made her a favorite subject for sentimental painters and engravers in Britain and the United States.

137.24–27 some that they called crayons . . . blacker, mostly, than is common] "Crayon" was the term used for a drawing executed in pastel or paste. Mark Twain said that the House Beautiful had "framed in black mouldings on the wall, other works of art, conceived and committed on the premises, by the young ladies; being grim black-and-white crayons; landscapes, mostly . . . name of criminal conspicuous in the corner" (*Life on the Mississippi*, chapter 38).

137.27–35   a woman in a slim black dress . . . Never See Thee More Alas."]
Although new to Huck, this picture would have been familiar to any
middle-class reader. It includes the "stock elements" of standard nineteenth-century mourning pictures: "the weeping willow, tombstone,
and pensive mourner leaning on the monument. Even the style of dress
common in mourning pictures is accurately reproduced" by Huck's
description (Strickland, 228). Huck's allusion to this woman's "very
wee black slippers, like a chisel" echoes Mark Twain's previous characterization of illustrations in *Godey's Lady's Book*: "each five-foot
woman with a two-inch wedge sticking from under her dress and letting-
on to be half of her foot" (*Life on the Mississippi*, chapter 38). See the
illustrations.

Left: Mourning print, by D. W. Kellogg and Company, lithographers (Hartford,
ca. 1835); the purchaser of the print wrote the name and death date of the
deceased on the tombstone. From the collection of Professor Barton Levi St.
Armand. *Right*: Mourning print, by William S. Pendleton, lithographer (Boston, ca. 1836), with a handwritten inscription on the tombstone. Courtesy of
The Harry T. Peters "America on Stone" Lithography Collection, Smithsonian
Institution, Washington, D.C.

137.38–138.4   dead bird laying on its back . . . tears running down her
cheeks] Magazines such as *Godey's Lady's Book* frequently illustrated
children mourning their dead pets, particularly pet birds: for example,
"The Dead Dove" in the February 1852 issue, or "The Dead Robin" in
The Ladies' Repository (Cincinnati) for May 1855. Engravings depicting
bereaved women—often using narrative details like the black sealing-
wax—were likewise commonplace. See, for example, "The Widow" in
the 1847 *Friendship's Offering*; "The Empty Cradle" in *Godey's Lady's
Book* for 1847; or "Woman's Grief" in the 1842 *Friendship's Offering*,

reproduced below. In this case the accompanying verse solemnly indicates that the bereaved woman broods "Over one only thought,—the stunning thought | That *he* was dead, who loved so long and well!" (Esling, 33).

138.18–22   young woman . . . on the rail of a bridge all ready to jump off]
Portrayals of women in despair, appealing to heaven for relief or threatening suicide, were less than commonplace in the ladies' magazines and annuals; nonetheless the genre of even this outlandish drawing can be identified with the following, called "Supplication," in the November 1848 issue of *Graham's Magazine* (Robinson, frontispiece, 267).

139.8   the *Presbyterian Observer*] The *Presbyterian Observer* (Baltimore and Philadelphia) did not begin publication until 1872, but there were numerous newspapers and magazines with very similar names at the time of the story; for example, the *Christian Observer*, subtitled " 'A Presbyterian Family Newspaper,' founded at Philadelphia in 1813" (Mott, 137), and the *Presbyterian Sentinel*, published in Louisville, 1841–44.

139.12   ODE TO STEPHEN DOWLING BOTS, DEC'D] Sentimental obituary verse was ubiquitous in American magazines, annuals, and gift books at the time of the story. Like many fellow humorists, Mark Twain accepted the invitation to burlesque this form, beginning when he published his first parody of an elegiac poem at the age of seventeen ("The Burial of Sir Abner Gilstrap," *ET&S1*, 106–9). In 1854 he became familiar with doggerel of the mortuary kind, published routinely in the death notices of the Philadelphia *Public Ledger*, and almost certainly "set up some of that poetry" altered for comic purposes while working as a compositor on the *Ledger* (Branch 1984, 3). He eventually published two brief articles in 1870 and another in 1880 on the subject (Clemens 1870b and Clemens 1870c; Budd 1977, 2). A number of "sources" for this "Ode" have been proposed, ranging from the poetry of Julia A. Moore to the hymns of Isaac Watts to the columns of the Philadelphia *Ledger* itself (Blair 1960a, 209–13; Byers, 259–63; Branch 1984, 2–3). But Mark Twain's "Ode" is a burlesque of the form, not a parody of any particular obituary verse or writer of such verse, and given his long acquaintance with such poems, it is unlikely that any single "model" can be identified.

140.1   Emmeline Grangerford] In the library of the Clemens family's Hartford house was an "impressionist water-color" of the "head of a beautiful young girl, life size, called Emmeline, because she looked just about like that." The Clemenses had purchased this portrait by Daniele Ranzoni in Italy in 1878 (AD, 8 Feb 1906, CU-MARK†, in *MTA*, 2:73; *N&J2*, 187 n. 50).

141.8–10   They kept Emmeline's room . . . just the way she liked] This procedure, common in the period of the book, received the ultimate endorsement in 1861, upon the death of Prince Albert. Queen Victoria kept his room at Windsor Castle unchanged and, like Huck and Mrs. Grangerford with Emmeline's room, visited it and meditated there.

141.17   little old piano, too, that had tin pans in it] The piano may actually have had tin pans in it: "Piano-makers of the early nineteenth century, responding to the programmatic demands of the battle-pieces and to the popularity of Turkish music and instruments, introduced devices for the production of a variety of unusual musical effects. Extra pedals were constructed which permitted the pianist to embellish his performance with the sound of cymbals, drums, and bells" (Slater, 111). See also the note at 141.19–20.

141.18–19   "The Last Link is Broken"] A sentimental song written by William Clifton in about 1840:

> The last link is broken that bound me to thee,
> And the words thou hast spoken have render'd me free;
> That bright glance misleading, on others may shine,
> Those eyes smil'd unheeding when tears burst from mine.

In 1897 Clemens recalled that he associated this song with a Hannibal contemporary of his, Eliza Hyde, and he used it to illustrate his remark that "songs tended to regrets for bygone days and vanished joys" in the days of his youth (*HH&T*, 31, 34). In chapter 38, Tom will call it "painful music."

141.19–20   "The Battle of Prague"] A ten-minute piano piece of program music written in 1788 by Franz Kotzwara (1730–91) of Bohemia. It featured staccato notes to simulate flying bullets and a wailing treble figure to suggest the cries of the wounded. By the 1840s it had become an overworked standard (Slater, 108–9). In 1913, Clemens's childhood friend Anna Laura Hawkins (Laura Frazer) remembered how she and the twelve-year-old Clemens used to climb a hill to visit Mrs. Richard T. Holliday: "Her house, I remember, had a special attraction for us. She owned a piano, and it was not merely a piano; it was a piano with a drum attachment. Oh, 'The Battle of Prague,' executed with that marvelous drum attachment! It was our favorite selection, because it had so much drum in it" (Abbott, 17; Hawkins and Holliday are identified in notes to 47.17 and 1.15–16). In *A Tramp Abroad*—and in an 1878 notebook entry (*N&J2*, 142)—Mark Twain described a performance of this piece by an Arkansas bride which he had heard in a Swiss hotel drawing room:

> Without any more preliminaries, she turned on all the horrors of the "Battle of Prague," that venerable shivaree, and waded chin deep in the blood of the slain. . . . The audience stood it with pretty fair grit for a while, but when the cannonade waxed hotter and fiercer, and the discord-average rose to four in five, the procession began to move. A few stragglers held their ground ten minutes longer, but when the girl began to wring the true inwardness out of the "cries of the wounded," they struck their colors and retired in a kind of panic. . . . She got an amount of anguish into the cries of the wounded that shed a new light on human suffering. (Chapter 32)

141.20   The walls of all the rooms was plastered] Plastered walls were thought to be a sign of affluence or sophistication. In an 1870 reminiscence Mark Twain quoted a woman from Fentress County, Tennessee, who expressed the following opinion of what her son and daughter-in-law had done to their house: " 'They've tuck 'n' gaumed the inside of theirn all over with some kind of nasty disgustin' truck which they say is all the go in Kaintuck amongst the upper hunky, & which they calls it *plarsterin'!'* " (*AMT*, 23). Mark Twain later adapted this description for Si Higgins's "high-toned" house in *The Gilded Age* (chapter 1).

142.1–28   Col. Grangerford . . . loud.] This description is very similar to that of Judge Griswold in Mark Twain's unfinished novel "Simon Wheeler, Detective," written in 1877–78:

> He was sixty years old; very tall, very spare, with a long, thin, smooth-shaven, intellectual face, and long black hair that lay close to his head, was kept to the rear by his ears as one keeps curtains back by brackets, and fell straight to his coat collar without a single tolerant kink or relenting curve. He had an eagle's beak and an eagle's eye. . . . Judge Griswold's manners and carriage were of the courtly old-fashioned sort; he had never worked; he was a gentleman. (*S&B*, 313)

Forgetting that he had already described Colonel Grangerford as "gray and about sixty" (133.19), Mark Twain may well have borrowed from this unfinished work after a break in composition. He perhaps drew some details from descriptions of General Henry M. Darnall, whom he remembered from eyewitness and newspaper accounts (see Davidson, 88–89, 95 n. 36; Branch and Hirst, 54–55, 73). Evidently he gave the colonel some of his own father's characteristics: Judge Clemens often wore a swallow-tail coat with brass buttons, he was tall, slim, and smooth shaven, and he had elaborate manners, although unlike Grangerford, he was stern, unsmiling, and ungentle. But Grangerford is also a recognizable type: the southern aristocratic gentleman, who appears in scores of nineteenth-century novels in "the plantation tradition" (Blair 1960a, 214–19).

143.11–17   mixed a glass of bitters . . . sugar and the mite of whisky or apple brandy] In 1874, Clemens proposed to improve his own digestion by the regime of a morning "cocktail" made with scotch whiskey, lemon, Angostura bitters, sugar, and water (*LLMT*, 190). While "bitters" might mean almost any kind of alcoholic drink taken in the morning, ostensibly to stimulate the appetite, the Grangerfords' morning tonic appears to be comparable to a "whisky cocktail," which according to the *Century Dictionary* consisted of corn or rye whiskey, "water flavored with bitters, usually also with the peel of orange or lemon, and sweetened with sugar."

146.12–17   a feud . . . takes a long time] In response to an 1885 inquiry about the feud episode in *Huck Finn*, Clemens explained that "indeed, feuds existed in Kentucky, Tennessee and Arkansas, of the nature described, within my time and memory. I came very near being an eyewitness to the general engagement detailed in the book. The details are historical and correct" (Clemens to Reginald Cholmondeley, 28 Mar 85, CU-MARK, in Blair 1960a, 225). During his trip down the Mississippi River in 1882, Clemens had been reminded of his near "eye-witness" experience "on a Memphis packet" by a conversation with Horace

Bixby, who was able to supply the participants' names—Darnell (or Darnall, as the family preferred to spell it) and Watson—and recounted several incidents in the feud (*N&J2*, 567–69). The similarities between this historical feud, which Clemens described in *Life on the Mississippi* (chapter 26), and the episode in *Huck* are striking: their locations, for example, are identical (Blair 1960a, 225–27; Branch and Hirst, 69–80; see the notes at 131.14–17, 147.28–31, and the map of Compromise on page 369).

147.28–31   Next Sunday we all went to church. . . . The Shepherdsons they done the same.] In *Life on the Mississippi* (chapter 26), Mark Twain quotes a fellow steamboat passenger who lived in the neighborhood of the Darnells and Watsons:

> Both families belonged to the same church (everybody around here is religious); through all this fifty or sixty years' fuss, both tribes was there every Sunday, to worship. They lived each side of the line, and the church was at a landing called Compromise. Half the church and half the aisle was in Kentucky, the other half in Tennessee. Sundays you'd see the families drive up, all in their Sunday clothes, men, women, and children, and file up the aisle, and set down, quiet and orderly, one lot on the Tennessee side of the church and the other on the Kentucky side; and the men and boys would lean their guns up against the wall, handy, and then all hands would join in with the prayer and praise; though they say the man next the aisle didn't kneel down, along with the rest of the family; kind of stood guard.

147.35   preforeordestination] Huck's combination of terms for two theological doctrines, predestination and foreordination.

148.13   hogs likes a puncheon floor] In a reminiscence written in 1877, Clemens recalled the church in Florida, Missouri, where his uncle John Quarles had a farm:

> There was a log church, with a puncheon floor and slab benches. A puncheon floor is made of logs whose upper surfaces have been chipped flat with the adze. The cracks between the logs were not filled; there was no carpet; consequently, if you dropped anything smaller than a peach, it was likely to go through. The church was perched upon short sections of logs, which elevated it two or three feet from the ground. Hogs slept under there, and whenever the dogs got after them during services, the minister had to wait till the disturbance was over. In winter there was always a refreshing breeze up through the puncheon floor; in summer there were fleas enough for all. (*MTA*, 1:7–8)

158.32   I found a canoe] Mark Twain first wrote "I took the canoe," an error he overlooked until the publisher's proofreader noticed that the canoe had been "lost" in chapter 16 (129.39). Because the book was in page proof, almost ready to print, Mark Twain was obliged to make an economical correction. He therefore substituted "found a" for "took the." But this solution left a larger problem unresolved: why, when Huck finds a new canoe, does he say nothing about going north with it? Mark Twain's wish to write about the Mississippi he knew had, in 1876, collided with the implausibility of Jim's trying to escape slavery by

traveling south. The loss of the canoe had made continuing south tem-
porarily plausible, as Huck and Jim decide to go "along down with the
raft" and look for another canoe to buy for their northward journey.
Mark Twain's next solution, also temporary, was to have the steamboat
crash into the raft, shifting the action ashore. He evidently wrote a
portion of chapter 17 (Huck at the Grangerford house), but soon put the
book aside for three years, the basic problem unsolved. When Mark
Twain returned to his manuscript in 1879–80, he made a note about two
characters who would eventually provide him with the solution to his
dilemma: "The two printers deliver temp. lectures, teach dancing, elo-
cution, feel heads, distribute tracts, preach, fiddle, doctor (quack)." To
this note he added parenthetically, "Keep 'em along." Bringing the
tramps aboard the raft, where they could *enforce* a southward journey,
meant Mark Twain could continue to write about the river he knew, but
it also required resurrecting the raft, to which end he wrote another note
to himself: "Back a little, CHANGE—raft only *crippled* by steamer" (*HF*,
appendix A). Having at last devised a plausible motive and means for
sustaining Huck and Jim's southward journey, he had forgotten the
ostensible reason they were still drifting south: the lost canoe and the
need for a new one. When the proofreader caught the inconsistency,
Mark Twain concealed the oversight as best he could by the slight change
in wording (Smith 1958, viii–x, 263; Blair 1960a, 250–59).

160.4–9   One of these fellows . . . brass buttons] Details in the description
of this rascal—his age, his baldness and gray whiskers, and his coat with
slick brass buttons—cause him to resemble Captain Charles C. Duncan
of the *Quaker City*, whose picture appears in chapter 59 of *The Innocents Abroad* (1869). Ten years after the voyage, Clemens publicly
quarreled with Duncan, calling him a temperance advocate who tippled
in secret, "heartless enough to rob any . . . orphan he can get his clutches
upon; . . . a canting hypocrite, filled to the chin with sham godliness,
and forever oozing and dripping false piety and pharasaical prayers"
(Clemens to editor, New York *World*, 14 and 16 Feb 77, in *MTMF*, 213–
14).

160.15–16   take the tartar off . . . generly the enamel along with it] On 24
August 1871 the *New York Weekly* rejoiced because the peddler of a
similar dentrifice made of acid and potash, with an equally disastrous
effect, "obtained his deserts by being sentenced to a year's imprisonment" (Jones, 468–69).

160.32–33   they'd tar and feather me and ride me on a rail] Two common
mob-inflicted punishments in nineteenth-century America, especially
in the South. The first consisted of smearing the victim with hot tar and
shaking feathers over him; the second involved transporting him astrad-

dle the sharp edge of a split log, to the accompaniment of jeers and abuse. Both punishments were likely to cause serious injury, even death.

160.37   Jour printer, by trade] The wandering journeyman printer was common in the antebellum South, and a recurrent rascally figure in American humor. In 1886 Clemens would recall from his days in Hannibal "the tramping 'jour' who flitted by in a summer and tarried a day, with his wallet stuffed with one shirt and a hatful of handbills, for if he couldn't get any type to set he would do a temperance lecture. . . . All he wanted was plate and bed and money enough to get drunk on" (Clemens 1886, 1). Clemens himself had followed this trade from the spring of 1853, when he left Hannibal, until the summer of 1854. Working notes show that Mark Twain had originally planned to make both confidence men jour printers (see the note at 158.32).

160.37   do a little in patent medicines] Itinerant patent-medicine peddlers selling cure-alls regularly appeared in the work of nineteenth-century humorists (see, for instance, "The Erasive Soap Man," Hooper 1851, 109–11). During the summer of 1883, when Mark Twain was writing and revising *Huck Finn*, he read a typical advertisement from the Magnetic Rock Spring Water Company of Colfax, Iowa, which claimed that their product cured "Rheumatism, Dyspepsia, Liver Complaint, Constipation, Dropsy, Paralysis, St. Vitus' Dance, Delirium Tremens, Diabetes, Stone in the Bladder, Blood Diseases, Scrofula, Ulcers, Female Weakness and General Debility." He thereupon ordered a barrel with the comment, "I do believe that is what is the matter with me. It reads just like my symptoms" (Clemens to Magnetic Rock Spring Company, 1 Aug 83, transcript in CU-MARK).

160.38–39   mesmerism and phrenology] Mesmerism, or hypnotism, and phrenology, the reading of character from the shape of the skull, were popular forms of entertainment in the early nineteenth century, often used by traveling "Professors" to exploit the gullible (Field, 129, cited in Hearn, 189). Clemens himself had observed practitioners of both as a boy in Hannibal. In his autobiography he recalled acting as a willing and convincing confederate to a traveling hypnotist (*MTE*, 118–25). His 1879–80 working notes show that he considered having Huck play a similar role: "Do the mesmeric foolishness, with Huck ~~& the king~~ for performers" (*HF*, appendix A).

160.39   singing-geography school] A school in which facts about geography were rendered memorable by the singing of songs embodying them.

161.36–37   I am a duke!] The duke resembles Clemens's distant cousin Jesse M. Leathers, who claimed to be the rightful earl of Durham. In several letters to Clemens during the composition of *Huckleberry Finn*, Leathers often used a gaudy style similar to the duke's. For instance, "Owing to my impecunious condition I have done nothing to assert the rights of the American heirs," and (in response to Clemens's invitation to visit) "I . . . shall be only too happy if I can bring one little sunbeam to mingle with the pure light which brightens and cheers your humble hearth and home" (Leathers to Clemens, 25 and 29 Nov 79, CU-MARK). Clemens was long fascinated by the subject of the "rightful heir," and during his sojourn in England in 1873 he closely followed the trial for perjury of Arthur Orton, who claimed to be the heir to the great Tichborne estate.

163.9   Bilgewater] One of Mark Twain's favorite comic names: "Bilgewater . . . Good God what a name" (*N&J1*, 76). In this case, however, it may have acquired a satiric impetus because of Clemens's unpleasant experience in 1879 while visiting with relatives of Francis Egerton, third and last duke of Bridgewater, who was one of England's wealthiest peers when he died without issue in 1803, an event that eventually led to a long public quarrel about the inheritance and the title. During a weeklong stay at the home of Reginald Cholmondeley, who was married to an Egerton and was entertaining various members of his wife's family, Clemens had seen "two American women" rudely excluded from all conversation by the snobbish concentration on "wills & other family matters" (*N&J2*, 336). In 1885 when Cholmondeley read *Huckleberry Finn*, he took this satire directed at his relatives in good spirit, offering to present Clemens "to the original Bilgewater." Clemens replied, alluding to his earlier discomfort with Cholmondeley's family: "maybe I can meet the original Bilgewater; and if he is in *your* company, I'll be mighty *glad* to." Mary Cholmondeley (a niece) later explained the reference when she sent Albert Bigelow Paine a copy of Clemens's letter: "Reginald Cholmondeley had invited Mark Twain to meet his brother in law the late Lord Egerton of Tatton. There had been some question of Lord Egerton taking the title of Bridgewater, which Mark Twain miscalls so delightfully" (Cholmondeley to Clemens, 12 Mar 85, and Clemens to Cholmondeley, 28 Mar 85, transcript by Mary Cholmondeley, both in CU-MARK†).

166.12–16   Pike County, in Missouri . . . my brother Ike] Pike County, Missouri, on the Mississippi River below Hannibal, about forty-five miles north of St. Louis. In antebellum lore, this county was the birthplace of some of the most worthless characters on the frontier. A stock character, Ike, appears in popular songs from the Gold Rush days, such as "Sweet Betsey from Pike" and "Joe Bowers."

168.11   the middle watch] The middle watch customarily lasted from midnight to four in the morning.

168.37   Garrick the Younger] David Garrick (1717–79) was a great Shake-
spearean actor and manager of the Drury Lane Theatre; there was no
Garrick the Younger.

169.1   finding water and gold with a "divining rod"] In 1870, Mark Twain
wrote: "I have seen more than four hundred 'gold-finders,' first and last,
but I never saw anybody that ever heard of one of them ever finding
anything. . . . I recall how for four dreadful weeks I followed step by step
in the track of a 'Professor' with a hazel stick in his hand,—a 'divining-
rod'—which was to turn and tilt down and point to the gold whenever
we came to any. But we never came to any, I suppose" (Clemens 1870a,
cited in Hearn, 198).

169.8   sword-fight in Richard III.] In chapter 51 of *Life on the Mississippi*
Mark Twain recalled that during his boyhood "a couple of young Englishmen came to the town and sojourned a while; and one day they got
themselves up in cheap royal finery and did the Richard III. sword-fight
with maniac energy and prodigious powwow." The actor Edmund Kean
(see the note at 180.26) was largely responsible for the popularity of this
flamboyant way of staging the sword fight: "Every personator of *Richard*
must fight like a madman, and fence on the ground, and when disarmed
and wounded, thrust with savage impotence with his naked hand. . . .
Mr. Kean has passed this manner into a law and woe be to him who
breaks it" (*Champion*, 16 Feb 17, in Clarke, 15).

170.10–11   little one-horse town about three mile down the bend] This
rural village, later called "Pokeville" (173.3), lies some unspecified
distance south of Compromise, Kentucky, and north of Napoleon, Arkansas. The text does not make it clear whether it is on the right or left
bank of the river. It may be suggestive, however, that Mark Twain's
1879–80 working notes for the book mention an impoverished "white
family & cabin at woodyard in Walnut Bend." This note follows one
about a "Negro campmeeting & sermon" and precedes one about the
"Burning Shame . . . at Napoleon, Ark" (*HF*, appendix A). In Mark
Twain's notes, Walnut Bend, Arkansas, about fifty-five miles downriver
from Memphis, is consistently associated with countrified naiveté and
poverty: in 1882 he reminded himself to stop at "Walnut Bend or some
other wretched place" on his downriver trip; he later alluded sarcasti-
cally to "The Linsey Woolsey Beauty of Walnut Bend" (*N&J2*, 457, 571).
"Pokeville," at any rate, is in the same physical and cultural vicinity.
See the map on page 367.

170.21–22   king. . . allowed he'd go and work that camp-meeting] Johnson
J. Hooper's "The Captain Attends a Camp-Meeting," a story about a
backwoods gambler and confidence man, Simon Suggs, was published
in several editions during Clemens's youth, and he showed familiarity

with it in an 1880 note to himself (*N&J2*, 363). As a boy Clemens had attended camp meetings like the one described here; he recalled one in particular, when "farmers and their families drove or tramped into the village from miles around to get a sight of the illustrious Alexander Campbell and to have a chance to hear him preach" (*MTA*, 2:279). In an autobiographical fragment he commented further: "Campmeeting. Campbellite revival. All converted but me. All sinners again in a week" (CCamarSJ, in Wecter, 88).

172.10–16   come, black with sin! . . . be at rest!] The preacher's exhortations use the conventional language of salvation, and may echo Joseph Hart's popular hymn, "Come Ye Sinners" (1759):

> Come, ye sinners, poor and needy,
> Weak and wounded, sick and sore;
> Jesus ready stands to save you,
> Full of pity, love and power. . . .
>
> Come, ye weary, heavy-laden,
> Lost and ruined by the fall;
> If you tarry till you're better,
> You will never come at all.
>   (Byers, 15–16)

173.15–16   would he let them kiss him . . . and he always done it] When Clemens saw Kemble's drawings for this episode in June 1884, he told his publisher to "knock out one of them—the lecherous old rascal kissing the girl at the campmeeting. It is powerful good, but it mustn't go in—don't forget it. Let's not make *any* pictures of the campmeeting. The subject won't *bear* illustrating. It is a disgusting thing, & pictures are sure to tell the truth about it too plainly" (Clemens to Charles L. Webster, 11 June 84, NPV, in *MTBus*, 260).

174.22–23   they were going to pay in cord-wood and onions, as usual] Clemens in 1886 recalled that when he worked for his brother Orion's Hannibal newspaper, "The town subscribers paid in groceries and the country ones in cabbages and cord-wood—when they paid at all, which was merely sometimes, and then we always stated the fact in the paper" (Clemens 1886, 1).

174.27–28   "Yes, crush, cold world, this breaking heart"] In the unfinished "Simon Wheeler, Detective" (1877–78), Hugh Burnside had written a "ten-line deformity" called "The Crushed Heart's Farewell" (*S&B*, 360). At the age of eighteen, Clemens himself had written a number of highly conventional love poems for Hannibal newspapers (*ET&S1*, 88–90, 92–94, 100–101).

178.1   Capet] Thomas Carlyle, in *The French Revolution* (one of Clemens's favorite books), reported that after Louis XVI was dethroned, the

Revolutionists referred to him as Citizen Louis Capet. The Capets were a ruling family of medieval France.

179.10–39 To be . . . go!] Although the duke believes he is reciting the soliloquy from *Hamlet*, 3:3, he disarranges it, intermingling lines from *Macbeth* and *Richard III* (Kirkham, 17–19). Mutilated Shakespeare was a staple of nineteenth-century comedy. Charles Mathews (1776–1835), a British comic actor, offered an "irresistibly laughable performance" as Hamlet to London audiences in 1811, and during a trip to America in 1822–23 impersonated a "black tragedian" who tried to recite Hamlet's most famous soliloquy but similarly mangled it (Blair 1976, 6–7, 8). Dan Rice, an American circus clown whose performance Clemens enjoyed as a youth, also made comic use of Shakespeare (Wecter, 192).

180.8–9 pretty well down the State of Arkansaw . . . little one-horse town in a big bend] Huck's subsequent description of this town, later called "Bricksville" (241.20), shows that Mark Twain had in mind Napoleon, Arkansas, at the confluence of the Arkansas and Mississippi rivers (see the map on page 367). His 1879–80 working notes mention an "overflowed Arkansaw town" and specifically locate the "Burning Shame" (the "Royal Nonesuch" of chapters 22 and 23) "at Napoleon, Ark" (*HF*, appendix A). Mark Twain had written a very similar description of an Arkansas town, clearly from memory, in the "Tupperville-Dobbsville" fragment, sometime in the late 1870s (*HH&T*, 55–57). And his characterization of Napoleon as a "town of innumerable fights—an inquest every day" in *Life on the Mississippi* (chapter 32) also had to be from memory since the town itself had disappeared by the time the author revisited the river in 1882. Typically, the use of such a prototype for Bricksville did not exclude his drawing embellishments and even factual details from other sources: see, for example, the comparable description of Pilcher's Point, Louisiana, in chapter 33 of *Life on the Mississippi*.

180.26 Edmund Kean the elder, of the Royal Haymarket Theatre] Edmund Kean (1787–1833) was a famous British actor who performed primarily at the Haymarket, Drury Lane, and Covent Garden theatres in London. He was sometimes called "the elder Kean" to distinguish him from his son, Charles John Kean (1811?–68), who was also an actor but considered a lesser talent.

181.26–183.3 loafers . . . gimme the *chaw*, and you take the *plug*] Antebellum travel books and humorous writings were packed with depictions of lazy loafers in sleepy southern towns. Tobacco chewers resembling these occur in an often-reprinted 1844 sketch, "The Mystery Revealed," by William T. Thompson, a Georgia humorist well-known to Clemens (Thompson, 60–61). The chaw and plug incident evidently derives from a western mining-camp anecdote (Eby, 11).

186.9–11   Boggs throws up both of his hands . . . Bang! goes the first shot]
The shooting of Boggs by Sherburn was based upon an actual incident
that occurred in Hannibal in 1845, when Clemens was nine—the shooting of Sam Smarr by William Owsley. Clemens recalled in 1900, "I can't
ever forget Boggs, because I saw him die, with a family Bible spread open
on his breast. . . . Boggs represents Smarr in the book" (Clemens to Miss
Goodrich-Frear, 11 Jan 1900, ViU†, noted by Howard Baetzhold). Smarr,
whom one neighbor had called "as honest a man as any in the state"
though "a little turbulent" when drunk, had ridden through Hannibal
shooting his pistol, and had several times publicly insulted Owsley.
After the incident, an eyewitness recounted to Judge Clemens that
Owsley had called out, " 'You Sam Smar.' Mr. Smar turned round, seeing
Mr. Owsley in the act of drawing a pistol from his pocket, said Mr.
Owsley dont fire, or something to that effect. Mr. Owsley was within
about four paces of Mr. Smar when he drew the pistol and fired twice in
succession, after the second fire, Mr. Smarr fell, when Mr. Owsley turned
on his heel and walked off." Smarr was carried into Grant's drugstore,
where he died (*MTA*, 1:131; Wecter, 106–8).

188.3   The people . . . said he done it perfect] In chapter 23 of *A Tramp
Abroad* (1880), Mark Twain recounts an incident he witnessed in Ger-
many, after the fall of a boy: "All who had seen the catastrophe were
describing it at once, and each trying to talk louder than his neighbor;
and one youth of superior genius ran a little way up the hill, called
attention, tripped, fell, rolled down among us, and thus triumphantly
showed exactly how the thing had been done."

188.6   somebody said Sherburn ought to be lynched] Lynching was a
common practice in nineteenth-century America, especially in the
South during Reconstruction, where it was rationalized as retaliation
for alleged crimes, but really was a form of intimidation directed against
blacks. Mark Twain had written an editorial in 1869 about the discovery
that a young black man who had been lynched for rape was innocent: "A
little blunder in the administration of justice by Southern mob-law; but
nothing to speak of. Only a 'nigger' killed by mistake—that is all. . . .
But mistakes will happen, even in the conduct of the best regulated and
most high toned mobs, and surely there is no reason why Southern
gentlemen should worry themselves with useless regrets, so long as
only an innocent 'nigger' is hanged, or roasted or knouted to death, now
and then" (Clemens 1869b, 2). When writing *Huckleberry Finn*, however, Mark Twain was aware that the violence he described was also
rooted in genuine frustration with the southern judicial system. In a
chapter written for—but excluded from—*Life on the Mississippi* (1883),
he wrote that southern juries "fail to convict, even in the clearest cases.
That this is not agreeable to the public, is shown by the fact that very

frequently such a miscarriage of justice so rouses the people that they rise, in a passion, and break into the jail, drag out their man and lynch him" (Clemens 1944, 414).

189.1–27 swarmed up the street . . . Sherburn steps out onto the roof]
Sherburn, although portrayed as a villain in the previous chapter, here plays a more sympathetic role, becoming to some extent a spokesman for the author's own viewpoint—a *raisonneur* whose scorn for the mob is nearly identical to feelings Clemens himself expressed in 1901:

> For no mob has any sand in the presence of a man known to be splendidly brave. Besides, a lynching mob would *like* to be scattered, for of a certainty there are never ten men in it who would not prefer to be somewhere else—and would be, if they but had the courage to go. When I was a boy I saw a brave gentleman deride and insult a mob and drive it away; and afterward, in Nevada, I saw a noted desperado make two hundred men sit still, with the house burning under them, until he gave them permission to retire. (Clemens 1923, 245)

Many narratives that the author read about the French Revolution recount the quelling of an irate mob by a forceful figure (for instance, Mirabeau, Marat, Robespierre, Danton). Mark Twain told a friend that such reading had confirmed his belief that "men in a crowd do not act as they would as individuals. In a crowd they don't think for themselves, but become impregnated by the contagious sentiment uppermost in the minds of all who happen to be en masse" (Fisher, 59).

192.25–26 all through the circus they done the most astonishing things]
The comic acts Huck describes here were a traditional part of the circus show in the "good old days of talking clowns": "Much as the court fool kidded kings, the circus fool made fun of the lordly master of ceremonies, the ringmaster. The latter was the butt or feeder for the comedian." For example, "Joe Pentland, a clown who cracked jokes with the ringmaster," disguised himself as a drunken sailor and

> shouted from the seats that he could ride "that danged fat nag." Amid the jeers of ringmaster and audience the sailor mounted the circus animal, only to fall off repeatedly. But while the audience still jeered at him the sailor doffed his uniform and rode superbly in spangled tights. . . . Disguised as "Pete Jenkins, from Mud Corners," the redoubtable [Dan] Rice staggered into the circus ring and, after clinging clumsily to a loping principal horse or resinback, shed countless coats, vests and pantaloons before, properly costumed for circus equestrianism, he pirouetted and somersaulted amazingly. (May, 70–71)

Rice visited Hannibal in 1852, and Clemens may have seen his act (Bowen, 29, 30). Descriptions of such traditional circus acts had long been standard material in humorous writings. At least four humorists known to Clemens had written about a purported drunk's disrobing on horseback—William T. Thompson in 1843, William Wright in 1867, George W. Harris in 1868, and Richard M. Johnston in 1881 (see Blair 1960a, 315–16).

195.1–4   Thrilling Tragedy . . . THE KING'S CAMELOPARD OR THE ROYAL NONESUCH] The exact nature of this performance, and its possible origins in western folk tradition, have been the subject of much speculation (see Blair 1960a, 317–20, and Whiting, 251–75). Mark Twain first called the skit "The Tragedy of the Burning Shame" but apparently altered it for the sake of propriety, for as he said in 1907, the "Burning Shame" was an indecent entertainment he had heard described in Jim Gillis's cabin on Jackass Hill in 1865: "In one of my books—*Huckleberry Finn*, I think—I have used one of Jim's impromptu tales, which he called 'The Tragedy of the Burning Shame.' I had to modify it considerably to make it proper for print, and this was a great damage. As Jim told it, inventing it as he went along, I think it was one of the most outrageously funny things I have ever listened to. How mild it is in the book, and how pale; how extravagant and how gorgeous in its unprintable form!" (*MTE*, 361). In fact, Jim Gillis's "impromptu" tale may have been a variant of a folk story with the same title, in which two traveling players stage a theatrical performance of a naked man on his hands and knees with a candle inserted in his posterior and then lit (Graves, 98).

198.35   Them rapscallions took in four-hundred and sixty-five dollars] An Elizabethan variant of the king and duke's scam occurs in a tale "laid somewhere about 1567." The London swindler, however, absconds with the proceeds and strands his audience in Northumberland Place before giving them even a single performance. John Chamberlain (1553–1627), "the letter writer," reported that "a precisely similar adventure" actually took place in 1602 (Hazlitt 1890, 203–4).

199.15   Saxon heptarchies] From the fifth to the ninth century England was divided into seven kingdoms known as the Anglo-Saxon heptarchy, or rule of seven.

199.16–23   Henry the Eight . . . Nell Gwynn . . . Jane Shore . . . Fair Rosamun] Although King Henry VIII (1491–1547) did behead two of his wives, neither is mentioned here. Eleanor (Nell) Gwyn (1650–87) was the mistress of Charles II; Jane Shore (d. 1527), the mistress of Edward IV; and Rosamond Clifford (d. 1176), the mistress of Henry II.

199.24–27   tell him a tale every night . . . Domesday Book] Huck confuses *The Arabian Nights' Entertainments* with the *Domesday Book*, a general census and survey of land holdings in England completed in 1086 for William the Conqueror. Neither book concerned Henry VIII, nor did any of the other events or persons mentioned in the rest of the paragraph: the Boston tea party (1773), the Declaration of Independence (1776), the duke of Wellington (1769–1852), or George, duke of Clarence (1449–78), reputedly drowned in a butt of malmsey wine in the Tower of London.

202.8–9   she was plumb deef en dumb] One of Mark Twain's 1879–80 working notes specifies that the child's deafness was caused by scarlet fever (*HF*, appendix A). In late 1882 or early 1883 the author noted to himself: "Some rhymes about the little child whose mother boxed its ears for inattention & presently when it did not notice the heavy slamming of a door, perceived that it was deaf" (*N&J2*, 510).

204.15–16   the Arkansaw village; and . . . t'other village] These two villages are on "each side of the river" (203.4–5) at some point south of Napoleon, Arkansas ("Bricksville"), and north of the Arkansas state line. In that stretch of river only Columbia, Arkansas, and Greenville, Mississippi (respectively above and below Point Chicot), correspond to this description (Howell, 168–69; James, 41; see the map on page 367). That Mark Twain may have had at least their basic geography in mind is also suggested by Huck's later reference to "a big steamboat laying at the shore away up under the point, about three mile above town," which he further says had "been there a couple of hours—taking on freight" (204.27–29). In the manuscript Mark Twain first wrote "taking on cotton"; Point Chicot was the site of a notable cotton plantation.

206.31–32   I'm going in a ship . . . for Ryo Janeero] In 1856 the twenty-year-old Clemens started a journey down the Mississippi River to New Orleans, whence he planned to sail to South America to make his fortune (*MTA*, 2:289).

211.4–6   some of them putting on their coats as they come] In chapter 55 of *Life on the Mississippi* and in "Villagers of 1840–3" Mark Twain recalled a Hannibal saddler who "always rushed wildly down street" to meet the boat, "putting on coat as he went" (*HH&T*, 37). For an acute analysis of the style in the opening portion of this chapter, see Smith 1958, xiii–xvi; see also Blair 1960a, 328–30.

213.15   hogwash] In a letter to John Horner of Belfast, Ireland, dated 12 January 1906, Clemens stated that this word was "a term which was invented by the night foreman of the newspaper whereunto I was attached 40 yrs ago, in the capacity of local reporter, to describe my literary efforts" (CU-MARK†). Clemens had evidently forgotten his discovery that one of his favorite writers, Horace Walpole, had used the word in a letter dated 22 March 1796 (Clemens's annotated copy of Walpole, 9:462, CtY; see Baetzhold, 274).

218.4–5   a word that's made up out'n the Greek *orgo* . . . and the Hebrew *jeesum*] Twice in Oliver Goldsmith's *The Vicar of Wakefield*, a book Clemens frequently read, sharper Ephraim Jenkinson supports claims to learning by tracing alleged etymologies (chapters 14 and 25). The use of big words to impress was an old device in frontier humor—for example, in "Stump Speaking in Arkansas": "Our carnal entranchasemen . . . depends on our heterognous exertions!" (*Spirit of the Times* 14 [13 Apr 44]: 81).

221.13   William Fourth] William IV, who became king of England in 1830, was succeeded by Queen Victoria upon his death in 1837.

224.10   I see it warn't nothing but a dictionary] During his first trip to England in 1872, Clemens wrote a note about the American consul's requirement: "If you want to ship anything to America you must go there & swear to a great long rigmarole, & *kiss the book* (years ago they found it was a dictionary)" (1872 "English journal," CU-MARK†).

232.12–13   He was the softest, glidingest, stealthiest man] In chapter 8 of *Quentin Durward*, a novel Mark Twain had consulted when writing *The Prince and the Pauper*, Walter Scott pictures an obsequious barber, councillor of Louis XI, as a little man who conceals his quick glances "by keeping his eyes fixed on the ground, while with the stealthy and quiet pace of a cat, he seemed modestly rather to glide than to walk. . . . [He] glided quietly back . . . everyone giving place to him" (see Baetzhold, 94–95).

233.1   "*He had a rat!*"] This episode was apparently based on an actual incident that took place while Clemens's close friend the Rev. Joseph Twichell was delivering a Decoration Day (Memorial Day) prayer in Hartford: "The 'He had a rat' story put into a funeral scene, where it actually occurred in this city, will be recognized by a number of Hartford people, who have had many hearty laughs at it in its chrysalis period" ("New Publications," Hartford *Evening Post*, 17 Feb 85, 3, in Fischer, 9). Clemens reminded himself in 1878 and several times thereafter to make use of the story (*N&J2*, 58, 343; *N&J3*, 16, 92).

234.30–31   I can't ever get it out of my memory] Clemens was similarly unable to forget the grief caused by the separation of slave families when they were sold. He wrote about it in "A True Story" (1874), chapter 21 of *A Connecticut Yankee* (1889), and chapter 3 of *Pudd'nhead Wilson* (1894).

246.24–25   the dreadful pluribus-unum mumps] Huck's source for this impressive diagnosis is the United States motto. In chapter 24 of *The Prince and the Pauper*, Miles Hendon similarly uses irrelevant Latin phrases to frighten a man.

248.27   Here's your two sets o' heirs] A chapter in Fuller's *Noted French Trials: Impostors and Adventurers*, "The False Martin Guerre," tells how an impostor, after passing himself off as a lost relative, disposes of most of the opposition and is about to establish his alleged identity when "a new Martin Guerre" arrives "just at the right time to drag the judges back into uncertainty" (Fuller, 21).

265.7–10   trees with Spanish moss on them . . . first I ever see it] According to 1848 and 1857 river guides the growth of Spanish moss (*Tillandsia usneoides*) commenced "just below" Columbia, in Chicot County, Arkansas, about thirty miles above the Louisiana border (Conclin, 96, 98; James, 38).

266.9–267.7   a shabby village, named Pikesville . . . Silas Phelps's place, two mile below here] Mark Twain consistently located Pikesville and the Phelps farm in southern Arkansas. References in the text likewise indicate the same location (Ensor, 7; see also Blair 1960a, 92; *TSA*, 112; *MTA*, 1:96; *HF*, appendix A; see notes to 265.7–10 and 274.15–16). If the identification of the Wilkses' village with Greenville, Mississippi, is approximately right, Pikesville must be still further south, though still in Arkansas—perhaps in the vicinity of Grand Lake Landing (see the note to 204.15–16, and the map on page 367). No evidence has been found that Mark Twain had this specific town in mind, and indeed he seems again to have drawn freely upon memories of other locales such as Lake Providence, Louisiana, which in chapter 34 of *Life on the Mississippi* he called "the first distinctly Southern-looking town you come to . . . [with] shade-trees hung with venerable gray beards of Spanish moss."

274.15–16   forty mile back here in the country, on the road to Lafayette] Lafayette County, Arkansas, in the southwestern part of the state, 135 miles away.

276.18   Phelps's was one of these little one-horse cotton plantations] Mark Twain explained in an autobiographical dictation that the model for the Phelps farm, which he placed in southern Arkansas near the Louisiana border, was his uncle John Quarles's farm near Florida, Missouri:

My uncle, John A. Quarles, was a farmer, and his place was out in the country four miles from Florida. . . . I have never consciously used him or his wife in a book, but his farm has come very handy to me in literature, once or twice. In "Huck Finn" and in "Tom Sawyer Detective" I moved it down to Arkansas. It was all of six hundred miles, but it was no trouble. . . . The house was a double log one, with a spacious floor (roofed in) connecting it with the kitchen. . . . The farm-house stood in the middle of a very large yard, and the yard was fenced on three sides with rails and on the rear side with high palings; against these stood the smoke-house. . . . The front yard was entered over a stile, made of sawed-off logs of graduated heights. . . . Down a piece, abreast the house, stood a little log cabin against the rail fence. (*MTA*, 1:96–99)

277.8–10   hum of a spinning-wheel . . . lonesomest sound in the whole world] In his description of the Quarles farm in his autobiography,

Clemens recalled the family room of the house, which contained a "spinning-wheel. . . whose rising and falling wail, heard from a distance, was the mournfulest of all sounds to me, and made me homesick and low-spirited, and filled my atmosphere with the wandering spirits of the dead" (*MTA*, 1:102–3).

279.19   Lally Rook] A sidewheeler named *Lallah Rookh* operated on the Mississippi between 1838 and 1847 (Lytle, 109). The name comes from Thomas Moore's epic poem *Lalla Rookh* (1817), and thus, like the *Walter Scott*, this boat got its name from a British Romantic.

281   *illustration*] In November 1884, when book agents were beginning their door-to-door sales of *Huckleberry Finn* with a prospectus containing sheets from the forthcoming first edition, a "glaring indecency" was discovered in this illustration—Uncle Silas appeared to be exposing himself ("Mark Twain in a Dilemma," New York *World*, 27 Nov 84, 1). The prospectuses were immediately called in and the page containing the picture excised so the sale could continue. Mark Twain's publisher offered a five-hundred-dollar reward "for the discovery and conviction" of the culprit who had defaced the engraving, but he was never found. The printers, using a re-engraved picture, repaired all copies of the first edition so far in print ("Tampering with Mark Twain's Book," New York *Tribune*, 29 Nov 84, 3; Blair 1960a, 364–67; Johnson, 47–49), although one copy of the proofsheets showing the defaced illustration survives (ViU; the defaced picture is reprinted in Meine, 32). This edition reproduces the repaired illustration, from a first edition in CU-MARK.

282.14   the mouth of the White river] Sixteen miles north of the mouth of the Arkansas River and Napoleon, Arkansas (Conclin, 96); see the map on page 367.

286.12   Hicksville, Ohio] A village in northwest Ohio, near the Indiana border.

299.14–15   Baron Trenck, nor Casanova, nor Benvenuto Chelleeny, nor Henri IV] Baron Friedrich von der Trenck (1726–94), a Prussian soldier and adventurer; Giacomo Girolamo Casanova de Seingalt (1725–98), an Italian adventurer; Benvenuto Cellini (1500–71), an Italian goldsmith and sculptor; and Henry IV of France (1553–1610). All made exciting escapes, and the first three wrote memoirs recounting them.

299.24–25   break your leg . . . nineteen foot too short] "Benvenuto Cellini's rope-ladder was too short. He fell into a moat, breaking his leg, when he attempted to escape from the castle of S. Angelo" (Moore 1922, 335).

299.27   Langudoc, or Navarre] Languedoc was a southern province of medieval France; Navarre, Henry IV's inheritance and refuge after his escape, was an ancient kingdom in the Pyrenees.

300.8–9   we can tear up our sheets and make him a rope ladder] An expedient described by Baron Trenck, Casanova, and Cellini, among others. (Moore 1922, 333–35, cites relevant source passages; see also notes to 302.2, 302.5–6, and 304.20.)

301.23–24   a shirt . . . for Jim to keep a journal on] In addition to the memoirs of the actual prisoners mentioned above, Tom may have been familiar with one or more books by Alexandre Dumas. In *The Man in the Iron Mask*, from *Celebrated Crimes* (1839), a prisoner at the Île Sainte Marguerite also wrote on a shirt; and in *The Count of Monte Cristo* (1845), the imprisoned Abbé Faria wrote a political treatise on two shirts.

301.25   *Jim* can't write] In most slave states, strict laws prohibited the teaching of slaves, mainly to prevent them from reading abolitionist literature. In 1836, after a purge of its abolitionist president and faculty by pro-slavery forces, Missouri's Marion College forbade its students to teach slaves to read and write unless they first secured the slaveowners' permission. In 1847, a Missouri state law was passed which made it a crime to instruct blacks in reading and writing (Trexler, 82–84; Holcombe, 230).

302.2   the best authorities uses their own blood] A practice followed by Baron Trenck and Abbé Faria.

302.5–6   write it on the bottom of a tin plate . . . Iron Mask] The Iron Mask scratched his name on a plate and threw it out of the window of his cell.

304.20   dig out with a caseknife] Baron Trenck sawed through iron bars with a pen-knife, and Abbé Faria, as Mark Twain recalled in chapter 11 of *The Innocents Abroad*, "dug through the thick wall with some trifling instrument which he wrought himself out of a stray piece of iron or table cutlery."

304.23   Castle Deef] Tom's name for the Château d'If, site of the Count of Monte Cristo's imprisonment and of a brief sojourn for the Iron Mask. Clemens visited it during the *Quaker City* voyage in 1867: "We saw the damp, dismal cells in which two of Dumas' heroes passed their confinement—heroes of 'Monte Cristo.' . . . They showed us the noisome cell where the celebrated 'Iron Mask'—that ill-starred brother of a hard-hearted king of France—was confined for a season, before he was sent to hide the strange mystery of his life from the curious in the dungeons of St. Marguerite" (*The Innocents Abroad*, chapter 11).

304.29   *Thirty-seven year*] Tom exaggerates: after digging for three years the abbé came up, not in China, but in another prisoner's cell.

311.8   make them a witch pie] Recipes for this dish (sometimes containing murdered babies or disinterred corpses) were so ancient and obscure that neither Nat nor Tom would know how to make one (Summers, 207).

314.38–39   Matilda Angelina Araminta *Phelps!*] In a footnote to chapter 11 of *The Gilded Age*, Mark Twain explained: "In those old days the average man called his children after his most revered literary and historical idols; consequently there was hardly a family, at least in the West, but had a Washington in it—and also a Lafayette, a Franklin, and six or eight sounding names from Byron, Scott, and the Bible, if the offspring held out." Matilda is the heroine of Scott's poem *Rokeby* (1813); Angelina is the heroine of Goldsmith's "The Hermit," included in *The Vicar of Wakefield*; and Araminta, the female lead in Congreve's *The Old Bachelor* (1693), as well as Moneytrap's wife in Vanbrugh's *The Confederacy* (1705). See also the name of Matilda Phelps's brother (329.9–11).

316.1   Acts seventeen] Mark Twain may have intended an ironic reference to either verses 24–26 ("God . . . hath made of one blood all nations of men for to dwell on all the face of the earth") or verse 29 ("Forasmuch then as we are the offspring of God, we ought not to think that the Godhead is like unto gold, or silver, or stone, graven by art and man's device"). Either statement can be understood as a condemnation of slavery, a practice which denies the brotherhood of mankind for the sake of economic gain (Arner, 12).

321.13–15   Lady Jane Grey . . . Dudley . . . Northumberland] William Harrison Ainsworth's popular romance, *The Tower of London* (1840), recounts the story of Lady Jane Grey (1537–54), her husband Lord Guildford Dudley (d. 1554), and her father-in-law, the duke of Northumberland (1502?–53), whose plot to secure the succession to the throne resulted in her reigning for nine days after Edward VI's death in 1553. All three were imprisoned in the Tower and eventually beheaded. In book 2, chapter 7, Northumberland is described "putting the finishing touches to a carving on the wall. . . . This curious sculpture . . . contains his cognizance, a bear and lion supporting a ragged staff surrounded by a border of roses, acorns and flowers intermingled with foliage."

322.1   coat of arms] Tom's design is described in a hodge-podge of sometimes colliding, though for the most part authentic, heraldic terms (see Birchfield, 15–16). Kemble's illustration on page 320 ingeniously incorporates most of the elements.

322.11   *Maggiore fretta, minore atto*] Literally, "More haste, less action."

326.11   Prisoners ain't ever without rats] Casanova complained of the huge rats in his prison, but Baron Trenck "tamed a mouse" and taught it to play with him (Moore 1922, 334).

327.21   Pitchiola] *Picciola* (1836) by Joseph Xavier Boniface Saintine. In this highly sentimental novel a prisoner carefully nurtures a plant and becomes obsessed with its survival; the watering with tears is Mark Twain's embellishment.

329.9–11   Thomas Franklin Benjamin Jefferson Elexander Phelps] Another Phelps offspring named after the "most revered literary and historical idols" of the time (see the note to 314.38–39). Samuel Clemens himself had been delivered by a doctor named Thomas Jefferson Chowning; he had a father named after Chief Justice John Marshall, a brother named Benjamin, another named Orion, and even an uncle named Hannibal.

332.8–9   Sometimes it's done one way, sometimes another] Carlyle's *French Revolution*, "Varennes," chapters 3–4, tells of both: a palace chambermaid informed Commandant Gouvion of Louis XVI's plans to escape from the Tuileries, and "a billet" warned "some Patriot Deputy."

332.13–14   it's usual for the prisoner's mother to change clothes with him] Many novels about the French Revolution tell of such exchanges, and for the flight to Varennes the dauphin actually dressed as a girl.

334.26   Ingean Territory] The area known as Indian Territory originally included all the present state of Oklahoma, except the panhandle, and was set aside by the federal government as a home for certain Indian tribes who had been forced to relocate there during the 1820s and 1830s. Never an organized territory, it became a haven for white outlaws.

340.27–28   I wish . . . 'Son of Saint Louis, ascend to heaven!'] Several historians, including Carlyle and Jules Michelet, whose *Historical View of the French Revolution* Clemens is known to have read, emphasized the fact that mistake after mistake occurred during Louis XVI's bungled escape attempt (Gribben, 1:466). The words that Tom quotes were spoken by Abbé Edgeworth just before Louis's execution (*The French Revolution*, "Regicide," chapter 8).

341.13–14   make him swear to be silent . . . and put a purse full of gold in his hand] Tom's suggestions are similar to details in Dr. Manette's story in book 3, chapter 10, of Dickens's *Tale of Two Cities*.

345.32   Well, sister Phelps] Mark Twain wrote in 1898 that "Sister" was a common form of address in the "Methodist, or Presbyterian, or Baptist, or Campbellite church" (*MSM*, 191). For the following description of the Arkansas gossips, Mark Twain may have borrowed some features from a story by Joel Chandler Harris, "At Teague Poteet's," which was published in the *Century Magazine* in May and June 1883, shortly before he wrote this scene. Harris's characters use expressions like "s'I" and "se' she," and one of them is even named Hightower (Carkeet 1979, 323–24; Carkeet 1981, 91).

346.4–5   Nebokoodneezer] Nebuchadnezzar (d. 562 B.C.), a king of Babylon who went insane (Daniel 4:33).

346.10   sister Utterback] Clemens was familiar with this unusual name from his childhood, when his mother took him to visit her friend Mrs. Utterback, a faith healer who specialized in curing toothaches (*MTA*, 1:108). He also used it in an 1866 sketch about "Old Mother Utterback," who lived "in the bend below Grand Gulf, Mississippi" (Clemens 1866b, 6). See also *N&J2*, 381.

347.34–35   I reckon they must a *been* sperits] Clemens, who was interested in (but skeptical about) spiritualism, may have read about the strange "haunting" of the Eliakim Phelps family in 1850 and adapted some of the widely reported supernatural occurrences for his tale. These included straw-stuffed dummies, anonymous letters, disappearing sheets and spoons, and "captious nails and candlesticks." The mysterious incidents of 1850 may well have been the work of enterprising, mischievous children (Kerr, 172–81).

361.7   go for howling adventures amongst the Injuns] In the summer of 1884 Mark Twain began the narrative forecast here, "Huck Finn and Tom Sawyer among the Indians," which he never finished (*HH&T*, 81–140).

GLOSSARY

Among the lasting achievements of *Huckleberry Finn* is the ready accessibility of its language: most of its one-hundred-year-old words and idiomatic expressions still require no gloss. We have, therefore, confined the entries here to words and phrases about which there is likely to be genuine doubt or uncertainty, or about which we have specialized knowledge pertinent to Mark Twain's meaning. When vernacular words or phrases (most oaths, for example) are wholly intelligible, we have not defined them. When words or phrases are to a degree obscure and are not readily found in *Webster's Third New International Dictionary of the English Language* (called by one expert "a masterpiece of the art of lexicography" [Landau, 352]), we have included them. If a word has more than one meaning (for instance, "spread-eagle"), some of which are in *Webster's* and some not, we define only the omitted meaning. A few troublesome dialect spellings are glossed only with the canonical spelling, as an aid to finding the definition in *Webster's*. A few words and phrases have proved more readily defined in the explanatory notes, to which the reader is referred in each case. All entries have been alphabetized letter by letter, always beginning with the first word of a phrase, even when that is a preposition.

The following dictionaries, glossaries, and other sources have been used to prepare the definitions:

Bartlett, John Russell.
    1896. *Dictionary of Americanisms.* 4th ed. Boston: Little, Brown, and Co.

Bates, Alan.
    1968. *The Western Rivers Steamboat Cyclopoedium; or, American Riverboat Structure & Detail, Salted with Lore, with a Nod to the Modelmaker.* Leonia, N.J.: Hustle Press.

Burchfield, R. W., ed.
    1972–. *A Supplement to the Oxford English Dictionary.* 3 vols. to date. Oxford: Clarendon Press.

Clapin, Sylva.
    1902. *A New Dictionary of Americanisms*. New York: Louis Weiss and Co.

Craigie, Sir William, ed., with James R. Hulbert.
    1936. *A Dictionary of American English on Historical Principles*. 4 vols. Chicago: University of Chicago Press.

De Vere, M. Schele.
    1872. *Americanisms; the English of the New World*. New York: Charles Scribner and Co.

Farmer, John S., comp. and ed.
    1889. *Americanisms—Old & New*. London: Privately printed by Thomas Poulter and Sons.

Farmer, John S., and W. E. Henley.
    1905. *A Dictionary of Slang and Colloquial English*. Abridged from the seven-volume work, entitled *Slang and Its Analogues*. London: George Routledge and Sons.

Gove, Philip Babcock, and the Merriam-Webster editorial staff.
    1961. *Webster's Third New International Dictionary of the English Language, Unabridged*. Springfield, Mass.: G. & C. Merriam Co.

Hunter, Louis C., with Beatrice Jones Hunter.
    1949. *Steamboats on the Western Rivers: An Economic and Technological History*. Cambridge: Harvard University Press.

Maitland, James.
    1891. *The American Slang Dictionary*. Chicago: R. J. Kittredge and Co.

Mathews, Mitford M., ed.
    1951. *A Dictionary of Americanisms on Historical Principles*. 2 vols. Chicago: University of Chicago Press.

Murray, James A. H., Henry Bradley, W. A. Craigie, and C. T. Onions, eds.
    1933. *The Oxford English Dictionary*. 13 vols. Oxford: Clarendon Press.

Neilson, William Allen, Thomas A. Knott, and Paul W. Carhart, eds.
    1945. *Webster's New International Dictionary of the English Language*. 2d ed., unabridged. Springfield, Mass.: G. & C. Merriam Co.

Partridge, Eric.
    1967. *A Dictionary of Slang and Unconventional English*. 6th ed. New York: Macmillan Co.

Ramsay, Robert L., and Frances G. Emberson.
    1963. *A Mark Twain Lexicon*. New York: Russell and Russell.

Thornton, Richard H.
    1912. *An American Glossary*. 3 vols. Philadelphia: J. B. Lippincott Co.

Watts, Peter.
   1977.   *A Dictionary of the Old West, 1850–1900*. New York: Alfred A.
   Knopf.

Way, Frederick, Jr.
   1943.   *Pilotin' Comes Natural*. New York and Toronto: Farrar and
   Rinehart.

Webster, Noah.
   [1870].   *A Dictionary of the English Language*. Rev. and enl. by Chauncey A. Goodrich and Thomas Heber Orr. 2 vols. Glasgow: William
   Mackenzie.

   1884.   *An American Dictionary of the English Language*. Rev. and enl.
   by Chauncey A. Goodrich. Springfield, Mass.: G. & C. Merriam & Co.

   1889.   *An American Dictionary of the English Language*. Rev. and enl.
   by Chauncey A. Goodrich and Noah Porter. Springfield, Mass.: G. & C.
   Merriam & Co.

   1894.   *An American Dictionary of the English Language*. Rev. and enl.
   by Chauncey A. Goodrich. Chicago: Webster's Dictionary Pub. Co.

Wentworth, Harold.
   1944.   *American Dialect Dictionary*. New York: Thomas Y. Crowell
   Co.

Whitney, William Dwight, and Benjamin E. Smith, eds.
   1913.   *The Century Dictionary: An Encyclopedic Lexicon of the English Language*. Rev. and enl. 12 vols. New York: Century Company.

Worcester, Joseph E.
   1863.   *A Dictionary of the English Language*. Boston: Brewer and Tiles-
   ton.

allycumpain]   Elecampane: hardy, European herb naturalized in the
   United States and commonly used in folk medicine. A white powder
   made by boiling the root is applied externally or internally, for lung
   diseases and for skin disorders, such as psoriasis and eczema. Spelling
   varied widely in the nineteenth century: elicampene, alycompaine,
   allicampane.

ash-hopper]   Funnel-shaped bin in which wood ashes were leached of their
   alkali, which was in turn used to make soap.

bar]   Sand bar, any deposit of river sediment that forms a shallow place
   (shoal) or an island.

beat]   Idler, loafer, good-for-nothing. Short for "dead beat."

beatenest]   Unsurpassable, not able to be "beaten"; hence, most extraordinary, inexplicable, unaccountable.

big water]   The Mississippi River, a translation of the Indian name for the river, from which "Mississippi" is supposed to derive. Huck also says "the old regular Muddy" to refer to the river (129.32).

bitts]   Sturdy posts for securing cables on a steamboat. They were fastened in pairs to the deck. About three feet high, the bitts had a crosspiece above the midpoint, forming an *H*. Kemble has drawn what a riverman would call a "kevel" (page 89).

blister]   Nuisance, irritating creature, characterized by an overweening, irrational persistence.

boom]   To go at full speed, roar along.

booming]   Splendid, grand, superb (135.15); very, extremely (208.35).

boss]   Term of address used toward ostensible superiors, strangers, often by blacks speaking to whites (103.20); best, first-rate, supreme (215.16).

bottoms]   Alluvial flood plain of a river, the "river bottom" during flood-stage. Usually fertile, low-lying, and flat. See Huck's description of the "Illinois bottom" (60.12).

break-down]   See the explanatory note to 112.18–19.

by de back]   Thoroughly. Possibly a reference to marked cards, as in *Following the Equator*: "I *know* you—I know you 'by the *back*,' as the gamblers say" (chapter 28).

captain's door]   Door by which the captain entered and left his room in the texas. Huck's description places it in the center of the forward wall. See diagram, page 391.

chimbly-guy]   Chimney-guy: a thin cable or wire used to steady the chimneys (or smokestacks) of the steamboat. See diagram, page 391.

chute]   Narrow channel or bayou outside the main part of the river, navigable only in middle to high water.

close place]   Uncomfortably delicate or dangerous position. Huck also says "tight place" (239.6) and "close-fit" (257.15) to mean the same thing.

coarse-hand]   Block, as opposed to cursive, lettering. Huck also says "coarse print" (242.20) to mean the same thing.

coase comb]   Coarse comb: a comb with large or widely spaced teeth, the opposite of a fine-tooth comb. Used as a crude musical instrument by wrapping it in paper and blowing against the side.

come any such game on]   To play any such trick on.

Congress water]   Mineral water bottled at Congress Spring in Saratoga, New York.

cross hall]   Narrow hallway at right angles to the texas hall, opening through a door onto the hurricane deck on both sides of the texas. Usually about two-thirds of the way from the captain's door to the stern of the texas. See diagram, page 391.

crossing]   See the explanatory note to 78.23–29.

cross off]   To thwart, obstruct, hinder.

dam]   To bear young.

dead beat]   Worthless idler who never pays his own way, sponger, loafer.

double-hull ferry-boat]   Steam ferryboat in which the deck is supported by two distinct hulls, with the paddle-wheel situated between them.

down in de bills]   Written down in the specifications, hence predestined, foreordained.

down the banks]   Scolding, reprimand.

fox-fire]   Rotten wood that emits phosphorescent light (caused by fungi).

freeze]   To yearn, long for intensely (169.15); to cling to, hold firmly or tenaciously (282.10).

gabble]   Intimate, eager conversation (264.25); to jabber, prate, talk rapidly and foolishly (274.20).

gar]   Long, spear-like fish of various kinds, commonly deemed inedible.

gone to grass]   Gone to the devil, expired, ruined.

grand bulge]   Most difficult or critical phase of an enterprise.

gumption]   Sense, practical understanding, quick perception of the right thing to do under unusual circumstances.

hark from the tomb]   Serious or earnest reproof, as in Isaac Watts's "A Funeral Thought": "Hark! from the tombs a doleful sound; I My ears, attend the cry— I Ye living men, come, view the ground I Where you must shortly lie."

have it for breakfast]   To save or postpone something.

hive]   To capture, catch, get (14.33); to appropriate, take without permission, steal (225.33).

holt]   Hold, grip, grasp. A "best holt" is one's specialty or title to attention (161.4); "let go all holts" means to relax one's grip, hence to abandon all restraint (284.23).

hollow]   See the explanatory note to 15.3.

horse bill]   Hand bill advertising a stallion available for breeding.

hunch]   To nudge.

jackstaff]   Pole on the bowsprit of a steamboat, used as a steering aid by the pilot, who aligned it with a given point on the horizon. See diagram, page 391.

janders]   Jaundice.

jour printer]   Journeyman printer: one who has completed his apprenticeship and is qualified to practice the trade, usually taking work by the day. See the explanatory note to 160.37.

juice harp]   Jew's harp.

law]   Lord (also "laws"). "Lawsy" (128.14) derives from "Lordy," "law sakes" (278.6) from "for the Lord's sake"; "laws-a-me" (278.18) and "lawsamercy" (348.38) derive from "Lord have mercy."

meeky]   To move in a retiring manner.

melodeum]   Melodion (or melodium): a reed organ, resembling a small square piano, popular in the nineteenth century. One variety, when the single foot-pump was operated inexpertly, produced a displeasingly uneven sound.

mud-cat]   Variety of catfish abounding in the Mississippi River, not highly prized for eating because of its coarse, muddy-tasting flesh.

mullet-headed]   Stupid, dull. A mullethead is a variety of freshwater fish known for its stupidity.

nigger-head]   Strong, black tobacco of an inferior grade, twisted or pressed into a flat cake or plug.

pat juba]   See the explanatory note to 112.18.

pilot house]   Topmost structure on a steamboat, housing the wheel and signalling devices used by the pilot. It was usually situated above the texas, far forward on the texas deck, with windows on all sides—all but the forward side glassed in. See diagram, page 391.

pow-wow] To hold a meeting for discussion, to confer (14.35); any kind of din, uproar, loud noise or racket (158.22).

puncheon floor] See the explanatory note to 148.13.

quarter] To sustain a position behind a vessel. The view from any vessel is divided into four parts: the port bow and starboard bow forward, and the port quarter and starboard quarter astern.

sand in my craw] Pluck, courage, determination. Huck also says "sand" for short (244.11). A bird's craw uses sand to digest hard morsels like seeds; hence, to have "sand in your craw" is to be able to digest or face something difficult.

scoop] To grab, gather up without ceremony, often surreptitiously (15.7); to vanquish, gain the advantage of, beat (326.24).

scrouch] Scrooch.

show up] To present (oneself) for scrutiny or examination.

size their style] To equal or match their characteristic manner, estimate correctly their level of sophistication.

skylight] Short for "skylight roof," the part of the texas deck covering the skylight, a row of transom-like windows (often stained or etched) that ran the length of or even wholly encompassed the main cabin. See diagram, page 391.

slept in our cravats] Were hanged.

soul-butter] Pious and sentimental words, perhaps in the sense of unctuous self-flattery.

spread around] To assume airs, show off.

spread-eagle] Extravagant (170.7).

stand from under] To avoid something falling or thrown from aloft, hence to get to a safe place, avoid danger or punishment.

swap around] To change from one place or subject to another (2.13) (also "swap about," 45.13). To "swap knives" is to change plans or tactics (282.4).

texas] Officers' cabin of a steamboat, situated on the hurricane deck, usually below the pilothouse and above the main cabin (see diagram, page 391).

tow-head] Small, recently formed island. Huck defines it as "a sand-bar that has cotton-woods on it as thick as harrow-teeth" (77.24–25). Mark Twain elsewhere wrote "tow-head (*i.e.*, new island)," a definition for which he recorded the supposed etymology: "Towhead means *infant*— an infant island, a growing island—so it is said" (*Life on the Mississippi*, chapter 23; *N&J2*, 471).

tow-linen] Coarse cloth woven from spun flax, hemp, or jute.

trot line] Long, sturdy fishing line to which shorter hooked lines are attached at intervals. Secured at one end to the river bank, it was used primarily to catch bottom feeders, such as catfish.

up to the hub] Deeply, fully, without reservation. The reference is to a wheel sunk up to the axle in mud.

valley] Valet.

whollop] Wallop.

without a jint started] Effortlessly, without strain, without displacing a single joint.

wood-flat] Raft or barge for transporting wood.

wood-rank] Stacked firewood, wood-pile.

yellow-jacket] Gold coin. Huck also says "yaller-boys" to mean the same thing (214.15).

REFERENCES

This list defines the abbreviations used in this book and provides full bibliographic information for works cited by the author's name, or by name and publication date. Any edition listed here known to be the one that Clemens owned is identified by an asterisk (*)—except for editions of his own works.

Abbott, Keene.
   1913. "Tom Sawyer's Town." *Harper's Weekly* 57 (9 August): 16–17.

AD   Autobiographical Dictation.

Ainsworth, William Harrison.
   1840. *The Tower of London. A Historical Romance.* London: R. Bentley.

AMT
   1959. *The Autobiography of Mark Twain.* Edited by Charles Neider. New York: Harper and Brothers.

Arabian Nights.
   *1839–41. *The Thousand and One Nights, Commonly Called, in England, the Arabian Nights' Entertainments.* Translated by Edward William Lane. 3 vols. London: Charles Knight and Co.

Arner, Robert D.
   1972. "Acts Seventeen and *Huckleberry Finn*: A Note on Silas Phelps' Sermon." *Mark Twain Journal* 16 (Summer): 12.

Ashmead, John.
   1962. "A Possible Hannibal Source for Mark Twain's Dauphin." *American Literature* 34 (March): 105–7.

ATS
   1982. *The Adventures of Tom Sawyer.* Foreword and notes by John C. Gerber; text established by Paul Baender. Mark Twain Library. Berkeley, Los Angeles, London: University of California Press.

Ayres, J. W.
1917. "Recollections of Hannibal." Letter of 22 August to Palmyra *Spectator*, undated clipping in Morris Anderson scrapbook, Mark Twain Museum, Hannibal. Partly reprinted in Wecter, 149.

Baetzhold, Howard G.
1970. *Mark Twain and John Bull: The British Connection*. Bloomington and London: Indiana University Press.

Baker, William.
1985, forthcoming. "Mark Twain and the Shrewd Ohio Audiences." *American Literary Realism*.

Bates, Alan.
1968. *The Western Rivers Steamboat Cyclopoedium; or, American Riverboat Structure & Detail, Salted with Lore, with a Nod to the Modelmaker*. Leonia, N.J.: Hustle Press.

Baughman, Ernest W.
1966. *Type and Motif Index of the Folktales of England and North America*. Indiana University Series, no. 20. The Hague: Mouton and Co.

Beidler, Peter G.
1968. "The Raft Episode in *Huckleberry Finn*." *Modern Fiction Studies* 14 (Spring): 11–20.

Belden, H. M., ed.
1940. *Ballads and Songs Collected by the Missouri Folk-Lore Society*. Vol. 15 (January) of *University of Missouri Studies*.

Birchfield, James.
1969. "Jim's Coat of Arms." *Mark Twain Journal* 14 (Summer): 15–16.

[Bird, Robert M.]
*1837. *Nick of the Woods; or, The Jibbenainosay*. 2 vols. Philadelphia: Carey, Lea and Blanchard.

Blair, Walter.
1957. "The French Revolution and *Huckleberry Finn*." *Modern Philology* 55 (August): 21–35.

1958. "When Was *Huckleberry Finn* Written?" *American Literature* 30 (March): 1–25.

1960a. *Mark Twain & Huck Finn*. Berkeley and Los Angeles: University of California Press.

1960b. *Native American Humor*. San Francisco: Chandler Publishing Company.

1976. "Charles Mathews and His 'Trip to America.' " In *Prospects*, edited by Jack Salzman, 2:1–23. New York: Burt Franklin and Company.

1979. "Was Huckleberry Finn Written?" *Mark Twain Journal* 19 (Summer): 1–3.

Blair, Walter, and Hamlin Hill.
1978. *America's Humor: From Poor Richard to Doonesbury*. New York: Oxford University Press.

Blathwait, Raymond.
1891. "Mark Twain on Humor." New York *World*, 31 May, 26.

Bowen, Elbert R.
[1959.] *Theatrical Entertainments in Rural Missouri before the Civil War*. University of Missouri Studies, volume 32. Columbia: University of Missouri Press.

Branch, Edgar Marquess.
1983. "Mark Twain: Newspaper Reading and the Writer's Creativity." *Nineteenth-Century Fiction* 37 (March): 576–603.

1984. "Three New Letters by Samuel Clemens in the Muscatine *Journal*." *Mark Twain Journal* 22 (Spring): 2–7.

Branch, Edgar Marquess, and Robert H. Hirst.
1985. *The Grangerford-Shepherdson Feud . . . with an Account of Mark Twain's Literary Use of the Bloody Encounters at Compromise, Kentucky*. Berkeley: The Friends of The Bancroft Library.

Brand, John.
1877. *Observations on Popular Antiquities*. London: Chatto and Windus.

Budd, Louis J.
1962. *Mark Twain: Social Philosopher*. Bloomington: Indiana University Press.

1977. "A Listing of and Selection from Newspaper and Magazine Interviews with Samuel L. Clemens, 1874–1910." *American Literary Realism* 10 (Winter): i–100.

1985. " 'A Nobler Roman Aspect' of *Adventures of Huckleberry Finn*." In *One Hundred Years of* Huckleberry Finn: *The Boy, His Book, and American Culture*, edited by Robert Sattelmeyer and J. Donald Crowley, 26–40. Columbia: University of Missouri Press.

Bunyan, John.
*[1678] 1875. *The Pilgrim's Progress as Originally Published by John Bunyan, Being a Fac-simile Reproduction of the First Edition*. London: Elliot Stock.

Buxbaum, Katherine.
1927. "Mark Twain and American Dialect." *American Speech* 2 (February): 233–36.

Byers, John R., Jr.
1971. "Miss Emmeline Grangerford's Hymn Book." *American Literature* 43 (May): 259–63.

Cardwell, Guy A.
1953. *Twins of Genius.* East Lansing: Michigan State College Press.

Carkeet, David.
1979. "The Dialects in *Huckleberry Finn.*" *American Literature* 51 (November): 315–32.
1981. "The Source for the Arkansas Gossips in *Huckleberry Finn.*" *American Literary Realism* 14 (Spring): 90–92.

Carlyle, Thomas.
*1856. *The French Revolution: A History.* 2 vols. New York: Harper and Brothers.

Casanova de Seingalt, Giacomo Girolamo.
*1833–37. *Mémoires de Jacques Casanova de Seingalt.* 10 vols. Paris: Paulin.

CCamarSJ   Estelle Doheny Collection, The Edward Laurence Doheny Memorial Library, St. John's Seminary, Camarillo, California.

Cellini, Benvenuto.
1851. *Memoirs of Benvenuto Cellini, a Florentine Artist.* Translated by Thomas Roscoe. New York: George P. Putnam.

Childs, Marquis W.
1982. *Mighty Mississippi: Biography of a River.* New Haven and New York: Ticknor and Fields.

Clarke, Asia Booth.
1882. *The Elder and the Younger Booth.* Boston: James R. Osgood and Company.

Clemens, Samuel Langhorne.
1851. "The New Costume." Hannibal *Western Union,* 10 July. Attributed.
1866a. "An Open Letter to the American People." New York *Weekly Review,* 17 February, 1. Reprinted in *ET&S3,* no. 181.
1866b. "Captain Montgomery." San Francisco *Golden Era* 14 (28 January): 6. Reprinted in *ET&S3,* no. 161.
1867. "Letter from 'Mark Twain.' " San Francisco *Alta California,* 26 May, 1. Reprinted in *MTTB,* 141–48.
1869a. *The Innocents Abroad; or, The New Pilgrim's Progress.* Hartford: American Publishing Company.
1869b. "Only a Nigger." Buffalo *Express,* 26 August, 2. Attributed.
1869c. "The 'Wild Man' 'Interviewed.' " Buffalo *Express,* 18 September, 1.
1870a. "A Big Thing." Buffalo *Express,* 12 March, 2.
1870b. "Post-Mortem Poetry." *Galaxy* 9 (June): 864–65.
1870c. Untitled article in "Memoranda." *Galaxy* 10 (November): 735.

1874. "A True Story, Repeated Word for Word as I Heard It." *Atlantic Monthly* 34 (November): 591–94.

1875. "Old Times on the Mississippi." Articles 4 and 5. *Atlantic Monthly* 35 (April and May): 446–52, 567–74.

1876. *The Adventures of Tom Sawyer.* Hartford: American Publishing Company.

1880. *A Tramp Abroad.* Hartford: American Publishing Company.

1881. *The Prince and the Pauper: A Tale for Young People of All Ages.* Boston: James R. Osgood and Company.

1884. "An Adventure of Huckleberry Finn." *Century* 29 (December): 268–78.

1883. *Life on the Mississippi.* Boston: James R. Osgood and Company.

1885a. *Adventures of Huckleberry Finn.* New York: Charles L. Webster and Company.

1885b. *The Adventures of Huckleberry Finn.* 2 vols. Leipzig: Bernhard Tauchnitz. Clemens's annotated copy of volume 2, in CU-MARK, to be reproduced in an appendix in *HF*, forthcoming.

1886. "The Typothetae." Hartford *Courant*, 20 January, 1. Reprinted in Fatout, 200–202.

1889. *A Connecticut Yankee in King Arthur's Court.* New York: Charles L. Webster and Company.

1894. *The Tragedy of Pudd'nhead Wilson and the Comedy Those Extraordinary Twins.* Hartford: American Publishing Company.

1895. "Fenimore Cooper's Literary Offences." *North American Review* 161 (July): 1–12.

1907. "Chapters from My Autobiography." *North American Review* 186 (October): 161–73.

1909. *Extract from Captain Stormfield's Visit to Heaven.* New York: Harper and Brothers.

1923. "The United States of Lyncherdom." In *Europe and Elsewhere,* edited by Albert Bigelow Paine, 239–49. New York and London: Harper and Brothers.

1944. *Life on the Mississippi.* Edited by Willis Wager. New York: Limited Editions Club.

1983. *Adventures of Huckleberry Finn . . . A Facsimile of the Manuscript.* Introduction by Louis Budd; afterword by William H. Loos. 2 vols. Detroit: Gale Research Company.

Clemens, Samuel L., and Charles Dudley Warner.
1873. *The Gilded Age, a Tale of To-day.* Hartford: American Publishing Company.

Colwell, James L.
     1971.   "Huckleberries and Humans: On the Naming of Huckleberry
     Finn." *PMLA* 86 (January): 70–76.

Conclin, George, comp.
     1848.   *Conclin's New River Guide; or, A Gazetteer of All the Towns
     on the Western Waters.* Cincinnati: George Conclin.

Cooper, Helen A.
     1982.   *John Trumbull: The Hand and Spirit of a Painter.* New Haven,
     Conn.: Yale University Art Gallery.

CtY   Collection of American Literature, Beinecke Rare Book and Manu-
     script Library, Yale University, New Haven, Connecticut.

CU-MAPS   Map Collection, University of California, Berkeley.

CU-MARK   Mark Twain Project, The Bancroft Library, University of
     California, Berkeley.

Davidson, Loren K.
     1968.   "The Darnell-Watson Feud." *Duquesne Review* 13 (Fall): 76–
     95.

Davis, Chester L.
     1955.   "Mark Twain's Personal Marked Copy of *History of European
     Morals* by William Edward Hartpole Lecky (Continuation)." *Twain-
     ian* 14 (September–October): 1–4.

Defoe, Daniel.
     *1747.   *Life and Strange Surprising Adventures of Robinson Crusoe.*
     London.

DeVoto, Bernard.
     1932.   *Mark Twain's America.* Boston: Little, Brown, and Co.

Dickens, Charles.
     1842.   *American Notes for General Circulation.* New York: Harper
     and Brothers.

     *1866–1870.   *The Works of Charles Dickens.* Household Edition. 55
     vols. New York: Hurd and Houghton.

     *1882.   *A Tale of Two Cities.* New York: J. W. Lovell Co.

DLC   United States Library of Congress, Washington, D.C.

Dorson, Richard M., ed.
     1967.   *American Negro Folktales.* Greenwich, Conn.: Fawcett Publi-
     cations.

Dumas, Alexandre.
     *[187_]a.   *The Count of Monte-Cristo.* London: G. Routledge and Sons.

     *[187_]b.   *Novels and Tales.* 14 vols. London and New York: George
     Routledge.

Eby, Cecil D., Jr.
1960. "Mark Twain's 'Plug' and 'Chaw': An Anecdotal Parallel." *Mark Twain Journal* 11 (Summer): 11, 25.

Eliot, T. S.
1950. Introduction to *The Adventures of Huckleberry Finn*, by Samuel L. Clemens (Mark Twain). London: Cresset Press.

Ensor, Allison.
1969. "The Location of the Phelps Farm in 'Huckleberry Finn.' " *South Atlantic Bulletin* 34 (May): 7.

Esling, Mrs. Catharine H. W., ed.
1842. *Friendship's Offering.* Boston: E. Littlefield.

ET&S1
1979. *Early Tales & Sketches, Volume 1 (1851–1864).* Edited by Edgar Marquess Branch and Robert H. Hirst, with the assistance of Harriet Elinor Smith. The Works of Mark Twain. Berkeley, Los Angeles, London: University of California Press.

ET&S3
1986, forthcoming. *Early Tales & Sketches, Volume 3 (1866–1868).* Edited by Edgar Marquess Branch and Robert H. Hirst, with the assistance of Harriet Elinor Smith. The Works of Mark Twain. Berkeley, Los Angeles, London: University of California Press.

Fatout, Paul.
1976. *Mark Twain Speaking.* Iowa City: University of Iowa Press.

Field, J. M.
1847. *The Drama in Pokerville; The Bench and Bar of Jurytown, and Other Stories.* Philadelphia: T. B. Peterson and Brothers.

Fischer, Victor.
1983. "Huck Finn Reviewed: The Reception of *Huckleberry Finn* in the United States, 1885–1897." *American Literary Realism* 16 (Spring): 1–57.

Fisher, Henry W.
1922. *Abroad with Mark Twain and Eugene Field: Tales They Told to a Fellow Correspondent.* New York: Nicholas L. Brown.

Fuller, Horace W.
*1882. *Noted French Trials: Impostors and Adventurers.* Boston: Soule and Bugbee.

Gardner, Joseph H.
1968. "Gaffer Hexam and Pap Finn." *Modern Philology* 66 (November): 155–56.

Gibson, William M.
1976. *The Art of Mark Twain.* New York: Oxford University Press.

Goldsmith, Oliver.
    *1882.   *The Vicar of Wakefield, a Tale.* New York: John W. Lovell Co.

Goodyear, Russell H.
    1971.   "Huck Finn's Anachronistic Double Eagles." *American Notes & Queries* 10 (November): 39.

Graves, Wallace.
    1968.   "Mark Twain's 'Burning Shame.' " *Nineteenth-Century Fiction* 23 (June): 93–98.

Gribben, Alan.
    1980.   *Mark Twain's Library: A Reconstruction.* 2 vols. Boston: G. K. Hall and Co.

Gunn, John C.
    1836.   *Gunn's Domestic Medicine, or Poor Man's Friend, in the Hours of Affliction, Pain and Sickness.* 8th ed. Springfield, Ohio: John M. Gallagher.

    1867.   *Gunn's New Family Physician: or, Home Book of Health.* 100th ed. Cincinnati, New York: Moore, Wilstach and Baldwin.

Hale, Mrs. Sarah J., and Louis A. Godey.
    1856.   "The Art of Making Wax Fruit and Flowers." *Godey's Lady's Book and Magazine* 52 (January): 20–22.

Hall, Edward H.
    1867.   *Appletons' Hand-Book of American Travel.* New York: D. Appleton and Co.

Hardwick, Charles.
    1872.   *Traditions, Superstitions, and Folk-lore.* Manchester: A. Ireland and Co.

Harris, Joel Chandler.
    1883.   "At Teague Poteet's. A Sketch of the Hog Mountain Range." Parts 1 and 2. *Century Magazine* 26 (May and June): 137–50, 185–94.

Harris, N. Dwight.
    [1904] 1969.   *The History of Negro Servitude in Illinois and of the Slavery Agitation in That State, 1719–1864.* Reprint. New York: Negro Universities Press.

[Hay, John.]
    1872.   "Mark Twain at Steinway Hall." New York *Tribune*, 25 January, 5.

Hazlitt, W. Carew.
    1890.   *Studies in Jocular Literature: A Popular Subject More Closely Considered.* London: Elliot Stock.

    1905.   *Faiths and Folklore: A Dictionary.* 2 vols. London: Reeves and Turner.

Hearn, Michael Patrick, ed.
   1981. *The Annotated Huckleberry Finn.* New York: Clarkson N. Potter.

HF
   1985, forthcoming. *Adventures of Huckleberry Finn.* Edited by Walter Blair and Victor Fischer. The Works of Mark Twain. Berkeley, Los Angeles, London: University of California Press.

HH&T
   1969. *Mark Twain's Hannibal, Huck & Tom.* Edited by Walter Blair. Berkeley and Los Angeles: University of California Press.

Hilton, G. W., R. Plummer, and J. Jobé.
   1976. *The Illustrated History of Paddle Steamers.* Drawings by Carlo Demand. Lausanne: Edita; New York: Two Continents Pub. Group.

Hoffman, Daniel G.
   1960. "Jim's Magic: Black or White." *American Literature* 32 (March): 47–54.

Holcombe, R. I.
   *1884. *History of Marion County, Missouri.* St. Louis: E. F. Perkins.

Hooper, Johnson J.
   1845. *Some Adventures of Captain Simon Suggs, Late of the Tallapoosa Volunteers; . . . and Other Alabama Sketches.* Philadelphia: Carey and Hart.

   1851. *The Widow Rugby's Husband.* Philadelphia: T. B. Peterson and Brothers.

Howell, Elmo.
   1968. "Huckleberry Finn in Mississippi." *Louisiana Studies* 7 (Summer): 167–72.

Hughes, Langston, and Arna Bontemps, eds.
   1958. *The Book of Negro Folklore.* New York: Dodd, Mead, and Co.

Hurd, John Codman.
   1858–62. *The Law of Freedom and Bondage in the United States.* 2 vols. Boston: Little, Brown and Co.

Hyatt, Harry Middleton.
   1965. *Folk-lore from Adams County Illinois.* Memoirs of the Alma Egan Hyatt Foundation. 2d rev. ed. Hannibal, Mo.: Harry Middleton Hyatt.

Inds
   1986, forthcoming. *Huck Finn and Tom Sawyer among the Indians, and Other Unfinished Stories.* Foreword and notes by Dahlia Armon and Walter Blair; texts established by Dahlia Armon, Walter Blair, and William Gibson. Mark Twain Library. Berkeley, Los Angeles, London: University of California Press.

James, U. P., comp.

    1857. *James' River Guide*. Cincinnati: U. P. James.

Johnson, Merle.

    1935. *A Bibliography of the Works of Mark Twain*. Rev. and enl. New York and London: Harper and Brothers.

Jones, Joseph.

    1946. "The 'Duke's' Tooth-Powder Racket: A Note on *Huckleberry Finn*." *Modern Language Notes* 61 (November): 468–69.

Kemble, E. W.

    1930. "Illustrating *Huckleberry Finn*." *Colophon*, Part 1 (February), 1–8.

Kerr, Howard.

    1972. *Mediums, and Spirit-Rappers, and Roaring Radicals: Spiritualism in American Literature, 1850–1900*. Urbana, Chicago, London: University of Illinois Press.

Kirkham, E. Bruce.

    1969. "Huck and Hamlet: An Examination of Twain's Use of Shakespeare." *Mark Twain Journal* 14 (Summer): 17–19.

Kruse, Horst H.

    1967. "Annie and Huck: A Note on *The Adventures of Huckleberry Finn*." *American Literature* 39 (May): 207–14.

Landau, Sidney I.

    1984. *Dictionaries: The Art and Craft of Lexicography*. New York: Charles Scribner's Sons.

Landon, Melville D. [Eli Perkins, pseud.].

    1891. *Thirty Years of Wit*. New York: Cassell Publishing Co.

Lecky, William Edward Hartpole.

    *1874. *History of European Morals from Augustus to Charlemagne*. 2 vols. New York: D. Appleton and Company.

LLMT

    1949. *The Love Letters of Mark Twain*. Edited by Dixon Wecter. New York: Harper and Brothers.

Lytle, William, comp.

    1952. *Merchant Steam Vessels of the United States, 1807–1868*. Mystic, Conn.: Steamship Historical Society of America.

McDougall, Marion Gleason.

    1891. *Fugitive Slaves*. Publications of the Society for the Collegiate Instruction of Women, Fay House Monographs, no. 3. Boston: Ginn and Co.

Mackay, Alexander.

    1849. *The Western World; or, Travels in the United States in 1846–47*. 2 vols. Philadelphia: Lea and Blanchard.

McKinney, John.
    1981. "Tom Sawyer's Island." *Islands* 1 (October–November): 60–65.

Marx, Leo, ed.
    1967. *Adventures of Huckleberry Finn*. Indianapolis and New York: Bobbs-Merrill Co.

Masterson, James R.
    1946. "Travelers' Tales of Colonial Natural History (Concluded)." *Journal of American Folklore* 59 (April–June): 174–88.

Mathews, Anne.
    1838. *Memoirs of Charles Mathews, Comedian*. 4 vols. London: Richard Bentley.

May, Earl Chapin.
    1932. *The Circus from Rome to Ringling*. New York: Duffield and Green.

Meine, Franklin J.
    1960. "Some Notes on the First Editions of 'Huck Finn.' " *American Book Collector* 10 (June): 31–34.

Michaelson, L. W.
    1961. "Four Emmeline Grangerfords." *Mark Twain Journal* 11 (Fall): 10–12.

Michelet, Jules.
    *1848. *Historical View of the French Revolution*. Translated by Charles Cocks. London: H. G. Bohn.

Miller, Michael G.
    1980. "Geography and Structure in *Huckleberry Finn*." *Studies in the Novel* 12 (Fall): 192–209.

Minor, Mary Willis.
    1898. "How to Keep Off Witches (as Related by a Negro)," in "Notes and Queries." *Journal of American Folklore* 11 (January–March): 76.

Moore, Chauncey O.
    1964. *Ballads and Folk Songs of the Southwest*. Norman: University of Oklahoma Press.

Moore, Mrs. Julia A.
    1928. *The Sweet Singer of Michigan*. Edited by Walter Blair. Chicago: Pascal Covici.

Moore, Olin Harris.
    1922. "Mark Twain and Don Quixote." *PMLA* 37 (June): 324–46.

Morris, Courtland P.
    1938. "The Model for Huck Finn." *Mark Twain Journal* 2 (Summer–Fall): 22–23.

Morrison, D. H., ed.
*1882. *The Treasury of Song for the Home Circle: The Richest, Best-Loved Gems*. Philadelphia: Hubbard Brothers.

Mott, Frank Luther.
1931. *A History of American Magazines, 1741–1850*. Cambridge: Harvard University Press.

MSM
1969. *Mark Twain's Mysterious Stranger Manuscripts*. Edited by William M. Gibson. Berkeley and Los Angeles: University of California Press.

MTA
1924. *Mark Twain's Autobiography*. Edited by Albert Bigelow Paine. 2 vols. New York and London: Harper and Brothers.

MTB
1912. Paine, Albert Bigelow. *Mark Twain: A Biography*. 3 vols. New York and London: Harper and Brothers.

MTBus
1946. *Mark Twain, Business Man*. Edited by Samuel Charles Webster. Boston: Little, Brown and Company.

MTE
1940. *Mark Twain in Eruption*. Edited by Bernard DeVoto. New York and London: Harper and Brothers.

MTHL
1960. *Mark Twain–Howells Letters*. Edited by Henry Nash Smith and William M. Gibson. With the assistance of Frederick Anderson. 2 vols. Cambridge: Harvard University Press, Belknap Press.

MTL
1917. *Mark Twain's Letters*. Edited by Albert Bigelow Paine. 2 vols. New York: Harper and Brothers.

MTLBowen
1941. *Mark Twain's Letters to Will Bowen*. Edited by Theodore Hornberger. Austin: University of Texas.

MTMF
1949. *Mark Twain to Mrs. Fairbanks*. Edited by Dixon Wecter. San Marino, Calif.: Huntington Library.

MTS
1910. *Mark Twain's Speeches*. New York and London: Harper and Brothers.

MTTB
1940. *Mark Twain's Travels with Mr. Brown*. Edited by Franklin Walker and G. Ezra Dane. New York: Alfred A. Knopf.

Murray, Charles Augustus.
 *1839. *Travels in North America during the Years 1834, 1835, & 1836.*
 2 vols. London: Richard Bentley.

Musick, Ruth Ann.
 1948. "The Tune the Old Cow Died On." *Hoosier Folklore* 7 (December): 105–6.

Nathan, Hans.
 1962. *Dan Emmett and the Rise of Early Negro Minstrelsy.* Norman: University of Oklahoma Press.

N&J1
 1975. *Mark Twain's Notebooks & Journals, Volume I (1855–1873).* Edited by Frederick Anderson, Michael B. Frank, and Kenneth M. Sanderson. Berkeley, Los Angeles, London: University of California Press.

N&J2
 1975. *Mark Twain's Notebooks & Journals, Volume II (1877–1883).* Edited by Frederick Anderson, Lin Salamo, and Bernard L. Stein. Berkeley, Los Angeles, London: University of California Press.

N&J3
 1979. *Mark Twain's Notebooks & Journals, Volume III (1883–1891).* Edited by Robert Pack Browning, Michael B. Frank, and Lin Salamo. Berkeley, Los Angeles, London: University of California Press.

NN-B   Henry W. and Albert A. Berg Collection, The New York Public Library, Astor, Lenox and Tilden Foundations.

Northup, Solomon.
 1853. *Twelve Years a Slave.* Auburn, N.Y.: Derby and Miller.

NPV   Jean Webster McKinney Family Papers, Francis Fitz Randolph Rare Book Room, Vassar College Library, Poughkeepsie, New York.

O'Connor, William Van.
 1955. "Why *Huckleberry Finn* Is Not the Great American Novel." *College English* 17 (October): 6–10.

Ottley, Roi, and William J. Weatherby, eds.
 1969. *The Negro in New York: An Informal Social History, 1626–1940.* New York, Washington, London: Praeger Publishers.

Paine, Albert Bigelow.
 1923. Introduction to *What Is Man? and Other Essays,* by Samuel Langhorne Clemens. Vol. 26 of *The Writings of Mark Twain,* Definitive Edition. New York: Gabriel Wells.

[Pease, Lute.]
 1895. "Mark Twain Talks." Portland *Oregonian,* 11 August, 10. Reprinted in Budd 1977, 51–53.

Pettit, Arthur G.
 1974. *Mark Twain & the South.* Lexington: University Press of Kentucky.

Pike, Martha V., and Janice Gray Armstrong.
  1980. *A Time to Mourn: Expressions of Grief in Nineteenth Century America*. Stony Brook, N.Y.: The Museums at Stony Brook.

Radford, E., and M. A. Radford.
  1969. *Encyclopedia of Superstitions*. Westport, Conn.: Greenwood Press.

Reade, Charles.
  1861. *The Cloister and the Hearth*. London: Trübner and Co.

Reed, E. J., ed.
  1861. *Transactions of the Institution of Naval Architects*. Vol. 2. London: Institution of Naval Architects.

Robinson, Fayette.
  1848. "Supplication." *Graham's American Monthly Magazine of Literature and Art* 33 (November): frontispiece, 267.

Roueché, Berton.
  1960. "Annals of Medicine: Alcohol, III—The Bird of Warning." *New Yorker* 35 (23 January): 78–106.

Rulon, Curt Morris.
  1967. "The Dialects in *Huckleberry Finn*." Ph.D. diss., University of Iowa, Iowa City.

Saintine, Joseph Xavier Boniface.
  1848. *Picciola. The Prisoner of Fenestrella; or, Captivity Captive*. Philadelphia: Lea and Blanchard.

S&B
  1968. *Mark Twain's Satires & Burlesques*. Edited by Franklin R. Rogers. Berkeley and Los Angeles: University of California Press.

Scott, Walter.
  *1827. *The Poetical Works of Sir Walter Scott*. 5 vols. Philadelphia: J. Maxwell.

  *1842–47. *Quentin Durward*. Vol. 8 of *The Waverley Novels*, Abbotsford Edition. Edinburgh: R. Cadell.

  *1871. *The Lady of the Lake*. Edinburgh: John Ross and Co.

Sharp, Cecil J.
  1932. *English Folk Songs from the Southern Appalachians*. London: Oxford University Press.

Siebert, Wilbur H.
  [1898] 1967. *The Underground Railroad from Slavery to Freedom*. Reprint. New York: Russell and Russell.

  1947. "Beginnings of the Underground Railroad in Ohio." *Ohio State Archaeological and Historical Quarterly* 56 (January): 70–93.

Simpson, F. A.
    1929. *The Rise of Louis Napoleon*. London, New York, Toronto: Longmans, Green and Co.

Slater, Joseph.
    1949. "Music at Col. Grangerford's: A Footnote to *Huckleberry Finn*." *American Literature* 21 (March): 108–11.

Smith, Benjamin E., ed.
    1902. *The Century Atlas of the World*. New York: Century Company.

Smith, Henry Nash, ed.
    1958. *Adventures of Huckleberry Finn*. Boston: Houghton Mifflin Company, Riverside Press.

Smith, Solomon.
    1868. *Theatrical Management in the West and South for Thirty Years*. New York: Harper and Brothers.

Strickland, Carol Colclough.
    1976. "Emmeline Grangerford, Mark Twain's Folk Artist." *Bulletin of the New York Public Library* 79 (Winter): 225–33.

Summers, Montague.
    1946. *Witchcraft and Black Magic*. London: Rider and Company.

Thomas, Daniel Lindsey, and Lucy Blayney Thomas.
    1920. *Kentucky Superstitions*. Princeton, N.J.: Princeton University Press.

[Thompson, William T.]
    1845. *The Chronicles of Pineville*. Philadelphia: Carey and Hart.

Trenck, Friedrich.
    1853. *The Life of Baron Frederick Trenck*. Albany: J. Munsell.

Trexler, Harrison Anthony.
    1914. *Slavery in Missouri, 1804–1865*. Baltimore: Johns Hopkins Press.

TS   Typescript.

TSA
    1982. *Tom Sawyer Abroad; Tom Sawyer, Detective*. Foreword and notes by John C. Gerber, text established by Terry Firkins. Mark Twain Library. Berkeley, Los Angeles, London: University of California Press.

TxU   Humanities Research Center Library, University of Texas, Austin.

ViU   Clifton Waller Barrett Library, University of Virginia, Charlottesville.

Walpole, Horace.
    *1861–66. *The Letters of Horace Walpole, Earl of Oxford*. Edited by Peter Cunningham. 9 vols. London: Henry G. Bohn.

Waterman, Miss Catharine H., ed.
    1841. *Friendship's Offering*. Philadelphia: Marshall, Williams, and Butler.

Way, Frederick, Jr.
    1943. *Pilotin' Comes Natural*. New York and Toronto: Farrar and Rinehart.
    1972. Diagrams, *S&D Reflector* 9 (June): 24.

Wecter, Dixon.
    1952. *Sam Clemens of Hannibal*. Boston: Houghton Mifflin Company, Riverside Press.

Wells, David M.
    1973. "More on the Geography of 'Huckleberry Finn.'" *South Atlantic Bulletin* 38 (November): 82–86.

Welsh, Donald H.
    1962. "Sam Clemens' Hannibal, 18[4]6–18[4]8." *Midcontinent American Studies Journal* 3 (Spring): 28–43.

Westerhoff, John H., III.
    1978. *McGuffey and His Readers*. Nashville: Abingdon.

White, Gilbert.
    *1875. *The Natural History of Selborne*. London: Bickers and Son.

Whiting, B. J.
    1944. "Guyuscutus, Royal Nonesuch and Other Hoaxes." *Southern Folklore Quarterly* 8 (December): 251–75.

WIM
    1973. *What Is Man? and Other Philosophical Writings*. Edited by Paul Baender. The Works of Mark Twain. Berkeley, Los Angeles, London: University of California Press.

Wolford, Leah Jackson.
    1916. *The Play-Party in Indiana*. Indianapolis: Indiana Historical Commission.

Wright, William [Dan De Quille, pseud.].
    *1877. *History of the Big Bonanza*. Hartford: American Publishing Company.

Wyeth, John Allan.
    1914. *With Sabre and Scalpel*. New York and London: Harper and Brothers.

NOTE ON THE TEXT

The text of *Huckleberry Finn* published here is identical in every respect, including pagination, with the text of the novel to be published shortly by the University of California Press (in cooperation with the University of Iowa) in The Works and Papers of Mark Twain (volume 8). Both that volume for scholars and this Mark Twain Library volume have been edited by Walter Blair and Victor Fischer in collaboration with associate editors Dahlia Armon and Harriet Elinor Smith, assisted by Richard Bucci, Paul Machlis, Kenneth M. Sanderson, and other members of the Mark Twain Project. Fischer and his colleagues in The Bancroft Library have established the text from the pertinent documents in accord with the standards of the Center for Scholarly Editions (CSE). Editorial work on both volumes has been supported by a generous grant from Hedco Foundation and by matching funds from the Program for Editions of the National Endowment for the Humanities, an independent federal agency. (It may be useful to note here that the University of California Press has recently published a third edition of *Huckleberry Finn*, illustrated by Barry Moser, that was typeset from the Mark Twain Project's established text but is not otherwise a part of its publishing program.)

Fischer established the text principally from five authoritative documents: (1) Mark Twain's holograph manuscript for the last three-fifths of the book—all that is known to survive—now in the Rare Book Room of the Buffalo and Erie County Public Library, Buffalo, N.Y. (William H. Loos, Curator); (2) the first American edition, published in February 1885 by Mark Twain's own publishing house, Charles L. Webster and Company; (3) excerpts from the novel prepared from first-edition proofs and revised in part by Mark Twain for publication in the *Century Magazine* for December 1884, January and February 1885; (4) a partial set of page proofs of the first edition, occasionally corrected by Mark Twain, now in the Mark Twain Papers, The Bancroft Library; and finally (5) chapter 3 of *Life on the Mississippi* (Boston: James R. Osgood, 1883), the only surviving text of the so-called Raftsmen's Chapter, a passage written for but removed from *Huckleberry Finn* at the suggestion of Mark Twain's publisher, Charles Webster.

The following history of the publishing process derives in its entirety from the original research of editor Fischer, soon to be published in the textual introduction and apparatus to the Works edition of this book. The story of how Mark Twain composed *Huckleberry Finn* which Blair published in 1958 still stands virtually unchanged, despite twenty-five years of critical scrutiny and the Mark Twain Project's intensive search for new documentary evidence (Blair 1958, 1–25; see also Blair 1960a, passim). Mark Twain began his manuscript in 1876, carrying the story perhaps as far as the start of chapter 17 before setting it aside. He returned to it three years later and wrote perhaps as far as chapter 21 by the end of 1880; and he probably completed the remaining chapters (adding an interpolation that comprised half of chapter 12, and chapters 13 and 14) in the spring and summer of 1883.

Mark Twain had this holograph copied in two stages on the typewriter: the first two-fifths of the manuscript, which was completed by 1880, in late 1882 or early 1883; the remainder, possibly in batches as he composed it, during the summer of 1883 when he first completed it. The typed copy, not the manuscript, became printer's copy for the first edition—but only after Mark Twain meticulously and rather thoroughly corrected and revised it, and only after the first two-fifths—evidently revised heavily and therefore harder to read—was *re*-typed under William Dean Howells's scrutiny. Howells had offered to read the printer's copy in his usual fashion, and on 22 April 1884 Mark Twain told Webster, "Yes, I want Howells to have carte blanche in making corrections." Less than a week later, Howells returned the final three-fifths of the book, presumably with his suggestions and corrections, to Mark Twain. But at the author's request, he held on to the first two-fifths in order to have it retyped for the printer. Howells spent nearly three weeks overseeing this task, proofreading the original against the copy so carefully that he considered both equally "ready to go into the printer's hands." None of these typescripts is known to survive, and Howells's "corrections" are not now distinguishable from revisions Mark Twain himself made.

Mark Twain chose the young *Life* illustrator Edward Windsor Kemble to draw the illustrations for *Huckleberry Finn*. Kemble was provided with a complete copy of the text and he decided, for the most part, what and how to illustrate. Nevertheless, Mark Twain closely monitored each batch of drawings as they were produced. At first he felt unenthusiastic about the result: "The pictures will *do*—they will just barely do—& that is the best I can say for them." But two weeks later, having urged his publisher to "punch him up to improve more," Mark Twain found Kemble's work delightful: "I *knew* Kemble had it *in* him, if he would only modify his violences & come down to careful, pains-taking work. This batch of pictures is most rattling good. They please me exceedingly." Mark Twain did, however, ask for revisions occasionally, and he went so far as to veto one drawing altogether: "you must knock out one of them," he wrote the publisher, "the lecherous old rascal kissing the girl at the campmeeting. It is powerful good, but it mustn't go in." It was omitted. A little later he noticed that Kemble had drawn the name of the wrecked steamboat in chapter 13 as "TEXAS—having been misled by some of Huck's remarks about the boat's 'texas'—a thing which is a part of *every* boat." This error, too, was eliminated. Even so, some mistakes persisted, despite the author's close scrutiny: the definite article in Kemble's rendering of the book's title (chapter 1), for instance. But on the whole, Kemble did a highly conscientious job in representing the text, eventually contributing more than 175 drawings in a matter of weeks.

Mark Twain was unusually fortunate to have *Adventures of Huckleberry Finn* transmitted from manuscript, through typescript, into the first edition, as accurately as it was. Both the typists he hired to copy his manuscript and the printers who set up the text for Webster were, by and large, unusually rigorous. Still, the author, as was his habit, complained of the printers' mistakes. These evidently varied in frequency from chapter to chapter: "Most of this proof," he told Webster, "was clean & beautiful, & a pleasure to read; but the rest of it was read by that blind idiot whom I have cursed so much, & is a disgraceful mess." A little later he added: "If all the proofs had been as well read [by the proofreader] as the first 2 or 3 chapters were, I should not have needed to see the revises at all. On the contrary it was the worst & silliest proof-reading I have ever seen. It was never read by copy at all—not a single galley of it." Mark Twain's own proofreading was rather hurried and incomplete, in part because at the time he was undergoing extensive and very painful dental work. To Howells, who would help out on a part of the book, he complained that the printers "don't make a very great many mistakes; but those that do occur are of a nature to make a man curse his teeth loose." One month later, he wrote to Howells: "I am sending you these infernal Huck Finn proofs—but the very last vestige of my patience has gone to the devil, & I cannot bear the sight of another slip of them. My hair turns white with rage, at sight of the mere outside of the package." Partly because of this particular tantrum, the author never read portions of the text in galley proof, and may have skimmed them only very lightly in page proof. Corrections made during this late stage were, for the most part, prompted by the thoughtful queries of an editor or proofreader employed by the printer.

Even so, the first edition contained a number of purely typographical errors, as well as mistakes traceable to Mark Twain's (rather than his typesetters') carelessness: "Bessie" for "Becky" (47.17); "meet again" for "meet" (211.25); and "the nigger woman's gown" for "aunt Sally's gown" (333.10–11). These errors, as well as several that presumably *were* caused by the typists' or the printers' mistakes, are corrected in the present text. For instance, when Huck rows the skiff over to a ferryboat in order to get help (chapter 13), he seems to go from his skiff to the deck of the ferryboat as if by magic—at least he does so in the first edition. This effect is probably the consequence of an error made by a typist who overlooked two sentences now restored to the text: "Everything was dead still, nobody stirring. I floated in under the stern, made fast, and clumb aboard" (88.15–16).

One major flaw in the text of the first edition arose, paradoxically, from Mark Twain's desire to accommodate his young publisher on a practical matter. Webster had been charged with, among other duties, finding a way to publish *Tom Sawyer* and *Huckleberry Finn* as a matched set. One of the difficulties this assignment posed was that the two books were of very unequal size. This problem led Webster to suggest that Mark Twain omit a long passage where Huck visits a lumber raft in order to find out how far he and Jim are from Cairo, a passage Mark Twain had already published as an extract from his book in *Life on the Mississippi* (see pages 107–23 of the present text). Mark Twain replied to this suggestion on 22 April 1884: "Yes, I think the raft chapter can be left wholly out, by heaving in a paragraph to say Huck visited the raft to find out how far it might be to Cairo, but got no satisfaction. Even *this* is not necessary unless that raft-visit is referred to later in the book. I think it is, but am not certain." Even without taking the precautionary steps he mentions, Mark Twain accepted Webster's suggestion: the passage was removed from the printer's copy, Kemble prepared no illustrations for it, and the author seems never to have complained about its omission from the first edition, still less to have restored it in subsequent editions.

The omission of the Raftsmen's Chapter has been a notorious crux even long before 1942, when Bernard DeVoto (then Editor of the Mark Twain Papers) first restored it to the text. Most later editors have declined to follow DeVoto's restoration, continuing instead to exclude the passage or, at most, to print it within typographical warning flags, or as an appendix, thereby treating Mark Twain's act of accommodation as an inviolable sign of his intention. It was DeVoto, however, who first pointed to a mistake in the text that Mark Twain's omission had created: Huck's plan to "paddle ashore the first time a light showed" and ask about Cairo (106.28–32) was made to precede an inexplicable change of plan, "There warn't nothing to do, now, but to look out sharp for the town" (123.30–31). Moreover, among those critics who agreed with DeVoto, several further problems caused by the omission have since been identified, and restoration of the passage has been vehemently advocated because, in one way or another, it improved the text of Mark Twain's book.

The editors of the present text restore the passage, but not because it improves the book. The passage is restored by Fischer because Mark Twain intended to publish it in *Huckleberry Finn*, but changed his mind *only* to accommodate the publisher's convenience—a decision roughly akin to accepting the publisher's censorship. This analysis, it should be noted, rests upon the currently available evidence. It is therefore always possible that Mark Twain's intentions for his text just happened to coincide with his publisher's needs—but for the present, the editors find no documentary evidence that such was the case.

The edited text published here is the first ever to be based directly on the author's manuscript of *Huckleberry Finn*, thereby preserving many hundreds of details of punctuation and spelling, as well as several dozen words and phrases that were omitted from or otherwise distorted in the first edition because the typist, typesetter, proofreader, or even the author, mistakenly changed or omitted them. In addition, Kemble's original pen-and-ink drawings (rather than the first edition engravings) have been used wherever possible to produce the illustrations. Most of these original drawings are in the Vassar College Library, and were made available to the editors by Lisa Browar, the curator in charge. Two drawings are in private hands and were made available to the edition by their owner, Peter A. Benoliel.

Finally, the text is made more intelligible to a modern reader by the Explanatory Notes and Glossary, which derive from ongoing work on the forthcoming scholarly edition, and by various maps of the Mississippi River, prepared by the editors and drawn by Mark Ong. Priscilla Botsford drew the floorplan of the steamboat "texas" which accompanies the note to 81.20–28. All of the editorial matter for this book was prepared on a Zendex computer system generously donated to the Mark Twain Project by Robert Livermore, a long-time Friend of The Bancroft Library. Fran Mitchell expertly and cheerfully shepherded the entire volume through the press. The editors wish to thank these individuals for their contributions, and to remind the reader that a complete record of acknowledgments will appear in the Works volume later this year.

Robert H. Hirst
General Editor, Mark Twain Project

July 1985